CALIFAX

TERINA ADAMS

Petrice

For the kick up the bum I needed

Author's Note

I can only assume, since you've downloaded Califax, you've read the first in the series, Dominus. I will also assume that if you've moved on to Califax, Dominus was your cup of tea. Yippee!

So glad you enjoyed it. There is plenty more in store for Sable and the team.

Happy reading

Chapter 1

HE COULD'VE BEEN LOOKING at me right now, obscured within the heaving crowd of gawkers bustling for the perfect vantage point. I glanced around, scrutinizing the faces of the crowd pressing into me. I'd see Carter if he wanted to be seen. And what about Holden? Would he bother to show his traitorous face?

Jax sat alone on a bus bench across the street, slumped forward, elbows on knees, wrapped in a black overcoat, looking like some misfit suffering from a heavy night on the drink. He was suffering, but the results were not self-inflicted. He stopped taking the pain suppressants, because apparently, they dulled the mind and senses, which meant he'd be feeling the effects from his fight with one of Carter's Aris minions.

I'd known Jax only a couple months, and of all the people to betray me, he would've had the greatest reason, but he didn't. According to the twisted principles in his world, we were enemies, yet here Jax and I were, two opposing factions, relying on each other to get through this mess. For me, he promised to help his greatest enemy—Dad.

The lady beside me elbowed me in the side as she raised her phone to take a photo of the missing top of the Amex Tower. What was once one of the most impressive buildings in the city, the tower now looked like an ugly scar on the landscape, a survivor of some unforgiving savagery. The needlepoint spire that made the building the second-highest building in the city lay blocks away. The top point pierced the paving as if a giant used it for a javelin.

The police had erected yellow tape three blocks back, while essential personnel moved around the disaster site. Less than twelve hours since the devastation, but already men and women in jumpsuits and booties were combing the area for survivors and clues. This far back and the dust coated all surfaces. It still hung in the air, leaving a chalky smell that scratched the back of my throat. The buildings adjacent suffered damage with a few blown windows but appeared to remain structurally sound.

The crowd jostled, curious onlookers hoping for a better view. The camera rolled on a news reporter standing just inside the barrier tape. I was keen to hear the latest update on what they knew so far, so I relinquished my spot and shuffled farther right—a tight squeeze by any standard. Desperate to hear her report, I ducked under the tape and stumbled over the debris, making sure to keep close enough I wouldn't be easily spotted as being on the wrong side of the barricade.

"No deaths have been confirmed as yet. Initial reports claim everyone on the top floors had already evacuated due to a fire alarm."

"Hey, lady." On hearing the shout behind me, I ducked under the barrier tape and disappeared through the crowd. I heard all I wanted to hear. No deaths so far. It was as good an outcome as I could have hoped.

The immensity of the destruction ran a slow, winding hand of dread around my heart. No one should be able to do such a thing, at least not with their mind.

There'd been the slimmest hope I would succeed in stealing the grafter. Even so, I'd been prepared to do it. If not for Tyren's betrayal, I may have succeeded. What about Holden? I believed in him, believed he meant every word of his lies about factional family being stronger than blood. After everything he'd done for Dad, everything he said to me, I thought I could rely on him.

Jax didn't bother to look up as I slid down beside him. He wanted me to stay in his world. He feared Carter would still be around, but Dad was languishing in jail, and Mum and Ajay were missing. Our argument spun in roundabouts until Jax finally gave in when he saw I wasn't going to change my mind. My home world was the only place I could think of finding answers.

He'd made a remarkable recovery thanks to the pills. Even so, he looked like the loser in a heavy-weight championship gone wrong. I couldn't shift, so I dragged him, sagging sack of bones and all, back to earth with me, driven by selfish reasons. I gained one thing from Dominus, but I lost everything else—everything worth living for. Carter would be stopped, but I needed to find Mum and Ajay first. Until I could hug them both again, nothing else mattered.

It was only after my terrible act of destruction that I began to understand what Jax meant when he said we weren't nice people when we became our true nature. On numerous occasions, I'd witness the soulless desire of bloodlust Jax took on when his factional nature won through. I felt the lure to become destruction many times while in the game and then during our fight with Carter at the top of his tower. Jax was right. Releasing the constraints on my ability felt like a sudden injection of something wild and vital, something addictively delicious.

The shock of Jax's injuries and a narrow escape from Carter's control dampened my need to continue destroying. But while I had laid beside Jax, listening to his steady breath, the power coursed through my veins, fighting to engulf my rational mind and turn it into a weapon I could wield. In equal measure, the idea attracted me and repulsed me, but at times, the attraction felt greater than the repulsion.

"What do you think of your handiwork?" He used a flat tone devoid of sarcasm or smile.

I looked at the back of the crowd then ran my eyes up the tower to the gaping wound at the top.

"It will get better."

"What will?" I snapped at him, which wasn't fair. The weight of the last six hours came out as one long sigh, sounding as heavy as the feel of my body.

Jax ignored my outburst. "Over time, you'll become stronger at controlling your ability, not just in use, but also in desire. The hardest part is the beginning, accepting what you're capable of and the yearning to allow that side of yourself through. The first acts are the hardest to face. At some point, you become numb to the shock of what you're doing. That's the dangerous time. Allow yourself to be consumed, and your factional nature's all you'll become. Find the balance, and you don't have to be a monster. It's not easy, but you can do it."

Only days ago, Jax confessed his pain at being Aris. To him, allowing Aris free was to become a monster.

"Do you still believe it's important to release everyone from their grafts?"

Jax wouldn't meet my eyes, nor did he seem in any hurry to reply. He winced as he moved on the seat, making me wince too. I rested my palm on his upper arm. "Are you all right?"

"Recovering with each minute."

I was about to apologize for dragging him back here, when he said, "Carter freed me of my graft, and then he stuck me in Dominus. Maybe it would've been different if I'd not been forced to use my factional nature in such a way. It made me believe I was nothing else but the desire that consumed me."

"You don't believe that now."

"I'm here with you, not with him. That means something."

"It means you're good inside. That's the real you, not bloodlust."

He flashed me a small smile. Hopefully because it hurt to do anything else and not because he thought me sentimental. I had to resist offering my hand as he inched up from the bus seat. I wanted to help him, but he would appreciate the sentiment as much as he would appreciate a poke in the eye.

"We should go. Every moment we linger, Carter moves closer to his goal. I need to get to the warehouse and see if Dominus is still there."

"Maybe Carter's monitoring the place for our return."

"Or perhaps not. It's stupid to return there. He wouldn't think me that foolish, so it may work."

"What does it matter if Dominus is still there. Who are you going to train?"

"I want to go back inside. I need to train myself."

"I don't think *you* need any more training."

"I need to enter the tunnel. It's something none of us did. Carter forbade it."

"You've never been down there at all?"

"Sure, some parts. I helped build the real tunnel back in our world. But we were all assigned to building separate parts. That way, no one would know the whole route. He planned for only a certain few of us to ever enter the tunnel and then on to the Dome when the final confrontation came. No one but the Senate of Factions and staff have entered the Dome. The staff are grafted individuals. They work within the Dome in strict confidentiality, with harsh penalties for any who slip up, so no secrets ever come from them. It's impossible to breach from the outside. That's why we built the tunnel, so we could enter from underground. Carter and Nixon designed that part of the Dominus program; no one else knew what it looked like."

"But what about your tattoo?"

"It's a faithful representation, but I've never used it."

His coat disguised the map snaking up his forearm. Otherwise, my eyes would be walking over it right now.

"It doesn't make sense. Why would he be so secretive about reaching the Dome?"

"You should know by now that there's no trust between anyone. Not even those who are on your side. Not even amongst your family."

"I wish I didn't know."

Jax gently squeezed my arm. "It happened. There's no point dwelling on it, only in changing the outcome."

I inhaled big, taking his words in, forcing them deep within my body so I could believe them enough to know we would change the outcome.

"Are you the only one with the tunnel tattooed on your body?"

He nodded. "In our world, the Dome has always been shrouded in secrecy. Few questioned why, as that's how it's always been. I hope to learn the secrets the Dome holds before we enter the place for real. I don't want any surprises, especially from the senate. Hopefully, Carter and Nixon stayed true to our world when they created the replica in the game."

"How long will it take you to get through the tunnel?"

"To be honest with you, I'm not sure. I don't expect you to follow."

"I want to see my dad."

He shook his head. "It's too dangerous. Carter may have planted spies at the prison waiting for you to do just that. As Nixon is still in jail, he will be wondering why you have not used the grafter yet to reverse your father's graft and set him free."

"I have to see him. He'll be wondering what's going on."

"No."

"I have to let him know I failed. And what Holden did." Jax may not have liked my idea, but I wasn't going to let it go. "This is my family."

"You want to care for your family, then keep your head down. Don't let Carter know where you are. Don't forget your father's vulnerable too. He's grafted, but Carter isn't, nor are a lot of his followers. Now that you've escaped his noose, Carter has no reason to keep him alive."

The realization turned my legs to lead. "Jesus."

"As long as you stay away from him, Carter will see no point in touching him."

"I can't leave him. I have to know he's all right."

"You could be signing his death warrant."

"But he's my dad!"

"And he killed my family!"

And there it was, brought out in the open in harsh shouted voices. The ugly wound I was afraid would surface at some point to drive a wedge between us. No matter what Jax did for me, the truth would never go away. I was the daughter of the man who murdered his family. There would be no real forgiveness.

Both of us stared at each other before Jax collapsed into the seat again like a balloon figure of a man deflating.

I didn't have the luxury of stressing over the divide between us, something we would perhaps never be able to erase. There was no time to regret the past, especially actions I had no control over. "Please, Jax."

"Going to see your dad is a bad idea. Every part of me says so."

"I can say the same about entering Dominus, but I know I can't stop you."

"Ditto for you."

I couldn't help but smile. Jax looked at me from his better eye, the other still visibly injured. I wanted to run a gentle hand down the side of his face and with one magical touch make it all better. He suffered because of me. I remembered that one horrible moment when I thought he betrayed me. Never had relief felt so immense and beautiful as it did when Jax walked through Carter's office door. Without his interference, my confrontation with Carter would've ended badly. Instead of being caught in his web, we were fighting against him.

All of this because my enemy, someone I was supposed to loath—an Aris—saved me, while a member of my faction—what Holden called family—betrayed me.

"All right. We'll get this over and done with. Your father first, and then we go to the warehouse. I also want to find Elva and learn who else is on our side." The decision seemed to rally his strength, dragging him to his feet.

"Maybe she went with them."

"No, I know her well enough to know she would not do that."

"She followed Carter in the first place."

"No, she followed me."

I tried my hardest, but the look on Jax's face said I failed. He should never know how I felt. I didn't even understand the depth of it myself. But when my heart exploded with relief at seeing Jax walk through the door of Carter's office, to know he hadn't betrayed me, it had exploded with something more.

Jax said he and Elva had never been romantic, and she was obsessively stuck on Holden. So stupid, but jealousy was the first emotion to flood my insides. The first emotion was always raw and honest. Only later, when your mind churned through the situation, could you alter your perception and distort how you felt. Yet I had been jealous. Bad, bad timing. These were the wrong emotions to feel. He'd hate them too.

"We've known and trusted each other since we were kids."

"Then I'll trust your belief in her." Our surroundings became more important to stare at.

"Months ago, I would've said you were foolish to trust me."

This drew my attention back. "And what do you say now?"

"It's the only thing that will help us survive."

Chapter 2

FROM THE PRISON PARKING LOT, I scanned the wire fence and the surrounding area. Jax disappeared ten minutes ago to skulk around the perimeter, checking the prison surveillance plus any extra surveillance the prison may not be aware of. Carter was too shrewd to make obvious mistakes, so I doubted Jax would find anything.

Ten minutes, that was all, but the minutes were more like hours. I shifted my weight from foot to foot then paced under the canopy of a large tree. A lusty bloom of wide leaves flowing to the ground from thick boughs created a secluded nest. Parting the leaves, I could see the camera towers at the four corners of the parking lot. According to Jax, they wouldn't be a problem. Carter's surveillance system was all we had to worry about, but maybe Dad was no longer of interest to him. Jax scoffed when I made the remark.

After too much time elapsed, Jax made his way back toward me, taking a different route from the one he departed on. His gait reminded me of what he suffered to get here, a place he didn't want to be, to see a man he loathed. I could think of no words that would express my feelings adequately enough. Best to focus on what needed to be done.

"The place looks clear as far as I can see."

How confident was he in that assumption? Best not to ask. We both knew how thin the path was we'd chosen to take. Nowhere was safe. No one was our friend. Nothing was reliable. They were the only truths we had left—live by the moment, the only reality we faced.

"Come." Jax led me out from under the canopy. For one startling moment, I expected men with blood-red eyes to emerge from the parked cars or from behind the building and charge toward us in a death run. I clutched Jax's hand. He stopped, looking down at me, an expression asking questions I ignored. The terrible bruising on his face was the first thing my eyes settled on before I forced them to his good eye. What was ahead for us? How many times would Jax suffer before this was over? How many times would I?

I shook my head. I would not voice my apprehension or give him any excuse to call it quits.

"Let's go." This time, I led the way, only to be yanked back by Jax's strong grip.

"I've got an idea. Let me go first."

"Why...? W-what?"

He silenced my awkward stuttering with a figure over my lips. "You've trusted me so far."

"I can't stay out here any longer."

"I won't be long."

"Jax," I groaned, but he was gone. Not gone, as in sprinting across the parking lot at top speed; gone, as in vanished. He crossed, leaving me alone. This was my world, but I backed up under the tree canopy like I was an alien and the world an unfamiliar and hostile place.

It took moments for Jax to return, but long enough for the tension to twist my muscles into tight knots. I jumped at his arrival, mainly because he appeared beside me and placed a hand on my shoulder. "Jesus. A little warning next time."

"Sorry. I've located your father."

"Is he all right?"

"Yes. I'm not sure why that is."

I was not going to ask him if he was disappointed. "You think Carter would've done something to him by now."

"If Carter felt his plans were unraveling, he would act decisively and swift. The fact he's left your father tells me he's not bothered by what we've done."

"Or he knows something we don't." I grasped his arm. "What if they have Holden? What if he never managed to escape, and my mum and Ajay?"

"The text he sent says otherwise. Holden's smart. No one survives Dominus without cunning and tenacity. Holden planned for this to happen. Perhaps he wasn't expecting the extra load, but he knew his escape route."

The breath I held slowly seeped out, some of the tension along with it.

"I've got a better way in to see your father."

"We're going to shift to the in-between."

"He was in the library. He wasn't happy to see me. I've warned him you're coming, so he's returned to his cell. I'll take you there, but I'm not hanging around. You've got ten minutes to talk; that's all he can guarantee before they come and drag his ass back to the library. I'll be back in that time to get you and your father, if that's what you want."

He took my hand. I tugged on it so he would look at me. "I know what he means to you. And yet you're still willing to do this. Thank you." So lame.

I stared at a blank expression, because even after everything, Jax could still hide. He wore a wall of granite, because it protected the vulnerability inside, and in his world, those weaknesses destroyed a person. He buried the depth of his pain deep, but I caught a fleeting glimpse when his defenses slipped.

"I'm not sure how far I can take this, so don't thank me yet."

Always the threat of deception. How could anyone live a life locked within themselves?

The warping tug of shifting to the in-between still made me woozy, but we didn't hang around long in the one place that gave Jax and me peace. Jax pulled us through the bands, and I was spat out inside a small, stark room that smelled of bleach and stale air. At some point, Jax had let me go, choosing not to follow me through.

Dad stopped midpace and rumbled toward me. With no time for

words, he swept me into a tight embrace, engulfing me within cheap lemon laundry powder and a strong astringent smell, like the feeling bleach leaves in your nose but accented by a tinge of rotten fruit.

This was the first time in… I couldn't count when, that we touched. Because it was him, because it reminded me of my former life, because habits could be so strong they swept aside my intentions to keep Dad at arm's reach, I hugged him back. The hug grew tighter, springing tears to my eyes. When I was young and the world a complicated place, Dad's hug made me feel strong. I thought him a hero. I thought he made the world a better, safer place. I believed in him, because I didn't realize how much people could lie.

We had ten minutes. I would give myself a little longer to be that naïve child before I pulled away and became the wounded, mistrusting adolescent.

"Jax has a few bruises," Dad said.

"Things didn't work out the way I planned. There was little chance I would succeed."

Dad inched down onto his cot, locking his eyes to mine, waiting for the painful words he expected to come. His fear mirrored my own; Mum and Ajay sat heavy in both our minds.

The pull of his eyes drew me down beside him. "Tyren betrayed us. Carter wasn't even there, but he returned when he found out. The grafter was locked in a drawer, so I never would've been able to touch it."

"None of that matters."

"You haven't heard the worst of it. We got the grafter. I destroyed the top of the Amex in getting it, but Holden betrayed me. I gave the grafter to Ajay and told him to give it to Holden. He took it, Mum, and Ajay and disappeared. We have no idea where he is."

He was on his feet, giving me his back. With each step he took, the fury seeped through his pores and bled into the air. Like a rapid drop in air pressure before an impending storm, his fury sucked the oxygen from the room. He hulked across the small space, strides decimating the distance to the metal chair. One swipe, and the chair impacted into the wall with a reverberating *twang*, followed by his fist, the sound a dull crunch of bone cracking against bone.

It was over. The violence expelled the fury, which released the taut twist of my muscles. Dad collapsed forward, forehead to the plaster, fist locked to the wall, knuckles white. I endured too much to feel pity for his pain. There was no righteousness in his feelings, for he'd driven it upon himself by betraying his own people, betraying Jax's family, betraying his family.

"He left a text on Jax's phone, saying Mum and Ajay were safe."

He absorbed my words without releasing his fist from its vice or lowering it from the wall.

"What am I supposed to do, Dad? I don't know where to start looking."

"What's Carter up to now?"

"I don't know. Jax took me back to his place… the place in his… your world. We've only just returned. I don't know—"

"You need to distance yourself from him." He looked over his shoulder. Steel met my eyes, the sort of steel a person infused into their soul to survive. Instead of my father, I stared into the eyes of a senate member, the head of Persal.

I rose off the cot. "He saved my life."

"This time." His fist relaxed to his side as he turned to face me, the moment empowered by the silent force of wills personified in the rigidity of our bodies.

If I'd been in Dominus, I would see the digital clock ticking the seconds away from our conversation. I broke first. "Tell me, Dad. Who would you have allowed to survive if you would've won?"

He took a placating step toward me. "Your naivety places you in danger."

"I'm not your little girl anymore. You've seen to that. Dominus has changed me in ways you would approve. But it has also changed me in ways you wouldn't like. In my veins runs Persal, but in my heart, I'm none of you, and that's what counts."

Another step toward me, a desperate, pleading stride with arms thrown wide. "Baby, I never chose this for you. I would've shielded you from this."

I backed up, avoiding his reach. "You can only be one thing in your heart. You can't kill people and profess to feel deep love and compassion at the same time."

An emotion wiped down over his face, washing my father away. "There is no black and white. That is the belief of the innocent, and I know you are no longer that innocent girl."

The pounding in my chest thinned my breath.

"To survive Dominus, you have to become another person. It was designed for that purpose. You stand here before me a survivor with only months of training. And so I know, Sable, you have blood on your hands."

I took another step back when my breath wouldn't come at all. Covering my lips with my palms, I turned from him and breathed out the sting in my eyes.

"I know the goodness in your heart. You are not evil. But there is so much cruelty in both our worlds. We can't push for justice when we are weaker than our enemy."

I covered my ears as my only escape then slowly lowered my hands over my lips before dropping my arms to my sides. Clarity was a bitch. I didn't want it. The understanding made the decision too painful. If I let Dad go, if I made Jax fulfill his promise, I would unleash him onto both worlds. Carter, we had to fight, but would I end up fighting Dad too?

"You can never trust another faction, especially Aris."

It took courage to turn and face him, courage because I didn't know what I should do. I could not focus on the decision my heart would make, only the right decision. "You only say that because Carter outsmarted you."

"I say it, because it's true."

"Holden left me to die."

"He knew Jax would save you."

"But Holden didn't save you."

Dad exhaled the depth of his tension. It fled his body, taking with it the strength he needed to keep himself tall. He collapsed onto the cot, elbows to his knees, face buried in his hands. "Holden is an idealist. He's also the last person I expected to betray me."

At last we reached a point in the conversation I would readily engage in. "So, what happens now?"

"We need to find out what Carter is up to."

"What about Mum and Ajay?"

"Holden will see them safe. He may have betrayed me, but he is not a murderer for no reason."

Like you.

"You won't succeed while you're with Jax. He's cunning and unpredictable. There is nothing about him you can trust."

"I think you're wrong."

"He won't accept you, Sable. Not the way you hope he will."

"What are you talking about? We're allies. That's all."

"He will never forgive me. You know that. Every time he looks at you, he will remember what I did."

Damn his perceptive eyes drilling into my heart. Exposed and raw, there was no point in looking away or armoring my emotions. To hear him say it exposed the truth from deep inside. The fear bled me dry. How could Jax ever look at me and not see what he lost? I would become the symbol of his pain. I would always be the daughter of the man who destroyed his life. I would always be Persal. Maybe once he returned to his world, back amongst his people and living with the daily reminder that he was alone, he would remember his torment, remember why the factions stayed apart. Perhaps in our darkest hour, he would decide forgiveness cost him too much. Perhaps then he would hate me.

Dad placed a hand on my shoulder. "I do not say these things to hurt you. I say them to keep you safe. Do not make the same mistakes I've made. The alliance with Aris is over. You're on your own."

Alone. The word rattled around in my heart. "I can't do this on my own."

"You have me. You will always have me."

Not if you're stuck in here.

"Outside the city of Califax, there are villages full of Persal, and they are waiting for my return."

"They knew what you planned on doing?"

"Of course. They have been preparing. These are people you can put your faith in, not a kid from Aris. When we find out what Carter is doing, we will return to Persal HQ. I will make sure you are safely transferred to Uradra, our stronghold outside Califax. It is there Holden would've taken Lila and Ajay."

"And what will you do?"

"Make Carter pay. Then finish this."

I couldn't do this. I pulled away from his hand. "I can't shift. I have no choice but to be with Jax."

My revelation froze Dad, froze time. "There was only the slightest hope," Dad said as he patted my knee, but his weak smile and the way he avoided my eyes told me the truth.

Dad's fate was mine to decide, so too the fate of both our worlds if I set him free.

The sound of movement on the other side of the door was Dad's signal to stand.

"He's returned." I glanced over my shoulder to see Jax's face through the small slot in Dad's door.

Jax would free Dad if I asked. He'd do it, because we put our trust in each other. But if I told him not to, he'd gladly do that too.

What if Carter returned to *finish this*, finish Dad as he would do Carter—without thought or remorse?

"Jax will help me, but he won't help you." My voice broke at the end. I couldn't be faithful to everyone, not when they all insisted on choosing sides. I could only be faithful to my heart.

"I can understand that." He swept me into a fierce embrace and whispered in my ear. "Remember what I told you. Persal HQ. They will see you free." The hug was over with my next inhale. He pushed me away toward the exit. "Don't trust your faction if you choose, but you can trust me. I want you to believe that. I would risk my life to keep you, your mother, and Ajay safe. If anything happens to any of you, then my life is over."

No, Dad, don't say that. Don't say that when I just betrayed you.

I couldn't swallow the pain in my throat nor wipe the sting from my eyes. I had to make a choice that was above my fear and beyond my own self-interests.

I stared at Dad as I backed toward the door, writing the memory of him as it was now, the tight clench in his jaw and broad expanse of his chest, imposing defiance, and yet the soft, loving pull of his eyes asking my forgiveness.

This felt like the penultimate moment, the final outcome at the end of the war, the time to remember those sacrificed.

I was sure I would never see him again.

Chapter 3

JAX TOLD me to stay put, which I did for a whole three minutes before I spied someone mounting the steps to the front door of the warehouse. I left my hiding place on the other side of the road and sprinted across, hoping to catch the door. The guy carried a bag of groceries in each hand and was having a hard time keeping his bundle while backing through the doorway.

I raced up the steps. "Here, let me help you."

"Thanks. I'd curse if my bottle of red ended on the pavement."

Once inside, he juggled the bags to one hand and offered me the other. "Ned. I don't think I've seen you around."

I scooted around him and dashed for the elevator. "I'm not around much," I yelled over my shoulder.

I first rode this elevator with Jax a couple months ago. A lifetime of experiences spanned the distance of that first moment to now. I shed the naïve girl the moment I crossed the threshold into Jax's apartment. Time would not unwind. I'd seen, done, and knew too much. But I would not rewind if the choice was mine. Innocence was a hidden cage. The truth was no greater pain than the entrapment of Dad's lies.

This is the moment your life began. Jax's words the second before he jumped from the Amex Tower. He was right. And I was glad, because I was no longer a victim. I could fight.

The lift doors slid aside. Jax turned to look at me, the brow above his good eye furrowing. I slowed at the sight of Elva, but my heart was bathed in relief. I prayed she would be here, free of Carter's hold, because I needed people to believe in. Trust was an illusion in their world. But I needed it as much as I needed the air to breathe. Despite growing up believing strangers were a threat, there were always three people, my family, I trusted unequivocally in this world. And even now, after it all, I still trusted Dad with my life. But perhaps not with my heart, because I knew what he was capable of; his family were the only people who weren't expendable.

"I told you to wait until I came for you."

I shrugged as I moved closer. "I don't know why you wasted your breath."

Elva's Icelandic glare chilled the air between us, the silence saying this was all my fault, which I accepted. "You're not welcome."

"Elva." Jax let off a warning grumble, but his heart wasn't in it.

"Have you looked in the mirror?"

"Who needs a mirror?" He slumped down in the closest couch. "I can feel it."

Elva stomped past Jax, who was resting his head in the crook of his thumb and forefinger. "You've ruined everything. We had our plans." She pointed behind her at Jax. "He looks like the walking dead. Carter's disappeared, taking his followers with him." She jabbed me in the chest. "You started it."

"We weren't getting anywhere." We both turned to Jax as he spoke. "We were no further in making a successful plan. Perhaps this is for the best."

Elva stomped back to stand in front of Jax. "It's going too fast."

"Wait… you were planning to betray Carter?"

She spun around to face me. "But he's likely to win, thanks to you."

"Holden betrayed us all," I said.

Elva joined Jax on the couch, arms folded across her chest. "He wasn't part of our plan." She looked away, shutting herself up tight behind her pain. Maybe he didn't want to be part of their plan, because he had plans of his own, or his prejudice prevented him from working with them.

"Holden's not our concern. We need to finish what we started," Jax said.

Elva snapped out of her gloom in seconds. She pushed up from the couch. "I'll call Striker and Nuke. They've been waiting to hear from me."

"What have you told them so far?"

"That you're still alive. They told me Reg and Malvo are missing."

Jax snorted an unconvincing laugh like he was questioning her assessment about him being alive, or perhaps it was because of Reg and Malvo. "They'll be with Holden. We've got no time to waste. The other two need to be here ASAP. The longer we delay, the farther Carter moves out of our reach."

Elva punished the screen of her phone with vicious swipes as she searched for their team's cell numbers.

Anyone who looked like Jax did now would be holed up in bed for the next week or checking themselves into the closest emergency department. Not wanting to disturb him, I inched down beside him. My presence was perhaps disturbing him; my next question would disturb him more, but he was stuck with me.

Staring at his profile, the good side of his face, I could be forgiven for forgetting the last few days. I wanted to forget the last few days, the fight, the betrayal, but there was no going back to that girl anymore. The chasm within split me in two. On one side stood the girl I knew. On the other, a sacrifice, and from that sacrifice rose a girl I loathed but longed to be. That girl understood the risk, made the choice, committed the unthinkable, and found her strength. But she had to squash the shame and abhorrence for the things she did in order to succeed in the things she had to do. That girl was the side of me Carter had cultivated into being.

I swallowed. "What's the plan?"

"It doesn't involve you."

"I'll pretend you never said that."

We locked eyes, mine the stronger, because he only had one with enough penetrating power. I no longer had to try for one of Dad's death stares. Anger and determination were the driving force behind all my facial expressions now.

"I haven't just betrayed my father so you can leave me behind, chewing my nails on the couch."

"Why did you want to leave him there?" His voice softened.

"You were right. He would've done the same as Carter. I didn't want it to be about me, but my reason is also a selfish one."

"That's nothing to be ashamed of."

"I don't want to fight my dad, not like we will have to fight Carter."

Jax rested his hand over mine. "That's a better reason than saving the world."

"I hate that you always say the right things." It was the perfect thing to say. *Just like he is.* "What's your plan?" *Don't, don't, just don't. It will hurt you too much.* I forced myself to look away from his good eye. How long could I deny that my feelings for him had changed?

"We must reach the Dome."

"I can't believe you haven't done that already."

"Carter monitored each game. We had no way of reaching that far without him knowing."

"I don't understand why it's necessary. It's a game. Carter's not in the game. Everything he plans to do is here, real life."

"The Dome is the end. It's always been the end. We need to know what we face. In this game, surprises are deadly. And I'm not just talking about Dominus."

"The final confrontation." I echoed the words he spoke the first time I entered Dominus.

Elva returned, the high heels of her boots puncturing the wood floor with her forceful strides. Was it that she infected my mood or the other way around? "They'll be here soon. One thing I should tell you—Carter turned up here a couple hours ago."

"I would've been surprised if he hadn't."

"He was only interested in Dominus."

Jax waited silently for her to elaborate.

"I'm not sure what he did; he was in there a while. I stayed upstairs. I couldn't face him. At that point, I wasn't sure what happened to you."

Jax pushed to his feet. When he reached halfway, he slowed and gripped his side. "There's only one way to know what Carter did."

No point asking him if he felt strong enough to enter Dominus, for I knew what sort of answer I would receive. I followed him into the gaming room, surprised to see everything looked untouched. At the very least, I expected tables overturned and monitors smashed, not the room looking as it did the last time I was here. Perhaps he stripped the game from the computer.

Jax headed to the terminals, Elva to the cupboard. "Everything's still in here." She pulled the equipment out.

"What if we entered without the suits? Wouldn't we be invisible?"

"To ourselves, yes." Her voice was laced with the sarcasm she nurtured especially for me. "The computer would still register our movement."

"We're in."

The word *Dominus* filled the screen, a magnet that had my feet moving to stand beside Jax.

How long had it been? Forty-eight hours, more, less? Time coalesced, but the feelings did not. As I stared at the word *Dominus*, each discrete memory brought its own suffering. Finally, this was our choice, and we were choosing to enter. I wanted to hunt Holden down, rescue Mum and Ajay, not enter the game. But to find my family, I had to be in Jax's world, and I needed him for that. Besides, he stymied his plans so I could see my father first. To follow without complaint—that's what I owed him.

The game came to life, but rather than bark the orders to gear up, Jax stared at the screen. This dragged Elva over, jumpsuit in hand. The silent exchange between them ran heebie-jeebies up my spine.

"What is it?"

Ignoring my question, he fingered the jumpsuit in Elva's hand. "It looks fine. At least he left the equipment alone."

I captured his attention by pushing in front of Elva, separating the two. "What is it?"

"You can't come. The four of us will enter. We'll move quick, find what we need to know, and then return."

"What? I'm not staying here on my own."

"Carter won't come back. This is the safest place for you."

"I'm coming with you."

"Sable, don't. Now is not the time to fight me."

"Let her come… if she so desperately wants to," Elva said.

Despite his damaged features, I could still read the frustration on his face.

"Tell me why you don't want me to come."

"Carter has messed with the game. The lowest level we can enter is Level Nine."

"At least the game is still active."

Jax shook his head. "You don't understand me. You can't play at Level Nine."

"And you can?" I flicked a glance over his wrecked body.

"You can't keep protecting her." I'd never heard softness in Elva's voice. I looked over my shoulder to remind myself it was her who spoke and was surprised to see the softening of her voice had followed through to her expression. Was it Jax's compassion for me, the daughter of the murderer, that strummed the note on her fierce loyalty and deep passion?

"She's involved. You want to protect her, then get out of her way."

Wow, was I hearing this? Elva on my side. And it didn't sound like she wanted me dead. The opposite, she wanted me to thrive.

The damage to Jax's face distorted his expression, but there was no hiding the defeat, it echoed through his body, rounded his shoulders, and forced his gaze to the floor. I hadn't realized until now how nice Jax's hand felt cradled in mine as I folded my palm around it. "It's time you trusted me."

"You've played a handful of times."

"You're not in the best shape, Jax. It's me who needs to protect you."

That one eyebrow rose again. Even his mouth twitched into a pained smile. "How about we protect each other? All of us." His gaze expanded to sweep Elva in then came back to me. "We enter in game mode. Once you're in Aris HQ, the computer will launch a major attack."

Ouch. Not something I wanted to be reminded of. "You need Persal on your side if you want to reach the Dome."

"I can't believe I'm saying this, but a Persal would come in handy," Elva said.

The moment was diffused by the entrance of Patrick, aka Striker, and Nuke. Patrick's jaunty strides as he crossed the floor eased the suffocation in the air, the result of our conversation. His warm smile beamed across the room and right into my heart. "Jeez, girl, that's some handy work of yours."

I'm not sure my replying smile matched his enthusiasm. "Thanks. As impressive as it may look, I failed."

"Not from where we're standing," Nuke said. "Carter's unhinged."

"Perhaps we could save awarding gold stars until after we exit Dominus," Elva said.

"Wow, man." Ignoring Elva's verbal stab, Patrick came alongside Jax. "You look like hell."

"We going in again?" Nuke asked.

Elva threw Nuke a suit. "Level Nine."

Nuke caught his suit one-handed. "And the reason for the high-level fun?"

"Carter's messed with the game," Elva replied as she tossed me a suit.

Jax pulled the silver dots from a metal box, handing some to me first. "For you."

"Why just me?"

"It's not just for you. We all have to wear some; otherwise, we can't control our avatars. And it would be good to keep tabs on your power status. The rest of us are experienced enough with our ability. But I would feel better if you had a way of monitoring what's going on up here." He tapped the side of his head.

"I already know what's going on in my head. I don't need a computer to tell me. I know what it feels like now. I know when my power's coming through, and I know how to moderate it."

"It can get tricky in Dominus."

"I know what it's like. I've been inside, remember?" There was an edge of defense in my voice. Was he questioning my ability to control myself, because of what happened last time?

His one-eyed gaze lacked power. "We won't get through this if we can't agree."

"Nor will we if you don't trust me."

"This is not about trust."

"What're we playing, footsies or Dominus?" Elva's dry tone pulled us out of our stalemate.

Jax leaned in close. "I know what it's like to lose people I love." And then he left me. I watched his back as he crossed to the mat. Once zipped up in his white jumpsuit, he merged with the back wall.

What did he mean? Sure, I knew what the surface statement meant. But was there something deeper? Or was it me peeling through layers that didn't exist? He'd set my mind spinning. Did I want there to be something deeper? Jesus, I did.

Life has meaning because our hearts dictate it so. Take away that one truth and we function; that is all. But our true purpose is to thrive, and to thrive is to share our heart, stitch the tears, patch the wounds, and risk doing it again and again and again.

"Our objective is the Dome," Jax said, cutting through my epiphany.

Nuke released a low whistle. "We're going to be running in circles down there."

Jax pulled the arm of his suit up to his elbow. "Not if I can help it."

"Thank God someone thought ahead. Hope it's accurate enough," Patrick said.

"Is anyone worried about the Persal?" Nuke looked at me. "No offense, but the tunnel is in Aris HQ."

"Discussion's been had. She's coming." Elva strode across to the mat, minus her high heels but no less imposing.

Jax hid the map beneath his jumpsuit again. "Business as usual. We've done this before. Nothing changes. The Dome has its weakness; we've just got to find out where." He switched to game mode. As in his voice, his mind no doubt switched too.

I followed everyone across, taking my position. There was just the five of us on the mat facing each other in a circle. As if sensing some profound moment, Jax stayed quiet. Before we lowered the goggles, I glanced at everyone's faces, but saw nothing in their expressions to reveal the secrets of their thoughts. Elva stared at Jax with her usual barbed expression. Jax was a wall, and the other two looked like they were preparing for a parachute drop or some other similar harmless high-octane sport. We were strangers, Jax and Elva so far apart from the rest of us they were from a different world. Four Aris and one Persal. I would choose to enter the game with these four and no one else. This moment was like the in-between, where nothing happened but anything was possible, the place where our differences were shed and we stood as equals. This was a time where we could all be family.

"How many kills to get out?" I asked.

Jax rested his hands on his goggles, about to lower them into place. "Just keep killing."

Chapter 4

ONCE THE GOGGLES WERE DOWN, we ran. I staggered for a moment when I glanced to the corner of my vision to see my kill quota. Sixty. The digital clock stayed at zero, which was something, I guessed.

"What happened to landing us where we wanted to be?" Nuke asked.

"I don't have control over our location." Although we were at the beginning of the game, Jax already sounded strained.

"I can't wait to torch that asshole," Elva said.

Despite her acidic words, stirring the fury she no doubt cooked inside, she slowed her pace to keep in line with Jax. We all did. How long could he keep this up and still expect to fight? I'd suggest walking to spare him, but that would be like throwing gasoline into flames. Jax would hate the suggestion of weakness.

The tri-blade nudged against my left thigh as I ran, the dagger against my right, both vital to my survival, but more so what swam below my skin. Inside the game and destruction roamed the entirety of my body, tensing muscles coiled to spring. In the real world, I shied from that part of myself. In Dominus, I wrapped it around me like a cloak. Destruction was me, and I was that other girl who risked all for what she believed in.

The Central Airways terminal loomed over the buildings ahead, its bulbous top soaring toward the giant moon. Skytrains swarmed around the platforms, messing up the view with their metallic bodies. Behind that was the Dome, dwarfing the terminal with its cruel, spired majesty. Its glass glistening like dew on spiderwebs in the morning sun.

Everyone diverted left across the street, which gave me hope we were near Aris HQ. As if my thoughts jinxed our progress, a harsh cry sounded from behind. I spun to find a large warrior pounding up the rear like the Terminator on steroids. My tri-blade found my hand when a blur knocked past me and descended on the warrior. The speed at which Jax dispatched the huge warrior by ripping his head from his body could only mean I had to be moving in slow motion. This was Level Nine. I had to remember that. The skill and speed of our opponents would be considerable. What the hell had I walked into?

Because I missed the kill, my skills status bar, having risen, slid back out of orange. I spun away from the carnage, preparing for the onslaught. All it took was one attack, and the rest followed. Ordinary people became our enemy.

An Amazonian woman sprinted ahead of the pack. She was mine, because my tri-blade planted itself deep within her chest. The reaction natural, I barely had to think. Like a gentle caress, destruction soothed along my skin, the feel an addiction. My power status bar registered the caress and shot through to red. I inhaled the metallic smell of blood and flexed my fingers. And there was that feeling again. The same one I felt the last time I played—the feeling of mastery. I was someone now. That's how destruction made me feel.

The coolness of my tri-blade as it appeared in my hand grounded me back into the game.

The game had just begun.

Chaos surrounded me, but I dragged my focus back inside and concentrated on the calm spawned from destruction, my true nature. My mind shut out the peripheral and tuned to the necessary, picking off my next target. And that one act sent my skills status bar through halfway, nudging up to tinge red.

Elva rode the back of a warrior dressed in blue. Her teeth sank into his neck, her nails piercing through his throat. The other three were similarly engaged. They had their game to play, so I shut them out. My eyes fell on the woman in green. The tattoo behind her left ear told me she was one of my family—according to Holden—just like he was supposed to be.

This time, I used the dagger, taking her through the back of the neck, because I needed the tri-blade to cut the maroon warrior off as he ploughed his way toward Nuke.

Level Nine and the game was fast, which meant the return of my weapons came just as fast, but faster still, I released them again. My body was not my own. It moved in a way I'd never possessed before. My weakness in sport, coordination, was now my strength. But through the bellows of war, the snapping of bone, and the cries of anguish, I had no time to marvel at my skill.

I couldn't help but glance to the right of my vision. The digital clock stayed motionless; we weren't on a timer, and our enemies were NPCs, which meant they were easily dispatched without consequences.

The moment that thought flicked into my brain, any courage and skill I felt I gained withered as the memory of my last fight arose.

Not your fault. Not your fault. Not your fault. I continued the mantra as I aimed my tri-blade once more. To end this fight, all I had to do was release destruction, send a lethal injection through the closest warrior, and let it infect the rest. Destruction agreed, tumbling along a restless path beneath my containment.

His name was Harris, but I couldn't speak the name, not now, maybe not ever. His eyes still bored through mine, his blood-soaked breath still brushed my cheeks, and his blade still marked my stomach. But he would never do any of that again. I had seen to that. The claim of self-defense wasn't easy to accept because he was not evil. We'd both been victims. But staring into his eyes, I'd known in that moment only one of us could survive.

Plagued by the past, my body kept moving. I released my weapons without focusing on my aim. I twisted, dodged, ducked, aimed, sliced, kicked. These were motions my body followed, fueled by the violence surrounding me, fueled by an internal instinct, fueled by another force separate but a part of me. Until someone wrenched my arm down.

"Fun's over. Let's go." Wasting no time, Jax headed off down the road, hand clutched to his side in his pained run.

I easily moved alongside him, casting surreptitious glances his way. With the fight over, slain disappeared, clean-up complete, I looked for real wounds, blood seeping through from anything reopened. But of course there would be nothing to see, not in Dominus. Everything real was magically wiped clean. His bare torso wasn't even glistening with sweat, just filled with ridges that announced his muscular frame. It was as false as the depiction of him striding tall. He had popped another couple of tablets he stowed in his pocket before we entered his apartment. And I was supposed to feel confident the tiny tablets would be enough to hold his insides in place, keeping infection at bay. Sure, his facial wounds healed faster than possible, but we were in Dominus; one false move, one lapse of concentration, and anyone of us would be dead.

Aris HQ loomed into view a few blocks away, but before we made it there, a warrior dropped down from the roof of a building and landed on Patrick. Elva sprang, as did Nuke, and that was the end of the opponent, but his efforts drew more. Pedestrians turned into warriors, pulling weapons absent moments ago into their hands. The odds were never in our favor, but this time, it looked grueling. There had to be at least thirty at a rough count. Behind them, more transformed. Perhaps our location, close to Aris HQ, home base, had drawn the computer into attack overload.

Pain slammed into the side of my head, sending my health status bar to red, the indicator I did not want to see topping out to that color. The next thing I knew, my face kissed the paving. Despite the shock and pain, I retained enough sense to know lying still would get me killed. I rolled as a blade embedded in the paving with a *chink* where my head had been. On my back, I stared into the face of a bearded warrior the size of a house. We were moving at triple the speed, but my mind slowed the moment enough for me to stare into his eyes, eyes that should contain no depth, because they were nothing more than a programmed design, but they looked as dark and dangerous as Harris's eyes the moment before I killed him. As his blade rose up again, I rolled to my front, gathered my feet, and sprung out of the way. The slice of his second attack skimmed the small slip of material on my ass.

My blade left my hands as I spun, but before it met its mark, a bolt, looking like lightening, shot from the warrior's free hand and disintegrated my blade. The smell of ozone washed back over my face, singeing my cheeks. I glanced to the faction indicators. Perun was in charge of lightening. Asshole. I'd just have to reply with some juice of my own.

The warrior swung high with his blade. What I caught was the flick of his other hand. The bladed hand was a distraction to what he really intended to do. The bolt jagged across the gap between us. My own ability met it halfway. When the two powers met, it triggered an energetic explosion, with rays of lightening radiating upward to the sky. The force of my destructive nature sent a shockwave blasting outward, the sound a deafening roar. I shielded my ears with my hands and crouched to the ground.

Something the size of a truck—that's what it felt like—knocked me sideways, and I rolled, banging knees and hips and elbows until I finally came to a stop. Joints protesting, I looked back to see Jax finishing some guy off. Sloppy, that's what I'd been, leaving him to down the warrior who'd no doubt been close to downing me. My skills status bar agreed, sagging back from red.

Jax fought with vigor, but how much longer could he go on?

Time to even the battlefield. Destruction wanted to play.

My focus was the warrior closest to me. A funneled stream kept the area of effect contained to just him. With his messy demise, I moved on, dodging blows myself, embedding my tri-blade in one fighter at the same time I kept up my steady annihilation. It took concentration to keep destruction within a certain radius, and it was just as hard to keep myself from being staked, sliced, or fried.

Destruction moved as quick as the Aris team until we freed our path. At the left side of my vision, the digital numbers on my kill quota counted, flipping through ten and kept going, topping out at twenty-four. Jesus, killing had become too easy.

"We have seconds before we're attacked again," was all Jax bothered to say. He was panting, something I rarely heard him do while in Dominus.

"It's just a few blocks; let's go." Elva led, sprinting off down the road in the direction of HQ. Perhaps she noticed Jax was struggling and wanted to take the pressure off him by taking command of our party. Even in the lead, she kept a close eye on Jax, occasionally casting glances his way.

Watching her, a yawning gap cleaved my heart. Dad's words would remain as a shadow of doubt. Dominus forced us to work together for our survival, but what would happen when the game no longer existed, when we returned to Jax's world? I couldn't be with any of them. Aris and Persal couldn't exist together, even if their hearts wanted it so.

Elva's focus was Jax, her lifelong friend, and Carter, as was Jax's. They stood to suffer more from Carter's actions than the rest of us. I could understand their narrow focus. Nuke and Patrick would follow them. While Carter was my focus too, my family came first. Mum and Ajay were my concern above all else. Perhaps the four of them would understand. But they would follow their path, and I would have to follow mine.

Maybe Dad was right. Maybe I needed to think of my own survival and that of my family. The thought weighed my legs, made my body feel like a sack of rocks too heavy to drag around. I didn't want to do this on my own. My throat thinned to a tube, thinking about it. How could I succeed? Where would I even start?

Just finish the game. No point diverting my concentration unless I wanted to find myself speared on the end of some warrior's sword. Dominus was deadly enough without feeding myself more fears and doubts.

Closing off my wandering mind, I picked up my pace, keeping stride with the others as we fast approached Aris HQ.

Chapter 5

ELVA WOUND us to a halt across the road from Aris HQ. The building rose like a beacon of doom. We had to enter, for it was our exit out. Jax would never leave without his answers. The only way to get those was to fight through to the Dome.

Pedestrians remained pedestrians for now, filling the street like a toxic spill, each a potential lethal threat, which would trigger a cascade effect. We had seconds, only that, to stand around stressing on how bad it was for a Persal to enter Aris territory. The computer would launch a major offense, as if what we survived so far was outside that category.

"How bad will it be?" Did I really want the answer?

"Stick to your training and keep together. That's about all I can say," Jax replied.

Nuke turned to me. "Confined spaces and explosives don't work well."

I gave him a wane smile. Jax intervened before I could tell Nuke my control on my factional nature was better than that. "Check your weapon."

"The Perun blew it to pieces."

"And you bested him a beauty, which means you earned your weapon back," Patrick said.

Both blades hung from their holsters at my hips.

"Big brownie points for the winners. Give us more fireworks, and you'll earn yourself extra. Although don't get too fancy. I'd rather the roof didn't cave in on us."

"Don't linger once we're inside. Staying topside will likely get you annihilated," Jax instructed.

"As will hanging around here any longer," Elva said.

Snapped to game reality by Elva's call, Jax turned and jogged across the street without another word. Sandwiched in the middle of Nuke and Patrick, my pulse jacked with each stride I made.

Pedestrians forked around us. My party's eyes followed each one. No one's attention stayed on our path, because the threat loomed at either side. Despite the easy gait, everyone's bodies moved with rigidity, tensed and coiled, ready for a fight. This close to Aris HQ, a Persal amongst the bunch, and we wore a bullseye on each of our chests.

Jax punched through the door to HQ and sprinted down the hall. I slowed to allow the others through first, hoping to delay lethal attacks until everyone was well on their way to the tunnel. Once I crossed the threshold, I was knocked sideways and into the wall by an invisible force. Like being caught in a slow-motion movie, I watched Patrick, who entered just in front of me, turn in a slow arc toward me, yelling something nonsensical. I could've filled a sentence in the time it took him to say one word.

My body moved no quicker than Patrick could speak, but my mind raced ahead on fast-forward. My entering Aris HQ had triggered a reaction none of us anticipated. Fighting in slow motion would be all right if everyone else moved at the same speed. If not, we were screwed.

Watching Jax push past Nuke, who stood in front of Patrick, turned into a slow agony. He too yelled at me, but I understood his garble as much as I had Patrick's. His avatar, which was normally blank, lit up with anger-fueled panic. If Jax was panicking, everyone else should be panicking. Not that it would make our situation any better.

I pushed off the wall, feeling like I moved through thick molasses. The fact that my mind remained unaffected made the struggle of forcing myself into action torture. This was Dominus. Nothing I experienced was real. The computer was warping my perception. If my mind worked at normal speed, then the rest of me would do the same. I just had to fight through the delusion to the truth.

I closed my eyes. *This is not real. This is a delusion.* A few more of those mantras, and I opened my eyes. Jax still pushed past Nuke. Patrick's face remained frozen in shock. *Dammit*, my mind wasn't strong enough. I doubled my efforts to move from the wall, fighting against the invisible energy that held me in place.

My attention was drawn from Jax's stricken face to movement behind me. A huge warrior, head encased in a black-and-red mask, leaving the gray-blue of his eyes to burn through the line of my party directly to me, chopped his way through Elva on a headlong charge down the hall. His blade, the curved bow of a cutlass, sliced with clean efficiency, turning meat and bone to paper then sparking off the walls once through because of the strength at which he swung his weapon.

My horror poured out in one long scream that took eternity to leave my mouth. The party moved in slow motion, but the warrior had the advantage, moving at top speed. Swinging his sword left to right, he ploughed through the rest of my friends in a rampage directed toward me, his eyes the merciless rage of a ferocious churning sea.

Unable to move any faster, I watched in terror as everyone I depended on and cared for were sliced down with brutal skill. Each slice of the warrior's blade tore at me as if I were the one being stripped layer by layer, limb from limb. I sucked in the horror so totally that I became the agony, but not in my body, in my heart.

My health status bar zoomed up to flashing. My skills status bar drained to nothing. Arms felt stapled to my side, legs glued to the ground, I was bound, caged. The suffocating feeling so real my heart just about busted out of my ribcage in my effort to break free.

I tried to scream, but the word came out in one long, drawn-out syllable.

I ducked my head, mustering my strength, and forced against my binds, tensing so hard my veins would burst at any moment. *It's not happening. It's not real. It's not real.* The mantra poured out through a pain bursting through my chest, welling up my throat, and spewing out of my mouth.

When I looked, it was carnage. It was agony. It was too unbearably real to comprehend and stay sane. It was the end.

The silver of the blade became my view. A trickle of blood dripped like tear drops through the vacancy, the stillness so immense I swear I heard them hit the tiled floor at my feet with a *plop*. The blade arced high, spraying the blood drops into a fine curtain across my face.

The snap in my mind like a thump to my head was forceful and absolute. Destruction came through, sharpened with malice, tipped with fury, wielded with calm precision, searing a hole through my brain, which felt so good. The release was a great outpouring of energy.

The sword splintered through the middle. The metal drooped down either side like melting plastic. Destruction continued to splinter up his arm and into his body, splitting him in half. But it did not finish there. With the warrior gone, it ran along the tiled floor, creating one long crack that spread with rapidity. More masked warriors appeared, cramming the hall. Destruction overran them, slicing them down the middle with as much proficiency as the warrior had displaced my friends. None could pass without meeting a similar fate.

When the last defender of Aris HQ lay in a bloody pile on the floor, I collapsed to the tiles, bled dry of emotion. Though not for long. Someone yanked me to my feet. While they did that, my mind scrambled to relay an important fact; I slid down the wall at normal sped.

Jax shoved his face into mine, all beaten up, bruised, yet alive, so very alive. I'd be jubilant if the shock of what I'd seen hadn't sucked my emotions dry. A rough shake of my shoulders as an extra wakeup, he yelled, "What's going on?"

My mouth moved, but my words had taken flight.

Jax pushed me down the hall. I staggered, nearly tripping over the dead. Dead, yes, there had been a fight, but half of them were mutilated, something only Aris could do. The rest were carved cleanly in two. That had been my doing.

As Jax dragged me past, the dead warriors disappeared, clearing our path. Fifty-two, the number of my kill quota, hovered as a faint acknowledgement, siphoned to the back of my mind, because my concentration remained disoriented. I staggered, relied on Jax to keep my legs going. My mind floated, body weakened by the ebb of my adrenaline, but Jax's grip on my arm became my anchor. Someone needed to slap me back into the now.

The painting of the tunnel maze flashed into my consciousness as we passed it by. Jax didn't let go of my arm as he steered me down the next hall. A sudden halt, then Jax said, "This is it."

His one good eye swirling more blood-red than white, it bored into me, saying something he didn't want to repeat out loud. Then he let me go, half shoving me back as he burst through into the room. Elva barged past me and leapt at a warrior waiting inside while Jax busied himself with the other. With both of them engaged, Patrick rushed for a certain place on the floor and crouched, resting his hand on the tile. The floor vortexed inward, tiles falling away, sucked below as a gaping hole revealed a steep stairwell into darkness.

With Patrick's foot on the top step, a glow illuminated our descent. Nuke gave me a gentle push from behind, telling me not to linger. I followed Patrick down, with Nuke close behind. The cold wall chilled my palms as I traced my hand along the rock for balance. There was no wall, no stairwell, no slow-motion fight, and yet I was descending, fingers freezing, relaying a fight that left my body trembling.

I glanced over my shoulder to see Jax coming up behind, Elva bringing up the rear. The knot in my stomach uncoiled a couple of rounds seeing Jax's face, but my limbs still tremored. With everything moving so fast, my body had yet to shake off the fear. My mind still swam in a haze, trying to grasp the reality that everyone was still alive. I glanced to my status bars, finding solace in seeing my power status bar in red. But I didn't need the visual to know my factional nature stayed close within reach. I could feel it wandering below my skin.

Once we reached the bottom of the steps, the tunnel lit up, showing the way. No fighting room in here with the low ceiling almost touching the top of Jax's head and the width less than an arm's span. The cold crept under the small scraps of fabric that hid my private parts. I breathed it deep into my lungs along with the dank, musty smell.

About to comment on how thoroughly my senses were hijacked, I was stopped when Patrick turned to Jax. "Perhaps you should lead the way."

While not as big as Jax, Patrick wasn't small, which meant shifting positions within the tunnel took some awkward maneuvering. Jax squeezed my arm as he pushed past me. A minor touch, but after seeing his body sliced in half, I shuddered an exhalation and wiped some strands from my brow with a faint tremor in my hand, streams of adrenaline still working their magic.

Jax studied his forearm, running a hand along the tattoo. "We have about a hundred paces, and then the tunnel branches. While we go, I'll try to work out the right path, but I'll need to follow the other paths to rule out the dead ends." He craned his neck to look to Elva at the back. "There's no guarantee we won't have visitors from the rear, so keep alert." He looked at me. "I think you've bought us some time. The stunt you pulled back there has earned you more brownie points. Check your belt." His gaze did just that.

I looked down to find a small axe resting alongside my tri-blade. "Why this?"

"You've earned some extra weapons thanks to your skill with your factional nature in scoring kills. You'll also find your skill level with the weapons has improved."

"More brownie points," Patrick said.

"We're also likely to get a head start," Jax added. "Which we shouldn't waste."

"I saw you all being killed, in slow motion." The words left a foul taste in my mouth. Just uttering them sent me back a few short minutes to being pressed up against the wall, unable to move, unable to fight. Once again, my body responded, heartbeats fracturing like the strength of the rhythm would falter any minute. The tremor through my body was so violent I was sure everyone could see.

Patrick, directly in front of me, frowned. "Not us, baby, but the warriors didn't stand a chance."

"I don't understand what happened," I said.

"That was Aris's defense and something I have to admit I didn't expect, not like that. You have to remember not everything you see will be shared by the other players," Jax explained.

"You're lucky none of you witnessed what I saw."

The conversation descended us all into silence as if we were paying respects for the fallen. Nuke placed a hand on my shoulder. "I guess that means your initiation is over. At some point, everyone faces a gruesome lesson alone. Dominus can affect the mind of each individual differently while still displaying the overall game stage to every player."

"Carter is one sick bastard," I said.

No, not just Carter. Dominus was not Carter's idea alone. Dad played his part too, demanding the creators—of which Elva and Jax were two—to produce the sick and twisted special effects they wanted, each idea designed to strip a person of their humanity and mold them into the perfect tool.

As if sensing the uncomfortable silence, Jax said, "We're eating into our head start." He set off, going as fast as the narrow tunnel would allow, as fast as his body would allow.

We crowded along behind him. The narrow walls felt protective; how could we be attacked down here? Sure, we didn't have room to fight, but neither would whoever came after us. But this was Level Nine. No time for complacency, for it was akin to an early death.

"How's it going down the back, Elva? Clear?" Jax asked, almost as if he read my mind. His cautious tone wiped the security I felt from our confined space. "Try not to become too strung out." Another warning that gobbled up my confidence. Lesson understood—in Dominus, expect anything.

We finally reached the fork Jax had spoken of earlier. We gathered in the space now widened to accommodate the extra direction and waited for Jax as he ran a finger along the branching tattoo, trying to find our route. The other three flicked glances down each tunnel. Always alert. My lack of training and experience meant I readily relied on Jax to give the signal. But being a member of the party, I needed to be an active player, not a passive participant. Besides, I had to wipe out my memory and concentrate on the game, my surroundings, and any noises I heard. Hopefully, this would keep my mind from recalling what I'd seen.

Our avatar faces were distinct in the mysterious glow of light that shone the way. We were nothing but sharp juts and chiseled angles, defined muscles and ridges. Everything about us was a fabrication, like Dominus, and as real as the slow-mo fight I'd experienced moments ago. All in my head, but close to killing me.

My party, the bond we shared, felt like the only real thing at this moment. But that too could turn into a fabrication when the right moment arose.

"This way." Jax headed left. We followed without question, me safely sandwiched between my Aris friends. For everything they did for me, I would not let them down. If there was only one promise I could make, that was it.

Chapter 6

We all skidded to a halt with the rumble beneath our feet.

"Anyone care to guess what that was?" Patrick said.

Silence from the two who helped design Dominus did not bode well.

"Felt like an earthquake," Nuke said.

"In a game?"

"Really? After all this time, you're going to start questioning the reality of what you experience inside Dominus?"

"How about you children shut up and keep your pace." Elva's voice of reason, brittle as new-season ice, cut through the squabble.

"Just keeping the tension light," Patrick said.

"We'll take the next left." Jax peered in close to his forearm. "Looks like it widens out into a cavern not too far ahead."

I wasn't about to point out how neither Jax nor Elva bothered to answer Patrick about the rumble. They either didn't know or think it important. And given everything we had to worry about, the question was best left behind us.

The tunnel ceiling glowed a mysterious dull blue-white. Without it, the tunnel would be a black hole forcing us to move with caution, using the wall as our guide with no hope of finding our way. "Where's the light coming from?"

"We programmed the lighting into the game to help those who made it this far, back when we thought Carter and Nixon would allow us to enter the tunnel. In the real tunnel, we've buried trylite into the walls and ceiling. It's a special rock that is mined in the deserts thirty miles sunder of Califax. The Senate of Factions control the area. It's mined under strict regulations to ensure no faction contains the monopoly. It's expensive stuff because of its natural illuminance. Our cities are lit by the usual means, because the cost of buying trylite makes its wide-scale use prohibitive. Plus, it doesn't give a bright light. Ironically, it's cheaper to use in the long run. Thanks to Carter and Nixon, we were able to source an ample supply of the rock for the tunnel."

"That, I would like to see," Patrick said.

"It would mean leaving your world for ours," Jax replied.

"Hallelujah, show me the way."

"You wouldn't be so ready to give up your world if you understood mine."

"If you knew my life, you wouldn't question my desire."

The quiet hung in the air like smoke, suffocating and persistent. Except Jax and Elva, we knew little about each other and the experiences that warped us for better or worse. Inside Dominus was not a time to explore our diversity, but his comment reminded me there were many ways to suffer, many people who'd suffered, and many paths that enabled finding commonality with others. But in Jax's world, factional differences overshadowed everything else.

"Oh, God, I just remembered," I said, coming to a halt, banking up the three behind me. "Carter said he and Dad made changes to the game, so it would hijack everyone's free will, forcing them to belief only in his vision, just like brainwashing. It's the reason no one has questioned the sanity of what we're doing."

"He did?" Elva's question speared through the dull light.

"It doesn't work on anyone native to his world. I wasn't playing long enough to experience any effect. Patrick and Nuke, both of you were, but you've betrayed Carter to help us."

"I don't feel any different," Nuke replied.

"Me neither," Patrick said.

"But this is great. It means Carter's tweaks weren't foolproof. There has to be others free from his control," I added.

"If there are, once they're in my world, it won't make any difference," Jax said.

"But it does. They'll refuse to fight."

"I'm not sure they'll have a choice. Not once the senate finds out. Fear is the greatest influencer. And the senate isn't known for their leniency. Carter's plan will be the more attractive option."

"Maybe the senate finding out will be the better option," I said.

"I'll be glad when you reach our world. Then maybe you will stop being so pathetically idealistic," Elva said.

With the dull blue light from above, Jax's features looked ghostly. "The senate usually acts with retribution. And they cast a wide net. Many innocents will be caught inside. It's not something you want to happen."

He continued on, leading the way through the small tunnel. I followed after with my head twisted in conflicted knots. Carter's war was wrong. But the senate didn't sound much better. Who could blame people for wanting to free themselves from suppression and tyranny?

I didn't get to argue with myself over whose war would be more just, because the tunnel widened out into the cavern Jax mentioned earlier.

"'Bout bloody time. My neck's developed a crick from being bent so long," Nuke said.

We fanned out in a semi-circle, attention centered on the pool of water in front of us. The mysterious glow from the cavern ceiling ran in a blue line across the surface of the water. Like a map showing the way, the line of light, sharp and smooth in the ripple-less pool, revealed the only tunnel exit on the other side.

"Before we get in that water, I want to know for sure this is the right way," Patrick said, but Jax was already scrutinizing his forearm, holding it up close to his face, because the dull ceiling glow provided little in the way of a torch for map reading.

"Can't swim?" Nuke said.

"It looks cold, and yes, I know it's all in my head, but we all know how much Dominus messes with our heads. I'm not keen on making the trip back because we made a wrong turn."

Elva moved to stand beside Jax. "Well?"

"It's the only way. When we get beyond this, there will be a myriad of choices. Things could get a little tricky."

"Tricky! What do you call this?" Patrick said.

"We've come this far unmolested. I'd say that's thanks to our efforts in cleaning out Aris HQ. But we've still got a long way to go."

"I'm a good swimmer." I smiled at Elva. I meant I was willing to take the plunge, but her snarl told me she thought I was boasting. Would we ever be friends? Probably not. And why should I be able to read her avatar facial expression easier than I could read Jax's?

Like a good leader, Jax plunged in first, sinking to his waist in no time.

"This sucks," Patrick said as he waded out after Jax.

I touched my toes in the shallows and gulped in a sharp breath with the feel of ice-cold water penetrating through my shoes. *I'm not really about to enter a black lagoon.* The shiver that raced up my spine told me otherwise.

"How deep is it?" I asked.

"Don't know. Elva and I weren't responsible for designing this."

"You don't suppose there is something in here?" Nuke said.

"We're in Dominus. Of course there will be monsters in the water," Patrick responded.

I was the only one not up to my waist, so I held my breath and waded forward. The cold rushed around my ankles, down into my shoes. Farther in, it gripped the calves of my legs and sent shards like ice up my inner thighs. By the time the water reached my waist, my breath wheezed in and stalled. "I hope we'll dry off automatically once we reach the other end."

"You've got nothing on that'll weigh you down when wet." Patrick's words came out choppy through chattering teeth.

He had a point. My bra and briefs were like bathers.

No good thinking about the hidden depths of the black pool and what could be lurking. This was the only way across, and the others were leaving me behind. I pushed off from the rocky bottom and settled into freestyle to catch up. Not wanting to put my head under the water, my strokes were awkward and slow. Like an optical illusion, the gap between myself and the others increased with every stroke I made. The pool itself appeared to stretch farther into the tunnel mouth, which had to be all in my head, another Dominus mind game.

I abandoned my vigil on the whereabouts of the others and concentrated on increasing the speed of my strokes. My weapons felt like anchors at my sides. The battle axe banged against the front of my left thigh as I kicked my legs, trying to gain the extra speed. At this rate, the others would reach the other end while I was still at the beginning.

The cold was a vice around my chest. My inhale was a gasp sucked up a tube the size of a pin head. I slowed to scan for the others, who were now just small heads bobbing through the water as they disappeared to the other side.

In the dim light, the digital display messed with my night vision. Stupid bloody status bars. And all the info on the factions was cramming up one side of my vision. If only there was a way to turn it down.

I stopped, my legs spinning frantic pinwheels to keep me afloat. The axe had to go. I wrenched at the stone head, but it wouldn't budge. The handle had to be caught in the fastening. Since the thing appeared at my side, I had no idea how it latched to my belt. What special clips or tags held it in place?

Legs going like a beater, I attempted to yank the axe from its place. "God dammit." It wouldn't move. Without my hands helping me stay above water, I sunk to my chin. The churn of the water and a mouthful, feeling like ice sludge, rushed down my throat. I let go of the axe head and flailed my arms, coughing and splattering the ice sludge out of my mouth. The cold so deep. There was no flavor to the water, no stagnant or putrefied taste that would make me wretch, just the feeling of a knife slicing down my throat and into my chest.

A slimy slither brushed across my right calf. "Jesus, what was that?" I flapped backward, making enough noise to echo back up the tunnel to Aris HQ.

"What did you feel?" Jax was the first to respond.

"Something slimy, like a tentacle."

The mention of it had my stomach zipped up to a small bag.

"Swim." Jax only needed to say the command once. Everyone

splashed through the water in an uncoordinated race to get out, including me, the weight of my weapons forgotten.

The inky black of the water fed horror scenarios through my head. I felt a million slimy tentacles crisscrossing my body, wrapping around my legs, tugging, tugging me under. I gasped and spluttered, swallowing mouthfuls of water—which weren't real—because my mad dash churned the water like rapids.

Jesus Christ, get a grip, Sable.

The unknown was the terror I faced. It took hold, kidnapping my sanity. I splashed about without making progress, because I couldn't focus on saving myself when my mind was constantly constructing the feeling of something grabbing my legs and pulling me back.

"Nuke." It was Elva's voice.

The single cry stilled me. I tried to count heads, but the damn digital display crapped up my vision. Jax was waist deep on the other side of the pool, but with Elva's cry, he splashed back into the pool.

"No!" Patrick yelled at him. "No point in you risking yourself."

Someone bobbed down beneath the surface. At least I hoped they bobbed down and had not been yanked.

I held my breath, trying to peer through the light show in my way. I flicked a glance to the bottom left of my screen, scanning down the list of factions. Phonus ruled the night. There was nothing darker than underground. This had to be one of Phonus's night pets.

"There has to be a Phonus warrior close by controlling it!" I yelled.

Jax backed out of the water, skimming the cavern for movement.

With a sudden splash, Nuke shot to the surface, gasping for air.

Next to him, another head popped up. "Oh god, Nuke." Elva swam toward him. "Are you all right?"

"You need to ask the critter that," Nuke said between gasping breaths. "I know you want to kiss me right now, Elva, but how about we leave that until we're on the shore?"

"Finish the crossing. Get out of the water!" Jax yelled from the shore. How did the injured amongst us manage to reach the shore first?

I followed the other three, pounding my arms that were fast losing their sense of touch through the cold. I managed a few strokes, when a wall of fire corralled us backward from the shore.

I scanned my left vision for the culprit. Negal, fire and pestilence. And knowing that didn't help me any. While I was at it, I risked a quick look at my status bars to see my health status bar inch higher with each breath I made. The chill was working its way deep within, freezing me from the inside. Soon, I would be frozen in place.

Splashes just outside the wall of fire meant something was rearing out of the water or something was coming in. The wall was too high for me to see Jax on the shoreline. The intensity of the fire created its own wind. I squeezed my eyes tight as a hot gust burned my face and funneled down my throat to scorch my lungs. The pain constricted my windpipe. But the instant heat did nothing to soothe the cold in my heart.

I gagged on water and surged to the surface only to have my face dried in a nanosecond. Someone grabbed my arm and tugged me around.

"Turn your back to the flames" Elva yelled over the roar generated by the scorching wind.

We all ended up facing each other in a circle, Patrick opposite me. Behind him, I spied someone emerge from the flames, a face half-masked by leather. Small spears like needle-sharp teeth protruded from the leather on his cheek. The nightmare deepened with the appearance of a ring of warriors, silent assassins swimming through the flames, gliding with the grace of sharks.

In the water, what use were weapons? And I wasn't sure if in my panic I could control my factional nature enough to prevent the cavern roof from coming down.

A thick arm grabbed me from behind, clamping me around my throat, cutting off any scream. My struggles were pathetic, legs banging helplessly against the warrior's large body. In one firm tug, the warrior pulled me under. I flailed, using up my energy and my breath without succeeding to free myself. The idea broke the mental restraints I used to keep my factional nature in. I cloaked myself in its lure, warming from the strength it gave. But what did I fear more, drowning or bringing the tunnel ceiling down on our heads?

Before my ability punctured a hole through my control, the arm around my throat lessened. Not waiting for the warrior to gain a better grip, I swam to the surface. Someone burst from the water in front of me. I whipped my dagger from my belt in one smooth action that impressed the hell out of me and jabbed the dagger in a downward motion to pierce the warrior's skull. A hand manacled my wrist.

Jax pulled me close, his face shoved into mine. "Swim for the flames. When you're close, duck under the water and pass underneath. We'll take care of this."

"Jax," I gasped, fingering his face.

He released my wrist and pushed me away. "Go!" he shouted at me.

"You're not giving me a chance." None of them understood how much I'd made peace with my destruction, how much the two of us worked together, most of the time.

"It's not that. I wouldn't put it past Carter to construct this part of the game with paper-thin walls. We're in Level Nine, which places constraints on what we may and may not do."

"That sucks."

"It's called Dominus. Now get out of here." Without another word, he swam back into the fight.

The flames flicked and danced across the surface of the pool, creating a light show that would be stunning anywhere else. The sound of fighting cornered me. My factional nature did not want to leave. Destruction thrived on the swirl of chaos. All around me, the grunts and noise of fighting, the guttural cries of death, fed my need to destroy. The ache of withholding my power seized my limbs. I trod water, fighting with myself.

My inertia broke when I spied a dip in the wall of flames. It took immense effort to force my arms to obey. Destruction wanted to hijack my body, turn me around the other way. While in Dominus it felt like that side of me became the bigger part.

With the first few strokes, my saner side won, destruction subdued. I swam like it was the last act I would perform. This close to the flames, my eyes dried, blurring my vision. My skin felt ready to peel. I inhaled a deep breath and ducked below. Underneath the flames, the water boiled like hot lava. I pushed to the surface again, shielding my face. There was no going under unless I wanted to cook the flesh from my bones.

Behind me, the fighting continued. The wall of flames spiraled tighter, forcing us into a burning soup in the middle. This was the only way out.

Nothing is real. Why did I bother to tell myself those things? It never made any difference. I would have to swim like hell and forget the rest.

I took two breaths then ducked under the water again. Swimming forward was like swimming into the center of a volcano. The skin on my fingers burned first. The spear of heat shot up my arms and rushed over my face. The scream bulged my cheeks. Eyes squeezed shut, I blew hard through my nose to keep the lava out. My lips felt like they were being peeled away. The burn moved over my body, scorching my flesh. The urge to open my eyes and look at my health status bar nearly overrode sense.

The swim turned into the rest of my life, which shortened by the second. I was engulfed with the fiery agony of being burned alive, skin stripped, bones charred. But still, I swam. And that was it. I could still swim. If I could still swim, my mind had not shorted out with the overload of pain.

Jax said experienced players were able to blanket Dominus's control over their deaths. I felt every inch of this torture, yet I was still alive, which had to mean Dominus could no longer convince me I was dying. The idea gave me the power I needed to push through the wall of lava and reach the other side.

When the temperature cooled, I swam upward and surfaced into the dull blue-white light from the ceiling of the cavern, the shore not far ahead. The flames were gone. I straightened to find my feet hit the bottom of the rocky pool. Once I reached waist height, I spun, searching for the others.

"Is everyone all right?" Jax's yell echoed around the cavern.

With each reply, my exhale grew deeper.

I crawled up onto the bank and collapsed with my head against the smooth stone. Tension gone, I felt limp.

With the sound of the others splashing to shore, I slid farther down until the entirety of my body lay on the cold rock. The cold was the elixir I needed. I'd even enjoy lying on a slab of ice right now.

After a few more calming breaths, I raised my arm so I could see my flesh was intact. I even ran my hands over my waist, savoring the feel of smooth skin, all thanks to Dominus's mind control; in reality I was wearing a white jumpsuit.

"How much longer do we have to go?" Nuke asked.

Jax had collapsed beside me. He continued to stay on his knees and elbows, head bent. I listened to his harsh breathing. How much more did he have left in him? Elva shuffled over and ran a soothing hand down his back. "It can't be much farther."

Jax gave himself the time for one more breath before he sat up, heaving himself over onto his ass like he aged a hundred years in one fight. "This is all too easy."

"Not according to my status bars," Patrick said from his position on his back.

"This is Level Nine, yet we've made it this far underground and only once faced an attack."

"Carter and Nixon never anticipated anyone ever getting this far, so they didn't bother creating extravagant defenses," Nuke suggested.

"Carter never underestimates anyone," Jax said.

And with that pronouncement, we all fell silent, except for someone's stomach, which decided to growl in the quiet.

"Now that's something seriously missing in this game," Patrick said. "Don't you guys have vending machines in your world? If you don't, I'm in no hurry to visit."

With the mention of food, my stomach joined in. As if the grumbles spurned him on, Jax launched to his feet. "I think that's enough sitting on our asses."

Elva followed, giving Nuke her hand. He groaned as he accepted her offer.

"Are you sure you're ready to continue?" she asked once Nuke released her hand.

"I'm always ready." Jax patted her shoulder. "We're going to win. You know that, right?"

She reciprocated with an insipid smile. "We always do." Her voiced sounded tired to me.

Chapter 7

JAX DROVE OUR ARDUOUS PACE, now that the tunnel widened, speeding up with each scan of his forearm. I would like to think it was because he saw the end around the next bend and not because there were far too many forks left to take. I breathed deep through the stitch cramping up my left side. After feeling my skin burned from my body, I was not about to complain about something so insignificant.

We were nearing our end goal, according to Jax some turns back, which felt like hours ago. The grumble in my stomach had turned into the sort of sickly churn you get when the stomach acid has nothing to dissolve but your stomach lining. If we didn't reach the end soon, I would likely start gnawing on someone's arm.

On the next divide in the tunnel, Jax halted us with a raised hand. "Straight ahead and we're there."

"Feels like we've been training a lifetime for this moment. Anyone want to say something on this momentous occasion?" Patrick asked.

"My guess is entering won't be easy. The point of Dominus was to train us to reach this goal. Don't think the hard part was the journey here. I would say our work has just begun," Jax said.

"Just as long as they have food in this place." And to illustrate my sentiment, my stomach grouched loud enough for everyone to hear.

"You best stay here then. We wouldn't want you messing up and keeping us stuck in Dominus, because you were distracted by your stomach." As always, Elva injected enough nasty tone to leave me in little doubt she spoke down to me, not at me. I swear she blamed me for Holden's treachery, possibly even twisting the stupid factional mess enough to make me responsible for his inability to love her.

Jax came to stand between us. "No one gets left behind." He glanced down at me. "One more push and it will all be over."

"One way or another," Nuke muttered.

Jax led the way. Patrick waited for me to go in front, and Elva once again came behind. She'd proven more than capable, so chivalry wasn't needed here; I'd say her skills in a fight outmatched Nuke's and Patrick's put together.

Around another bend and we came to the base of a steep stairwell, much like the one at Aris HQ.

Jax placed a hand on my shoulder and gently squeezed. "Up there is our way out."

"At least we don't have to retrace our steps. I say let's mount them damn stairs and get this over with. I'm not a mole," Patrick said.

Jax looked at the others then down at me. "Try not to destroy anything too early. We need to learn as much as we can about the place before we demolish it." He smiled, which was encouraging, the first genuine smile I'd seen on him for a long time, the first real expression I'd been able to detect on his avatar face. The openness of his expression made me realize how much of his peace was eaten up by Carter's demands. There was no need for pretense anymore. He was as close as he'd ever come to beating Carter—nowhere near close enough, but he was finally trying to carve his own hope for the future. Once we smashed our way through the Dome's defenses, he would learn the secret he spent years preparing to understand, something he seemed to feel was the key to our final success and Carter's downfall.

Jax spun, about to mount the stairs, when something fell from the ceiling on top of him, dragging him down the first step and onto his back. In the blue-white light, black engulfed him like a shroud.

Elva moved first, crashing me out the way as she sprung toward Jax on the ground. Before she reached him, another black shape dropped down from above, knocking her over before encasing her in a black cloak. The two writhed helplessly on the ground, their legs poking out the bottom, the only parts of them we could see. Muffled cries and grunts of strain sounded from the struggles as the shapes of body parts protruded through the black coverings, which looked more like a PVC blanket contouring to the outline of their bodies than a creature. But the way they moved over Jax and Elva's bodies, sliding and slithering, repositioning themselves whenever they slipped, there was no doubt these things were alive.

"What the hell?" Nuke yelled, as he leaped forward.

I reached for his arm but missed. "No, wait. The same will—"

Too late. Nuke was engulfed in the same blackness that entangled the others. I could see the outline of Elva's face project through the covering, the black adhering to her nose like cling wrap. Her next inhale sucked the black into her mouth.

"It's suffocating them," Patrick said, surging forward.

"Be smart about this." I stalled him. "These are night creatures."

Patrick craned to the ceiling as I looked over my shoulder. The muffled cries of the others slowly suffocating under the tight wrap of the black creatures caused destruction to rage beneath the boundaries of my skin. The marker on my power status bar couldn't move any higher. But there was no visible opponent.

"Do you see anything?" I asked.

"The bastards are keeping well hidden. We've got to get that stuff off of them."

"You move and they'll have you too."

Patrick spun on me. "We have to do something."

"You want to be a victim, then do it. There's an invisible boundary in front. Go over that and you'll trigger another one to drop down on top of you."

"Then get fancy," Patrick said.

But where were the Phonus warriors? How could I destroy them if I couldn't even see them?

Jax had shielded his mouth with his forearm, preventing the black from suffocating him, but Elva had not reached up in time. She arched her body off the ground, flailing her arms while the black sucked up her nostrils and caved into her mouth. Nuke was on his side, so I couldn't see how he faired.

There was no time left.

"We're going to lose Elva if you take any more time."

My eyes ran the length of the steps, which cut up into the ceiling, up into the darkness that lay hidden at the top. "She's too tough to allow Dominus to rule her mind like that," I said. Either way, I was going to waste these Phonus bastards.

There was nothing to see up there, which meant our not-so-friendly friends had to be hiding in the darkness at the top of the stairs.

I funneled destruction up the steps, flowing it out like a gushing flood of water. It tumbled forward, a waterfall running backward, gaining momentum as it coursed up toward the door at the top. The blast channeled through my ears. I ducked, shielding my face, but the only thing that poured down on top of us was a blinding ray of light.

The black creatures were gone, leaving Elva, Jax, and Nuke like newborns rolling on the rocks, blinking in the bright sunlight.

"How did you know?" Patrick asked, bending down to offer his hand to Elva.

"Lucky guess. We couldn't see them anywhere, so I figured they had to be hiding behind the door. If we'd made it past their creatures, then they would be the first thing we encountered."

Elva humphed as she glanced sideways at me. "Thanks."

I tried to keep my triumphant smile to a small crease.

"The walls aren't coming down around us, so I'd say our cautionary measures so far have been unnecessary," Jax said, rubbing his side. "But don't let that fool you into thinking there'll be no more surprises." He spared a moment to meet each of our eyes. "You did good, Sable."

The bright light meant I could finally see his features properly, but anything special on his face was buried below his avatar expression.

"Let's finish this," he said.

"Seventy-two," I said, which made everyone stop and turn to me.

"I've got seventy-two kills now. That means I'm out first opportunity."

"Anyone else not at their quota?" Jax asked, glancing around.

"I'm good," Nuke said.

Patrick gave a thumbs up. "Me too," Patrick

Elva moved toward the stairs. "You need ask?" She smiled at Jax as she placed her foot on the first step.

Jax bounded up the stairs, the rest of us close at his heels. By the time I neared the top, I gasped for air. My fingers went to my weapons on my belt, fingering each for reassurance. The tri-blade first, my preferred weapon, then the dagger and the axe. Or maybe I would forgo all of those and let destruction have its way.

First to the top step and out into the blinding white light, Jax staggered to a halt, blocking our entrance.

"What the hell?" he said as he moved away from the entrance and into the Dome.

Given his slow exit from the tunnel and no obvious sounds of fighting, I eased my hand off my tri-blade and followed Nuke up into the light.

I stepped into the void, expecting to feel some form of delineation, a marker as to the pinnacle we reached. Nothing. I stumbled into Nuke's back and found the other three standing just in front, turning slack-jawed at the sight surrounding us.

The Dome was a void. No warriors appeared to defend against our attack, no marble halls with expansive ceilings, no glass windows towering to the sky. There was nothing.

"This doesn't look right." Patrick spun in a slow arc.

Jax shielded his eyes with his hand as he ducked his head. Elva touched his shoulder as she walked past him, turning circles as she went.

"There's nothing at the Dome. Is this what it means?" Nuke said.

"No, dumbass, it means Carter wiped the Dome from the game. That's what he did when he returned here after the fight at the Amex," Elva replied.

"He sure didn't want anyone getting in," Patrick said.

"What do you suppose he's hiding?" I asked, glancing at Jax, his head still buried in his hand.

"If we knew that, we wouldn't be here." Yet another moment Elva could enjoy spearing me with her sarcasm. But she was right—dumb question on my behalf, yet surely one of them would've heard rumors.

"How many people work at the Dome who are not a part of the senate?"

"What's that got to do with any of this?" Elva said.

"You're telling me not one person has let slip why the senate keeps what's inside the Dome a secret?"

Elva let me know what she thought of my questions by turning her back on me.

Jax dropped his hand. The next minute, he disappeared from in front of me. Elva did too. I ripped my own goggles from my eyes and blinked in the normalcy of the white room, Dominus left behind. Hopefully for good.

Jax threw his goggles on the mat and strode across the room, climbing out of the white jumpsuit as he went. I hastened after him, jumping on the spot for a moment while I slipped my own jumpsuit off each leg. No one bothered to be neat, so I left everything where I stripped and headed out of the gaming room after the others.

"Maybe there never was anything at the end of the tunnel."

"No." Jax shook his head. "It wouldn't make sense." At least he was back to talking again. "That was our end goal. Why create a game for that reason alone and not bother to detail the finish?"

"He doesn't want us getting there first," Elva said, slumping down into the closest seat and folding her legs over the armrest.

"Carter has lied all along. We know that for sure. Maybe he never intended for any of us to survive the initial fight," I said.

"We're the weapons, and weapons are easily disposed of when they reach their use-by date," Nuke said.

Jax stared off into space, keeping himself separate from the conversation, his face the usual impenetrable wall. His hopes in our future success had ridden on our final push.

I placed my hand over my stomach as it churned then growled. Now was not the time for mundane activities like eating. No one reacted to my stomach's plea, so I ignored it and slid onto the armrest of a vacant couch.

"What's our plan?" Patrick eased down onto the couch next to Elva.

Like he hadn't heard the question, Jax stayed quiet, either thinking or stymied. The last time I'd seen him hopeless was when I left to blow the roof off the Amex Tower. I'd been fueled with my conviction, which had given us both a vehicle through which to act. But there was nothing left in me now to drag him out of the quagmire of his mind. Our situation looked bleak at any angle. Never accept defeat; Dad taught me that. Five against Carter's army, odds were against us, but the smartest survive; Jax taught me that.

"Weren't you the one who told me I had to push beyond the boundaries of my limitations and master my fears? Well, I've done that, and I'm still here."

In unison, their faces turned to me, expressions telling me I'd just spoken a weird dialect.

"What are you talking about?" Elva said in the same tone she'd use to ask, *Are you two?*

"The four of you look defeated."

"How 'bout you let us suck up some inertia for a while. I think we've earned it," Patrick said.

Maybe I was the only one willing to function, because my plans hadn't involved the Dome. Finding it a void did nothing to ruin my path. I slid down onto the couch. "The Dome was Carter's end. But it doesn't have to be your end."

"What's your plan, Einstein?"

I ignored Elva and looked at Jax. His eyes were on me.

"Dad told me there were Persal waiting for his arrival in a village called Uradra. That these people knew everything about his and Carter's plans. Maybe Carter did the same. Maybe the reach of this plan is wider than either of you anticipated. I'm counting on neither Carter nor my dad telling anyone, including each other, the truth of what they hoped the outcome would be and their plans to fulfill it."

"Do you think there would be anyone else from the senate who knows?" Nuke asked.

"No way," Elva and Jax chimed together.

"The senate would've had both of them and their families killed plus half of either faction's HQ wiped clean just to make sure," Jax said. "They would also send out emissaries to village strongholds to monitor for any rebellion."

"Real friendly world you've got there," Nuke said.

"Dad could tell me what Carter wanted to hide."

Jax's gaze wandered my way. *Do I really want to do it all again?* That was the question in his eyes. Yes, if it gave us the clue we needed.

He slid up from the couch and passed me, heading for the kitchen. "Anyone else need something to eat?" he called over his shoulder.

"I thought we'd never get around to the serious stuff," Patrick said, climbing out of his seat.

Nuke was on Patrick's heels, which left Elva and me. Only a few times I'd been stuck alone in her company, and those had been some of the most uncomfortable moments of my life. On the verge of following the others into the kitchen, I stalled, not wanting it to look like I was using them as a shield between the two of us. Emotional transparency was great when the other person only had good words about you to reveal; otherwise, it sucked. Especially when whatever had to be said would be delivered with barbed words.

"If you cared for Jax just one bit, you'd stop bringing your dad into this." A lip curl from her would've been perfect at this moment.

"It's because I care that I mentioned it. He didn't get what he wanted from Dominus, but my dad could give it to him."

Looking like she'd eaten rotten fruit, her lip did curl. "Then you know little about Jax. He'd rather play Level Ten in Dominus than accept your father's help."

So Jax had not told her about his willingness to help my dad escape jail. And that it was only because of me he remained incarcerated.

"You want to help, go join your own faction. Give Jax some space."

Was this the same woman who stood up for me before we entered the game a few hours ago? Her mercurial moods toward me made knowing where I stood with her like walking on fractured glass. It was her loyalty to Jax and fierce love for Holden that made me willing to be her friend, but her prejudice against me, formed from the start, was an obstacle she seemed unwilling to overcome. Despite her caustic attitude toward me, I admired her. She held more integrity than all of us. "Carter has an army. We only have each other. It's best not to make enemies out of the few friends we have."

"My trust is earned, not granted."

"Haven't I proved myself these last few months?"

"You've proven you are your father's daughter."

Was this about Harris? "Why did you bother to stick up for me back there if you don't want me around?"

"Because you have a strange hold over Jax." She slid forward in her seat. "But listen to me, girl. I'll bring you down if you hurt him. That, I promise. You're Persal. You'll always be Persal. Nothing changes that."

"You didn't seem to hold any bias when you were dating Holden."

Oops. I'd say by the sting in her expression that was not a good thing to say for nurturing a bond.

"I've learned a powerful lesson since then."

"But I'm not like Holden."

"Words are like paper—no substance underneath."

"My enemy is the same as yours. I promise you that."

"I learned long ago that promises are as short-lived as the breath wasted saying them."

In one graceful glide, Elva swept from her seat and strode across the floor to join the rest in the kitchen, leaving me sucking in breaths like I'd gone a round with Mike Tyson. Verbally sparring with her was equivalent, as far as I was concerned.

I pressed back into my seat, ignoring my stomach's ache with the smell of frying bacon filling up my nostrils, and wrapped my hands around my waist in a pseudo hug. The four Aris stood in the kitchen talking. Patrick laughed and playfully shoved Nuke in the arm. The ever-present tension Jax carried across his shoulders and the hard set of his jaw eased free. He smiled at Elva, pointing to something on the bench behind that he wanted her to hand him. Another session over, another mission completed alive, another moment the Aris party solidified their bond and trust in each other. Was it only Elva, or were the others wary of me after what I had done to Harris? Or maybe wary of me because I was Persal? Surely not Nuke and Patrick, neither having spent a lifetime burdened by factional prejudice. And what about Jax?

I stared at my feet, bare because I'd not bothered to slip back into my boots once I stripped off my white socks, and now curled them up on the couch with me. Where did I belong?

Chapter 8

I LOOKED DOWN over a world beautiful yet cruel, a place where the leaders locked themselves in their glass towers, morbidly afraid of their people. Loitering in the street was enough to have you arrested. Befriending or falling in love with the wrong person would get you killed. This was the world Jax grew up in; they were the rules he trusted.

In the distance was the Califax Dome, a majestic sight rising stories above the city surrounding it, gleaming glass and spires reflecting the orange glow of the sun, combined with the blue of the moon. I'd been close to the Dome, but from below ground and never in real life. Awe and loathing made for an uncomfortable partnership inside my head. Within the Dome's stunning glass walls, policies were made to keep the people subjugated. Burying secrets was done to maintain power, not for the good of the people.

I looked over my shoulder when I heard Jax coming up behind me.

"How you feeling?" he asked.

"Do you want me to lie?"

"There's been too much of that. Let's make a pact." He held out his hand. "From now on, we speak the truth."

I looked at his hand. "You sure you can keep to that?"

"Isn't this what you've wanted all along?"

Yes, and look what I got. Did I really want to risk hearing how Jax truly felt about a Persal, the daughter of his family's murderer? The truth is what everyone demands, but the reality is most people just want a truth they can live with.

There was nothing left of who I was, the life I had. Maybe I had the ability to make myself anew. But to make a home, I needed people I loved. At the moment, I lost the two most important people, which left one I cared about, Jax. I needed too much from him—and I wasn't prepared to unpack the extent of everything I did need from him. I doubted I'd have the strength to accept the truth if he decided to walk away.

He quirked an eyebrow, glancing down at my hand still resting by my side. "What sorts of secrets do you plan on hiding?"

I palmed his hand with a wane smile. "You got yourself a deal." Even though I planned to focus on hunting Holden down and finding Mum and Ajay, while Jax planned on stopping Carter.

He ran a finger across my brow, which made me jerk a fraction. "What's this for?"

I shook my head as my reply, because too many words needed to be said as explanation, and I wasn't sure if I would choose the right ones or say it the way it should be said.

It seemed I didn't need to say anything; either that or ignoring my lack of answer made ignoring the tension thickening the air easier for him. "You need some tattoos. That's the first thing. After that, I'll head to Aris HQ."

My stomach tightened at the name. The memories were fresh and all too willing to spew out on replay. You can never unsee something, never undo something, and that small truth could alter a part of you that would never be altered back. We surfaced from the game only a day ago, and here we were in another dimension. It had been me who kept us moving. If we did, I could stay ahead of the memories, maybe.

"If I had an Aris tattoo, would I be able to enter?"

"No. You can trick the people on the street, but you can't trick the sensors." He placed a hand over his chest. "It's in here that can't be hidden. The sensors will detect the fabric of your factional nature. Anyone can fake a tattoo."

"I'll be an anomaly, fooling most, but never really being what I want to be."

"And what is that?"

"Free to choose my own path."

"In my world, that can never happen." He turned away, running his fingers through his hair, drawing my attention to the black band on his wrist. "Elva would've taken care of Nuke and Patrick's tattoos by now. I think it's best we get this over with."

"Is that what you were looking for?" I pointed to the band.

"Yeah." He held his arm out, inviting me to take a closer look.

"What did you call it?"

"It's a cephulet. Think of it as a computer and smartphone rolled into one. It connects us to the biostream, which is our word for internet."

"Where's the screen?" It was a flat black band, which wrapped around his wrist like a leather bracelet.

Jax tapped his temple. "The cephulet acts like the silver dots in Dominus. It taps into your neural frequency and displays the screen in front of your eyes, much the same as in Dominus. Your brain waves are transformed into commands. All you have to do is think, and it does."

"Does that mean you have a whole computer screen in front of your eyes all the time?"

"No. You can regulate what you see and at what time. You'd go crazy otherwise."

"Can I get one of those?"

"It's too dangerous. People need to be registered to wear one so their use of the biostream and all communications can be monitored. As I said, factions are not allowed to communicate with each other unless it's within work channels. Some have managed to alter the cephulet, making it unreadable while still remaining connected to the biostream, but their successes have been short-lived. Carter and Nixon tried it for years. In the end, they gave up and used an old-fashioned prototype cephulet, which kept them outside the biostream but limited their application."

"What happens if we get separated?"

"I'll try to get you the prototype. They're illegal, so they're hard to come by now. I may be able to find one."

"So black markets exist in your world?"

"Black markets will exist anywhere you make something illegal."

A low tone hummed through the apartment. The alien sound amped me to high alert. My factional nature ceased its slow rolling path around my body and zapped to life.

"Delivery." Jax moved past me, heading for the door.

"Already?"

Not long after we arrived, Jax turned on a wall screen and browsed through catalogues of clothes. He made me watch an animated woman stroll across the screen dressed in the latest fashion, proper fitting clothes at least and not the pathetic wisp of fabric that failed to cover my body in Dominus. Some clothes were as outlandish as the couture that paraded the catwalks back home. But I was happy to see the army-style cargo pants and jumpsuits also seemed popular over here as casual wear for the everyday person.

Once I made my choice, Jax told me to stand directly in front of the screen, and a green beam scanned me from head to feet, taking my measurements for an exact fit. This was the way people shopped, because apparently simple pleasures like sauntering the aisles of a retailer, feeling the fabric and trying on outfits, encouraged too much interchange between factions. There were a shops that catered for specific factions, but the habit of physically shopping was a quaint pastime for the wealthy and not the norm.

The face of a young guy appeared in a large screen to the left of the door. Much like Jax, Holden, and Elva, the guy looked like he'd been beamed directly from earth. He could be any delivery guy from back home.

I inched into the bedroom when Jax opened the door, shy of being spotted in case the guy had some telepathic way of seeing right into my mind or soul.

I peeked around the doorjamb when I heard the suction noise as the front door closed and Jax heading back into the apartment. He handed me the small package. "Go change." For a brief moment, his eyes focused ahead, seeming to look straight over me, before he said, "I'll give you five minutes."

"What was that?"

His gaze refocused on me. "What?"

"Just then. It looked like you zoned out."

"I'm checking the communication channels. I'm also running a biostream search, looking for a tag from Elva."

I frowned as I gave a small shake of my head meaning, *What the heck?*

"We've got to be careful how we communicate. Elva may think it's not safe to go directly through the coms channel and instead leave a tag in the biostream. It's like a snippet of code we devised as a way of letting each other know there was a message to relay. It's nonsensical to monitors, which are mostly bots."

"And is there anything?"

"Not so far."

"Is that good or bad?"

"It means you have to change out of your clothes so we can get going."

"Where?"

Jax used his finger against my forehead to push me backward into his room. Once inside, he turned away, but as he was turning, his focus shifted to look at the screen only he could see.

I stared through the gap that was the door to his room, not seeing a way to close it. "Umm... I need a little privacy."

He spun back with a blink to bring his eyes back into focus.

"That's easy." His smile was welcoming after the twenty-four hours we all had so far. He waved his hand chest-high at the left side of the open doorway. Without sound, a door slid out from a slit that appeared in the doorframe. Before the door closed, his gaze once again turned to his screen, shutting me out.

I'd chosen a simple, deep-green jumpsuit made of soft, lightweight fabric, which fit like a glove and easily stretched when pulled. I fingered the material, trying to determine if it was made from similar fabric as back home. The soft durability felt otherworldly. The jumpsuit had been the least outrageous outfit; plus, it gave me room to fight. I didn't expect to be fighting

—I hoped I wouldn't be fighting—but since I spent the last few months battling in the streets of Califax, I couldn't scrub the idea a warrior would appear from out of nowhere and attack. The shoes were also lightweight, boots with soles that could be from rubber but gave more when pressed.

I pulled my hair up using an accessory I found in the packaging, some fancy metal clasp that managed to hold all my long hair in a comfortable, loose bun, then surveyed myself in the mirror. I didn't look any different, which meant I looked human. So had the guy at the door, which meant I had nothing to worry about.

I scanned the left side of the door for the mechanism that would open it, saw nothing obvious, so I headed for the right side. Much like glass doors at offices or shops back home, the door slid across in silence as I walked in front of it. Jax, looking out of his expansive window, spun when he heard me exit. His eyes wandered slowly up my body, and then he quirked an eyebrow. While his eyebrow went up, so did my heart rate and a thousand butterflies in my stomach while my steps slowed to a crawl. The sudden flight of the butterflies had been so unexpected it left my head spinning. I wanted to about-face and scurry back into his room, press my back against the shut door, calm my breath, and analyze what the hell I was supposed to do now. These were powerful, raw feelings, as open, honest, and frightening as the horror and terror I faced in Dominus. I wasn't ready to be hammered by yet more intense emotions.

"Passable."

The slow smile softened his features, and I heaved out my sharp inhale. "Is that good or bad?"

"There's little difference between your kind of human and mine. Don't worry about blending in. People don't strike up a conversation with complete strangers like they do in your world, so you shouldn't need to speak too much, if that's got you worried."

The moment of seconds ago passed. We were back to talking about necessary and safe topics, such as my predicament. "Comforting to know."

"You'll be fine. But we might just leave your hair down for now."

Instead of waiting for me to do it, Jax reached his hands behind my head and gently tugged the fastener out—quite a feat without hurting me, as my hair was bundled up in a messy bun. In order to deal with my hair, we were forced to stand close. Reaching forward as he did put us even closer.

Jax needed a shower—Christ, I probably needed a shower—but the smell of his sweat was too familiar for me to think it unpleasant. We both fought hard to be alive, to be here now. I found a safe spot to stare on his shirt, but I itched to look up. Just one look. So I did. Jax stopped what he was doing for a moment and looked down at me. We were caught in an awkward moment of forced intimacy.

Maybe I was fooling myself, reading more than what was there, lost in my own stupid girlie excitement that I saw the mirrored need in his eyes. I say maybe, because it was gone so quick. As if shaking himself out of a daze, his expression shifted back to the blank canvas I knew so well from a place of soft vulnerability of a moment ago. "There's a lot we need to do to survive." He backed away.

"Yeah, I know." I caught the disappointment in my voice. Would he? We were in Califax for real. This wasn't a game. The cost was perhaps too great. In his world, it was time to play by his rules. Time to learn what it really meant to be a faction member.

Jax handed me the metal clasp and motioned that I should bring some hair over my shoulders. "Make sure you keep behind your ears covered for now, or at least the right one. Keep your wrist covered for the same reason."

"Will you do my tattoos?"

"No. I'm not great."

I lifted his arm up between us. "But the detail on this is amazing."

"It hurt like hell. With a professional, you won't feel a thing."

"But we'll get caught. What if the tattooist reports me?"

"I know somewhere we can go."

"Are we talking somewhere illegal?"

"He's not sanctioned by the senate, if that's what you mean by illegal."

"This guy doesn't know Carter, does he?"

"I'd never take that risk. Carter never used the sorts of people I will take you to see."

Who was the real Jax? Not the boy who accosted me in the convenience store all those centuries ago. Nor the boy who jumped from the

Adolphy Tower and dragged me into Dominus to watch me fail as revenge for his family's murder. But a part of him was that boy. There were many shades in all of us.

The longer we spent together, the more it would hurt. I just knew it would, because this wasn't a fairy tale, and bad things happened all the time in real life. Idealism bled from the wounds created by Dominus, Carter, and my dad until there was nothing left within me but the strong will to survive.

"We gotta go. Elva will be waiting for me at Aris HQ."

"What about Nuke and Patrick?"

"She'll leave them at her place. And if they are smart enough, that's where they'll stay."

To cut our conversation off, Jax moved around me and headed for the kitchen, where he rummaged for things in a drawer, which he then slipped into the pocket of his clothes. He changed from earth clothes shortly after we arrived into a navy-blue jumpsuit teamed with black boots, which looked made for running and reminded me of the STU from the last game we played in Dominus.

With a hand out, he signaled for me to join him. It was time to face my new world.

Chapter 9

DOMINUS GAVE Califax the familiarity of a frequently visited city, but the people made it foreign. No warrior-clad fighters here, but normal human lookalikes dressed in outfits recognizably earth-like to weird. We exited Jax's apartment onto a boulevard of broad-leafed trees. With no cars on the street, boarded gardens pockmarked the pedestrian walkways, filled with a rainbow of color. This was not the Califax I knew. There was little difference between Jax's street and many of the others I moved through while in Dominus, but the air smelled alive with floral perfume, the wind tickled the hairs around my face, and the sun bathed my cheeks. Real sensations, not a mockup from a computer plugged into my neural pathways to convince me what I tasted, smelled, and touched were real.

"It's beautiful."

Jax snorted his reply.

"You don't think so?"

"Beauty never penetrates very deep."

"I never realized Califax smelled so good."

He huffed. His mouth remained tight. Small creases etched fine lines across his forehead. Best to leave the conversation where it stood, behind us.

Skytrains crisscrossed overhead like dozens of spiders busily creating an invisible web. Their metal hulls glimmered in the sun, the light reflecting onto the tops of the highest buildings, so they sparkled like jewels.

"Do they every collide?"

"No. They're equipped with advanced avoidance systems. It would be impossible."

"Nothing's impossible."

He slid a sideways glance my way. "Normally, I would agree with you, but it would be incredibly hard. The system requires authorization to override. And central command have the ability to override all controls if the system is hijacked. It's one of the reasons Carter and Nixon decided to go underground rather than overhead. The senate controls the airways."

Jax set a brisk pace, forcing me to jog the occasional step to keep up. Rejuvenated from a concoction of tablets he'd taken when we first returned to his world, Jax hurried us along the street, heading for the Central Terminal, which reared up over the surrounding buildings like an alien from *War of the Worlds*. I couldn't help but groan at the irony of how close we were to living out a real-life *War of the Worlds*.

The swelling on Jax's face had disappeared, leaving minor bruising and a few remnant scabs from cuts. He felt healthy enough to set a punishing pace, and given that I was on another world, I couldn't help but tread on his heels while I gawked at everything around me but the direction we headed. He was polite enough to keep his cool about my clumsiness.

"I keep expecting one of these people to transform—"

Jax lurched to a stop, rearing on me. Alarmed by his sudden action, I jumped back a pace, but the one thing that echoed through my head was the way his hand halted inches from touching me. He looked over my head at the people passing as he said, "We won't talk about that in the open. Come, let's keep moving." Just like Dominus, fear and vigilance followed our every step.

The crowd of pedestrians now became a crowd of enemies. The people around me looked as human as anyone on a city street back home, and yet I remained alert, tense, waiting for someone to lurch my way while pulling a weapon from their belt. My factional nature prowled under my skin. I dared not reach within and soothe the wild call. Any acknowledgement of what crept inside fueled my need for release.

No eyes met mine, and I was perhaps drawing attention to myself by staring at each face, scanning behind each ear for the revelation of who they really were. Jax increased his pace, forcing me into a light jog. Did we keep moving for fear the police would arrest us for standing too long in one place?

Close beside him, the tension in his body radiated through the space between us. I didn't need to look at him to know his own factional nature pestered him as much as mine did me. Too much time spent beside each other fighting, and I could practically taste the vibe of his feral nature. It ran along the outside of my skin as if enticing destruction into a deadly game, which would see us both killed at the hands of the senate.

"Relax," he breathed with as much strain as I felt.

"If you want me to relax, perhaps we can slow down. That way we don't look like we're on the run."

He slowed a smidgeon, enough so I could catch my breath. I leaned in close. "I'm alien. Give me a chance to look."

He snorted but made no other comment, just directed me across to the other side of the street, which was easy to do when you didn't have to dodge traffic.

"We're going to take a skytrain. I'm not overly comfortable with the idea, being crammed in with so many people, at least while you're design-free"—still so cautious, he avoided using the word tattoo in case someone passing overheard—"but it will take too long to walk where we're heading."

"Why can't we just zap ourselves there, like you did at the prison?"

"I don't want to risk it. There have been some unregulated shifts by some senate members to other dimensions in the last year or so. According to Carter, the last time he was back here, the senate ruled to increase research into a way of monitoring shifting by listening for the echo of any warp along the seams of the dimensions and time. It wasn't so long ago that Carter returned with that information, so I doubt they've made a lot of headway. Up until now, I've been careless in the way I shift. But I'm not willing to risk it now."

"What information could they get?"

"It's too early to say. A rough location of where the warp began would be a logical guess. They would be keen to know the destination as well. I'm sure they will succeed in the end. It's only a matter of time."

"What will that mean for you?"

"It means I will no longer have the option."

"You will have to make a decision as to where you want to be."

He nodded.

"And where would that be?"

"Here, of course." He spared me a quick frown before glaring ahead.

Stupid me, stupid question. This was his home. Of course he chose to remain here. Why had I thought he'd think otherwise? Because I would choose to remain in my world.

The triangular black shadow of a skytrain swept over us and raced along the ground toward the terminal. The first time I'd ridden in one of those, I blew it out of the sky in order to exit Dominus. The idea of boarding one again wasn't high on my list of must-dos, even if they did look like a carnival ride.

A memory flashed forward so real and fast I sucked in a breath. *The metal door divides the cockpit from the passengers. Jax's hands rest on my showers as he whispers in my ear, "I believe in you." A bright white flash blinds me, and a roar explodes through my ears.*

"Sable?"

I blinked, blinked again, then shook my head. "I'm fine." The power of the memory had sent me reeling back a few paces. Destruction punched a beat through my chest. "Dominus has gouged the memories in too deep."

"Just as long as you don't start fighting phantom bad guys."

"I make no promises."

"Hold out until we get where we're going. Then you can freak out all you like, and no one will notice."

"That doesn't comfort me any."

That earned me a quick smile, but Jax spared no time for anything else before he hurried off down the street once more.

"This is the only way?"

"We need you decorated ASAP. Haven't you flown before? Outside Dominus, that is."

"Yes, but are these things air-worthy?"

"They have a spotless record. More so than I could say for what you'd call an aircraft."

"How do I know you're not just saying that to get me onboard?"

"You'll have to trust me, Sable." And with that, he flashed another quick smile, and I forgot about our surroundings and goal for one moment.

Trust was what he asked of me from the start, when his intention was to get me killed. I'd given him my trust, and he saved me. He wasn't looking at me now, so my smile was for myself.

People scurried around the tripod legs at the base of the terminal like busy ants seeming to have no direction. They crammed into the lifts, which then shot through the floor of the first platform in a blink before returning to the ground a short time later.

God, I remembered this. I turned away, but Jax snagged my elbow and pulled me along with him to join the waiting line. Once in line, he took a thick strand of my hair and brushed it down over my right shoulder in a slow caress, like he was fascinated with the texture, but his eyes weren't on mine. It made his gesture seem unconscious.

"Have you heard from Elva?" I kept my voice low.

Jax's focus returned to me. "She's busy with Nuke and Patrick."

"Have they been taken care of?" I couldn't help but glance around me.

"It's happening as we speak. Don't worry; we're on target."

Don't worry? What would happen to me once I was tattooed a Persal? Where would I go? How would I survive in this world if I was not alongside Jax?

The swift movement of the line meant I didn't have to bother Jax with my fear. Besides, I knew what he would say. A life of living on this earth and the senate's rules had permeated deep. He rebelled enough to side with Carter, but there were perhaps perceptions too pervasive to release.

The line grew short, and in no time, Jax placed his hand feather-soft on my back, encouraging me inside. A waterfall of people flowed into the lift, sandwiching us in the middle—my preferred place, as it meant I couldn't see us rising off the ground. Even when I thought enough people entered, more kept coming. Hopefully, we wouldn't exceeded our capacity. I was pressed back into Jax as, unbelievably, more decided there was room to spare. If we'd not been packed tight, I would turn and ask him if he was worried about the amount of people the lift would have to carry. Just when destruction's urge to create a few windows in the glass and get some fresh air became too great, I was whizzed out of my body when the lift left the ground and slowed at the first platform before I had time to inhale.

About a quarter exited. Jax slid his arm to my waist, pressing his fingers firm into my side, keeping me from following the third out. The doors closed, and my stomach was left behind once again as we moved to the next tier. Here, Jax dropped his hold, so I shuffled forward with the exiting handful out onto the platform and the sea of people.

I faltered to a stop amongst the throng crisscrossing the platform to reach their skytrains before they departed. Jax moved beside me and took my hand, guiding me forward away from the lift entrance.

People pressed past us, faces of humans wearing clothes of varying designs, from the commonplace, like my outfit, to the outlandish, such as starched high collars, bowing outward and down from the neck, and weird ribbed fabric bunched around the torso. Each rib rippled discretely as the person walked. One lady wore boots that reached to the top of her thighs and finished off with PVC style underpants. When it came to clothes, it seemed anything was acceptable.

Jax said nothing as he led me through the crowd. Unlike in Dominus, no one parted to allow us through. Forced to make our own path, we bumped and squeezed our way past groups who gathered to chat.

I was swallowed by the crowd, drowned by the babble and laughter, and assaulted by the strong combination of smells that either tickled my nose or burned the hairs and scorched the back of my throat on the way down. Bumped and pushed, destruction responded, firing along my arms, chest, and torso. Feeling the ignition, I looked down my body, expecting to see my jumpsuit alight or at least my body glowing through from underneath. Nothing, my ungrafted factional nature remained concealed.

A laughing woman tripped into me and sent me staggering backward into someone behind, ripping Jax's light hold on me free. The woman's makeup—bold hues, heavily applied—flashed in front of my eyes before she disappeared. Her open mouth, white teeth gleaming sharp and straight, had my heart racing to a manic pace.

Around me, warrior's clash with the reverberating sound of metal on metal, the harsh grunts of fighting, and the harrowing cries of agony. Chaos spins me in circles until I spy a warrior break free, sprinting across the platform then diving for the opening door of the skytrain.

There was pressure on my upper arm, and my attention struggled to return. My breath came through in short, sharp pants driven on the wave of destruction's path under my skin. On autopilot, my legs did as told, stepping one after the other, but my mind ran in confused circles. If not for Jax's hand, my anchor, moving me forward to where we needed to go, I would've tripped over whomever got in my way and ended up groveling at people's feet. Destruction flirted on the edge of eruption. In the end, I closed my eyes and focused on Jax's touch, shunting the dangerous part of me deep inside.

"Are you in control?" His breath tickled wisps of hair around my neck.

His voice was like an elixir, firm and demanding, snapping me back to myself, grounding me within.

I would've nodded, but I felt verbalizing it was stronger. "Yes." I heard the steel in my voice, putting destruction in its place.

When I opened my eyes, I stared into Jax's dark pits, both his eyes clear and menacingly sharp thanks to the concoction of pills.

"It's all right. I've got everything under control."

"We need to reach our destination, so keep the skytrain intact."

Jax making a joke? At such a crucial moment as this? He backed up his remark with a budding smile, so I would have to say yes.

I looked past him at the skytrains docked around the perimeter of the platform. "Which one is ours?"

"We want the blue one." He pointed to the farthest from the lift. Of course. "If you're ready, we should go."

People sat on large, round, cushioned seats looking like giant mushrooms in the center of the platform. They either chatted or stared into space, perhaps browsing their cephulets like people on earth did their phones when they were bored. No doubt, those who talked were from the same faction, and those who stared into space were not.

I glanced behind people's ears where I could see, looking for the one thing that segregated them into categories and forced them to live a certain way and love certain people. If their arms were bare, I glanced at their wrists to see the tattoo that protected them from the senate's fear and retribution.

I saw a few I knew. Phonus, Perun, Negal. My pulse quickened when I discovered a group of Persal, two men and women, standing in a huddle laughing. The women wore lavish clothes, something you'd see on the latest catwalk, with draped shawls that trailed along the ground behind them like a wedding train. The men dressed equally smart. Perhaps these people were the elite of this world, rich and influential, like my father had been. They reminded me of the sorts of people Mum and Dad entertained. I knew how to mingle with the likes of this group, because up until months ago, I grew up in that life. I attended the same school as their children. I'd been content in that life, because I knew no better.

The old me was pathetic and weak. I longed to see my family again, to overcome this feeling of vulnerability and chaos, but I would never choose to rewind time to the safe place where we were still a family, to believing Dad would always protect me. That life was more a fabrication than the game. I didn't need Dominus to teach me that. Fate—destined to outrun us and end our charade—would've taken care of it.

Jax led me around the mushroom seats and up the few steps to the waiting skytrain. I slowed as we neared. There was nothing below the skytrain but an endless supply of air. The wind rushed over the side and into my face as if pushing me back from the edge. We'd ridden the lift in lightning time but ended up so high the horizon expanded to the city limits.

"The docking arm is solid enough to support the weight. It's not about to fall off the edge of the platform."

"How about out of the sky?"

"No one in Califax has a problem using skytrains."

Which meant I was drawing attention to myself. Jax had taught me to find the other side of my fear. I followed him over the edge of his apartment to do just that. He was right. It made me stronger. But it didn't mean I had to look.

When we neared the skytrain, I ducked my head and closed my eyes, using Jax's firm hold to guide me across the threshold. I'd already plummeted from a STU utility through a busted skylight. Perhaps this would be like knitting compared to that experience. As if hating this fear, destruction burned across my chest. I clenched my fists and teeth to force it down then remembered Jax held my hand. He didn't say anything, and I kept my eyes closed, because it was easier to concentrate on controlling destruction that way.

The air changed from a cool invasion through my clothes to warm and still. I opened my eyes to a sea of faces, but no one bothered to look at us.

Only half the seats were taken, but Jax led me toward the far right, the least populated part of the skytrain. Each seat faced inward, but down this end, we stared ahead at the vacant seats opposite. Behind them was the metal hull of the craft. The light came from above with the top third of the skytrain made from glass. It was perhaps a good thing I couldn't see the ground.

"Do we have long to go?"

"Long enough."

"Are you going to tell me where we're going?"

"The outskirts of the city, where the senate's reach is weaker."

"And where black markets thrive."

"All manner of things thrive there."

"How do you know about these people?"

A woman made her way down toward our end, choosing a seat opposite us and halting our conversation. Jax turned away from me, placing an invisible wall between us. I did the same, fixating on the metal hull over the woman's head. According to Jax, this was a long journey, so I would be staring at that spot for quite some time.

Chapter 10

AFTER LOOKING up through the skylights of the skytrain, catching the occasional flash of another skytrain passing overhead, I longed to see the ground. Blind to any view, it had taken a little getting used to the maneuvers the train made as it ferried us along. Although the skytrain moved with smooth efficiency, my body had become sensitized to the small movements.

The train lurched to the side, and I was pushed tight alongside Jax with a gasp. He reassured me with a squeeze of my hand before taking his back. The woman opposite stared through us, her eyes focused on more interesting things. Mechanical whirring sounded from behind our seats, and the train returned to smooth flying.

Jax leaned over to whisper in my ear. "Sometimes, that happens. Violent downdrafts or updrafts. The sound you hear is the stabilizers recalibrating."

I nodded and schooled my face to boredom, like everyone else.

We made numerous stops so far. At a guess, we'd been traveling about one hour. By now, the skytrain was emptied of all but the woman opposite us and a handful of people toward the front dressed in no-frills overalls, which looked well-worn and in need of a wash. Given it was mid-morning, they could be the equivalent of nightshift workers heading back home to sleep it off before they started again. Maybe I had it all wrong, but I couldn't help making up stories for this new world and drawing parallels with my own. And I didn't know why I bothered. It wasn't like I was hoping to make this place my own.

"We're here."

I went to slip the latch to the harness but found it wouldn't open.

"Like I said, the skytrains are safer than your aircrafts, but there have been incidents on docking. The harness is locked until the train comes to a complete standstill," he murmured close to my ear so the woman wouldn't hear.

I settled back, not at all calm as I felt the descent and simultaneous slowing of the train. The whirring kicked in again, followed by some other mechanical sounds and the train began to maneuver through small adjustments in direction before it began to vibrate slightly.

I had to swallow what I was about to say out loud. Then, in a low voice spoken from the corner of my mouth, I asked, "Is that normal?"

Jax leaned close again. "It just means there is some low-level turbulence. At this slow speed, the train's controls can get a little sloppy. The sounds are the stabilizers again, compensating for the lack of precision in the steering and the turbulence. The extra noises are the ultralight stabilizers. A good pilot can maneuver a train at low speed and height by ultralight stabilizers alone."

"You seem to know a lot about skytrains."

"I wanted to be a pilot when I was young."

"What happened?"

There were a few soft bumps and more whirring noises before we came to a halt.

"I became a pilot," Jax said as he unclipped and pulled his harness over his head.

The woman opposite us stood and hurried from the skytrain the moment the door slid open.

"Jesus, you're joking. I thought you said you couldn't fly one of these, and that's why I had to…." I darted a look up the end of the skytrain where the last were exiting and new arrivals were boarding.

Jax jerked his head toward the door with a smile. "You're like a child. Everything is surprising and new. It's refreshing to a jaded person like me."

The harness latch was a complicated mess of buckles and clasps. I grinned up at him with an apologetic smile before flicking a glance to anyone close by. How many people had problems getting themselves out of a harness? Probably few, if any.

"Press this," Jax said. The silver button undid everything else, and the harness clasp peeled away as if on command, releasing me. Jax lifted it over my head then helped me to my feet.

I looked through the metal grille on disembarking and saw nothing but gray. The Dome and the Central Airways terminal were no longer visible on the horizon. We'd left the treed boulevards behind and entered into a place that held no color... or cheer, by the looks of it. The beauty of central Califax did not extend to the outskirts.

I leaned over the railing and glanced below. People, like ants, scurried along the narrow alleys that wove like warrens between the flat-roofed buildings. Dotted here and there, the alleys opened out to court-yards of gray. It was here I found splashes of color, not from flowers but what looked like stalls. A marketplace?

Jax gave me enough time to absorb the sight in a fraction before nudging my elbow. "Let's go."

Our boots *clanked* along the platform and down the stairs. I grabbed the railing for balance, as my eyes were too busy looking at the scene below me rather than at where I was going. Jax slowed, creating distance between us and the people who'd disembarked with us. "This is the fringe."

"And the Senate of Factions don't bother too much with the upkeep," I observed.

"In more ways than one."

"Meaning?"

"The fringe would be the equivalent of your slums. I lived long enough on your world to understand the effects of poverty are universal, even in different dimensions. The influence of the senate is weak this far out, so there is a lot of illegal trade."

"Such as false tattoos."

"Factions mix readily, because there is less policing. They also trade directly with the country provinces, which is forbidden. Normally, there are nominated parties that deal with trade to prevent the factions from dealing with each other. The provinces are separated into factions, and while they sustain themselves on their own form of agriculture, each province specializes in specific manufactured goods."

He pointed toward a ridge of mountains in the distance. "Those are the Eliqua Mountains, Set province, and where they mine most of our metals. And behind us is the Ulridian Desert, Persal province, and where they mine trylite, the rocks that glow."

"Dad thought Holden would return to a village within the Persal province called Uradra."

He looked ahead, seeming to find the final decent more important than what I said, which meant I was not about to tell him I planned on going there, something likely to fork our paths.

The neglect toward the fringe became apparent once we reached the ground, but Jax wouldn't hang around long enough for me to comment. Without hesitation, he headed off down one of the many alleys branching away from the platform. The buildings pressed close on either side, arrowing toward the mouth, forcing us into single file and cutting off any conversation. Jogging behind, I felt the beginnings of a stitch, because I was holding my breath too much.

We burst out into an open space cluttered with stalls and fringe dwellers cramming the laneways as they inspected what was on offer. The placed hummed with a low chatter, devoid of the energy I felt in central Califax. While most of what I'd seen of the fringe from above was gray, these pockets vibrated with color from the fabric hung on lines, stretching the width of the lane to the woven baskets of spices raised off the ground on roughly hewn logs. Insects buzzed around carcasses laid out on thick blocks, but the air smelled of fresh blood, not rancid meat. The crowds hid most of the stalls, but they could not suppress the aroma of roasting spiced meat or sweet baked goods. It must have been only hours ago I last ate, but the saliva pooled into my mouth when I passed a rich toffee, buttery caramel smell.

The vibrancy of the market space did not transmute into the fringe dwellers. For many, their faces looked as faded as the colors of their clothes; they also smelled just as worn and dusty. Judging by their expressions, I'd say their spirits were no better than their clothes.

I was bumped and jostled and forgot to keep my hair in place over my shoulder to protect the secret of what was not behind my ears; maybe out here it didn't matter.

Once we entered another alley, wider than the first, I caught up with Jax. "You move through the fringe like it's your second home."

"I know my way around." He increased his pace.

"And that's all I get?"

"For now."

"You're worse than Carter and Dad for secrets."

"And you're nosey."

"Curious, you mean. You must have felt like this when you entered my world."

That earned me a sly smile. "Just a little. Although I was more curious about one person in particular."

"Who was that?"

"You."

My mouth clammed shut on what I was about to say. It took a few steps more before I said, "Curious is not the way I would describe you when I first met you. Predatory, hostile. Those are the first words that come to mind."

Jax ignored me.

"Not that I blame you."

He ignored that too.

There were metal doors with big metal latches on either side of the alley. "Are these people's homes?"

"Yes," was all Jax had time to say, when a man entered the mouth of the alley and headed toward us. Jax dropped behind but nudged me in the back so I would not lose my pace. The man shuffled along, hugging the wall, keeping his gaze to the dirt ground. Oversized trousers, shirt-sleeves covering his hands, he appeared to have shrunken in his clothes. He wore a turban like brown cloth low over his forehead and ears, partially concealing his tattoo. Set. I'd not seen too many of those tattoos before.

We exited one alley and turned left into another, equally as narrow, dark, and dirty as the last two. The walls on either side were crumbling with age. Bricks of unequal size were stacked upon each other with no mortar to glue them together. Piles of refuse created mounds for us to weave around. I covered my nose and mouth with my hand to reduce the stench from the waste of living.

Halfway down, Jax stopped at a metal door with a rusted gouge running from midway to the ground and pounded with his fist. Feeling like we were being watched, I glanced up and down the alley then ran my eyes up the brick wall to see a child's face peering over the roof. The moment our eyes met, the child darted away.

I stared back at the door when the *click* sounded. A small portion of it opened at eye level, reflecting the dark from inside. Seconds later, the peekaboo hole disappeared, followed by a loud *clunk*, and the door opened.

A short, portly man, no taller than my shoulders, stood in the door-way. His bottom lip, swollen to twice the size of his top lip, drooped down toward his chin, exposing his teeth and an intricate tattoo on his gums. The pattern continued across his lip, ran in channels to his chin and down his throat to disappear in the V of his shirt front. We'd found our tattooist.

He stood aside without a flicker of recognition or welcome. As I passed, his dirty-green eyes travelled the length of me without leering. Good thing, as I was sure destruction would rally in the face of a threat. All I saw was simple curiosity. Once we were inside, he stuck his head out, glanced up and down the alley, and then bolted the door.

I followed Jax down the windowless passage and into a bright, airy atrium at the center of the house. The place reminded me of Aris HQ on a smaller, less opulent scale. One story up and a balustrade wrapped around the circumference of the open space. A young boy peered through the railings, and when I met his stare, he ducked his head back and hid himself behind one of the metal poles. The man followed my gaze and, seeing the boy, barked something incoherent. The boy scampered, his bare feet slapping on what sounded like concrete.

Satisfied the boy had gone, the man hobbled off down another passageway. One leg appeared shorter than the other, accentuating the bow in his spine. Movement for him looked painful, but his speed suggested otherwise. In no time, he waited at the door to a dimly lit room, hands on hips as a silent reprimand for our tardiness.

"Could you give us a moment please?" Jax turned his back to the stout man, blocking him from my view. "What's your tattoo going to be?"

I'd pushed this decision to the back of my mind, but now I had to face it. To be tattooed Aris meant I could stay with Jax. To be tattooed Persal meant I could enter Persal HQ, gain their protection, and be taken to Uradra, where I would be reunited with Mum and Ajay. To be tattooed a Persal meant Jax and I would no longer fight together; we would fight as enemies.

"Why can't I have both, one behind each ear?"

He shook his head, a tired smile on his face. "If only the decision were that easy." For the first time since we left his apartment, Jax took my hands in a solid grasp. "You will never be an Aris. The tattoo will never eradicate what is within you."

"You think I don't know that?"

"I think your family means more, as it should. You'll never be safe by my side."

"Is this you pushing me away?"

"This is me wanting to see you survive. It's going to get ugly. People fear dissent as much as the senate does. It upsets the balance. Most in Califax are happy with the way things are. They benefit from the peace the senate enforces. That's why Carter and your father kept everything a tight secret. One sniff of trouble creates widespread panic. A Persal caught tattooed an Aris will trigger alarms akin to a full-scale war. Never forget what a war would mean."

"When factions fight, nothing is left."

"The foundation of our peace is built from fear of factional war."

The small man behind us cleared his throat, the signal to finish up our conversation.

"I'll wait for you out here."

I moved around Jax and down the passage. The man watched me pass with his observant eyes.

Inside was a low wooden table, and beside that a chair. In the dim light, I couldn't make out what filled the rows of shelves behind. My nose clogged with centuries of dust and the musty smell of damp clothes and books.

The man hobbled around me and patted the table. "Lay." His heavy accent twisted the word to almost indecipherable, but the pat was enough for me to understand.

I slid on and lowered myself onto the cold surface while he busied himself at the shelves. Once he had everything he needed, he returned to the table. A harsh light glared just above my face, forcing me to turn away, shielding my eyes.

The man grabbed my left arm and turned it up to examine my wrist. He spoke a few words, but I shook my head, unable to understand. Instead of repeating himself, he tapped my wrist, because sometimes actions were clearer than words. He was asking what type of tattoo I wanted to cover my supposed graft. The fact I had no mark to indicate I was grafted seemed a moot point to him.

I hadn't thought of that. I waved my hand over my face, feeling for whatever it was that shone the light in my eyes. The man rescued me, pushing the arm of the light aside so I was able to look around the room, my mind scrambling for inspiration, conscious that he would perhaps want this over with and us out the door. My eyes fell on the cuff link at my wrist that acted like a button on a shirt.

"You have a pen? I will draw it for you." I mimicked writing. Hopefully these people wrote using similar instruments. He frowned then spun and rummaged through his shelves. When he came back, he held a small, sharp metal poker like the sort Mum used to test whether cakes were cooked all the way through and pointed at the table.

Understanding what he wanted me to do, I sat up and etched my drawing into the wood. Crude as it was, he nodded, his lower lip flopping up and down with the movement. Whether he understand or not, the exact design of the tattoo on my wrist didn't really matter.

I undid the cuff link and rolled up my sleeve then lowered myself back down onto the table while a gentle whirring came to life.

As Jax promised, I felt a faint drag on my skin and nothing more. I resisted the urge to watch, instead staring at the opposite wall, my eyes traveling the cracks while the whirring played in my ears.

When my wrist was complete, he laid my arm gently by my side and moved up to my head, bringing the harsh light with him. He brushed my hair away from my ear and tapped the skin with his finger. "Here?"

As if to remind me of who I was, destruction flared briefly as a hot arrow before settling into its ceaseless roam through my body. I hesitated for two breaths then told him what faction I would become.

Chapter 11

WHEN HE WAS DONE, the little man left the room without a word. I pulled the metal clasp that Jax removed from my hair earlier out of my pocket and attempted to tie my hair back without a mirror. Now, there was no reason for me to hide behind my hair. Once done, I ran my hand over the tattoo behind my ear, expecting to feel something. The skin was smooth. There was no pain.

At the door, I bumped into Jax. He looked at my hair pulled back then into my eyes for so many breaths I lost count. With a gentle hand at my chin, he turned my head to the side so he could see the tattoo.

With my chin free, I turned back into eyes swimming in their fury. Without a word, he spun and stormed down the dim passage, leaving behind the lead weight of his disapproval. He might as well have punched me in the gut for the same effect. My head felt heavy, and for one brief moment, I lost the will to follow. The conviction I used to tell the tattooist in which faction I would belong fled. Had I made a dreadful mistake?

The desolation lasted a second before destruction raged through to sweep my weakness aside. How dare he judge me like that?

At the end of the passage, I found Jax shaking hands with the stout man in the atrium, the gesture filled with familiarity and fondness. Both looked at me when I appeared. Jax dropped his eyes, but the stout man continued to watch me as I approached, eyes set to neutral. I wasn't even a curiosity to him.

Jax said a few more words to the man before he released his hand.

"Thanks for this." I pointed behind my ear. "And this." I pointed to my wrist.

For the first time, the corners of his mouth creeped into a smile, but his drooping bottom lip made the smile heavy. Encouraged by his sudden warmth, I stepped closer holding out my hand, returning my own smile and hoping he would do likewise. No hesitation, he clasped my hand in both of his. This close to him and the dusty smell, which seemed to permanently live in the air, mingled with a subtle musky-earthy aroma like wet soil.

No tattoo on his wrist. Without thinking, I grasped his wrist and turned the underside facing up so I could see the clear, pale skin underneath. "You don't have a graft." Not sure he understood me, I ran a finger down the inside his wrist. "Where is your graft?"

He turned his head to look over his right shoulder, revealing the skin behind his left ear. No tattoo there either. This man was free.

"I don't understand."

He nodded as if agreeing to something I said as he settled his gaze on me. The softening of his eyes spread to the rest of his expression, continuing farther to diffuse through his body, crossing the connection of our touching hands and into me. It was like a great exhale had swept us in, stripped us of our rigidity and strain, then released us back into this room. My first desire was to hug him close, a thank you for understanding and accepting the choice I made without judgment. With the gentleness pouring from his eyes, the lump welling up my throat made me want to cough. I'd not realized how much Jax's reaction to my tattoo upset me. I would've chosen another, but in the brief seconds as the stout man peered down at me, I'd been swamped by my fear.

I heaved out the truth on a long sigh. The stout man continued to hold my hand, accepting the light tremor that rushed through my body with a gentle squeeze.

"Sable."

I wasn't sure if Jax was warning me to stop or calling me over. "Thank you once again."

I left him smiling his funny, almost smile to join Jax at the entrance to the passage that led to the front door.

"That man has no tattoos… well, except for the obvious ones on his face."

Jax looked over my head. The man eased himself down on a metal chair at the far side of the atrium.

"He can't leave his home."

"Why? Because he has no tattoos?"

"It's his silent rebellion against the senate, but his choice imprisons him. If he dares to spend too much time out in the open, the senate's sweepers will find him. And out here on the fringe, they are merciless."

"Sweepers?" I'm sure I heard the name before but couldn't remember when or where.

"Don't worry about it. Look, I have to leave you for a while. The tattooist has agreed to keep you safe until I return."

"Where're you going?"

"I have to do something. Nothing important, but it will be easier if I go on my own."

"What am I going to do?"

He shrugged. "Sit, wait, whatever you want. Just don't leave. I'll try to be as quick as I can."

As if to stop me from asking any more questions, he fled down the passage and out the front door.

Once Jax was gone, the stout man rose awkwardly from his chair and hobbled toward me, waving his hand for me to join him. He took my hand like we were old friends and led me up a wide flight of stairs built from light-colored stone. On the second level, I was able to look down onto the atrium and only now noticed the outline of tiles in the shape of a scythe. The tiling of the scythe was a few shades darker than the rest of the tiles blending the pattern into the floor when viewed from ground level.

"You're Aris."

The man nodded.

"What's your name?"

A gulf of silence, so I patted my chest. "Sable." Then I pointed to him. "And you?"

He straightened as best he could, dropping my hand. "I know what you're say. My name is Islia." Because of his lower lip, his words were jumbled, but I still understood. "Yes, I am Aris."

"But you choose not to wear a tattoo."

"I am old. When I was young, there were no grafts."

"You hid when they tattooed everyone?"

"Like a few, I escaped to the fringe when they did. But many who made the same choice as I did have since died because of their choice."

"You were born in central Califax?"

"To a very prominent family. I had a wonderful job I enjoyed very much. I was a pilot, would you believe?"

At his height, I wouldn't, but I guess things were different over here than back home.

"But this is my home now. Has been for many a year."

"Has Jax told you anything about me?"

"You're not Aris. Come." Islia guided me to a spiral staircase sandwiched between two rooms. "Up here, you will see the place we call home."

At the top, I stepped out onto the flat roof. Clothes flapped in the gentle breeze on a line draped between two poles. It reminded me of Jax's apartment back in my world, minus the comfortable cushions, the chaotic city noises drifting up from below, and the fateful night when he first showed me the in-between. I crossed to the edge and looked down over one of the marketplaces. Instead of horns, screeches, and sirens, stall holders announced their latest sale and people haggled for a decent price. Somehow, everyone managed to find a spot to display their produce in the small open space crammed between buildings.

"How many of these markets are in the fringe?"

"Enough to meet our needs. Each free space sells something different. The location of space granted to a particular stall holder will depend on what they sell. Similar stalls are clumped together."

I looked down on the earthenware pots filled with colorful powders surrounded by sacks filled with vegetables.

"This would be the grocery free space. Convenient for you. Where is everything grown?"

"In the country provinces. The senate controls agriculture, but we have our own network that supplies the free spaces with enough to keep us fed."

"Why doesn't the senate put a stop to your networks, if they're so paranoid of mixing factions?"

"Logistics and cost. We also keep our heads down and our channels closed. They don't appreciate the extent of what we do out here."

"What about in the countryside? Do the factions mix there?"

"No. Most stick to the old ways. Only those who benefit financially from trade are willing to mingle. Califax is the only city where the factions live side by side."

"Because they are grafted."

"There was a time in the distant past when there was little segregation. Turbulent times, or so we're told. There are great monuments left from the destruction to be seen in the outer provinces. We're taught our segregation is our evolution to civility. It began many a lifetime ago.

"Representatives were elected to trade with other regions, other factions, for anything they were unable to produce themselves. Califax was the first of our cities and the first to form a senate of mixed factions. It sits within the confluent of the surrounding factional regions and is still the only city where mixed factions live together. But the first people to populate Califax were ungrafted because the technology did not exist."

"Were they peaceful?"

"Not quite. The city has been rebuilt numerous times. With each destruction of Califax, it proved harder to repopulate. People were afraid. It was not until the graft was developed did anyone feel comfortable enough to live side by side with a different faction. In the regional areas, people mostly cling to the old ways even though the senate ruled they too would be grafted."

"If they lived segregated from each other in their factional regions, why did the senate graft them all?"

"A graft takes away their ability to revolt."

Of course. Why had I even bothered to ask the question? "Why do you oppose the grafts if it's the only reason you can live side by side?"

"Look around you." With a sweeping wave of his arm, he encompassed the expanse of the flat-topped rooflines that formed the outer fringe. "Some of these people are like me. We hide to protect our freedom. We are not grafted, and yet we live here amongst each other in relative peace."

"Why in the fringe? Why now, if it's never been achieved before?"

"Hardship gives us a commonality, so too a shared enemy. We've forgotten to hate each other. But it's not just here. Although the senate would have us believe our history is full of nothing but violence, there are shared stories from our past that tell us some of our ancestors lived in harmony.

"When the grafts were first legislated, the senate promised they would be temporary, that Califax would move toward a peaceful solution of living together without altering the people's nature. But the people became dependent on the grafts. They believe it is the only way for any of us to survive."

"What do you believe?"

"I believe everyone is frightened. They no longer know what it means to live with a factional nature, to be in control, to live with choice. The senate tells them they are incapable of controlling their true nature, so they fear themselves, unable to make their own judgment. They alienate us from our own bodies."

"And if they were freed from their grafts?"

"History would say we cannot survive together that way, and yet us fringe dwellers do."

"But if you had wealth with no common enemy, what would happen then?"

"That, I cannot tell you. I can only tell you what I hope for now, and that is to see us all free. These grafts are a cage."

"If you are graft-free, why don't you leave? I gather you can shift."

"My family is here, as are my memories. This is my home." He placed a hand on my elbow. "I am sorry, but I must leave you. I will send my grandson, Nada. He can take you down into the market and buy you something to eat."

I nodded instead of refusing, because Jax told me to stay put. "I'd like that." The market was just below, so we weren't wandering far. How could it hurt? And if Islia saw no problem in me going to the market, then there was no danger.

Islia hobbled back toward the stairwell and called to his grandson, who had to be the boy I spied hiding behind the railing. Within moments, he appeared, a smile across his innocent face as he looked at his grandfather. An emptiness opened inside me. It felt like my heart had fallen into a big crevasse. Mum and Ajay were supposed to fill that empty place.

Nada appeared about Ajay's age. Another year of growth and he'd be looking down on his grandfather, just like Ajay would soon be looking down on me. His short-cropped black hair exposed the symbol of Aris tattooed behind his ear. Islia was willing to make a stand, but he would not risk the safety of his grandson.

Islia rested a hand on Nada's shoulder as he spoke to him, but I didn't hear the exchange. Nada glanced at me, sharing the same broad grin he'd given his grandfather, and my heart fell a little further into the crevasse.

"Trust Nada to find you something good to eat. He will take care of you." Islia flicked a finger under Nada's chin. "Not far. Do not take risks." We both watched him shuffle to the stairs and disappear inside, and then Nada turned to me, his eyes roaming over me with boyish curiosity.

At that moment, my stomach decided to grumble.

"Your stomach's saying something." He had a high, boyish voice like Ajay.

"That it needs to eat."

He slipped his hand in mine, the feeling warm and welcoming. "There's a great place we can go." He already smelled like he'd been rolling in cinnamon sugar, but underneath the first hit of saliva-inducing sweet spice was the ever-present smell of dust and staleness.

"It can't be far. My friend told me I wasn't to leave your grandfather's house. I'll get in trouble if he finds out."

He screwed up his face. "That's stupid."

"Didn't your grandfather just tell you to stay close?"

"That's different. I'm a child."

"And I'm a stranger. I could get easily lost."

His nose pinched up. "Not with me you won't," he said as he pulled me forward. Because I had a child as a guide, we rushed down the stairs, ran across the first level, and jogged down the last set of steps to the atrium. His eagerness to show me the fringe incited my own anticipation. It would be the first time I was able to wander around this alien world.

Out in the alley, I attempted to draw him back to his departing words on the roof. "Why is it important you stay close to home?"

"The sweepers take children."

"Children in particular?"

His head bounced up and down with big, exaggerated nods, and he widened his eyes to affirm the importance of his answer.

"Do you know why?"

Maybe I shouldn't ask questions like I didn't know anything about this world. How much did Islia know about me? Was it dangerous if he knew I was an alien?

"Something to do with our tattoos." He sounded vague in his reply, his attention snaffled up by the market we just entered. "Do you like hot or cold things to eat?"

"Anything filling. I'll trust you, like your grandfather told me to do."

If his smile was any indication, he liked being boss.

The idea this was another world ignited my senses. I wanted to slow enough to touch the vegetables and fruits piled high in barrels, smell to see if their flavor was familiar or exotic, but Nada wasn't interested in giving me the time. None of this should be strange to someone from this world.

"Here." Nada dragged me over to another stall. "These are good."

He pointed to small white pastries.

"I trust you."

He haggled the price with the stall holder, while I browsed along the row of other treats the owner sold. They all looked like pastries, varying in shapes and sizes, but their crusts weren't brown.

A darting figure in my periphery caught my attention. I turned in time to catch the skirt of a young girl disappearing between the crates stored underneath the stall next door. I headed over, interested in the idea of finding another child, when the rest of the marketplace was packed with adults, something I may not have noticed had Nada not mentioned the sweepers taking children.

I crouched down and peered through the crates to spy big, round black eyes staring back at me.

"Hello." I offered the warmest smile I could find, even though the smell that wafted out to greet me was like a bucket full of rotten vegetables. "I'm here on a big adventure to find something good to eat, but I'm new, so I don't have much idea about what to buy." I don't know why I felt the tug to befriend her.

"You're with that boy." Her voice was small and tight.

"Nada. Do you know him?"

She shook her head then changed her mind and gave a slight nod. "Kind of."

"I gather you two aren't friends."

She shook her head again.

"Would you like to be friends? I could introduce you."

This time, she gave an emphatic shake of her head.

"Does he frighten you?"

"I'm not allowed to speak to strangers."

"You're speaking to me, and we don't know each other."

"I'm not allowed to speak to you."

"Well... I'm glad you are, but I hope you don't get into trouble."

"Hey, what are you doing?" Nada came up behind me, which frightened the young girl. She darted out from under the stall and ran down the street on dirty bare feet.

I straightened and caught Nada watching her dart away with a slight crease in his brow.

"You frightened her."

"Not me, really." He handed me some of the white pastries wrapped in a netted fabric.

"What do you mean?"

"We're not allowed to make friends."

"*We*, as in the children?"

"It's safer when we're frightened of everyone, when all we want to do is hide at home. That way, the sweepers won't find us. Sometimes I see her in the market when I come shopping with my grandfather. She follows me but never comes up to say hello."

"Nada, where are your parents?"

"Dead." Said with all the world weariness of an adult. "The sweepers got them. That's why my grandfather did me this tattoo."

"But you said the sweepers were after children because of their tattoos."

He shrugged and popped a pastry into his mouth, putting my questioning to an end. Only a child could reduce such a repressive life to a mere inconvenience.

"Do you know what faction your parents were?"

"I was seven when they died."

Should I dare ask the question? "Were they both Aris?"

"We don't talk about the dead," he replied then turned and headed back to his grandfather's house, seeming to have lost interest in shopping anymore.

Chapter 12

JAX RETURNED HALFWAY through a game Nada taught me. It involved the knuckles from animals, a quick eye, and an even quicker hand. Nada beat me every time but admitted to being impressed with my skill, for an amateur.

Jax ruffled Nada's hair and said to me, "We best go. I want to speak with Elva before the end of the day."

For a few hours, I'd been somewhere else with a small boy not too unlike Ajay, losing myself in the simplicity of childhood. I hadn't thought my mind would ever let me forget, but it had let go easily, willingly, quite desperately, until I was happy. With Jax back and talking about Elva, I was back too, in an alien world, pretending to be someone else.

Jax rested a hand on Nada's shoulder. "Thanks for babysitting Sable."

Nada's grin split his face. He straightened, expanding his chest like he'd been given the biggest compliment. My gaze wondered from the pride on Nada's face, along Jax's hand still resting on his shoulder, to Jax's face and the loss forever cast as a shadow on his expression. His loss was eternal. Unlike my struggle, his fight would not return his family.

"Thanks for the food and the company. I hope we see each other again."

I caught Jax's brow pinch at what I said. The familiarity in the way he spoke to Nada and Islia, I thought he visited regularly, which meant we'd be this way again enough times for me to make friends. Maybe I was wrong.

Islia ghosted into the doorway of the passage that led to the exit and the alleyway. Jax joined him, and they turned and disappeared into the dim light heading for the front door.

"I meant what I said. I hope we see each other again." It was my turn to rest my hand on Nada's shoulder.

"It may not be safe," he said with the courage of an adult.

"Friends are worth visiting, no matter what."

"You bring danger to the fringe."

Jesus, I'd not been expecting that. "I'm sorry…." *What do I say?*

"This is not who you are. I know that. It's a matter of time before they know that. And here in the fringe, we're not treated like everyone else."

I'd been slapped, gut-punched. It felt like the biggest rejection I received in forever—actually, since I first met Jax, but I hated him too much to care back then.

One mental slap later… "You're right. I'm really sorry. I never thought about the danger of coming. Jax should never have brought me here."

Nada shrugged. For the second time since coming to Islia's home, the heaviness of my pain turned me into a lump of rock. All Nada needed to do was roll his eyes at me, and I'd be fighting the swell of tears. I resisted wiping the few small strands of hair from his forehead, resisted a gesture so familiar to me yet loaded with memories. When destruction seared hot through my heart like a warning lance to my fragile feelings, I spun away and headed after Jax and Islia.

Jax stood in the alley, Islia holding the door like he was waiting for me to leave so he could lock it behind me. I slipped past him but faced him halfway out. "Thank you for what you've done."

"I can't decide if you are foolish or brave."

"I'm anything but brave."

"Sometimes, the foolish become the brave." His dirty-green eyes became my conscience, my reality, my fear.

What were we doing? What did we hope to achieve? An impossible task. We could not hope to win. Carter had an army; the senate had more. What did we have but just a handful of people with hope?

"We have to go, Sable."

Islia tilted his head in a gentle gesture of respect then closed the door.

Jax was already walking, forcing me into a light jog to catch up.

"Next time, you listen to me." His voice short, terse.

I wouldn't tell him it was Islia's suggestion. "We went to the market for only a few minutes."

Jax kept a mean pace, nothing unusual there, but this time the march was coupled with heated vibes emanating from the rigid swing of his arms and the piston-punch of his legs through the dirty alley.

"Why do the sweepers target the children?"

"Let's just clear the fringe first."

"You can't talk while you walk?"

"There's too much to say." His words were staccato as we stormed along.

We passed through market spaces puncturing the gray of the fringe with their dazzle of color, tuning my senses, into many alleyways, suffocating, dirty, and dull, which sucked the life from my breath. I had no hope of finding my way to Islia's on my own… or the platform. I quickened my steps to keep close to Jax.

My head spun at the speed in which Jax snapped me back from the mouth of the alley. With one arm across my stomach pushing me in the gut, the other jabbing at my shoulder, I was hustled backward until I tripped over my feet. A hand under my shoulder, Jax hoisted me up like a rag doll, propelled me around, and sent me stumbling back the way we'd come.

"What's going on?" My question was left behind as Jax pulled me into another alley.

"Move it," he barked, pushing me in the back.

The steel in his voice sent me scurrying as best as I could around the debris and rubbish that littered the alley. Panic-laced anger, that was the emotion behind the force in his voice, which had me break into a jog. My feet obeyed my own welling panic, rushing up behind me like some black messenger of death. The hard pump of my pulse would likely burst a vein, but destruction would burst through me first.

Holding back destruction became my biggest fight, and our mad flight through the alley wasn't helping.

"Jax, stop." I fell sideways, slapping my hands onto the rough, cold brick wall. A rush of heat scalded my palm as a fine fissure split the brick under my fingertips, zigzagging up the face of the wall. "Jesus." I jerked my hand back, curling my nails into my palms until it hurt.

Too busy looking behind us, Jax had not seen. "We don't have time for this." He wrenched me off the wall.

"What's happened?"

"Sweepers are combing the fringe. We nearly ran into one just now."

I pulled out of his hold. "Does Islia know? What about Nada?"

"I've warned him."

"How?" *Of course, stupid.* "Your cephulet. But wouldn't that mean the senate can keep track of him?"

"His is a black-market variety, which keeps him off the senate's grid, but the particular sort he has is unreliable and prone to frying your brain."

"Are they here for us?"

He glanced in the direction we'd come. "They come all the time to harass the people. It doesn't have to be about us." He swung his attention on me. "You don't know how to act around sweepers. Out here, your tattoo alone is not enough to protect you. The senate is aware of the trade in illegal tattoos. Your naivety will raise their suspicions, and that alone will have you taken."

"But they wouldn't guess I'm an alien, surely?"

"There are other more serious reasons for being taken."

"I have the tattoo of Aris. We're allowed to be together."

A muscle twitched in his left jaw.

He did not understand the depth of my need, so he had no right to judge.

"What's done is done. Get over it." My blood thrashed through my ears followed by a sudden wave, which swept out of my body. Chips of brick flung off the wall to the left and right of us, showering us in a fine spray of dust I inhaled deep then coughed out. Caught in his own anger, Jax did not seem to notice how close destruction was to doing major damage.

He took a stride toward me. "You don't understand what you've done. You're locked out of the one place you may have been safe, and you've limited your ability to finding your mum and brother."

No, he was wrong. I had not made that mistake. I couldn't have. "No one cares who or what I am in the fringe." This great rush of emotion poured through me, sharpening my voice. Did Jax hear the accusation I'd not bothered to disguise?

"What are you going to do, Sable? Hide here until it's all over?" He took another step forward, spearing his face too close. Destruction took it as a threat. I bit my inner cheek until I tasted blood. My vision swam with tears of pain, but it was what I needed to make destruction back down.

"Nowhere is safe, especially not the fringe." He seized my chin between his fingers and forced my head to the right. "This tattoo, this lie, will get you killed." He released my chin. "You could cost everyone their lives for being here." The expulsion of his anger thrust him backward away from me, thrusting destruction deep down inside.

The fight drained through my pores, destruction defeated. Standing there with hands on hips, eyes to the ground, there wasn't any fight in Jax either.

"My world will twist your soul," he said.

"It hasn't twisted yours."

He hmphed a sarcastic laugh. "That's debatable."

What did we say, now that the tension eased from the air? Jax wouldn't look at me, staying behind his wall of complicated emotions.

I wanted to ask him what he thought would make this world better, but I got the feeling he was lost. Dad's actions were the trigger that drove his conviction. But without his revenge, what kept him going was what kept me going; there was no way out. Fight or die, they were our two choices, just like in Dominus.

"Sweepers will be stationed at the platform. Our best hope is to head back to Islia's."

"Don't they check the houses?"

"Most homes have false floors or walls. If you can find shelter, you're rarely detected."

He drew me back the way we'd come, but we managed a few steps before fringe dwellers ran past the mouth of the alley. The expression of fear on each face hammered my heart. With a violent wrench, Jax spun me toward him and shoved me up against the wall. My breath *oomphed* out. I was about to spit a protest, but he pushed his body up against mine and pressed his lips against my neck before his hand wandered down to my hip then snaked around to my ass.

"At least pretend you're enjoying this." His whisper tickled my skin.

Pretend what? How? Oh, Jesus. There was no escaping, no hiding, except for this. I wrapped my arm around his neck and tilted my head to the side, exposing more of my neck, which gave me a good view of the alley entrance.

A lone figure passed up ahead then jerked to a stop and looked our way. The man was dressed similar to Jax, in all black, including his helmet, which disguised his face, thick-soled combat boots, and a belt from which dangled a variety of implements—my guess, weapons. A shimmer of air surrounded him, like hot air rising off asphalt on a summer's day.

"We've been spotted. Someone's coming toward us, all black."

Each step he took rose destruction inside me. "There's something surrounding him."

"It's a sweeper." Jax lifted his head. Rather than look at the sweeper, he stared at me. "That's a protective barrier." We were close. He only needed to whisper. "The barrier's to protect against factional nature attack, giving the sweepers the upper hand." He gave up the pretense of our intimate interlude and stepped back, leaving a cold emptiness to take his place. He'd yet to face the sweeper's way. "Let me talk. If things get ugly, you need to run. Do you think you can get back to Islia's?"

I nodded, a lie, but I didn't want Jax worrying. "And, Sable, don't allow your factional nature through. I'm serious. I can't begin to explain how bad that would be."

I closed my eyes as if to suck his words from my memory. Too late, he already uttered the call, and destruction obeyed. The taste of blood lingered in my mouth, a reminder. It did not have to become me. We were one, but I was the greater. I had to believe that.

Jax turned to meet the sweeper, stepping in front of me, which only strummed the strands on my flimsy control of destruction. I peered around Jax to see the sweeper had stopped. As if sensing a threat, he raised his weapon. "What is your purpose for being here?"

"Looking for somewhere secluded."

"You're not from the fringe. Why are you here?"

In the silence, my factional nature tickled along the underside of my skin.

The sweeper waved his weapon at Jax to help loosen his tongue.

"We're here on a dare. And then we found this alley and... it looked private enough...." He let his sentence trail away, indicating the sweeper should fill in the rest with his imagination.

As he didn't question further, the sweeper was likely consulting his cephulet. Then he barked out, "Name."

The sudden shout made me duck behind Jax again to see his fists ball. I wanted to rip my heart from my chest to give me some peace. The rampage of its beat harnessed destruction, rallied it into a wrecking ball.

"I want your name."

"I'd rather not. There are certain people who are better off not knowing I'm here."

Jax glanced back at me, whispering the words, "Now's a good time to run."

"You're kidding." Like that wouldn't trigger the sweeper into action.

I was at war within myself. The threat from the sweeper, the tension from Jax, my mind tumbled with the pressure of withholding destruction. But the danger was immense. He was not the only sweeper. He couldn't be. If I used destruction, how many more sweepers would arrive?

"Trust me," Jax said.

"Have the girl move around to the front where I can see her."

Jax turned back to the sweeper. "That's not such a great idea."

The sweeper raised his voice and his weapon to his eyes, both a death command. "Move to the front."

I came around beside Jax, but he snapped his arm out to block my path. Under his breath, he said, "Can you at least do one thing I ask?"

Hearing the exasperation in his voice, I obeyed, moving back behind him, then inching farther away. On edge like this, my mind tittered on instability. The adrenaline dancing its merry tune throughout my body warped destruction to near uncontrollable.

And what did Jax hope to do? Why speak the question? I already knew the answer.

The sweeper reacted to my insubordination by waving the barrel of his weapon as he held it up to his line of sight. "Come out where I can see you, now."

Jax became fluid in one partial inhale. Too quick for the sweeper to register, he spun, gathering momentum, and aimed a kick at the sweeper's head. Apparently, the shield surrounding the sweeper was good against a factional nature attack, but useless against bodily attack, because he staggered backward under the assault, his arm with the weapon flung wide.

Not giving the sweeper a chance to recover, Jax launched another kick, foot to chin. And then again. Jax's onslaught turned ruthless. He pummeled the sweeper with enough blows to send anyone to their knees. His swift attack left the guy with little room to defend.

With the brutal fight in front, the running footsteps behind me caught me by surprise. I spun to see the little girl who'd hidden under the table at the market, racing toward me. For one dazed moment, I stared at her, unable to convince myself she was here in the alley when a sweeper was so close behind.

Forgetting the fight, I rushed to her, conscious of her vulnerability. "What are you doing here?"

She grabbed my hand. "Come."

I tried to pry my hand from hers. "This is dangerous. You shouldn't be here."

"Neither should you." She bit back. "Don't you know the rules?"

"What rules?"

"Fringe rules."

"Which are?"

"Run." To make a point, she pulled my hand extra hard, and I was jerked forward. "Run," she said again, echoing Jax, but if I did, wasn't that being a coward?

Behind me, the only person I knew in this world, the only one I trusted, fought for his life. Either I followed my desire and stayed, or I trusted Jax and went with the girl.

"Come on," she said.

I looked over my shoulder to see the fight evened out. The protective shield surrounding the sweeper was gone, as was his helmet. The sweeper, as he'd been, was also gone, replaced by an Aris immersed in bloodlust. I didn't need to see Jax's face to know what he'd become.

Upon seeing the enemy, destruction swept forth.

Chapter 13

WITH HEAVING BREATHS, I tried to push my factional nature down into my body to hold it in.

The little girl pulled on my hand. "You can't help."

"No, wait." I tried to take my hand back from her vice grip—I couldn't flee and concentrate on holding my ability in check—but her torn nails dug into my wrist deep enough to pebble blood around her fingers.

"Come. On."

With the brutality of the fight raging behind me, destruction forced itself through the cracks it found in my mental armor. My body felt zapped with electricity as destruction charged out of me. Through gasping breaths, I tried to suck it back, stemming the immensity of the flow. Too late, a fracture raced in a ragged line in front of us as we fled, splitting to a foot wide. The little girl dodged the gap and kept her pace. On seeing what I'd done, I redoubled my efforts to contain destruction. I thought I'd mastered it, but there was a new level of control I had yet to reach.

The crack was a flag to the sweepers; someone lived here ungrafted. But they would already know, or else why harass the fringe dwellers as much as they did? I now understood the danger I placed everyone in by being here.

We burst out of the alley into a deserted market space looking like the action had already passed this way. The owners had up and fled, leaving their stalls overturned, baskets scattered, fabric ripped from the lines to lay trampled under the stamped of desperate feet. Soft fruits oozed their insides. Luscious white pastries similar to the ones Nada had bought us, plus other baked food, had tumbled and minced together as they were ground into the dirt. A big boot print sliced through the corner of one pastry, the rest sticking to the bottom of my shoe as we ran by.

I surrendered to the girl's vice grip and scurried along beside her, weaving around the chaos then into another alley.

Finally, she stopped, releasing my wrist, and knocked twice on a metal door in quick succession. After a heavy *clank*, the door swung wide, sucking in a small gust of wind. The woman in the doorway measured to my nose, but her face radiated a fury suited to someone twice her size. Fury transformed to surprise at seeing me, and then her blue eyes narrowed as they honed in on the little girl.

"Azrael, no." The words were emphasized with a violent shake of her head.

Ignoring the woman, Azrael grabbed my wrist again and pulled me inside. I half expected the woman to close the door on me before I made it through, but Azrael moved quick, tripping me up the small lip at the door so I clumsily crashed inside. Not waiting for any terse words from the woman, Azrael kept her firm hold and pulled me along a narrow, dark passage with the heavy *clank* of the door being locked behind us, which had to mean the woman was not about to scream at Azrael to kick me out.

With the front door closed, we plunged into darkness if not for the lamp hanging from the wall in a large bracket of twisted metal. We finished up in a small room furnished with the bare essentials and a few comforts like cushions and throws to prevent the room from appearing austere.

The woman entered the room with the cautious eyes of someone who managed to survive the constant harassment of the sweepers. Peacock-blue eyes lasered over me before settling on my tattoo. For someone who looked as old as my mum, she was still attractive, although the buckle of lines at the corners of her eyes and across her top lip, plus the creases gouged into deep scars between her eyes, said her life had not been easy. The way she moved, alert with every step across the room to stand by her daughter—there was no mistaking the resemblance—eyes on me like I was a feral animal, spoke of a life in the fringe. As she'd done to me, I darted a look to the tattoo behind her ear when she glanced down at her daughter. Perun, no mistaking the jagged bolt of lightning.

"You know better, Azrael." The fury had subsided. Her voice now quivered with the outpour of relief.

"She needs our help."

Her mum shook her head. "We can't help her. She can't stay here."

"But we have to. The sweepers will get her otherwise."

"That is not our concern."

Azrael puffed herself up, on the verge of arguing some more.

"Your mum's right."

Azrael's angry little face snapped to me.

"It's not safe for anyone at this moment. You shouldn't be rescuing strangers," I said.

She looked nothing like Ajay, but she made me think of him all the same. I would be repeating her mum's command if this were my family. "Besides, I need to find my friend. He may need my help."

Azrael grabbed my hand, shaking her head. "You can't go out there. You can't stop yourself from being Persal. The sweepers will see."

My eyes widened at her honesty. Her mum's expression had not altered, no surprise at the shocking revelation. It was like she expected it all along, or she'd seen the lie many times over. There was nothing friendly about the woman, but I would act prickly too if my family was at risk and harboring someone wearing a false tattoo, which would see everyone punished.

I gave Azrael a weak-smiled apology and turned to leave, but she snagged my hand. "No."

Her mum sighed. "You can stay for a while. There is no point walking into danger."

"I'm worried about my friend. I left him fighting a sweeper."

Her peacock-blue eyes kept everything she thought inside. Then finally, she said, "Did Islia do that?"

No point in lying. She was hiding from the sweepers, so the senate were no friends of hers. Besides, Azrael, in true child style, had already revealed my secret.

"Yes."

"That is why you are here?"

"Yes."

"Perhaps you are in more danger than us. Come, we cannot stay out here." She glided past me, moving toward the opposite door to the one we'd enter by, disappearing farther into the house. Azrael, deciding it was safe to let me go, dropped my hand and followed her mum through another dark and narrow passage smelling of damp clay. Closed doors on either side broke up the earthen walls. We ended up in a cheerless, dank room with cracks running from ceiling to floor and dirt under our feet. Three cupboards lined the back wall, each uniquely carved out of smooth-looking stone. From the belt of her pants, the mum pulled a set of keys and unlocked the smallest, a waist-high cabinet, with something similar to a metal poker.

"Azrael, you go first."

Seeming content now that her mum was on her side, Azrael ducked and stepped through. My turn to follow was announced by a terse jerk of the mum's head toward the cabinet.

With my hand on the doorframe, cold seeped through my fingers. The surface of the cabinet was cool and smooth, like marble. But the door looked built from metal beaten thin to make it light yet durable. The back of the cabinet opened out into a dark space, but the big surprise was the floor, which disappeared downward into a stairwell. Below, a dull light flickered like a small flame. Azrael appeared at the bottom in silhouette, some ten steps below. "Come on." She impatiently waved me down.

The room at the bottom was big enough to accommodate a group of people comfortably. Jagged rock walls, it would've been a laborious task to cut this room into shape. Three beds and a small table with a single drawer were the only pieces of furniture. The air smelled like it had been locked away for centuries with little disturbance, but with a cold earthiness that comes from underground.

With a muted *click*, the light from above disappeared. The mum's footsteps scuffed down the rock steps. In the flicker of the candle flame, she looked younger. The golden light hid the gray flecks around her ears, so all I saw was a mane of black hair.

When Azrael opened the drawer of the table, a cast of soft light shone over her face and up to the ceiling. She pulled a glowing lump from the drawer and placed it on the table then blew out the flame with an exaggerated huff. Trylite. The same rock that had illuminated the cave as we moved through the dungeons in Dominus. Only this was the real thing and not a simulation. But Jax had said trylite was expensive, its mining and sale strictly monitored by the senate. How was it a fringe dweller had themselves some trylite in their escape room?

The only noise was our breathing, the only light the dim, golden glow of the rock. It made it seem like we were the last people to survive. The room shrank. I couldn't think of anything to say that would not expose me as being off-world. Strangely, despite the mum's defensive expression, I wanted to befriend her. Maybe it was because she was my mum's age. I'd forgotten what it was like to trust an adult, but confronted by her calm strength, I couldn't help feeling like a child.

"Can you buy trylite around here?"

"No. It was gifted to me."

By someone with a lot of money and influence, most likely. What woman from the fringe knew the right sort of people well enough for them to supply her with such a valuable gift?

I wouldn't question her. Who was I to delve into her secret? And she was unlikely to tell me the truth, if anything at all.

Azrael slid onto one of the beds. "What was that boy's name?"

"Be quiet, Azrael. That is none of your concern," she said.

Azrael's mouth drooped at the corners. Her head dropped, so she was staring at her hands in her lap. Her mum sat next to her and patted her thigh then covered her hands with her own. "You know why I say these things."

Azrael rolled away from her mother and stretched out on the bed with her back to us. What her mother did was for her safety, but it would be a prison for a child.

"What's your name?" I asked.

After a decent wait, she said, "Alithia."

I took a seat on the next bed. "How long do we stay here?"

"Until nightfall."

As much as that? "But I can't. I have to find my friend."

"He will find you."

"He doesn't know I'm here."

She turned away from me and stared at the wall opposite.

"Do you know him?" I said.

She leveled her gaze at me. "I took you in because of my daughter's pleas." She returned to staring at the wall. End of conversation. This was going to be a fun time, but I couldn't fault the woman's caution. After all, she had a daughter to think about.

I slid farther onto the bed, leaning against the wall, which made for an uncomfortable backrest due to the jutting rock. No way would I last until nighttime sitting here staring at the wall. At some point, Azrael was bound to get restless, or maybe she'd been conditioned to sit through long periods of confinement. Her escape was likely sleep.

The utter stillness in the room twitched my legs. I had a roving energy gliding ceaselessly through my body, which seemed to get worse the longer I stayed put.

"Is it just you and Azrael?" I needed distraction.

She nodded. Was it the question or the fact she wasn't interested in any conversation? People living in the fringe were perhaps intimately associated with death, regardless if it was a conversation no one wanted to have.

"I'm sorry."

"If you were from around here, you'd know not to pry."

A distant bang silenced us both. Azrael rolled over and looked up at the ceiling. The whole room seemed to hold its breath. The bang sounded again.

"It's him," Azrael said, climbing from the bed.

Alithia hitched her around the waist. "You can't be sure. It's not the knock."

"It has to be. I know it is." Azrael pleaded, "You can't leave him."

"What if it is not him?"

"The two of you wait here. I'll go," I said.

Azrael froze in her struggles. Alithia's eyes were dark in the dull light, dark enough I couldn't read them.

"No. There will be less trouble if I go." She swung Azrael aside. "You wait here," she ordered, jabbing a finger at her daughter. But the moment she was up the stairs and out of the cabinet, Azrael bounded after her. As if I'd be left behind.

I rushed on Azrael's heels. I caught up in the first room, latching onto her arm, hauling her to a stop. "Get behind me." Destruction loomed deadly close to release. If I were to look in the mirror, I'm sure I'd see its turbulence churning up my irises.

"No!" she yelled, attempting to drag herself free.

"Don't break your mum's heart." I said back with equal ferocity.

Her face was a puffed red flush of anger, but she relented all the same. With the sound of commotion up the passage to the front door and her mum's gasps of dismay, Azrael was off, pattering across the floor in her bare feet.

"Help me!" cried Alithia up the passage. I was in motion in seconds flat.

The dim lamp gave me little light, but I didn't need much to see. Jax had slid down the wall, leaving a thick smear of blood trailing after him. I'd seen this all before. No, this time, he looked worse. It wasn't possible he was still alive. *He is, he is, and bleeding out fast.*

Azrael collapsed on her knees in front of him. "Jax," she cried with a childish voice full of desperation.

I wasn't gentle when I wrenched her out the way; nor was I conscious of where she tumbled.

"We need to get him inside, lying down." I hated the fear in my voice. I swallowed the big ball of panic in my throat, hoping it would take destruction down with it. "Take his other side. Gently." Good, a harsh tone in my voice. It's what I needed to fool myself. "Where can we take him?"

"The escape room." Good to hear Alithia sounded calm too.

"We can't get him down the stairs while he's like this."

"And we can't hide him quick enough if the sweepers come."

No arguments from me.

Jax was a big guy, which meant it was going to be hard. When he scrambled his feet under him to give us a hand, I had to bite my bottom lip to stop from whimpering with his pain, but we needed his help if we had any hope of getting down into the escape room.

I ignored the tacky feeling of his clothes and the wetness that spread to me and concentrated on shuffling us step by step down the passage. At the first room, I refused to look at him for fear of what it would well up inside me. Destruction hated any weakness. It hated awkwardness and shame and confusion and fear, writhing like a caged animal teased with a hot poker.

It took an eternity to reach the room with the cabinet, during which Jax must have trailed most of his blood supply, leaving the rest on me and Alithia. A handful of times, his legs buckled, and it was only our combined strength that kept him upright. Azrael opened the cabinet door, staying amazingly controlled and quiet for someone so young seeing something as terrible as this, but she was a fringe child. I had to remember that.

"You'll have to bend down," I whispered close to Jax's ear. Not even I wanted to hear the suggestion that someone as badly injured as Jax had to contort himself to climb into a small space.

He tried but collapsed forward onto his knees in the entrance with a groan of pain. Both Alithia and I cried out when he went down. His weight too heavy, neither of us could stop his momentum.

"We'll have to drag him down," Alithia said.

My mouth dropped open, about to protest, but her eyes flashed warnings. I shut my mouth and nodded.

Working together, we turned him onto his back, and I tried to ignore how feeble he'd become in the time it took us to get him here from the front door. Only now did I get a good look at him, and again, I had to swallow that hard ball of panic made bigger by my tears. I swallowed it all down, punched it deep into my stomach. "We'll both take an arm."

Dragging him down the stairs was agony, but watching his wounds seep was worse. We needed to get him safe. That's what I told myself for ten steps, and when we reached the dirt floor, Alithia and I collapsed down to our asses panting with more than the strain. But Alithia was a survivor, and in no time, she recovered, waving her arm at Azrael. "You know where things are."

Once Azrael disappeared, Alithia turned to me. "He's as good here as on a bed for now. Azrael will give you what you need. I'll be back soon." Then she was gone.

In the gentle glow of the trylite, I assessed his wounds, pressing my lips tight at the sight of him. There was nothing I could do for him now but soothe my hand over his brow and down his arm so he would know I was here until Azrael came back.

There was so much blood left in a trail down the stairs and on the floor to here, caking the dirt into clumps. How much of that was his own? If he opened his mouth, would the blood stain his gums, his tongue? I closed my eyes as I stroked his arm, seeking solace in touching him as much as to give it in return. For one moment, I felt as though gravity pulled me down into the center of this alien world, crushing me with its intensity. This wasn't a game. We were no longer in Dominus racking up kills so we could escape with our minds intact. Outside the game, how much of our sanity would remain if we continued to be who we were?

Azrael clambered noisily through the small doorway and down the steps. She cradled a box in her arms.

"I got you this." She set the box beside me on the floor then sat next to Jax's head.

"You should wait outside." After years of protecting Ajay, I didn't like the idea of her witnessing the mess Jax was in.

She shook her head. "No. I can help."

This was one stubborn child. "Do you have any tablets. You know… coagulants?"

"Like this?" She opened the box and rummaged inside. The bottle she showed me looked different to the ones Jax had in his apartment.

"We're not allowed to use them usually. They're for special cases."

"Sounds like the right ones." I hadn't thought Alithia would have the right medicine, being in the fringe and all, but it seemed her benefactor was as generous with medicine as they were with the trylite.

My hands shook when I took the bottle. There was so much going on inside me; not the least was my factional nature clawing at the walls.

"How about some water?"

Azrael scuttled up the stairs once more.

Shaking hands made the bottle hard to open. I tapped gently, not wanting to spill any of the precious pills. He looked so bad three would do to start, especially since there was no one around to judge how many I wasted.

"Jax." I cupped his face. "Jax, I have the pills for you."

He lolled his head toward my voice then tried to reach out his hand, but it flailed beside him. I clutched it in mine. "Open up. I'll put them in your mouth."

"I had no choice." His voice was tired, weak.

"It's all right. You're safe. You're going to be all right."

"Sable."

"You don't have to talk. Let me give you the pills."

Jax slowly turned his head away when I touched a pill to his lips. I couldn't see his eyes clear enough through the blood and open wounds to enforce my will with my glare.

"I didn't have a choice."

I placed a hand gently on his throat, because it was one of the few places with intact skin. A tear followed from my eye, landing on his chin. "I know."

I knew this heaviness, this horrible weight that sinks you down to the depths of yourself and makes you want to drown. "None of us do, Jax."

"Committed..." His Adam's apple moved under my palm. "You can't back out."

I had to lean lower to hear him. "Don't talk. I understand."

"They'll never stop."

"Jax, you don't need to tell me this." I squeezed the hand I still held.

"They won't relent."

More of my tears dropped on his face.

"Kill or be killed."

I lifted my hand from his throat and touched lightly over his lips. "Stop, please."

"I've never killed in real life before."

"I have. I'll never judge you." I leaned down and pressed my lips to his forehead.

Chapter 14

THE SILENCE of the empty streets belied the savagery of the hunt, which had taken place only hours ago. With Jax's rebellion, more sweepers were sent to the fringe. Alithia had returned with news that four more utilities had landed. She assured me the fringe dwellers were good at hiding and most had disappeared by the time reinforcements arrived. The clash between the sweepers and those who had remained to fight was brutal but swift. That was all Alithia would tell me. Hours later, and I couldn't tell if she blamed us for what happened.

From her rooftop, the fringe looked peaceful in the twilight. The soft yellow glow that flickered through open windows was like a signal of survival. From the chaos and violence, to this, where not even the wind disturbed the quiet. The night became a glow of fireflies.

I pulled my legs to my chest and rested my chin on my knees as I stared out over the roofline. Due to the heat, in the warm months, a lot of living was done on the rooftop, but in a place like the fringe, a worn rug and a few tattered cushions were the only comfort you would find. Was this the reason for Jax's rooftop room back in my world?

The high-rise apartments in central Califax did not look like the sorts of places people would gather on the roof, but the fringe was like another world, and I could only wonder how close Jax had been to this way of life. It didn't make sense. His apartment screamed wealth. His family was obviously connected with the senate—or else why had Dad targeted them—and that could only mean money. Yet this family seemed to know him intimately, plus he moved around the fringe like it was his second home.

I glanced over to the fire burning in a large bowl in the center of the rug. I stared into the dancing flames, remembering the conversation Jax and I had on his rooftop. I remembered the glow of the firelight on his face, softening the hard edges, which had etched permanent lines on his brow, making him handsome yet unreachable. I remembered the haunting of his eyes as he told me Dad was not human, not earth human anyhow, and that he was a part of this whole elaborate and deadly design to get us all killed.

Alithia returned to the roof, carrying a tray with two mugs. She said little to me since her return, staying long enough in the escape room to check on Jax and gain Azrael's assurance she would remain in there with us until she gave the all-clear to come up top. It was only after the sweepers departed that she'd given me a terse and abbreviated account of what she learned and saw. I couldn't fault her attitude. This was her home, and this was what Jax and I had done by being here.

I took the hot drink from Alithia and cradled it in my hands, using that to push away the memory of Jax's tortured confession. This was only the beginning. What world of pain and regret would we face before we reached the end? Who would we be when we got there?

"It's so peaceful at night," I said, but I didn't expect an answer from her.

She sat beside me on the edge of the small brick wall and looked down on the street below. I followed her gaze to see a figure shuffle silently down the alley. In the moon shadow cast by the buildings, his slow, hobbled gait made me think he was wounded or old, someone lucky to be alive.

"Triptophia is full tonight. In another hour, a third moon, Iridiaus, will rise sunder. Though it is only small."

"You have three moons."

"Four. Eurodus is the closest and largest. It is the moon that follows the sun. It would light the night as day, but it is the day moon. The smallest, Iridiaus, is the last to rise and is still there first thing in the morning, although you barely see it with the naked eye. The fourth, Riddean, also a giant, only comes into view at night every couple months. It is usually in the sky during the day but hidden by Eurodus. In fact, it should soon be seen in the night sky."

I'd given up the pretense I was from this world. Alithia accepted the quiet revelation with equal amounts of silence. Perhaps there were ungrafted people in the fringe who'd experienced shifting. Maybe she was ungrafted herself, though she wore a tattoo on her wrist.

"Why do the sweepers come?"

"It is the senate's attempt to control the outer fringe with terror. Their power is limited in its reach this far out. The only way they can maintain their authority is to keep us living in fear."

"They come and terrorize the people and leave?"

"No. They come looking for children. Early on, it became apparent those living in the fringe did not uphold the same prejudice as the rest of Califax. Living so close together, relying on each other to survive, the factions mingled, and many fell in love and had children. To prevent mixed births, all baby boys were marked for forced sterilization at puberty. Soon, many parents refused to register their child's birth. And with the constant flow of illegal immigration, the senate soon realized the problem had stretched beyond their simple means of control. That is when the sterilization clinics stopped and the sweepers arrived. It is a crude, brutal threat to our continual defiance."

I could've asked why anyone in the fringe bothered to risk so much by defying the senate and having children, but I was too young to appreciate the biological drive, and I didn't want to offend her. A subject change was best. "How many of you are grafted?"

"Most, but not through choice. I was born in a more respectable sector, where all the people are grafted and tattooed upon birth. I dishonored my family by chasing my heart. My parents disowned me, because the young man was from another faction. They feared punishment and so reported me to the senate. They took him away." Her voice remained flat, because the past could no longer affect her, or she'd cried too many tears to shed anymore. "His parents blamed me, but not as much as I blamed myself." Her gaze rested on the fire. The golden glow rewound the years on her face, but her tone was anything but young. "I never saw him again. My parents were driven from their comfortable life, ostracized for the part they did not play in the ruin of his family. They claimed they no longer had a daughter."

"That must have hurt."

"It was a mercy. Had they remained by my side, the senate would have likely executed me. Since I was not pregnant and now abandoned by my family, they miraculously let me go. I was a great example. This is what happens to those who disobey the senate."

So he was not Azrael's father. And *young man* meant this happened long ago.

"You haven't bothered to have Azrael tattooed."

"There is no point. They would take her regardless. They do not trust the tattoos out here."

I understood the reason for her leveled gaze. My first instinct was to look away rather than at her penetrating glare. Jax already made me feel inches tall for my choice. I didn't need a stranger reducing me more than I already was. Too late, my throat constricted up with the choke I felt when people made me believe something about myself was wrong, and I always feared they were right, no matter how much I told myself otherwise.

Rather than look away, I focused on the flames, but the silence thinned the air between us until it felt like we'd be snapped together, bashing heads on the recoil. How dare she judge me? I should just leave rather than put up with her silent inquisition. But I couldn't make myself move. She'd become an enigma in the confusing paradox that was Jax. No, that was too simple an explanation for what drew the confession up my throat. Alithia faced fear with courage and survived through tenacity. She was a mother. The hardship of her life did not diminish her desire to love.

"As a Persal, I would be alone in this world." Jesus, that sounded so pathetic.

Finally, she dropped her gaze to the fire. With that small gesture, which was no movement at all, she pushed me aside. Alithia followed her heart, damn the consequences. She forged a life here, because she believed it had meaning. And I caved, because I was afraid.

"Not out here you wouldn't."

The welling in my chest made me feel like a child having just received praise. She had not pushed me aside.

"But I have to find my mum and brother, and I need to be in central Califax to do that. That's where I'll find the information I need to locate them."

She took a slow sip of her hot drink, not bothering to reply or ask questions about me, like who I was, where I came from, or why I was here. Maybe fringe dwellers knew not to ask questions, or maybe she already knew, which seemed plausible, given how much Azrael seemed to care for Jax.

The silence became awkward. "If you don't mind me asking, where is Azrael's father?"

"Buried." The word spoken like a sledgehammer struck on stone.

"What is her factional nature?"

Her gaze sliced to me. For a moment, I felt sure she wouldn't answer me.

"I am Perun. Her father was Aris."

A cross-breed, a child born with different factional natures. And that is why the senate sent the sweepers to round up the children. And I couldn't help but admire her more.

"How many children like Azrael are there?"

"A few. The senate have taken most, and the sweeper attacks grow more frequent with each year. The escape room is our only protection. They would like to see us eradicated. Removing our children is a start, but enough people from the inner sectors fall on hard times and find themselves out here. And although the senate control immigration from the outer provinces, enough slip through undetected and end up in the fringe as illegal citizens. Our numbers swell despite the senate's regime."

"What will the senate do now that a sweeper has been killed?"

Killed. Jax had killed someone. Remembering this, I couldn't stop the echoes of his despair, the plea that I understand why he did it, that I forgive him. In truth, he wasn't searching for my forgiveness, but he didn't realize that yet. He was searching for his own. I should know.

No, don't feel this. I ached for Jax, but those sorts of feelings only made destruction restless. I wasn't allowed to feel the gentler emotions, and taking on Jax's pain made destruction want to lash out.

"We cannot hide the fact that a sweeper has been killed." Alithia's response gave me something to concentrate on, allowing me to claw myself out of the deep well destruction would pull me into. "But we can hide the truth of how. And that is the most important thing. He could have died in a skirmish in which he became outnumbered. It is a possibility. It is important the senate do not know he was killed by an ungrafted Aris. That alone would bring the force of the senate's army into the fringe, something we could not protect ourselves against. Everyone in the fringe knows the importance of this secret. They will protect it." She placed her mug down on the brick wall and edged herself around to face me. "I can give you one warning. The most important warning you will ever hear. Never let them know you can fight. More importantly, never let them know you are not Aris."

The tone of her voice had altered little, but the force of her declaration washed through me, firing destruction to life. I buried my head in my knees as if that would hold the wall of my factional nature back. *Think of something else.* How much did she know of Carter and Dad's plan? No good, Carter's name reverberating through my head was enough to weaken my hold over my factional nature. "What about the crack along the ground in the alley?" I burst out like that was my salvation from the turmoil within me.

"It has been taken care of."

As if dismissing me, she shuffled around to face the fire. Could it be my being Persal made her uncomfortable, or more importantly, an ungrafted Persal? But no, she fell in love with a man of another faction. Surely that was enough to prove she didn't care about who someone was within.

"My mum and Ajay are on this world somewhere. I need to find them. There is a possibility they've been taken to a village called Uradra in the Persal province."

"I do not know that area."

"My mum has no ability. She's stuck in this nightmare because of her marriage to my dad."

"Who is your father?"

I'd learned little about who he was as a man in this world, but the few things I gleaned weren't good, so it was with hesitancy I told her. "He was one of the senate, Nixon."

An ice wall descended between us so sudden yet so forceful I felt hypothermic in seconds. Along with the glacial shift, a twitch in her jaw and the rigidity of her shoulders revealed her anger. Feeling the force puncture through me, destruction rallied in defense. *God, it's not an attack.* But the swift change in her demeanor, coupled with the topic of our previous conversation, and I had little defense against my factional nature.

I uncurled and turned, dropping my legs to the floor, fists clenched tight so my skin could feel the sharp pain of my nails. Pain brought me back from the edge.

Alithia stood, her movement so swift destruction reared beneath my skin. *Jesus, cool it.*

"What's wrong?" My voice quivered through the strain of holding destruction back.

"I shall check on Jax." She turned her back on me, and I was on my feet before I realized I had any intention of doing it. "Alithia." I did not mean to sound harsh.

She did not turn around. "Right now, Jax is more important."

"Why are you shutting me out?" *Not you, please.*

She spun around. Destruction reacted so quick I could only catch the end, slamming down on the leak with such force it felt like I dropped a thousand feet. Too late, the bowl of fire shot skyward and exploded into a dazzling display of fireworks.

Alithia staggered backward with a gasp. I palmed my mouth as horror brought a sting into my eyes. "Jesus. I'm sorry."

"What are you doing with him?" She took two strides toward me. Not my sudden and violent release of destruction, nor the embers falling to the rooftop, diminished her.

"I don't understand." Faced with her venting fury, I took a step back.

"How can you be so selfish?"

She didn't wait for my reply, striding away from me across the roof and down the stairs.

Feeling weak, I stumbled backward to the wall. She knew. But it wasn't my factional nature that made her hate me. It was my dad. I slumped down but missed the brick wall and instead slid down the face to land heavy on my ass. Cradling my calves, I buried my face away. If only I could bury myself away.

Chapter 15

IN THE DULL light of the trylite rock, Jax appeared better than when he first staggered through Alithia's door. A constant diet of tablets and sleep through the night created miraculous results.

I slept rough on the bed next to him, waking regularly to check on him, then wasting precious sleep time as I sunk into the swelling hatred of myself, which had no place in the fringe, in this world, in my heart, while I struggled to stay undetected and alive. Now was not the time to beat myself up for every decision I made.

Forever prowling below the surface, destruction loathed my pity party; I should loathe it too. At least I had an internal alarm bell for every time I focused more on myself than on what was important, and it was about time I paid attention. I had to stop feeling like this. Get smart, get tough, because that's how people survived.

"You're quiet."

I jerked at Jax's voice filtering through the silence.

I shuffled across my bed and sat gently on his, not wanting to disturb him in case he was still sore from the fight. The tablets had done wonders, but they weren't a total miracle cure that had him back to normal in one night. "I'm glad you're alive."

"Only just," he replied. I wouldn't be able to tell if he smiled, because his face still resembled a boxing glove, puffed and raw, but the bleeding had stopped. In the dull of the light, I couldn't see if any of the wounds already knitted back together.

I finally managed to dig out a smile. "You look terrible."

"I feel better than when I first arrived. How long has it been?"

"Not sure exactly. Maybe twenty-four hours."

Jax suddenly rolled to the side then froze mid-roll. "Ouch, that hurt."

"Fool, why did you do it?"

"Elva will be worried."

"True, but you need to be worried about yourself first. You can't help anyone until you're strong."

He inched himself onto his back. "We should get going. We risk being confined to the fringe the longer we stay here. It could already be too late."

"What do you mean?"

"After what I did…." Jax swallowed, his eyes fixated on the ceiling.

"Don't worry. Alithia told me it was taken care of. The senate will never know the truth."

"But they will know one of their own is dead. They each wear tracking monitors, which means they were alerted the moment he died. He would've disappeared from their grid."

"But as long as they don't know how he died…."

Jax shook his head then clutched at his temples. After a few calming breaths, he said, "That's not enough. They will suspect that someone used their factional nature. It's how the senate works. They will increase patrols at the exit points from the fringe. The fringe itself will be under constant surveillance."

"Isn't it always?"

"Not as much as it will be now. They will not let this pass without severe punishment. It's how they work. Retribution."

"I really hate to admit this, but I'm starting to understand why Carter and Dad did what they did. If this was my world. I'd want to fight."

Jax eased his head to the side. Because of the dull light, his eyes, visible now that the swelling of his cheeks had subsided somewhat, lacked the penetrating glare he usually arrowed at me. "You don't mean that."

"How about what happened to Alithia? Her parents disowned her, because everyone was scared. That's what the senate has done. They've built a culture based on fear, so that parents can be turned against their children, neighbors against each other."

"And you'd be willing to do what it takes to change that?"

"Weren't you? Isn't that why you became a part of Dominus?"

Jax slowly turned his head away to the ceiling. "I don't know why anymore. I just know I can't live like this. But now I know what it really means to fight."

I should drop the topic. He probably didn't want to think about it so soon after what happened.

"It's what Carter and Nixon trained me to do. They trained us to succeed. Both knew how the sweepers were taught, so they did things differently with us. We were given Dominus, which gave us the edge. It's the only way I could've won against that sweeper. It's only now I truly understand what I've been trained to do," he said.

"None of this is your fault."

"I feel trapped within my body. I can't stand to be the half of me they allowed free."

"Weren't you the one who said it didn't have to define us, that we could choose?"

"That was before."

I didn't know how to deal with this Jax, only the Jax that had all the answers. All I could ask was, "What do we do now?"

"What we planned. We head back to central. I need to reach Aris HQ. Find out if anyone knows of Carter. You'll want to hear word of Holden or your family."

"Will that be easy?"

"No. Holden's not going to alert anyone to his hideout."

"What about Uradra, the Persal village Dad told me about?"

Again, Jax rolled his head sideways to face me. "According to your tattoo, you're Aris, Sable. You won't get within miles of Uradra."

Oh, sweet Jesus. What had I done? I bowed forward, burying my face in my palms. *Stupid, stupid, foolish girl.* But instead of another dose of self-pity, destruction washed through, sluicing any doubt and replacing it with some mega volts of electricity. Instead of digging my nails in deep, I sat up, separating my hands, palms facing each other, then inch by inch allowed destruction to flow from one hand to the other. The air between heated with the exchange, warming the skin. But the more destruction flowed its invisible web, the hotter my palms became. They should've glowed red with the heat, but they remained a dull pink in the trylite. When the heat became unbearable, I channeled it around and around my body in a dizzy swirl that felt like I was in a whirlpool. There was no outlet for the buildup, which grew with the race around my body. Soon, my body felt like it was pulsating like a living heart.

"Sable." Jax touched my arm.

My eyes flew open. Concentration gone, destruction shot forward like a blade, splicing the rock wall adjacent us. Shards of rock exploded toward us. A second ticked as I lurched on top of Jax. The wind of the shards passing sliced the ends of my hair.

I peeled up, glaring down at him. "Dammit, Jax. Don't do that." Then remembering he was injured, I leaped off of him. Destruction simmered.

The silence between us smacked me back. "Sorry. Did I hurt you?"

Dust hung in the air, climbing into the back of my throat as I inhaled. Behind us, a small piece of loosened rock fell to the dirt floor with a soft *thud*.

At first, Jax didn't respond, which made me think I hurt him enough he couldn't speak. Then I saw his shoulders quiver and heard the chuckle. This was followed by a groan as he gently lowered a hand over his chest. "God, my insides don't like it." He wiped at his eyes with his other hand. "But my soul does. I needed a laugh."

"I'm glad I could provide it." I sat back, not bothering to hide my stupid grin.

He huffed another small laugh. "You're lethal. You know that? It may not seem like a compliment given... well, you know. But I mean it as one."

"I don't have control, not enough."

"The roof is still over our heads, not *on* them. I'd say that's good progress from someone who only gained their factional nature a few months ago. For many, it can take years. You make me believe there is hope."

"Me? Hardly."

"You and the people here in the fringe."

The door at the top of the stairs *clanked* open.

"Looks like my renovations were detected."

We both smiled at each other, listening to the feet slap down the stairs. I looked over my shoulder as Alithia appeared around the corner.

"What's going on? Jax?" Seeing him awake, she forgot what dragged her down here, thank God, and hurried across to him.

"I'm fine."

She pulled up short like he'd just sworn at her. Becoming all business-like, she said, "Maybe you should take another tablet."

"I don't want to use up anymore of your supply. You need them more than I do."

"Don't be a hero." Her tone was dismissive as she headed across to the box of medical supplies I left on the small table. The atmosphere in the dank room transformed into jagged pieces of glass. This was the first time I'd seen Alithia since her dismissal of me on the rooftop last night—or had more time elapsed—and even now, the prickly heat radiated off her. The swelling hatred for me transferred into her feet, into the way she held her body, erect, rigid as she moved toward the small table of supplies. She would love to see me gone, the enemy, but had yet to toss me out, because of Jax.

"Is it all right to take so many of those pills? Back home, you take the dose prescribed, no more, or you may suffer something worse than your initial ailment." I didn't want to question her judgment; God knew she hated me enough already, but what if it were possible to OD?

"Our medicine is obviously far more advanced than your own." The prickly heat made it up into her voice.

I glanced at Jax. The swelling subsided enough for me to see his eyebrow rise. Anyone, sick or not, would feel the tension in the room.

Alithia stopped before she reached the box. I followed her gaze to the lump of rock that had made it this far across the floor. She looked back over her shoulder to the hole in her wall and the debris littering the floor.

I was about to say the lamest word invented—*sorry*—when Jax spoke up. "It was my fault."

Alithia swiveled back to the box and rummaged through the contents until she found the pills. Her lack of response hitched the tension up a couple notches.

She tapped out a dose and held out her open palm.

"Alithia," Jax said, looking up into her eyes.

"Shut up and take them."

He did as she demanded, swallowing them down dry, which was how he'd been taking them since we first gave them to him.

Once he got them down, he said, "We have to get going."

"You're not strong enough yet. Have something to eat first. And you need a change of clothes. Besides, it's too early in the morning. No good moving around just now."

"She's right." I didn't say it just to get on Alithia's good side. I couldn't help but swivel my head toward her. She refused to meet my eyes. I still wanted us to be friends, despite everything, but that didn't look likely.

"How long have I been asleep?"

"Twenty-four hours," she said.

Jax shook his head. "That's too long. We have to go."

"You can eat first."

"I'm not taking any more of your supplies."

"We won't get far if you look like that," I said. "Give yourself a few more hours. It won't hurt."

"Every hour counts." God, he was stubborn.

Alithia's mouth pinched tight enough her lips were disappearing. This is what Jax meant to her. A stranger to her, she hated me, because I was the daughter of the man who killed Jax's family. She was outraged for him.

"What is it?" Jax asked, his perceptive gaze darting between the two of us.

I shook my head to dismiss his question. He pushed himself up to his elbows, smoother than he would've when he first woke. "Relax." I pushed him gently by the shoulder. "Lie down again."

"I'm not an invalid," he snapped at me then hoisted himself up to sitting. "I want to know what's going on here. Has something happened I need to know about? Have you heard from Elva?"

"I would've told you as soon as you woke up." The defense in my voice pulled destruction out of slumber.

"Then why do I feel like the temperature in the room has dropped below freezing? And what's with the furtive glances between you?"

"It's nothing—" I started.

"Why, Jax?"

He turned to Alithia while I heaved a silent breath and closed my eyes.

"Why what?" he said.

"She's Nixon's daughter." I swear the venom in her voice was more lethal than a cobra.

Jax hung his head, his breath trailing out, hunching him forward.

"How could you bring her here?" Her words rose at the end, and she palmed her mouth, turning her head away.

Jax shuffled around, forcing me to get up while he fumbled himself off the bed. I clamped my mouth shut from telling him to stay put. Something was going on here. Since I was already a pariah in her eyes, no way should I intervene.

Jax swayed a little once he was on his feet. My arms jerked toward him, an instinctual grab to help him, but he shot me a sidelong look that let me know what he thought of that. Without words, he still managed to inflict barbs upon any who treated him like an invalid. With her head turned, Alithia did not see, or I'm sure she would've barked at him to get back in bed.

Once steady, Jax crossed the room and pulled Alithia into his arms. She went into him, her body sagging into his, her face finding his chest. I never thought I would see her collapse. The strength within her made her emotional crumble too sad to witness.

I swung away, giving them space and what privacy I could. I walked across to the pockmark I'd made in the wall, crunching on the debris. An ugly emotion stirred inside me, beyond destruction, and possibly just as destructive. Hands akimbo, I stretched my neck back and stared at the ceiling while I turned my concentration inward to the constant vibration of my factional nature as it migrated around my body. Jealousy was a sickness.

One small glance over my shoulder only stabbed the stake in deeper. Was that a lover's embrace?

"Mum wouldn't let me keep it," Azrael babbled on happily as if we hadn't just spent more than twenty-four hours hiding in the escape room because sweepers had moved through the fringe causing chaos.

"Your mother's wise," Jax said, gently cuffing her under the chin.

I forced my eyes away on seeing the playful gesture. Besides, I'd been scrutinizing Azrael's young face all this time, looking for signs of similarity between her and Jax, which was bad of me, because it twisted the knife and spewed out the jealousy, something I'd spent the last hours trying to pack away.

Alithia said Azrael's father was buried. But what did that really mean? Buried for real or in her heart? Something she would have to do if he disappeared into another world, lost to a cause greater than their love.

The eyes were the same, as was the dark hair. And her defiant and courageous nature, but that was also her mum. When I caught my eyes straying to Jax with all the wrong questions in my mind, I rose and headed for the next room.

None of this made sense. Jax had always been passionate about factions staying apart. He was adamant any love between them would never last.

"Where are you going?" Jax asked.

"Do I need to tell you?" Let him think I was heading to the bathroom.

He pulled a dramatic face, an *oops, I'm in trouble* as he turned back to Azrael, then tickled her, which made her curl up in giggles and roll to the floor. My heart twisted up into a tight knot, gripped in this horrible vice that spread through to my stomach, pouring the acid through until I felt sick. But I found myself lingering in the doorway, captivated by this side of Jax I never knew existed. All I'd ever seen were hard lines, sharp eyes, ruled lips, never this lightness, which had swept all the dark broodiness from his features. Less than thirty-six hours ago, Jax nearly died. He crossed a line no one should be forced to cross. Azrael's gift was to take that memory away. Maybe it was only a temporary gift, but it was a gift all the same. I had no one to give me such a gift.

With him busy, I stole a look at him, mapping every crease and line —of which there weren't many—every inch of skin down to what I could see of his collarbone. How old was he? I'd always assumed he was around Holden's age, twenty-two. But he could pass as older. But not old enough to…. I swiveled away, heading anywhere that wasn't where they were and ran into Alithia coming through with a tray of drinks.

She'd already plied Jax with more food than I'm sure she could afford. The spicy smells started the saliva in my mouth, but I swallowed it all and sat back on the couch while Jax refused to eat her supplies. The argument ended with him eating most of what was in front of him, offering me plenty, but with Alithia in the room, I couldn't accept. She rose from her seat, saying, "Don't martyr yourself," directed at me then left the room. Even with my mouth watering, my stomach churning acid, I couldn't eat a lot, but Alithia was right. I needed to be strong to succeed, so I forced chunks of spicy meat into my mouth. And despite the way I felt, I closed my eyes and floated on the strong, delicious flavor.

I stood aside to let her pass then eased myself into the passage, far enough I could still see them, the three of them. Jax took the offered mug, his eyes lingering a moment on her face. But I couldn't read the silent words they spoke. Flicking a look to her face, neither could I read her expression as she'd already turned to hand Azrael her mug.

I focused on the rough plaster rather than them. *Don't be so stupid.* What they had, if there was anything at all, was none of my business. I had no right to sneak around like this, fostering suspicion, letting it color my heart all shades of gray. And the pretense I used to get away was childish. Instead, I headed back into the room. An extra mug sat on the tray, now placed on the floor beside Azrael. She was gracious enough to bring me a drink despite her feelings toward me, and all I could do was twist myself up in ugly feelings.

I took the floor next to Azrael, who in child-like innocence slid herself closer to me so that our arms pressed against each other. She rested her knee across the top of my thigh once I folded my legs. Ajay wasn't even this cuddly with his own family. It would be easy to wrap an arm around her shoulders and pull her closer. Alithia would likely prickle. And what would Jax think?

I took a sip of the warm, sweet drink when Alithia spoke. "I know you will not listen to me."

"You know the danger if we stay longer."

"The danger is no more now than it was when this first began. Another twenty-four hours will make no difference."

"It's not just the senate's reaction I'm thinking about."

Along with Alithia's sigh, her body collapsed back into her seat. For this moment, she looked defeated. How much sleep did she get last night? Before I could stop myself, my eyes roved over her face, scrutinizing her anew, reassessing her age. I first thought she looked closer to Mum's age, but if she and Jax were an item, she couldn't be as old as that. Living on the fringe would not be kind. It's not like she could pop out to the local health spa for a treatment. It could be she was much younger than her lines would have me believe.

"I don't want you to go." In the stretch between conversation, Azrael decided it was time to have her say.

"I have to, Az."

I inhaled, hearing the pet name, the sort of thing close friends would use with each other, close friends, family, Mum and Dad.

Azrael made a show of folding her arms with great force across her chest. It worked. Jax slid off his seat to land in front of her. "Our being here will only bring you more trouble."

She shook her head. "No, it won't. We have the escape room."

"How long do you expect us to stay down there? The sweepers presence will increase."

"But they already do, even when you're not here."

Although no one was saying it, this conversation was really about me. I was the alien with the lie tattooed behind my ear. I was the risk. Jax was a registered citizen within this world. If he was caught, they'd send him back to his sector of Califax with a wrist slap. If I was caught, they would pull the fringe apart in their violent search for who was responsible for my presence in this world.

"Come here." Jax patted the floor beside him.

As Azrael shuffled on her ass to where he indicated, I glanced at Alithia, but she was staring into her mug. Her expression told me she was in another place. Another time. Just not here right now. What memories haunted her? Because her features were definitely not at peace. Was she steeling herself for Jax's departure yet again? Waiting, fearing he'd never come back?

"You know my promise," Jax said, leaning closer to Azrael.

She nodded.

"I will keep it. I always have."

Her bottom lip tightened in defiance. I could perhaps respond for her, even though I didn't know what the promise was, but I could guess. Not all promises could be kept, especially not forever. How many promises had I made to Ajay in the last year since our life spiraled into the gutter? And how many of those did I manage to keep, no matter how hard I tried?

Jax kissed her on the head then pushed up from the floor. The energy in which he did it, the sort that signaled departure, dragged me up as well. The other two joined us standing. Without preamble—easier that way—Jax disappeared down the passage to the front door.

Azrael grabbed my hand. "I don't want you to go."

"I don't want to go either." I bent down to her level. "But I have a family I have to find. I have a brother a little older than you, and my mum."

I fought to keep my eyes on Azrael and not allow them to wander to Alithia, who stayed standing close by.

"They're lost?"

"They are. And I have to go find them. Just like your mum would do anything she could to find you. I'm sure I'll see you again."

"That doesn't always happen."

Jesus, what could I say to oppose such wisdom? "You're right, but I never forget a friend. Even if I don't see them, I never forget them."

Her face remained a scowl at my clumsy and stupid attempt to make this easier. There was no removing her mood, so I squeezed her shoulder and followed Jax down the passage and out into the street. Behind me, Azrael's thumping bare feet followed as far as the door, but she was pulled from the threshold by her mum. "But I want to say goodbye."

"You can do it from the doorway."

Azrael yanked her arm out of her mum's grip, but she obeyed and stayed in the safety of the dim passage. Jax gave her a wink before marching off down the alley, keeping the goodbye short, always the best when it was hard to leave. I lingered, because I was terrible at saying farewell. Azrael stayed with her arms folded, face a scrunched wall of refusal at our departure. Alithia disappeared the moment Jax left.

"See ya." I gave a pathetic little wave and hurried after Jax.

We found the first market space we entered eerily quiet. No one bothered to return and right the chaos. Jax continued with his brisk pace, weaving around and over people's livelihoods now strewn in the dirt. No one in the fringe could afford this, but there was little we could do. Even so, I couldn't help but bend and scoop up a few things that weren't food trodden into the ground and placed them in woven baskets or wood boxes still sitting right-side up. No help really, nor did it lift the feeling that my limbs were wrapped in elastic bands and forced to move under tension. I was like a deadly virus to the people of the fringe. Once caught, it would spread its dire consequences to everyone who lived here.

After jogging to come alongside Jax, I said, "It's like the aftermath of an apocalypse."

"The fringe is waiting for continual retribution. I doubt the sweepers left with the answer to how their comrade was killed. They will return again in greater force. And we've wasted too much time hiding in the escape room."

"You needed your strength before we left."

"We could've left a day ago."

"With you looking like you did?"

Jax jabbed a glance sideways at me. Reaching the mouth of the alley, I gladly dropped behind as we entered the narrow gap. He was in a hurry. His brisk pace said so, but the pounding of his boots said some-thing else. Jax was angry, fueled by the pain of leaving Alithia and

Azrael? The delay? The devastation the sweepers left? When he walked away from Alithia's home, he walked away from the happy part of himself.

I kept behind and stayed quiet for the rest of our labyrinth jog to the platform. I craned my head up to the skytrain waiting at the top of the metal scaffolding. Seeing it made my stomach somersault, and I hadn't even left the ground yet. I really didn't want to get used to this.

Jax's boots were clanging up the metal grille already, snapping me out of my scaredy-cat headspace, not even stopping once to see if I was behind him. Destruction rose up, just like my eyes, glancing back up the face of the scaffolding. *Oh no you don't.* This baby needed to stay in the air. Any sudden release, even a small ejection, would be catastrophic.

As I climbed the stairs, I pumped my fists, curling them into tight balls and focused on forcing destruction into my feet, visualizing a release through my boots to see if that would help, which made me stomp harder with each stride.

Almost at the first landing, before the next set of steps, my gait faltered, knee buckling when I felt a sudden dip. I sprung up onto the next step, my heart choking up my throat, hands manacled to the railing. The step I'd just left bowed down; metal twisted like it had been melted in a hot furnace then reformed distorted.

Jesus Christ. I darted a look above me to the underside of Jax's boots pounding up the next level of stairs. There was no one coming up behind me, no one anywhere near the platform. But that would not disguise this mess. Did the sweepers use skytrains? If so, they would see this and know. Nothing could buckle metal except extreme force or extreme temperature. At least not back home. And we weren't near any furnaces, so the only answer was destruction. They would know the moment they found it. Everything I did put the fringe people at risk of retribution from the senate.

I jogged the rest of the way, gasping by the time I reached the platform. There, I stopped, holding the railing to catch my breath. One look over, and I spun away and hot-footed it over to Jax, waiting by the open door to the skytrain, my legs tremoring and not just because I'd ran all the way. Forgetting about the height, that was the only benefit to my mess on the steps.

An empty skytrain—not surprises, given the ghost town we left behind. Jax led us to seats down the back. Without a word, he pulled the harness down over my head and buckled me in. I would've told him to let me do it, but with the dark cloud engulfing him, and trying to work out how I would tell him about the step, he was done and buckling himself in before I composed myself.

"I feel guilty for what we've done. The people of the fringe are going to suffer because of us. Isn't there something we can do for them?" Even though the skytrain was empty, I still whispered.

"The best help we can give them is to end all this, which we can't do by staying here and hiding. If you live in the fringe, you know how to survive." He stared ahead at the seats opposite. "We need to change the rules."

"When did you decide on that? I thought your plan was to stop Carter from starting a war?"

Jax's face no longer looked like it had been used by heavyweight fighters for warmup. Wounds remained as scabs, but the swelling subsided, leaving a few blotchy yellow stains. Hopefully, that was enough to prevent any suspicious questions should we run into a sweeper. Alithia had found him clothes similar to those we arrived in, a little on the baggy side. My new clothes were more conspicuous. She managed to gather a simple fringe outfit in the time she disappeared. The clothes were supposed to be temporary while she tried to wash the blood stains out of mine, but she failed. My new clothes were not the sort of clothes someone from the inner sectors of Califax would wear.

"If we stop Carter, what changes?" He struggled to keep his voice even.

"All-out war, for starters." I did the same, still trying to keep my voice to a whisper, because the skytrain might have ears in the form of a high-tech listening device, which seemed in keeping with the senate's paranoia.

"That's inevitable."

"But it doesn't have to be."

"Don't be naïve, Sable. You've seen too much to think like a child."

I didn't expect the flare of anger that surfaced. "At least I'm not gunning for a fight." For the people of the fringe, I was, but as Jax asked, how far was I willing to go?

Jax swallowed his comment and closed his eyes. When he next spoke, it sounded filtered through a carefully thought process. "Do you really believe that's what I want?"

What had driven this division between us? Was it because of Alithia and Azrael, the crack I'd made, or the fact I'd chosen Aris as my tattoo and not Persal? Despite my best efforts to swallow the hurt and jealousy, it wouldn't go down. But the tension wasn't from me alone. Where was the man who playfully cuffed Azrael under the chin? "Of course I don't. But you've changed."

Jax's dark eyes penetrated right through like the sharpest knife. "I killed a man. How's that for change?"

I turned away, but everything in front of me was meaningless images and color.

I'm sorry. So lame. This had nothing to do with love, but everything to do with his heart.

I felt like I was shrinking small enough to slip between the gap in the seat, but the curse of my true nature fought me again. Mechanical whirring began then a loud *clank* below my feet. The sudden feel of movement as the skytrain pulled away from the platform distracted me enough that I lost my full grip on destruction. The press of the harness on my chest holding me in place loosened. At the same moment, the buckle flung outward and pierced the metal on the other side of the hull.

I shrieked.

Jax rounded on me. "What're you doing?" His expression was as dangerous as a sledgehammer.

"I..."

He jerked his head around with enough force to give himself whiplash.

"I hate flying." I closed my eyes.

Beside me, I heard Jax unbuckle. "Get up."

He crossed the aisle and slid into the seat a few places down. "Hurry." He barked the order as he lowered the harness over his head. "The system will register someone is unharnessed on takeoff."

I slipped down beside him, fumbling myself into my harness, but he pushed my hands away and locked it up himself. "No way will we get that out." He exhaled as if to even his breath, while he looked down the rows of seats to where the buckle sat embedded in the hull.

I couldn't say anything that would undo this, not without pouring out a whole heap of apologies and pleas, fast-tracking me into feeling miserable. I was lightning-quick sliding down into that dark well anyhow. But if I let myself sink, I'd likely blow the skytrain up, because destruction would claw its way up and out rather than wallow with me.

Chapter 16

THE SWEEPER WAS TALL, taller than Jax, and broader. He boarded at the next stop along with a half-dozen others. My eyes stayed focused on the seat opposite, but my body, my instincts, my innate warning bells followed his every move, heart a staccato beat as I prepared for the worst—that he would take the seat with the broken harness. He sat opposite us a few seats down. A deliberate taunt. With all the room on this skytrain, he decided close to us was best.

I kept my eyes straight as my skin felt tickled by millions of insects. The urge to look his way became an insistent knocking on my head. What about the buckle embedded in the hull, a neon for unregulated destructive activity? The moment it was discovered, the senate would know someone was moving about ungrafted, added to that the warped metal on the steps back at the fringe and the dead sweeper. I dared not think what this meant for everyone in the fringe. I was leaving more than breadcrumbs behind me.

The urge to look won out, more so because the stress of holding back made destruction jittery, roiling a great wave under my skin. The constant motion dizzied my head. One glance, that was all. Solid green eyes met mine at the other end, because he had bothered to remove his helmet. I felt forked through the head. Like the condemned, my eyes darted away. The great wave rose again. The tremor in my hands didn't show, but I pressed them onto my thighs all the same.

Jax nudged my shoulder as he leaned over. "We'll get off at the next platform."

"Isn't it too early?"

"We can catch the next ride."

So it wasn't just me with the heebie-jeebies. I was suffering a serious case of fight or flight, a natural human response, but my response was much deadlier.

Eternity passed, me struggling with destruction, forcing myself to sit still when I wanted to burst out of my seat. For some crazy and inappropriate moment, I thought of Holden—so not good, because any thoughts of him made me feel feral—and his teaching me to find my inner calm, to center on a state of inner tranquility, the opposite of chaos, my internal state right now.

I should've listened to that asshole more when I had the chance.

Eyes still on me, they peeled me open like an onion. Heat rushed into my chest then migrated up my neck. Good thing the fringe clothes buttoned up to a high collar. I touched it. Was he wondering what a fringe dweller was doing traveling farther into Califax?

My senses acute, this time I heard a small *click* at my buckle as the lock engaged to keep me seated during docking. Whirring, clanking, grinding, the skytrain maneuvered into place. I gripped the harness on my shoulder, ready to throw the cage off the moment the buckle unlocked.

A hand rested on mine, and I glanced at Jax. "Give us time to dock."

My panic was likely saturating the enclosed space. I couldn't even find him a wane smile.

When the skytrain came to a stop, Jax flipped his harness over his head and launched for the door as if driven by fire, but in my haste to remove the harness, the buckle caught in my hair. I was ready to yank the messy clump out regardless of the pain, when someone gently pushed my hands aside and began to pry the buckle from its tangle.

I jerked my head around. My eyes poured into the solid green of the sweeper standing next to me. Salted brown hair, trimmed mustache, normal-looking, nonlethal, he was anything but. A heavy dose of cologne wafted my way, and I thought of a weed that grew wild in our garden back home, the home we had before Dad went to jail. Invasive, but Mum loved the flowers and ordered the gardener to let it stay. That's what I smelled now, mixed with earthier tones that rooted you to the ground.

Not a crease or wrinkle out of place on his uniform or his face. No tech code or wiring evident within his pupils, just the dark depths of a normal human eye. If I touched his skin, would it feel warm and soft like Jax's, or rubbery and hard like a cyborg's disguise?

My heart took off on a chase as my mind wound to a halt. Distracted by his proximity, my factional nature burst the lid and swam a lap of honor through my veins.

"Keep still if you don't want to lose half your hair." He sounded amused.

"I can do it." *Cool it, girl.*

"Looks like you're making a mess."

Could this situation get any worse? Sweet Jesus, I was going to blow, which would definitely signify the situation spiraling to hell.

"I'm fine, really," I said as I lurched up—anything to get away from his touch—but fell back at the pain of almost being scalped.

"Steady up." Was he laughing at me?

"What's going on?"

Through a tangle of hair, I glanced up at Jax. His stern expression said *back off*, but this guy was a sweeper, someone not easily intimidated.

The sweeper ignored Jax. "We're almost done. If you wouldn't mind keeping your head still a little longer."

Jax's jaw twitched as he chewed on his emotions. His tension doubled my own, forcing me to forget about what was going on externally and focus internally. Dancing around my body, my destruction flicked flames down my arms, my legs, and up into my head, lighting me on fire. I felt whole, alive, and lethal.

"I've got this." This was not the voice I should use with a sweeper, but it was the voice destruction gave me, assured and determined. I pushed his hands away. "If you don't mind."

Dropping his hands, he took a step back then smirked. "If the lady insists." His tone was sarcastic. *God, asshole.* He returned to his seat.

Jax wasted no time diving in to untangle what was left of the mess, which took no time at all. What had the sweeper been doing if it took Jax so little time? He hauled me to my feet, not bothering to be gentle.

I spared a quick glance behind as we exited to make sure nothing was left—weird, given I carried nothing, but it was a habit I had from back home—and spied the buckle, but Jax jerked me around and pulled me forward. "The skytrain will be leaving any time."

Out on the platform, he hurried me down the stairs. Our freedom punctured my anxiety, so I was able to gain a mediocre of control over destruction.

"The buckle."

"Keep going."

"Do you think he saw?"

"Which buckle are you referring to? Besides, it doesn't matter. Any moment, he'll know you're not a registered citizen."

"Registered? How? Because of the buckle?"

"Save your breath for the run."

To say I was skimming the boarder of all-out panic was an understatement.

For once, I didn't notice our height and the long flight of stairs we jogged down, clanging noisily all the way, before we reached the pavement. Leaving the steps behind, Jax shot off at a brutal pace, which threatened to turn into a sprint at any moment. Already, a stitch stabbed me in the side, probably because I wasn't breathing.

This far from the fringe, and the slums transformed to clean streets and spacious apartments laid out in what looked like a grid pattern rather than unplanned urban sprawl. Not quite the leaf-lined streets of central Califax, but the buildings looked architecturally designed rather than cobbled together with dung and mud. There was space to live, breathe, and walk, no one shacked up close to their neighbor, no one forced to shop in crammed market squares.

I followed Jax's stare back over his shoulder. A handful of people came down the stairs and spilled in all directions. No sign of the sweeper.

"Perhaps the doors closed before he made up his mind," I said.

"It's best to assume the worst. We need to lose ourselves here for a while." Dragging me by the elbow, we headed for the other side of the street. Much like in central, the roads were paved for walking, so we crossed without needing to look.

"I don't know this sector, so we have to be careful. We're still a distance from central but close enough for the senate to flex its control, unlike in the fringe. This far out, the senate divides the factions in each sector into different housing estates to enforce separation. They allow everyone's natural mistrust of differing factions to keep them from mingling beyond what is deemed acceptable. We don't want to wander too far into another faction's sector. This road is the neutral passage between the quarters to the terminal, but we venture off this in anything but Aris quarter and we'll draw unwanted attention."

I welcomed the distraction of his conversation. "So living in harmony side by side works as long as they don't actually live side by side. Why even bother with the pretense?"

"For the sake of peace, the people need to believe it's possible. Panic can easily slide into chaos, chaos to anarchy. They need the pretense. Califax was founded on an ideal, and the senate needs to maintain that ideal, because without Califax, there is no Dome. No Dome, no senate."

"So you have no idea which way we should head."

"Away from the platform is my focus at the moment."

Jax stopped, his eyes doing what they did when he focused on his cephulet. "First left up ahead." He launched into his grueling pace again, eating up the distance until we reached our turn.

Ahead of us, the street opened out to a kind of boulevard, minus the trees and gardens at central. Green patches dotted the road where residents bothered to add a bit of color; otherwise, there was nothing but neutral tones.

"I'm hoping we can find an eatery. We can get lost in the crowd there," Jax managed to say through his unrelenting pace.

"I'm sorry about the buckle." This felt as close to home base as we would get right now, a good time to apologize for what I'd done, yet again. I seemed destined to make mistakes, and in this world, mistakes could be fatal.

"If he noticed, we would never have gotten off the train. At least you didn't send it across the aisle again."

"If you don't think he noticed that one or the other in the hull wall, why the rush?"

"I believe he had another motive other than helping you out of the mess you were in. You triggered his interest. He was focused on you most of the ride. It's likely the clothes."

"I felt pretty uncomfortable, believe me."

"Did you look him directly in the eyes?"

"Yes. But briefly."

"Retinal scan. He may also have collected some of your hair for marker analysis."

I halted. "What? You're joking."

"If he didn't manage a retinal scan, then he'd use the sample, hair, skin, whatever. Sweepers carry portable EPH devices for the analysis."

"I don't know what that means, but it sounds bad. What will he do?"

"Feed the results into a database on his cephulet. He would be able to determine your citizenship status within minutes, plus other things."

"Other things? What other things?"

"That you're not from here. A sweeper can detect a deception in minutes."

"But why pretend that's what he was doing? Why not ask me to surrender some hair to him?"

"Why do your intelligence services monitor certain people in the community?"

"So they can catch more than one criminal." I tugged on his arm, forcing him to face me. "By being with you, I'm putting you in danger."

"I can do that all by myself. Let's just focus on getting off the streets before we worry."

"But we're trapped. Surely they'll monitor the passengers on the skytrains departing from here once they realize I'm a non-citizen."

"Let's save the freaking out until we're safe. The most important thing right now is to protect your true identity. This is worst-case. I may be wrong about his motive."

Jax fell silent as we walked. I did the same, suspecting he was consulting his cephulet for a restaurant. I'm sure they would have apps or something that showed places to eat within the area.

"If we head left at the next turn, we'll cross over into the Aris quarter, which is where we want to be. Not far down that road and we'll find ourselves a place to eat. You hungry?"

"You've got to be joking."

"At least we can get off our feet for a while."

"I'm not going to settle until we're back at your place."

He didn't reply, so I glanced up at him, trying to decide from his profile if he was consulting his cephulet or unable to find something suitable to say. He caught me in his periphery and looked down. His eyes roamed my face, no doubt reading the silent question, because he said, "There's something else I should tell you, but maybe not just now."

"At a time like this, you don't say something like that and let it dangle."

"If the sweeper's purpose was for the reason I suspect, then he'll also be able to tell what your true factional nature is."

"I'm doomed."

"Only if you get caught."

"How am I supposed to evade a city of sweepers?"

"Maybe you don't have to. Perhaps it's time to leave Califax."

What? God, yes. I couldn't believe I was hearing him straight. This was what I wanted, but maybe leaving the city meant something different for him. And I couldn't enter Uradra, at least not with this tattoo on show.

I slowed. Did he include himself when he said that? I couldn't keep Azrael's big, round eyes out of my head. He wouldn't want to leave them behind. Maybe he would insist on them coming with us, if he planned on coming at all. I should ask him. If I did, I may hear an answer I didn't like.

There was no demarcation for the crossover into Aris territory except a stone tower standing about two meters tall. The stained red symbol of Aris was carved into its face. On the back of the tower was the symbol of Set. I thought there would be some greater divide, but it seemed the abhorrence the people held for differing factions was enough.

The modern modular houses were cozied up beside each other, leaving little space between. Aris neighbors could lean out their side windows and almost touch their Set neighbors' walls.

"What are you looking at?"

"I expected better segregation."

"This is one of the newer areas of Califax. The boundaries were better defined before, but most of it's been rebuilt under the new senate. This is their propaganda. They wanted proof that the grafting was a good idea, so the houses were built side by side along the boundary. The separation point was nothing more than the stone column we passed. It demonstrates how well everyone can live together once grafted without the need for walls, like cages."

"Why was this sector rebuilt?"

"Because of the wars."

"And yet those on the fringe have no boundaries at all."

"You can't compare the two. Those in the fringe are forced to live alongside each other and trust one another for their survival. They also have a lot more to lose if they can't get along. It's not the same here." He dropped silent, so I glanced at him. I must've had a questioning look, because he continued. "It's a mess, really. It's so complicated. When you used to argue about what Carter was doing, it made me start to think about the outcome if he succeeded. What would the people do if they were freed from their grafts? The people aren't even mixing, not really. How are they going to get along when the senate has continued to feed their natural dislike of each other? I don't know if it's in us to get along, not in the long run."

"You hate the division. I know you do." Alithia and Azrael were proof of that.

"I do not make up a city."

"What my dad did, was that the reason you joined Carter?"

"I was already involved before then. My dad got me involved."

I wanted to probe more, but the tight edge to Jax's words, sounding like they would screw his mouth shut at any moment, stopped me from questioning further. Alithia was the reason? Her and Azrael? A child of mixed heritage was a good reason to want an end to the divide, an end to fearing each other.

"Let's just focus on finding ourselves somewhere to lay low. We need to strategize." He sounded like we were in Dominus. "We'll find a mall next right."

Who heard the footsteps first, Jax or me? Almost there, a few more strides to make the turn, but someone was coming up behind us. There'd been no one in the street. We both spun at the same time. I inhaled sharply, more so to catch the tail of destruction.

The sweeper's weapon was already raised.

Chapter 17

DESTRUCTION SNARLED LIKE A WILD ANIMAL, the noise slipping past my lips. Jax's hand gripped my elbow, digging in to the point of pain.

He leaned close. "There's no running from this." His voice strained as he disguised what he said.

I turned to him, hiding my face from the sweeper so he would not see me speak. "What do we do?"

Always, I fell into the dark pools of Jax's eyes, but this time the flashing glare kept me out. He proved back in the fringe he would step over the line if there was no hope. But out here, that couldn't happen; we had nowhere to hide. There would be no help, no pills to put him back together. A fight was out of the question. Neither could we comply if the sweeper wanted us to go with him. That meant it was up to me.

The sweeper was disguised by his helmet and the ripple of air, like heat on a summer's day rising off the road, surrounded him. This time, the ripple appeared more substantial, not just a shimmering opaque film. It ballooned around him like frosted glass.

Jax avoided nothing, but he avoided my question. He wanted to keep destruction contained, wanted to spare me the truth, wanted to spare himself? Whatever the reason, his silence arced my factional nature. Soon, I'd have to open a small seam and release a little or risk detonating a lot and causing irreversible damage, and not just the physical kind.

"You will remain where you are."

The might of destruction hammered my pulse. With it came anger, not fear. The rush of my blood, the surge of adrenaline, and a coldness moved through my mind and heart. I turned to face the sweeper, squaring my body with his. The move must've looked threatening—it was—for Jax placed a hand on mine with a tight squeeze, a firm warning to keep my cool. It felt like a cage. The urge to rip my hand away from his burned hot through my heart, as did the sudden fire, flaring more adrenaline, surging a greater urge to react and an almost unbearable need to destroy.

Get your hands off me. I heard the words win my head before they came out. I pushed them down, choked on them rather than let them free, let the feral win dominance over me.

I glared at the sweeper, but not with the eyes of a good citizen, not with the eyes of the contained or defeated. Was this the sweeper from the skytrain? He'd seen the buckle, seen everything, including the truth within. He knew I was Persal. And as a Persal, I didn't need to touch him to do terrible things—if only we could make him lower his shield.

"You'll take your last breath shortly after you move… if you are foolish enough to do so," the sweeper warned.

"Timing and control are weapons," Jax whispered. His way of explaining the plan. Nothing needed to be said. There was no answer. We needed to stop the sweeper swift and silent if we were to disappear.

"Lie face-first on the ground. Do it slowly."

Jax remained standing, as did I.

"Lie down, now." The sweeper waved his weapon to remind us who was in charge.

Destruction would not reach him while his shield was up.

Jax nodded to me. "Do as he says."

He inched to the ground, placing his hands on his head, not an easy feat.

Destruction would not allow me to sink to my knees.

"Lie down on the ground or face the consequences." The sweeper raised his weapon, staring down the barrel.

"Sable." It was a warning, pitched to reverberate in my ears.

I will not kneel. But I had to. Could destruction breach this new more robust-looking shield? It would be a useless defense if one factional nature could win through. Maybe he couldn't fire his weapon with the shield up. Did I really want to risk it?

"Lady, this is your last warning."

I wasn't Sable, the girl dragged from riches to the slums, not anymore, not while destruction had control, and it would not let me do it. Jax was on his knees, which was wrong.

No, I should be there too.

Comply, comply. It hurt to think that. The thoughts built a wall. I could feel the casing, a hard layer locking the shadow of me out, the sensible part that wanted to follow Jax.

A high-pitched buzz split my ears. The sudden heat in front of my face was all the warning I had. Destruction moved just as fast. It wasn't me in control, but it was. This was the other part of me that had always been Persal.

A white light flared in front of my eyes the moment I felt the wave of energy release, channeling out of my body in an unstoppable gush. I shielded my eyes from the blinding light, unable to block my ears from the roar of the wind. Everything disappeared as fast as it came.

I felt the sudden movement, the eddying of air, and heard the crunch of his boots as Jax left my side. The blowback of energy caught on the shield rippled colors across its surface. It was still up. Jax launched himself at the sweeper. And now I could see what the visible difference of the shield meant. Impenetrable. Even to physical attack. He wouldn't win, but Jax would try anyhow, pounding against the shield with the force of bloodlust. I couldn't see his eyes to tell, but I knew the ferocity at which he hit.

This time, the whole of me was in control. The part of me that was from home, plus the part gifted from my father, very much of this world, welcomed destruction to rise. I savored the feel of it swelling within, charged and powerful.

Jax smashed into the shield, unable to reach the sweeper, but the force of his impact warped the shield inward, forcing the sweeper backward. He staggered a few feet then caught himself and aimed his weapon. Destruction was already released the moment the light from his weapon passed the shield. The two met, and a shower of light exploded outward in an arc of white and blue. Emboldened by the armor of protection destruction provided, Jax renewed his brutal attack. Lost to bloodlust, his pummeling on the shield became immense, cratering it inward, but still it would not break.

Electrical sparks flecked through the air followed by a loud crack the moment destruction made contact with the shield. One pulse, that was all, then Jax pounded forward again, growling out his fury as he battered on. Although hidden behind his barrier, our joint attack forced the sweeper backward. Destruction met the relentless fire of his weapon halfway, turning the lethal release into a harmless light show.

Engaged in the fight, we had no choice but to follow through to the end. Just like in Dominus, there was no backing out, no safe ground. The sudden expulsion of energy as the shield disintegrated threw us backward. I stumbled to my ass. The momentum kept me going until my legs went over my head. Destruction raged at my vulnerability, burning hot and white through my core. It swept the confusion of my fall, the disorientation of going over my head aside. I kept my mind enough to follow my roll back over onto my knees. All the while, I harnessed destruction into a thin stream. I stared into the barrel of the sweeper's weapon, funneled destruction up the shaft of the weapon, which then blew out the back of the gun and straight through the sweeper's eye. He recoiled, lost his weapon, and staggered back, but by now I was inside, tunneling toward his mind. Caught in the ecstasy of my power, I severed the synapse connections, electrical impulses, communication flow, everything that made his mind function.

Destroying his mind was easy, too easy. But it felt good, made me hungry. I wound my power into a tighter coil, searching out places untouched, driven by an insatiable desire. *More, more, more*, echoed through my head.

A sharp pinch on my upper arm, and destruction unraveled from the sweeper's destroyed mind, recoiling then rearing as Jax tore me around to face him.

A violent shake, his face in mine. "Look at me."

My mind felt wild, destruction uncontrollable. About to rip myself from his painful hold on my upper arms, a loud *crack* drew both our attention. The pavement at our feet spilt, creating a seam that ran away from us, widening as it went until it reached the sweeper's body.

Jax shook me again. "Sable, enough. Stop this."

I wrenched myself from his hold again as the windows of the house behind blew inward. Jax pinched me hard on the upper arm. And that was all it took. The shock gave me control to snap destruction back inside its cage.

I covered my arm where he pinched none too gently and glared at him, filled with residual energy from my factional nature. "Holden kissed me for the same effect."

"You were on the verge of destroying the neighborhood and everyone in it."

I shook my head. "No, I wouldn't." But it was true. I'd been lost.

The sweeper lay prone on the ground, staring blankly into the sky. Sweet Jesus, I'd done it again.

"He's not dead. But he might as well be."

I took a step back, palming my mouth, but that was not barrier enough to separate me from what I'd done.

Jax seized my arm before I distanced myself farther, pulling me along like a rag doll. "Don't. You had no choice. It was him or us. Sorry, but we don't have time to fall into a dark hole. If we move quickly, no one will know there were two of us. It's best the senate stay ignorant of the truth; that's if he didn't relay his situation to security control." He stripped the sweeper of his belt then yanked me away.

He kept a firm hold on my arm as we jogged down the street. "Are you okay?"

No. "Yes." But the word rattled around in an empty space.

"We couldn't have allowed him to repeat any of what happened."

"I know."

"If not you, it would've been me. Either way, one of us had to do it."

"I know." The words continued to rattle through space, my mind not on the conversation.

"Down here." We headed off down the next left onto a smaller street, like an alley, a clean one. The houses seemed to loom inward like pointing fingers. *We see you,* they seemed to say. The choking narrowness of the street, the imposing edifices of the apartments on either side, I was suffocating. The guilt chiseled through my sane mind now that destruction was spent.

"The noise is likely to attract people into the street. We need to disappear ASAP."

I'm not sure who broke into a run first. The sound of our feet echoing off the walls of the apartments sounded like an army on our heels. My pace quickened as we neared the mouth of the alley. Jax kept beside me. At the end, he threw out his arm to haul me back.

"See the glass building over there?"

Diagonally opposite us, a five-story glass-and-metal rectangle spanning a block diameter dominated the surrounding houses. Orange-and-red-tinged trees lined the pavement in front, a sight I would normally think beautiful. There was nothing beautiful about this city, about this world, about me.

"An Aris mall."

"You're not still thinking about food?" My stomach was stripped raw.

"I've got a plan."

"What—"

"We don't have time." Taking my hand, he pulled me out into the street.

The distance to the mall felt like an eternity. The small but steady stream of shoppers entering and exiting the glass doors looked like the enemy. Any minute, they would transform into fighters armed with blades or axes.

"You sure we should be in public?"

"We won't be for long."

My adrenaline inched higher the closer we came to the entrance. This was not the first time I'd been amongst people of this world, but this was the first time since the things I'd done, since we'd become fugitives. Jax had a plan. I had to trust him.

The doors slid aside as we approached, and a fragrant smell wafted out to greet us. It reminded me of home. The perfume and makeup counters were always the first you encountered when you entered large department stores. The smell, which did not come from a perfume counter but a group of Aris women standing in the entrance, was soon overwhelmed by the rich aroma of spicy and sweet mingled in the warm enclosed air. Like great arms, the smells welcomed me in. But there was nothing welcoming in here, only strangers. My tattoo was a lie. I was not like them. The hatred and fear they would feel for me if they knew the truth. And so they should, for I could level this mall if I wished.

What was I thinking?

Destruction massaged my thumping heart. Always there now, always bothering me, always trying to highjack my intentions.

"I'm not hungry," I mumbled.

"Good thing, because we're not stopping." He cut further conversation off by quick marching us across the expansive high-polished floor.

I glanced down at my reflection. Like Jax, I saw no indication on me that we'd been in a fight with a sweeper. It shouldn't be that way. It shouldn't be so easy to destroy someone's mind, but it was.

I didn't see where Jax led. Nor was my mind on the people around us. A part of me was struggling to keep up with what was happening now, because it was back with the sweeper, busy filling in the emptiness with guilt and self-loathing now that destruction had subsided. But another part of me was relieved. We were alive. We were free.

I should feel heavy-limbed thinking about what I'd done. I should feel like my heart was falling through the floor. But the jumble of my emotions cancelled each other out, so all I felt was numb. But he tried to shoot me, no hesitation in his mind. Them or us. That was the truth. This was the only way.

The mall opened out into a wide dome. Glass lifts, shaped like eggs, glided up and down between the five levels of the mall. Occasionally, one would disappear through a chute in the ceiling.

"You're joking," I said as Jax steered us toward them.

"We're not staying here."

"I thought you said we could bury ourselves in here for a while."

"We're not safe anywhere now. Since he's not dead, they won't be alerted to his predicament. But that's only true as long as he's not discovered by someone in the street."

"We should've moved him."

"And wasted precious time? Besides, we had nowhere to hide him."

We reached the cavity that housed an egg-shaped lift.

"Are you going to tell me what we're doing?"

"I'd rather wait."

"You're making me nervous. Destruction doesn't like me nervous."

"That's not funny."

"It wasn't meant to be."

A gentle breeze dusted my face as the lift returned. People's feet came into view as the lift descended in silence, not as fast as the lifts at the terminal, but these were fast enough to make my stomach curl into a tight ball.

"Hasn't anyone here heard of enclosing your lifts in metal so you can't see out?"

"I've never met anyone with a fear of heights."

Of course you haven't.

A group of smartly dressed Aris exited the moment the lift came to a stop. My eyes flicked behind their ears or to their wrists, but everyone scattered into the mall before my eyes could settle on the defining marks that labeled them good citizens of Califax.

The only marker to the doors of the glass lift was a strip of red glowing lights, which were green now that the lift had come to a stop. I peered inside the empty lift and saw the mechanics below floor-level. Jax bumped me through, soon followed by a stout woman who'd come up behind us. It was like walking on air. I huddled next to Jax, not wanting to touch the sides, as the only thing to indicate there was any glass there was the row of lights, now red because the doors were closing.

The lady got off at the first level. I looked at Jax, but he shook his head. By the time I glanced around to check out what was sold at this level, the lift slowed one level up.

"Where're we going?"

"To the roof."

I was about to ask why when we disappeared inside a brightly lit chute. A glow of flickering light messed with my sight. A breath later, butterflies tumbled through my stomach as the lift came to a rapid stop and the sun glared down at us. The lights turned green, separating through the middle as the doors slid apart to wrap around like the shell of the egg.

Unlike getting in, I jumped out the moment the red lights slid aside.

"How did the lift know to drop us off here?"

Jax tapped his temple.

"Do those things cook for you as well?"

He quirked an eyebrow at me. Strange earth humor was not appreciated at a time like this. But Jax was busy looking around the roof filled with personal transport. This was the equivalent of an earth parking lot, only on the roof. Instead of a variety of cars, there was a variety of flying vehicles, each as individually designed as any car back home.

"I'm getting a bad feeling about this."

"Given our run-in on the street, it's likely the sweeper on the skytrain sent through his findings. We can't use the skytrains now."

"We're going to hitch?"

"We're going to acquire a skycraft of our own."

"Steal, you mean."

"That's a matter of semantics."

I followed alongside him. "Won't that be hard to do? These things look well secured from the outside."

"The newer models, maybe. Few have the capability of stealing one. Owning your own vehicle is rare. They're expensive to buy, and you need room on your roof to park them, since it's forbidden to park them on the streets. Only sweepers are allowed to do that. But most importantly, you need to learn how to fly one. That in itself is financially prohibitive to most. It also means there are only a handful of people capable of stealing one. With so few having an air license, there are rarely buyers for stolen skycraft."

He passed the first but stopped at the second. "This one's an old model. Perfect for what we want. The newer models are a little trickier to steal anonymously."

"That's something I'll keep in mind."

Ironing over my sarcasm, he continued, "All vehicles are registered with the senate. Their movements are also tracked, as private vehicles are not allowed to leave the city limits. Add to that fingerprint analysis on primary surfaces and a few more modern tricks."

"In other words, impossible."

"The technology inside the older models means they're not traced as easily and easier to steal."

"Are they air-worthy?"

"Owners must adhere to a strict maintenance schedule, which is enforced regularly. That's part of what makes them so expensive to own. And since public transport is unrivaled, owning your own private vehicle is more about prestige than convenience." Jax smiled at me then stared off over my shoulder. I glanced in the same direction but saw nothing, which meant he was consulting his cephulet.

I was tempted to lean on the vehicle while I waited but was nervous it came with some form of security alarm I would set off if I touched it. "If there are only a few capable of flying these things, doesn't that narrow the culprit down?"

"It does. Handy for the senate."

"But not handy for us."

He was too busy attempting to break into the skycraft to look at me. "It makes little difference to us."

"How so?"

"I'm not a registered pilot."

"But... how is that?"

"You ask too many questions."

"And you're frustratingly cryptic at times."

He was too busy to glance at me, but his lips twitched at the corners. Playful Jax warmed my heart. When like this, he was someone I wanted to be around. That feeling was soon blown away by the thought of Alithia and Azrael. Jax was not the guy for me, an Aris in a world of division. More than that, his heart was already with someone else. God, I was stupid.

A soft *hiss* sound, and I spun around to find the door of the vehicle lifting up. Jax smiled at me then dropped the smile when he read my face.

"What? You're feeling squeamish about the theft?"

I straightened and unfolded my arms. "As if." Left off that sentence was *after what we'd done in the street.*

157

"I might not be registered now, but I'm a good pilot. We don't have far to go."

"Do you have to report to anyone before takeoff, let them know you're joining the airspace?"

"Private vehicles operate below a certain altitude, out of the way of the skytrains. We follow a certain grid pattern, which ensures separation. So you can enter and leave without a clearance. Never take your own route."

"But they'll be able to track where we land."

"Are you going to trust me, or is this you delaying the inevitable?"

"You should know the answer by now."

Chapter 18

ELVA MARCHED the floor of Jax's apartment, her body wired for a fight. She tossed her hair as she paced back toward us.

"You risked everything taking her to Islia." She placed the emphasis on *her* like I was the big problem in this equation; in Elva's mind, I was a big problem in every equation. "Look at you." She waved a dismissive hand in his direction. "You're lucky you're still alive, but if you do that again, I'm going to kill you myself." She spun and marched away, her heels smacking on the high polish. We all remained silent as if mesmerized by her forceful stomps. After enough pacing, she swung back to face us. Instead of nullifying, her pacing seemed to have arced her mood. "I could've told you the outcome. I did Nuke's and Patrick's tattoos."

"And my wrist is still smarting," Patrick said.

Elva rolled her eyes and adjusted her weight onto one hip. Like dynamite, I was sure she would explode with the right spark. Jax's apartment was huge, but with Elva here, the walls inched in closer, the air weighted, too thick to breath. Jax withdrew into himself, staring at the floor, wearing the mask he'd worn many times before.

Only an hour ago, Jax landed our stolen skycraft on the roof of the apartment opposite his own. Apparently, there were a few residents in those apartments who had one of their own, which meant it didn't look strange to see a skycraft land there. Landing incriminating evidence next door to his apartment felt too close, but Jax assured me they'd have no reason to assume it was him.

"God only knows what's made its way back to the senate. If the sweeper called in his findings, the senate will know enough."

I glanced to the sweeper's belt laying on the low table in front of the sofa. Jax had pulled the EPH device apart and sure enough found one of my hairs placed inside the receptacle. Not only did the sweeper know my true factional nature, but he'd also know I was an alien. And now the senate knew.

"So, we move faster with our plans," Nuke said.

Elva drilled him to his seat with her stare. "You have no idea how hard it will be to move around Califax if the senate knows about Sable. The city will be in lockdown, apartments searched. There'll be nowhere safe. I'm not even sure we'll get into HQ."

"Perhaps I should return to the fringe."

There were no words to describe Elva's expression toward me. Jax finally shifted from his marbleized position, eyes on the floor, to look at me. Nailed by two sets of eyes, I launched to my feet. "It's as you said, Jax. I need to leave Califax. I will head to the Persal village of Uradra."

Elva sauntered toward me. With each step she took, I prepared myself for her belittling sarcasm, which sliced in all the right places. I gasped when she gripped my chin hard and wrenched my head to one side. "What's this, honey?" The word honey came out barbed. "You think they're going to welcome you in a Persal village?"

"It wouldn't be hard for me to convince them otherwise. They'll understand once I explain." This close, I had to look up into her eyes.

"Why should they welcome a Persal desperate to be an Aris? You think prejudice is bad in Califax. This is nothing compared to the provinces. They will hate you for choosing another faction."

"I have my reasons for wanting this tattoo."

She leaned in close to ensure only I heard every word while she whispered. "When you asked to be Aris, did you stop to think what it would mean for Jax?"

"What are you talking about?"

Her eyes were arrows, poisonous ones.

"Jax now feels obligated to protect you. That's how he is. If it were me, I'd throw you out into the street and let you get on with pretending to be someone else. But Jax won't, because he's not as smart as me. He feels he has to babysit you, all because you have no spine. You'll slow him down. He doesn't even want you." She took a moment from her near-whispered rant to let everything she said settle inside. Her smug smile sparked the embers of destruction. "But listen, sister. If our lives are put at risk because of what you've done, I'll take you out myself."

I exhaled when she sauntered away, finally able to breathe. Eyes were on us, wary, so I swallowed my emotions down and forced what I hoped was a neutral expression. Since I'd made a mess of our safety so far, I didn't want to be the cause of friction between us all—there was nothing I could do about Elva. I'm sure no one heard our conversation, but Elva's loathing of me was no secret, so I'm sure everyone guessed at what she said.

Jax straightened from leaning against the bench. "Since we don't know what the sweeper did, we proceed with our original plan, although we proceed with caution. Elva and I will head to Aris HQ. It's the only place we're likely to gain any information." He looked at Nuke and Patrick. "You two stay with Sable. You don't know enough about how to act in this world to risk coming with us."

"I'm going to Uradra."

"How do you plan on doing that?" Jax asked, his sarcasm a rival for Elva's, his tone slipping over the cliff of tolerance.

"That's what she wants to do. Let her go," Elva said.

"Splitting up's not a good idea," Nuke replied.

I ignored all of them, keeping my eyes on Jax. "Your family would be your priority." *Is your priority*. He'd think of Alithia and Azrael first, as he should. I wasted too much time here. "Someone in the fringe will point me in the direction of Uradra. I made a mistake by choosing this tattoo, but the people in Uradra won't turn me away, as they are waiting for Dad. It won't be hard to convince them I'm his daughter, especially if Mum and Ajay are there. Holden will vouch for me too."

"And that will be that." Elva stepped forward. "That's your divide. There will be no coming back. You will be Persal for good then."

She was right. Like the crack I'd made in the fringe, a crack opened within me, growing wider by the second. But not just within me, it tore as an invisible barrier across the floor of Jax's apartment, a gaping chasm, me standing here, everyone else on the other side. "I will not choose a side." It felt like I was speaking from a distance, my words having trouble breaching the gulf between us.

"Too late, Mary Poppins. You already have."

"No, when the war begins, I will be on your side."

"The war has already begun, and you're heading to your side."

And there it was, the final split to sever our paths.

"Stop it." Jax stepped forward, cutting through the argument. He turned to me. "Let's talk." He glanced around at the others then back to me. "In my room."

Elva puffed out a breath as she spun away, slapping her arms to her sides.

"Give us a moment," Jax said. He strode to his bedroom door, slowing enough for it to open once it sensed his proximity.

I stared at his back as I followed him in. *You won't talk me out of this.* Not anymore. Our mission was compromised because of me. My inability to control destruction risked too many lives, put too many people in danger. I couldn't let it keep happening.

With extra creases forking his brow, hands on hips, Jax stared out the window. It felt like we were suspended in that quiet moment before the violence of a storm. I moved across to sit on his bed, watching his profile as he continued to stare at the view, but it was likely he didn't see the view with everything going around in his head.

"You won't find what you're looking for in Uradra."

"You can't say that for sure."

"You're right. But the people of Uradra were faithful to your father. I can't see Holden wanting to return there."

"But where else would he go? He wouldn't tell them the truth about what happened. Besides, they'd soon forget once they saw he had a grafter. He can build an army of Persal."

"It won't be that easy."

Of course, their reversed grafter had resulted in many fatalities.

He continued, "Why do you think your father and Carter took the risk and made the journey to your world if it was a simple matter of reversing people's grafts on their world? It's unlikely Holden will have as much success as he hopes. Once the fatalities rise, no one will believe in him."

"I have to try, Jax."

Was it my plea that brought him back into the room with me? He turned from the window and joined me on the bed. "I know you do. I understand that. It's why I won't stop you. I just want you to be prepared."

His sudden gentle words, after everything we experienced getting here—the cruel revelation of Azrael's parentage, my continual destructive actions, exposing us every step we made, the chase, the sweeper in the street, a man now better off dead than alive, and stealing the skycraft—made me stare at the floor. I felt a ball of lead fall through me, dragging all my organs down with it. I didn't have the strength to lift my head. "This is all Holden's fault." Because it was easy to blame someone else.

"Holden joined your father, because he believed in the reason. Not because he wanted Persal to win. He loathed the suppression of the grafts. He truly believes we have a right to live as ourselves, united with our factional nature."

"But he believes in division."

"There are few who would disagree."

"You would."

He gave a small shake of his head.

"I doubt Holden would be as caring toward a child of mixed birth," I added.

"Holden would never harm your mum and Ajay. He will make sure they're safe. He has more integrity than me."

"That, I don't believe."

"I wanted you dead."

"But I'm not, thanks to you."

"If you refused, I would've hunted your brother."

I arched my head back to the ceiling, not having the strength to argue anymore. "I wish you'd stop trying to make me hate you."

One huffed laugh, the most amusement I'd ever get out of Jax.

"Nuke and Patrick are going with you. At least as far as the fringe.

Neither are registered citizens, so they're in just as much danger. Go to Islia; he will help you. He'll introduce you to some of the provincial merchants. They have senate clearance to travel. Some are sympathetic to those in the fringe. He'll know the best ones. They won't ask."

My mind needed to catch up. "Do we go by skytrain? I know it's a risk—"

"I doubt you'll get beyond the first stop. Besides, none of you have a cephulet. The doors won't open for you unless you have one, unless someone else gets off at the same stop. And you can't guarantee that, since it's at the end of the line. You may be the only ones on the skytrain by then. Elva will take you."

"I doubt it. In case you haven't noticed, Elva and I aren't friends."

"That means she'll be all too happy to get rid of you. I'll be more useful at Aris HQ. She can shift you there, so you don't have to worry about long awkward silences or spiteful glances."

"I thought you were worried about the senate monitoring the shift ripples or whatever."

"Speed is more important now."

"The senate knows, don't they?"

"It's likely they do."

"This is all because of me. If only I weren't so hopeless in controlling my factional nature."

"We never would've gotten this far if you were any worse in manipulating your factional nature. It's like you've been using it since you were a baby. You're the best Persal I've met."

I don't know why I pressed my lips together as if to suppress a smile, because I sure as hell didn't feel like smiling, but the compliment found its way in regardless. "And how do I know you're not just saying that to cheer me up?" I wanted to shift us out of this gloom, but I sounded like I was sulking.

"I thought you trusted me by now."

I searched his eyes when he looked at me, hoping to see something written there that would give me a hint to his inner dialogue. He allowed me to look, even returned my silent inquisition with a similar look of his own, and then, as if snapping out of a daydream, he pushed to his feet. "You need to go. Ask Islia to hide Nuke and Patrick."

Without waiting for my reply, Jax strode for the door.

"I want to check on Alithia and Azrael," I called out.

Jax stopped, but he didn't turn around.

"I know she hates me, but I'm responsible for anything the senate throws their way. I want to make sure they're all right." I came up alongside him.

"Concentrate on what you have to do. Don't stay in the fringe."

Did he think I would do something else to put their lives in danger?

The door slid aside to the other three looking restless. Jax strode out of the bedroom. "Nuke, Patrick, you're going with Sable." He glanced to Elva. "I'll head to HQ. It'd be good if you gave them a lift. It's one quick shift. Then come straight to HQ."

"Are you crazy? What if the senate is monitoring the—"

"It's too late for us to worry about that. If they did receive the results from Sable's hair sample...." He faded off, because there was little point emphasizing what Elva, a citizen of Califax, would already know.

She pursed her lips and pushed past him. "Fine, if only to get rid of her."

Elva positioned herself in the center of the room. When none of us moved, she glared at us. "Well, come on."

Nuke and Patrick launched up and headed over to her. "What do you want us to do?" Nuke asked.

Elva's glare was enough to burn a hole through lead. She held out a hand on each side and wriggled her fingers then looked at me. "Looks like you're on the end."

Patrick squeezed my hand and winked.

Elva sneered. "Hold tight or we may leave some of you behind."

"Don't worry. I won't let you go." Patrick winked again. When would this stop being one big adventure to him?

Jax's eyes were focused on his cephulet, already moving ahead to the next important task. I should've done the same, but as I looked across the room at him, still looking semi-recovered from going a round with a heavyweight, that leaded feeling of inevitability sank through. Even though he wasn't moving, Jax began to recede from me as that gulf from earlier split even wider, so wide I felt there was no breaching it, no going back. I snapped my eyes away, no longer able to bare to look at him as the gulf split wide inside me. I wasn't going to see him again. The feeling was so sudden, so sharp, so final, so devastating.

How many sacrifices would we have to make before this was over, if it was ever going to be over? I was losing everyone around me.

Mum and Ajay would not be two of the many sacrifices I had to make.

"You know how it goes. Keep a hold if you want all your insides to follow you across. On the count of three, I'm off."

I closed my eyes, because I didn't want to see Jax's apartment disappear. I felt the tug inside, the usual weird feeling that lasted a split second as I was pulled from one place in time to the next. No lingering in the in-between. If we even reached that far. I wouldn't know, since I wasn't a shifter. I still didn't understand how it worked, how a mind could peel the fabric of space and time apart and move people through. But I could destroy with the simple flex of my thoughts. How could shifting be any more unbelievable?

When I opened my eyes again, I was standing in an alley of the fringe. Ahead, the alley opened up to one of those market spaces, still eerily quiet. From here, I could see the chaotic mess left by the sweepers as they scoured through the fringe. Everyone remained in hiding. The senate had yet to do their worst.

"Looks like earth is not the only place with slums," Nuke said, running his gaze up and down the alley then over the walls of the buildings hemming us in.

"The smell's no different either," Patrick added, making a point of scrunching his nose.

"I've fulfilled my obligation." Elva stepped away from us. "I suggest you get yourselves off the streets."

"What are we supposed to do?" Nuke asked.

"Stay hidden for now. It's going to get ugly. It's better you keep clear of central. The senate will target the fringe, but Islia will know how to hide you better than we could hope to do."

"Where is this Islia?" Patrick questioned.

"I know," I said, nodding toward his door. "This is his home." I'd ran through enough alleys in the fringe to know most looked like all the others, but I recognized the mark on Islia's door.

"I have to get back." Elva distanced herself from us a few steps more.

We were fragmenting, which was always going to be the case, only not as fast as I thought. "Hang on."

Elva gave a frustrated flick of her head before she leveled a deadpan stare my way.

I turned to Nuke and Patrick. "Can you give us a minute?"

The two exchanged a look between each other then between Elva and me. "Um… I guess," Patrick said, backing away.

"This won't take long, so don't go far," Elva said.

I watched Nuke and Patrick back away. Then once I thought they were far enough, I turned to Elva.

"This better be good."

"Why do you hate me so much?"

"You're not important enough for me to hate."

"I don't get it. I don't get you. I've done nothing to make you treat me like this."

"No, you haven't." She looked away. A small frown creased her porcelain brow as she thought.

"If I've done nothing, then why?"

She stared down at me. "Even in our world, Jax has stuck by you."

"You're jealous of Jax?"

She groaned a sigh then looked down at me with her usual scorn. "Not Jax, idiot." And with that, she was gone, leaving only a small disturbance of dust where she'd stood.

Holden abandoned Elva, and yet Jax was still willing to help the daughter of the enemy, the man who killed his family. Was she jealous of me?

Chapter 19

"Where are we?" Patrick spun in a circle, eyeing the crudely erected buildings.

"We're on the outskirts of Califax. This is the fringe and home to many like us ungrafted people. We'll find shelter here if the sweepers come looking. None of these people are friends of the senate." I pointed to Islia's door. "The guy who lives here is called Islia. He's the one who did my tattoos. He's a friend of Jax's, and Elva's too it would seem. He will hide you."

"You're not coming?" Patrick asked.

"I will, but not just yet. I have to see someone." Jax didn't want me visiting Alithia and Azrael, but I couldn't ignore them. I was responsible for the suffering they had experienced the last twenty-four hours and the great wave to come. They needed to be warned.

"Who could you possibly know on this planet that you need to go and see?"

"Just... go knock on the door. Islia is bald, about this high"—I measured my hand against my chest—"and full of tattoos. Tell him Jax sent you and that I'm coming. I won't take long. And warn him about what is to come."

Nuke grabbed my arm. "What do you think you're doing? We don't know what's going on with the senate. According to Jax and Elva, things are going to get ugly. You need to listen."

I pulled my arm from his grasp. "If you'd stop holding me up, I'd be back already."

"You've already gotten yourself in trouble here. Perhaps we should go with you," Patrick said.

"And get me in more trouble? Go knock on the door." With that, I took off down the alley at a sprint, disappearing around the corner before they could yell out. They were unlikely to follow, as the fringe would be nothing more than a dirty sprawling maze to them. It was little more to me, but I had some vague memories of the lefts and rights we'd made once we passed the market space close to Islia's home.

Patrick and Nuke were right. This was madness, but if I left without giving them a warning, and if something happened to either of them, I would spend the rest of my days knowing I could've done something to help. I had to lessen the fallout of what I started.

I veered down alleys that looked the same and passed empty market squares smelling rancid because no one had dared return to clean the mess. And the more I ran, the worse I felt. Every empty market space was a slash across my heart. Carter had weaponized us all. This was the outcome. Many innocents would die, because the innocent always suffered the worst.

But the fringe was a labyrinth, a confusing contortion of similar scenes blending into one. Feet pounding, my pace increased alongside my mind, scrambling with panic. I recognized none of this. Every turn looked the same, every market space a squalor of upturned debris abandoned like haunted remnants of fringe life. Where was I heading? And how did I find my way back?

A cry choked my throat. I swallowed it down with the spittle and gasped another breath. Another market space, another alley, and no one around to show me the way. Spidery tickles creeped along my shoulder blades. How much time had I wasted? The sweepers would find me in the open, with no chance of warning Alithia.

Out of one alley, I veered left into another and smacked into someone small, driving them down to the dirt as I tumbled over. My knee bit the ground first, followed by my hip, but the small child suffered the rest of my weight.

"Jesus, what—"

"Sable," Azrael squealed and threw herself into me.

I peeled her to arm's-distance. "Azrael." Then I dragged her close to me for a fierce hug. Floodgates opened; it felt like everything inside me gushed out. "I need to see your mum."

Released from my grasp, she scrambled to her feet. "Where's Jax?"

Was it my statement or her question that drew down the darkness? I stood. "He stayed in central Califax," I said as I climbed to my feet. "I don't have a lot of time. What're you doing wandering the alleys?"

She rolled her eyes at the accusation in my tone.

I gave her a gentle shake and lowered to her level, a tactic I had often used with Ajay to emphasize the seriousness of what I was about to say. "Azrael, you have to listen to me. Because you don't seem to be listening to your mum. Things are going to get bad around here."

She stepped back, telling me she wanted me to let her go. "Things are always bad around here."

"It's likely the senate know about me."

She frowned.

"What do you know about me?" Maybe I was saying things I shouldn't. I forgot for a moment she was a little girl, younger than Ajay —easily done, because childhood seemed nonexistent in the fringe.

"You're Jax's friend and that you need our help."

"That's true. But I'm your friend too, remember?"

"Why did Jax stay behind?"

"He had to deal with a few things. I came here to speak to your mum."

"I don't want you to speak to Mummy."

"Why not?"

"'Cause then she's going to lock me in the safe room again."

"It won't be forever."

She screwed up her face. "You're not my friend if you say that."

I reached for her as she turned to stomped away. "Hey." She shook my hand off her shoulder, but I had years of dealing with Ajay to know a thing or two about children. I jogged around to jump in front of her.

When she tried to duck around me, I grabbed her around the waist and tickled her. At first, she grunted angrily, but that lasted a full few seconds before she was giggling. When I'd gotten through to her, I stopped and let her go. "You know what?"

She shook her head.

"Adults do stupid things sometimes. They make everything more complicated than it needs to be, and they're silly enough to think they're making it easier. I'm talking about people like the senate. Problem is, when they do those stupid things, people like your mum and everyone here in the fringe can't do anything about it. And they get scared, because they're faced with something they can't control. The first thing they do is want to protect everyone they love.

"Every time your mum locks you in the safe room, it's a demonstration of how much she loves you. Yeah, strange, huh? Normally, you give people you love something delicious to eat, or—" I tried to search for something that would have meaning here, because there would be no such thing as lollipops or teddy bears. "—or a big hug, which I'm sure your mum gives you all the time, but when you live somewhere different like the fringe, then hiding people in the safe room is the biggest show of love there is."

She looked unconvinced.

"Still not happy?"

She shrugged.

"I've got to see your mum. Can you take me to her? I can't stay long, 'cause—"

"Why not? Why do you have to run away?"

"Maybe I can stay a while. But I've got people waiting for me." If only I thought to bring something for her. But in this world, I didn't know what options there were or how to get them.

I held out my hand. "Come on, let's go together."

She slid her small hand in mine and led me through the filth of her playground at a child's speed. I had to stop from telling her we should pick up the pace. Why though? She'd understand, having spent her life here, but I didn't want to ruin our short moments together and the innocent babble of conversation as she wove through the many alleys. I'd gotten myself so lost.

Azrael unlocked the door with a key she pulled from the deep pockets of dirty jeans. "Mummy!" she shouted the moment she burst through the door into the dim passage.

I shut the door behind her, making sure to hear the *clunk* of the lock taking before following after her.

"You haven't been outside, have you?" I heard her mum's warning tone as I followed behind. By the time I reached their living room, Alithia was already waiting, hands on her daughter's shoulders, pressing her close to her body. Shock, a shadow of fear, no doubt she was trying to think why I would be here. "Jax," was the first word she said.

"Not here, but he's fine." Was what I had to say something Azrael should hear? There were so many things I wouldn't tell Ajay, but Azrael was different, her circumstances different. Perhaps in the fringe, a child who knew the truth was safer than a child kept naïve.

"Honey, can you go put the pot on? Sable may like a drink of something warm."

Thinking she was helping me, Azrael hurried off without complaint. Once she left the room, Alithia turned to me, her eyes asking the questions. The hostility between us—all from her side—vanished, probably not from her heart, but Alithia seemed to sense it had no place at this time.

"Jax and I ran into trouble on our way back from the fringe. Another sweeper. I... incapacitated him. We were forced to steal a skycraft in order to reach Jax's apartment."

Alithia lowered herself onto the chair behind her, her action almost regal. I copied her, taking the chair behind me so we sat opposite each other.

"Before he was incapacitated, the sweeper managed to steal a strand of my hair."

Alithia's eyes widened.

"There's every possibility he relayed the information to the senate before we could stop him. With the missing sweeper in the fringe, and what happened on our way back to central, it's likely they will connect the dots."

She nodded. "Which means severe reprisals for those in the fringe. But this will spread farther. It will start in the fringe and spread to the inner regions of Califax, perhaps maybe into the provinces until the senate finds what they are looking for."

Me.

She didn't need to say my name, but it was there. Everything was on me. Guilt would not take hold; destruction would not allow it. I launched to my feet, needing the anchor of movement to help keep the deadly flow within, where it needed to stay. The feel of it slithering inside made my skin prickle, a combination of repulsion and anger. Destruction started this mess. Destruction was the problem.

The mention of the provinces made me pace. Mum and Ajay were out there somewhere in the provinces. If the senate sent out sweepers to check the villages for an alien, they would stumble on two. And what would they make of Mum, an innocent? I rubbed at my temples. How were her and Ajay coping with all this?

"I'm leaving for the provinces. I have to find my mum and brother. But I had to warn you first. You needed to know that what is coming may be worse than what you've normally faced."

Alithia's face was a blank slate. She and Jax were much the same in that regard, maybe in many regards, but there was no doubt what she would be thinking. "You want me to hand myself in."

She stayed quiet long enough for me to know what I said was true. "There would be no point in that. You'd sacrifice yourself for nothing. The senate would continue to raze the fringe until they found the culprit. There is no way you could've come to this world without help." She blinked, looked away. When she turned back to me, she said, "You hardly know us. Why do you care so much?"

Jax has already lost too much. I couldn't say it, so I said the next true thing. "I don't want you to die because of me."

"As long as the senate remains, our struggles will be eternal. This has nothing to do with you."

I shook my head. "Maybe not everything, but what is about to happen has everything to do with me." Azrael banged around in the kitchen. "Azrael should have the chance to be with her father."

The shock on Alithia's face made me want to claw the words back in. I hadn't meant to reveal that I knew.

"Why did you say that?" There was a quiver in her voice as her eyes filled with tears. She covered her mouth as she looked away.

Her reaction didn't make sense. "I'm sorry. I shouldn't have."

"Azrael will never know her father again."

"Maybe when the senate are overthrown and—"

"I told you, her father is dead."

"But...." What was she saying? Did I have it all wrong?

Azrael appeared, carrying a tray with three mugs in the center. Like the proper host, she settled the tray down on the low table. "This is yours." She handed me a deep-green earthenware mug.

I sat down, barely acknowledging her with a word of thanks as I stared at the contents in the mug. The steam winding its way up into my face brought with it the smell of something bitter and spicy, but I couldn't open my mouth to take a sip. I was filled with a knot of twisted emotions I couldn't pry apart. Was it wrong that in this desperate moment, the strongest emotion was elation? Jax was not the father.

"How about something to eat with our warm drink?" Alithia looked at her daughter.

"Okay." She put down her mug and trudged back into the kitchen.

I stared at her retreating back and knew the truth. I settled my mug in my lap. "Jax is Azrael's brother?" I asked.

"You did not know?"

I shook my head.

"When he found out, Jax came to see me full of rage, accusing me of destroying his family, for hurting his mother. I could not argue for myself, but it was not true. I loved Renus, and he loved me, and he loved Azrael as much as he loved his other children. I did not break Jax's family up, because Renus had stopped loving Lireea, and she had stopped loving him. Jax knew that. But he could not give up hope they would work through their differences and love each other again. Children will never give up hope.

"Renus and Lireea stayed together, because they were both employees at the Dome. If they separated, it would've caused friction at work, something the senate would not put up with. One of them would have been forced to leave, and of course no one leaves employment at the Dome—at least not alive or with their faculties intact."

Was she saying this to excuse her behavior? Or maybe Renus had lied about how he felt toward his wife to win her over. Guys did that sort of stuff, or so I heard through gossip.

"Renus and I would dream about what it would be like when the senate was no more and everyone was free. We could be together without hiding." She looked into her drink. "It was Jax who told me Renus had been murdered."

Guilt buried my eyes in my mug. Destruction riled against it. I stared into my mug, stared and stared, my fingers pressing hard against the sides until the mug suddenly broke, the warm, bitter drink soaking my pants. "Jesus, I'm sorry." I fell to my knees, scraping the pieces together.

"Leave it," she said around Azrael's gasp.

I looked up to see Azrael standing in the doorway, Alithia's lips pressed into a disapproving line. "It's only been a few months since I discovered my factional nature. I don't have good control."

Azrael was on her knees beside me, collecting the pieces herself. "We don't care."

The innocence of a child. I bit my inner cheek at the tightness in my throat.

Alithia waited for Azrael to clear the pieces. "Can you take them to the kitchen and perhaps get Sable another drink?"

I would've protested, but it wasn't the drink Alithia wanted to give me, just the truth.

"Jax always came. He snuck away from Carter, your world, to come here as often as he could."

"How did Jax find out about the two of you?"

"He was suspicious of his father's behavior. He followed him, saw us together."

"But did his mother know?"

"Absolutely not. She would've exposed us."

"And Jax never told her?"

She shook her head. "He knew what would've happened had our relationship been known. He loved his father, so he couldn't bring himself to hate him. But he needed someone to be the receiver of his anger. He hated me, but he would never expose me."

"He no longer hates you. It's obvious."

"He loves Azrael. She's all he has left of his family. We made a truce between us. He protects us now and supplies us with gifts and goods that we couldn't otherwise afford."

"He hated me in the beginning."

"I know."

"He wanted to see me fail in Dominus." Why was I saying this? Perhaps because I didn't want her to think Jax had betrayed his father by readily making friends with the enemy.

"I know. But I also knew he would never have gone through with it. It is not the sort of man he is."

Azrael trudged back in with a brown earthenware pot tucked under her arm and another mug in her hand. She handed me my drink then fished her hand into the container and pulled out what looked like a brown biscuit. "This one's for you."

Before I could take it, someone knocked on the door. Azrael dumped the container on the couch, with biscuits spewing from the top, about to run for the door, but Alithia snagged her around her waist.

"Don't you dare, young lady."

I took Azrael's hand the moment her mum let her go, which was hard to do as I placed my mug on the low table. "How about you keep me company?"

"No, go wait for me in the safe room," her mum corrected.

Azrael's eyes widened as my pulse climbed through normal. I inched to my feet. It was only once Azrael slipped her hand from mine did I realize I'd been squeezing it.

"Go." Alithia barked the command before heading for the passage and the front door. I tried to pull Azrael with me, but she was like a mouse, agile and quick, chasing after her mum.

"Azrael, no."

But the little girl beat me to her mum's side. As I approached, I heard a young boy's hastened words. "Tell her she must come now. I've got to go."

It sounded like Nada. Having said what he came to say, he scurried away, leaving the echo of his running feet.

Alithia turned to me, her expression filled with the sort of stoicism that lived within all who suffered without end. Before she could say anything, Azrael darted out the open door.

Alithia screeched and made a grasp for her daughter, but Azrael was determined to escape the dreaded safe room or maybe for once find the courage to say something to the boy she secretly followed.

I grabbed Alithia's arm as she was about to chase her daughter. "No, you stay. I'll get her."

"The boy came to say senate utility are heading this way. Six of them."

"Go to the safe room. I'll get Azrael."

"You don't know where to go."

I lifted her hand, wrist facing upward so the tattoo over her graft was obvious. "You can't defeat the sweepers?"

Alithia opened her mouth, about to protest, but nothing came out.

"Please, trust me."

And then I was off, running through the alley like I could fly.

Chapter 20

THEY CAME WITHOUT NOISE, passing overhead as I rounded the corner and broke out into a market space. Exposed and vulnerable, I stumbled backward toward the closest wall and stepped on the corner of something solid and round. It rolled out from under my foot, swiping my left leg from beneath me and sending me crashing into an overturned cart. My left wrist smacked into the edge of the cart and sent stars into my vision from the pain.

I huddled against the side of the cart, which offered no protection from above, and nursed my left hand as the skycraft maneuvered itself degree by degree overhead as if the pilot was looking for a place to land or spotted a victim to grab.

Destruction prowled, tail lashing in time to the beat of my heart like a caged tiger. Back pressed against the cart, I tried to soothe my wild side, the powerful part of me that itched to pull the skycraft apart in a fantastic display of fireworks. I could do it. *Too easy*, the darker side of me purred. Put an end to this assault. Save the people of the fringe. In doing so, I would condemn us all to war.

I rose an inch to peer over the cart, catching the bulky metallic ass end of the vehicle as it slowly disappeared from sight. Once it was gone, I slid down the wood of the cart and rested my head back. Yesterday, the sweepers arrived in small, narrow, zippy-looking vehicles, something easily maneuvered into tight spaces and small enough to hold a max of two maybe three sweepers. Today, they arrived in something else. Bigger, bulkier machines able to carry a high load. I knew these vehicles. I'd flown in one, or at least a virtual fabrication of one. STU utilities. The sweepers arrived for a fight and would not leave until they achieved what they wanted. The senate was on the hunt, and they'd sent a small army to make sure the job got done.

Time to move. Azrael hid somewhere in these alleys. I needed to find her. Although a fringe child, knowing her way through this maze and enough people to hide her, she lacked one vital weapon that I possessed—her factional nature.

My wrist hurt, but it was unlikely broken. I ignored the pain when I placed my weight on it to push to my feet. A noise to my right jacked my adrenaline, zinging it throughout my body as I spun. Destruction whipped out in an arc as if it followed my spin, impacting with an over-turned barrel, sending it skyrocketing into a mess of splinters, which rained down in deadly forks, pelting the already strewn debris on the ground.

A whimper close by had me on my knees. I peered under another overturned cart, one that had turtled onto its back over a log, leaving enough space for someone to crawl into.

"Azrael," I cried.

I crawled closer, then sat back on my knees when a man's face came into view as he pushed himself out from underneath. His eyes were on the scattered remains of the barrel before shifting to me. "You're—"

"What are you doing here? Go home, you're not safe." A fringe dweller, as if he wouldn't know that.

"My home is too far away. I won't reach it in time."

"Find a place nearby. Knock on some doors."

"No, it's too late."

"The STU utilities are too large. They will never find a suitable place to land, at least not in a hurry."

He shook his head, eyes wide. "You're ungrafted. You're Persal." He crawled toward me, reaching out for me.

"I can't stay here. I have to find someone." I stood before he grabbed me. "You know how to hide. Do it before it's too late."

"It already is." He pointed behind me.

I followed his outstretched hand, stared down the alley to see a STU utility hovering toward the mouth at the other end. The sides of the utility open and thick black cable unraveled to the ground. Soon after, black bodies abseiled like dozens of ants spewing from their nest.

"Hide yourself," I yelled as I set off at a sprint.

I headed down the opposite alley. *Where am I going, where am I going?* I ran blind, like the maze on the Adolphy Tower, driven by this hopeless need to save Azrael. A fringe child, she would be smarter than me, likely already in hiding. Maybe she'd caught up with Nada and he'd taken her to Islia's place. *Please let it be true.* I couldn't go back to Alithia. I didn't know which way to go, for starters, but I would never hide while there was no guarantee Azrael was safe.

The alley narrowed to shoulder width. I slowed my pace, forced to turn sideways to fit through. How many utilities had arrived? How many had descended? I'd been too distracted in Dominus to remember now how many seats those skycraft carried. *God, where are they now?*

At the end of this alley? I squeezed to a stop, the walls of the building on either side hugging me close as I listened for footsteps in the dirt, voices, even just whispers. The only sound that came back to me was the sawing of my breath, the thrashing of my blood through my ears. *Where are you Azrael, Nada?*

One... two....

I peeked around the corner of my hiding spot to two deserted alleys, forking in differing directions. Each way was the same, a dirty narrow path leading into another dirty narrow path. I glanced behind. *Which way do I go?* Never had choosing my direction meant more. And staying put made destruction press against its barricade.

I chose left for no other reason than it took me farther from the utility emptying its dangerous cargo. But perhaps this way led to another utility. Maybe the other fork would lead to yet one more. Suddenly, the alleys felt narrow, the fringe small, every turn a spiral in a web we were all caught within.

Each sprinting stride I made was a drumbeat until I slowed to a crawl, now slinking down the alley like a mouse. Was I still searching for Azrael, or was I moving to save myself with cautious steps in case sweepers waited at the mouth? Now reduced to heel-toe steps, I moved like a thief.

Destruction grew restless. It hated this self-preservation. But at the moment, the other side of me won. I managed to keep rational rather than rash. The saner side of my mind, which begged caution overruled the action destruction wanted to take.

At the end of another alley, I waited, pressed against the brickwork, holding my breath so I could hear clearer. There was nothing but a gentle breeze. About to slide my head around to take a peek, a hand smothered my mouth, another pulling me backward.

"Sable," came the whisper at the start of destruction's release. I slammed down hard on the escape as I stared into Nada's dark eyes, but already chunks of brick broke from the wall behind us rained lumps onto our heads and shoulders, spraying a fine power over us as well. I reeled both Nada and Azrael close, protecting them as best as I could from the crumbling wall.

"Go," I said, pushing them backward, out from under the painful shower.

Seconds after we left the spot, a thunderous *thump* followed the landing of a large chunk of crumbled wall, which left a hole in the side of the building. The three of us remained still and silent, gaping at the spot where we'd been, now hidden under the sizable chunk.

I spun on them. "Never creep up on an ungrafted Persal, especially one that is struggling to control her factional nature." With the realization of what nearly happened, I cradled my head in one hand. "Jesus."

"Cool," Nada said.

"Not cool. What are you two doing out here?" I swept Azrael into a suffocating hug, the sort I would give Ajay if he were here. Nada stood close, so he suffered the same fate.

Nada struggled away, no surprise, but violently shook his head as Azrael pulled hard on my left wrist. I bit back a groan from the pain, somewhat lessened, so the injury from the fall wasn't too bad. *Come with us,* their actions said. I allowed them to tug me back the way I'd come.

Was that footsteps? Coming fast. As I was about to whisper-shout at the kids to pick up their pace, Nada turned our jog into a sprint. Adrenaline, hot and burning, gave me the speed I needed. Lungs bursting, feet slamming hard on the dirt, my mind took it all in, moving ahead of my body, slamming into the blank void of the yet to be lived moment, careening through the choices I couldn't make.

Nada disappeared left followed by Azrael as the first shout came from behind. It was because of destruction, the noise of the fracturing wall likely heard from miles away. How fast could they run? Trained soldiers? Faster than me.

I skipped around the corner in pursuit of the other two and saw Azrael disappear inside an open door then stop to wave me forward.

I reached the door. "We can't just disappear. They will know we're here somewhere and search every building." The fear almost turned my tone to a high-pitched shriek. My body wanted freedom to run, not be confined within walls. The solemnity within Azrael's eyes stalled my wild panic, lashed destruction in place.

Nada pushed around Azrael. "Get in." He sounded like an adult. He sounded like Jax.

Nada closed the door behind me, drawing large bolts into place. The safe room. There would be a safe room inside this place. But the sweepers would've seen the children, which meant they would tear each building apart to find them.

"This way," Azrael whispered and took my hand.

Anyone from this house was already hiding, or maybe they never made it home in time.

Much like Azrael's place, we headed down a dimly lit passage and into an expansive room full of light. Overhead, there was no roof, which allowed the moon to shine down on the open-aired atrium, throwing a bluish hue like a delicate bruise across the tiled floor. Stairs led to a second story with a wraparound balustrade. Minus the deep-blue tiling on the floor and the draping plants from the story above, this was a replica of Nada's home.

The children moved with purpose. Asking questions would hold them up, so I followed but only made it halfway across the floor of the open space when shouts from outside filled the atrium. Nada acted like nothing happened. Azrael followed his example. Me, the only adult, froze like a spied rat. The sweepers knew we were hiding somewhere close. They weren't going anywhere.

A cylinder bounced beside me with a loud *thwack*. Two, three times it rebounded before rolling across the floor. Nada doubled back, his eyes going wide when he saw what caused the noise.

He hissed at me from across the open space. "Hurry."

The cylinder came to life, jerking up into the air once more. When it clattered to the tiles, it spun about spewing a dark mist ankle height. I remained locked as the mist rose and formed filaments that wound in a corkscrew fashion around the atrium.

Nada jerked my left arm, and the resultant pain from my wrist sent a sharp jolt to my brain, like the slap it was supposed to be. He'd pulled his dirty shirt up over his nose and mouth. Behind him, Azrael had done the same. Already, the air smelled like ozone mixed with sickly sweet treacle. I relented, running after Nada as he pulled me like a rag doll toward another passage. Where could we hide from something as thin as air?

More shouts studded the walls around us. A loud *thunk* hammered the door. Nada pulled to the mouth of the passage as a man's head loomed out of the shadows.

"Quickly," the man said, not bothering to hide his voice with the chaos erupting outside. I barreled toward him, driven partly by Nada's strong tug on my arm, until I was swallowed by the impenetrable dark.

I gripped the walls so I wouldn't fall over, because my eyes were useless to me now. Nada kept hold of one hand.

"Azrael?" I whispered. Someone touched my elbow. I fingered the air until I finally found the top of her head.

"You must put these on."

The man was close beside me. With surprising dexterity for being in the dark, he slipped something over my nose and mouth, securing the strap over my head. His hands disappeared. "Here, let me help," he said as he no doubt attended to Nada and Azrael.

There was nothing natural about the darkness. This man was ungrafted. Phonus. As Phonus, he saw through his fabrication.

"The safe room is this way." The man grabbed my hand, guiding me along at an uncomfortable pace for someone who was blind. I clenched my hand tight over Azrael's and dragged her along with me through the dark.

My other senses sharpened now that I couldn't see. I felt the roughness under my fingers as I ran my hand along the wall, heard our footfalls as reverberating smacks in the desolate darkness. Outside, the noise had diminished, shouts now the whispered communication through any tech they carried, the silence a prickle up my spine. It was better when they were yelling, providing us with a vocal map of their position.

I stumbled after the man, refusing to release my hold on Azrael's hand. Now that I'd found her, losing her would be akin to losing Ajay all over again.

Who was this man? An ungrafted, no friend to the sweepers. I had to trust him. But the dark made destruction twitchy. A little fireworks would make a terrible situation worse. It was already responsible for landing us here.

A loud *thunk* back down the passage made me jump, my shocked shout muffled by the mask.

The man grabbed my elbow, pushing my back against the wall. With my senses acute, I could feel his body in front of me even though his hand at my elbow was the only thing touching me. "Stand here."

I felt him leave me, swirling a soft feather wind the moment I heard another heavy *thud* from down the passage. The darkness turned my mind in on itself, spiraling into bad, bad scenarios. This was destruction's playground. My fear it loved best. Like a war cry, it rallied against those feelings that stifled me inside, constricted me, suppressed me. Destruction turned into a sea of wild waves, surging and relenting, surging and relenting, looking for the weakness in the dam wall.

With the noise overhead and yet more from down the passage, I pulled Azrael close to me, wrapping her up in my arms as if that would be enough to keep her safe. My next instinct was to call for Nada, but anything above silence seemed too loud.

When a hand touched me, I jerked, the mask muffling my cry. "You must duck low," the man said as he pressed down on my head. Creaking hinges followed his whispered warning. The pressure of his hand guided me into a semi-crouch. Cool air, saturated with the smell of confinement, touched my face.

"Go forward, there is nothing to trip on. After a few steps, you may straighten."

I did as instructed, shuffling forward into complete blackness. After counting a few paces forward, I straightened like my back had multiple aches. Behind me, the others came through, their feet the shuffles of awkward movement. With hands held out, feeling for anything solid, I moved away from the doorway to give them space. Someone brushed alongside me. I reached out and felt an arm then glided up to Azrael's head, her height and ponytailed hair the giveaway.

A soft breeze preceded a gentle *click* as we were locked in.

"Let me get us some light." At least the man had not locked us inside by ourselves in the dark. "The darkness in the passage was my doing, but alas, the darkness in here is outside my control."

Small crunching sounds helped me follow his movement through the room. He didn't go far, so the room wasn't large. He fumbled away in front of us before a low glow came to life, silhouetting his outline against the wall, perhaps a head taller than me, with broad, sloping shoulders. He turned with a candle in its holder—no gift of trylite from a lover—and came to us.

"You may remove your masks. No air from within the house will get in here. Ventilation is via ducts that open up on the roof."

I slid the mask over my head. "Thank you for your protection."

He crossed the room, his eyes crawling over my face as if I had facial features that were otherworldly and not the same as his. The candle cast shadows under his nose, his eyes caves set within the ridges of his cheekbones and brow. Scruffy hair stretched down to a long beard at risk of catching a light by the candle flame.

"It's been a while since they've treated us to such a spectacle." Amusement. Not the tone I expected to hear in a fringe dweller's voice, especially at a time like this.

He held the candle up to my face. With fingers on my cheek, he turned my head to the side. "Are you responsible for what is going on?"

"I don't know."

He removed his fingers but kept the candlelight close. He was close. Our eyes met. The candle flame was not enough to separate his eye color from hazel, brown, or black, but I was close enough to read what was written on his face. He was waiting—most of them were waiting—for a sign that would bring the day of reckoning, that would bring the storm of destruction, that would bring the end of their suffering.

I took the gamble to trust him. "Yes, I am. They're after me and my friends."

He glanced over his shoulder to a chair behind him then shuffled back and eased himself to sitting. My eyes followed him all the way then expanded to the rest of the room. Small and tight, like Alithia's safe room, but with enough furnishings to keep the occupants safe for days. Beds were pushed against the walls. There were even some chairs with hard-looking cushions.

"Then we must keep you safe," he said. "For anything the senate wants, we want more."

Chapter 21

TUCKED IN THE SAFE ROOM, we were sheltered from the looming threat outside.

"They will not find this room, so don't worry. I've lived through enough sweeps to know we're adequately hidden." He extended his hand. "Arlo."

"Sable." His fingers wrapped tightly around my own, his shake hard. "How often do they conduct these sweeps?"

"Enough times for everyone to keep their safe room adequately stocked. It's of great importance for the senate to keep us cowering. We're the unstable ground that could dismantle their control. They know that. They fear it. And so they send their might to remind us. But six utility? Now *that* is something I haven't seen in a long time."

"One of their sweepers is dead." Another might as well be.

"That's perhaps enough to warrant the show of force."

"What will happen?"

"Don't worry about that."

"But they saw us. They know we're here somewhere. And if they really want their target—"

Arlo gently patted the air to calm me. "We've lived through much. We can live through yet another sweep."

I flicked a look at Azrael and Nada who'd seated themselves on one of the beds, side by side, shoulders touching like brother and sister. Neither looked frightened, but both unconsciously sought comfort through bodily contact.

How long would it take before the not knowing drove Alithia out of her safe room and onto the streets? How much would the fringe people have to bear because of me?

The silence we sat in became a prison with no way to mark the passing of time. If there was anyone in the house, I couldn't hear them. Nothing came from outside, no shouts of command from the sweepers, no gunfire or any of the usual sounds that accompanied a war zone. As far as I could tell, no one in the fringe had weapons, at least not weapons that weren't in their minds, and some didn't even have that.

Noise would've given me a reference, but the eerie quiet prickled my reserve. My body wanted to prowl alongside destruction. I jerked up from the bed, a coiled spring about to unwind. Aware how that would've looked, I said, "I can't sit still."

Arlo opened his mouth to reply, but sudden harsh cries filtered down the air duct from outside, shouts and the unmistakable pleas of mercy.

I spun to Arlo. "They've caught innocent people."

"They're not who they want. They won't do anything to them."

"You can't be sure. They could use them to lure us out."

"Only if you let them get to you."

"But I can't just hide like this while they round up innocent people."

"Most here defy the senate, which means every day, every breath we take is a risk. To defy the senate means to accept that your life is a gamble. It's a silent oath we all take."

"I can't accept that. I can't allow people to suffer because of me while I hide."

Arlo stood. "If you can't, then you let the senate win, because that's what it means to fight a war. The silent oath is the choice we make when we choose to remain ungrafted, when we choose to love who we want, when we choose to lie by taking another tattoo." His pointed look was understood. "We all know we must accept to stand alone with our fate, however it may come, if we are to win. Because the senate will use the weakness within our hearts." He approached me. "The senate is powerful; we could not hope to go up against them as we are. The way to win this war is through silent rebellion. We work unseen. We build our knowledge first before we fight with our minds. The way to win is through stealth and cunning. The way to win is to accept sacrifice and be prepared to be that sacrifice."

I backed up, strangled by his declaration. He spoke like Jax when I first met him, holding strong to the same conviction Jax uttered when he explained the rules of survival in Dominus, but it wasn't just for Dominus that he'd spoken with such finality. I looked over at Nada and Azrael, who heard every grizzly word he said. How deep had those words sank into their psyche, so they too would feel this impassioned, this willing to risk everything?

More cries echoed down to us from outside, pleas from innocent people, people now caught in the net woven from my mistakes.

This couldn't be the only way. I wanted to argue against him. Tell him that losing everyone special wiped any meaning from life. To truly believe and to hold that belief to the end meant to sacrifice parts of myself, such as separating myself from the suffering of others when it was all because of me. I wasn't all right with that.

"I'm not one of you. I don't live here. I haven't made a silent oath."

The quiet settled like lead between us. "I'm not reason enough to allow people to die."

"We've all chosen our path."

"Then I'll choose mine. And it's not hiding here."

I spun and headed for the door.

"Wait." He pushed past me before I could turn back to him. "Stay here. I will see what is going on." He looked over his shoulder. "I *have* made a silent oath, so there is no reason to come looking for me."

He disappeared out the door so fast, closing it behind him, it was like he'd never been there. But his words remained an echo in my brain. Did Jax mirror Arlo's thoughts?

I gave Arlo a few breaths then unlatched the door.

"No, what are you doing?" Nada leaped to his feet, rushing toward me, Azrael on his heels.

I gripped his wrists tight. "Listen to me. You are not to come out.

Under any circumstances. You are to wait here until Arlo or myself comes and gets you."

"But you heard what Arlo said."

"I am not from your world. And so your rules do not apply to me. But they do to you. Is that clear? You are to stay here." I looked at Azrael. "Both of you. Do not leave each other."

"But you can't do anything. How can you hope to do anything?"

"Nada, please trust me. I can do a lot, and they don't know that, so it's my advantage," I lied. They did know, thanks to the sweeper, but Nada knew none of that.

"She's right." Azrael came to my rescue. "I've seen her. She's Persal."

Nada shook his head, pulling himself from my hold.

"Listen." I took his hands again. "The way to win is to stand together."

"Then why are you leaving us?" Nada asked.

I smoothed his hair on his head, something I often did to Ajay when he sulked. He hated it and would always jerk his head away. "I have to do something about this."

"No, you don't!" Nada yelled at me. "You don't have to do anything. You're not meant to. Arlo said so."

This was about his parents, people he loved and lost. Ajay would be the same way. He'd plead and plead with me to stay hidden. If it were Ajay, maybe I would listen, or maybe I wouldn't, not when the senate was intent on ripping the fringe apart because of me.

I wouldn't be able to make Nada understand. "You two can help by staying put."

At the door, I spared one look over my shoulder. Two mournful children stared back at me in the dull candle glow. They looked like ghosts. "For your mum and grandfather, stay put." It sounded weak to me.

Unlike when we entered the safe room, the corridor was lit by the large open atrium in the center of the house. The streets were now quiet. The worst possible scenarios built in my head. I headed for the sunlight streaming down onto the tiles but was brought up short with the sound of a frizzle and crackling like a strike of lightning sizzling the air. The noise came through from the roofless atrium, but it was also loud enough to penetrate the walls.

Steps slow, I made it to the end of the passage but stayed in the shadows as I peeked out into the sunlight of the atrium. My gaze followed a line of rope, the bottom coiled on the tiles, up to the roof as my pulse climbed higher. Someone had abseiled inside. I pressed against the wall and looked back the way I'd come, but the passage was dim enough to provide shadow for someone lurking down at the end. Sweepers wouldn't lurk; they would attack, so it was perhaps safe to say no one had seen my exit from the safe room.

I leaned farther out of the passage, scanning the surroundings, the balustrade to the second story, the roofline. Another fizzle and crackle had me dipping back into the dimness of the passage, pinning myself against the wall. Someone cried out, followed by angry shouts.

The sweepers were close. Fringe dwellers were suffering for each moment I stayed pressed against this wall. Destruction punched me through the chest, kicking me out into the sunlight, across the atrium, and into the short passage that led to the front door, but I slowed when I spied the door open. Arlo would not have left the door wide-open.

I inched to the opening and peered out. To my left, the alley was clear. At the other end, a gathering had crammed the mouth of the alley, pressing close to each other for a better look. Habit now, I scanned the rooftops, but saw no one. Another glance left and still the alley was clear, so I slipped out, shutting the door behind me, and slinked along the walls toward the small crowd.

I couldn't see past the group of tall men crowding the alley. I scanned the rooflines again. Since most of the buildings joined, you could use their roofs as a highway, but sandwiched between Arlo's home and the alley mouth was a building short enough to interrupt the trail, which meant I couldn't use the roofline to reach the end of the alley.

I felt too timid to ask to see, but these people weren't my enemy. "Excuse me," I said.

The man in front of me looked over his shoulder. "Are you mad? Go back to your home. This isn't the place to be." His voice trailed away to the clothes I wore, the result of a hurried change into a similar outfit as the one I'd first worn into the fringe. Jax had insisted, as there was no disguising me in central Califax wearing fringe clothes.

"Please."

I read the confusion then wariness as he shuffled aside, opening a small gap, which spread farther as the other men copied the first, driven by some silent trigger that made them think I was different. Behind their eyes, I saw questions asked, which might've led to many answers about the sweepers' sudden appearance in force.

The last man cleared for me, opening the view. Four men knelt on the dirt. Their hands were tied behind their backs, heads bowed. Two men already lay face-down in the dirt, unmoving. The stranger was right; this wasn't the place to be, but it was the only place for me to be. I was the one who started this. I was the one who could stop it.

A sweeper marched in front of the remaining four men, while a dozen other sweepers stood at varying positions amongst the crowd should anyone decide to act impulsively. Each sweeper, except the one marching out the front, wore their helmets and shields, and not just any shield. These were the heavy-duty, nil-penetration shield Jax and I encountered in the streets of the Aris quarter.

My heart punched along my ribcage. Destruction led the beat.

The sweeper without his helmet looked up at the crowd but said nothing. The moments coalesced to one long expanse of time as the crowd silently watched the watcher.

He shouted, "One more for your silence," then raised his weapon and fired at the next in line of the four. It was the same fizzle-crackle I heard inside Arlo's house, a sound that had been confusing although benign but would now ring through my ears, heralding a nightmare. A bluish-white light penetrated through the man's chest. In response, his head arched back, his mouth frozen in a cry that never came out. I gasped then smacked my hands over my mouth, turning away, but not before I saw the man's head loll forward to his chest, followed by his body crumpling to the dirt ground of the market space.

The fear spread through the crowd like a contagious disease, infecting me as well as everyone else. I hid behind a broad-shouldered man, numbed, hollowed, and falling down into the dark abyss of destruction. My hands shook with the adrenaline and panic, and more, a blinding rage and strong desire to teach a lesson.

I glanced around me at all the faces of the crowd, feeling a plea form in my mouth. I needed help. Destruction was taking hold. If it did, hell would rain down. My eyes swept onto Arlo, and for a moment, the buildup in me stacked to a grand halt. His eyes were on the enemy, no longer on the dead on the ground, expression set firm on his face. He could descend us into darkness, give everyone time to escape, just like I could bring the buildings down around us or shatter the mind of the marching sweeper. But what about the other sweepers hiding behind their shields? And any action from either Arlo or I would bring the full might of the senate down onto the fringe. The beginning of the war.

Do I just stand here and watch? Allow the sacrifices and become a part of the silent oath?

The sweeper pointed his weapon to the next man in line as he surveyed the crowd. "Will there be another lost to your silence?"

"No." I pushed past the last guy blocking my way and stepped forward from the crowd into the open space, making every effort to avoid Arlo's needle stare.

The sweeper raised his weapon, so the barrel pointed to the sky. "Well, this is interesting."

Whisperings and gasps rose around me.

This was not me being courageous, because I was as scared as everyone else. This was not me filled with destructive power. I wasn't looking to be a hero. Arlo kept silent and watched men die to keep me hidden. I just couldn't bear to live with the agony of seeing one more person die because of me.

The sweeper curled a finger, beckoning me forward. A smirk creeped onto his face. A dimple cut into his right cheek. Sky-blue eyes danced with the self-satisfaction that came with winning.

I resisted his contemptuous demand, which earned me a quirked eyebrow from him. He then cast a glance toward some of his comrades standing at the front of the crowd. That done, he returned to me, swung his weapon over his shoulder like he had little care, and lasered me with eyes more suited to a best friend or boyfriend, not a murderer.

This wasn't the first time I saw a sweeper's face. This sweeper was no different to the others—disturbingly human, disturbingly attractive, disturbingly boy-next-door, like a serial killer living quietly in your neighborhood, attending church functions, and helping elderly people across the street.

My arm was wrenched backward by someone behind me. I yelped, looked over my shoulder and into the blankness of a sweeper's visor, where his eyes would be. Funneling destruction deep, deep within his eyes, into his mind would be so easy—if I could get past the shield in time, which bent and warped to keep me on the outside of its protective fold and to keep him in. Besides, the effects would not end with him. No, they would only just begin, and the catastrophic results would decimate the fringe.

The sweeper behind pushed me toward the other sweeper, the one with the sky-blue eyes. He caught me with one hand like it was a game of catch, snorted a laugh, but didn't let me go. Fingers digging into my upper arms, he said, "I heard you had children with you."

I held his eyes. "You were misinformed."

"Is that so?" That smirk again, revealing him as a soulless killer.

He released his fingers from their painful grip on my upper arm and backed up until he was in line with the remaining three men, all the while keeping his sky-blue eyes on me. "Your silence brings death."

Do I spare a man's life to surrender two more, or do I allow this man to become that sacrifice? It was my choice. The life of a stranger for two children, my friends?

The sweeper lowered his weapon from his shoulder and nestled the barrel against the closest man's temple. "This life is on you," he said as if he could read my heart.

"Don't do this." It was all I could think to say. It was nothing more than a filler to slow time to the inevitable.

The sweeper spat out a laugh. He craned his head back and belted out another laugh, which rattled through the air like gunfire.

With the disturbance behind me, the sweeper's laugh cut off in an instant. I looked over my shoulder as a sweeper pushed through the crowd, dragging Nada and Azrael by their tatty clothes. A large knot welled up in my throat, chest seized in a vice as I watched them brought forward.

Nada would not look up at me. His features scrunched up in defiance. Maybe it was good he wouldn't meet my eyes, because he didn't need to read my horror. His stare matched Arlo's, seething anger, bubbling fury, too much for a small boy to juggle inside. Azrael's eyes filled with tears as she glanced at me. I reached out to take her hand, but the sweeper who brought them yanked the two away from me.

"It was only a matter of time before we had what we wanted." He waved his weapon. "Separate them."

Sweepers grabbed Nada and Azrael and dragged them one way, while another pulled me in the opposite direction. Azrael screamed and fought but was swept off her feet as the sweeper hoisted her under his arm. Nada swung out, his fist meeting air, powerless against the speed and skill of a trained fighter. The sweeper pulled him close, pinning his hands to his side, his shield descending again in case anyone in the crowd thought this was the time to defy, which left me powerless.

Destruction flashed hot in front of my eyes, disordering my mind. For one blurry moment, I lost sight of everything around me and felt like I was plunging into a deep abyss. I staggered forward only to meet a firm wall of resistance, but I didn't see what it was, because I closed my eyes, scrambling to claw my way out of this mental confusion and the slipping grip on destruction. Someone grasped my left wrist, and the dull pain gave me something to focus on. Pain was good for my control. Pain always brought me back.

Sky-blue eyes stared into mine, his fingers an uncomfortable manacle on my wrist. "Give me a reason, sweetheart," he whispered.

I turned around, but he jerked me forward. Stumbling along, I saw Nada and Azrael disappearing in the opposite direction. My eyes swept the crowd then caught on movement above. Up on the rooftops of a building, I saw the four of them.

Chapter 22

THEY GOT what they came for; perhaps I was the bonus add-on to the cargo they'd come chasing. At least for now, the fringe people would be left in peace.

The sweeper opposite me kept his face hidden behind his helmet. Although facing my way, his gaze could be turned inward to his cephulet. He wasn't sleeping, not with the rigidity in his body, looking like a predator ready to pounce.

There were five others in the utility with me, each concealing their face behind their helmet, the secret to their factional nature also hidden, but their shields were down. I wasn't threat enough. With six in the utility, I was helpless.

Shut tight with the enemy, destruction seared the underside of my skin. I'd be spiraling into a pit of manic despair if it deserted me. My passivity and weakness stirred its embers, but so too my fear. Destruction had no tolerance for those parts of me. It gave me courage, but it also wanted me fierce. Caught, confined, any possible solutions hopeless, and destruction rose within, consuming, magnifying, swallowing the sane side of me, electrifying my senses, charging my mind for revenge. It felt seductive but also dirty. The horrible things I'd already done. I couldn't open the gate to destruction and accept the courage it gave without being feral. I wasn't strong enough to resist. And so I accepted neither. I squashed destruction back down, suffered the pain like an unmet need, suppressed the part of myself that gave me strength.

The senate had me, thanks to another stupid mistake I made. Now Nada and Azrael, thanks to me, were in the senate's hands. What would Jax be feeling right now, seeing the last of his family disappear? Alithia would curse my name forever. I promised her I would keep her daughter safe. She stayed behind, because she believed in me, and all I did was get her daughter caught.

I managed to do the one thing Jax tried desperately to avoid. The senate now knew people were moving between dimensions, bringing others back into their world, others capable of the same strength as them. Was there any possible way the senate would discover Mum and Ajay? I didn't want to think about them; it hurt too much. It felt like I let them down, betrayed them.

They would graft me and replace the tattoo from Islia with the truth. Then the torture would begin. They would want to know everything, about my father, how I got here, my reason for being here, who I was connected with…. I buried my eyes behind my fists. If only I could shift. If only I'd been one of the lucky ones. I wasn't, because I'd never been lucky or special. Nothing came easy to me. Jax lied to make me feel better; I wasn't good with my factional nature. I'd been a clumsy mess.

I lowered my hands from my face when I felt the utility slow. The sweepers didn't respond in any way. They were nothing but statues… robots. Mechanical whirrs, small adjustments in positioning, next came the vibration, gentle enough it was like one of those massage chairs back home. A louder *clunk* thudded through the hull behind me and under my feet.

The six sweepers unbuckling their harnesses was the signal we landed. The closest to the exit punched a panel, and the door slid aside. One remained behind, the one who'd sat opposite me. With his approach, I pressed as far back as I could in my seat. He bent and unclipped the buckle. "Get up," he ordered with his weird tinny voice straining through his helmet.

"Where are we?" Not sure why I asked, as I didn't expect him to answer me.

"Home for you. Depending on how you behave, it could be a short time, or it could be permanent."

"Is it the Dome?" If only I could see his facial expression.

This time, his answer was to grab my upper arm and pull me to my feet. "How about you check it out for yourself?"

Destruction crawled its tentacles underneath the indent of his fingers. If I had the ability to ignite his skin, he'd be screaming right now.

So he'd release me, I walked ahead to the opening then out onto the platform where the other sweepers waited. No metal platforms here— under my feet was a solid, thick arm of concrete, giving it a sense of importance and permanency. There were a bunch more docking stations, but ours was the only utility here. The long arm of the plat- form extended around in an arc before being swallowed by a large tunnel protruding from the belly of a huge concrete block. Maybe it wasn't made of concrete, but it was just as ugly and desolate.

The remaining sweepers lowered their shields over their bodies. The guy who followed me out did the same. Protocol or caution? "Walk," he ordered.

The desert made the compound appear so barren, no Califax in sight. I glanced over my shoulder, more to check if I could see the city behind in the distance, but the sweeper must've thought I was checking him out. "Eyes front."

The blue moon, yellow sun, and an expanse of golden sand to the horizon, the only interruption were a few rocky outcrops. Flat, unwel- coming, deadly. No one could survive out here, which was why the compound was here. This was the only sanctuary, an ominous, forbid- ding sanctuary. A hot wind raced across the desert and barreled along the platform like a diesel, bringing with it grit and the smell of newly baked ceramics. An unforgiving heat, a life-stripping heat.

"Where did they take my friends?"

"It's not your place to ask questions," the sweeper beside me replied.

"Is there somewhere else they take kids?" This earned me a shove in the back from the sweeper behind. I got the message.

The domed tunnel loomed, a dark gaping hole, coming to life the moment we neared. Giant panels overhead flicked on in succession, creating an upside-down runway effect.

A woman in a blue jumpsuit much like doctor scrubs walked toward us surrounded by a halo of shimmering light. She wore her hair in a tidy bun on the top of her head, which suited her pinched expression, as did her straight back and purposeful stride. Both communicated military-style competence and a lack of humor, and most likely a lack of compassion as well. Her critical eye swept the entirety of my body in a blink. Judging by her expression, she wasn't impressed with what she saw.

"Has she been screened?" Even her austere tone matched her appearance.

"All data has been sent through."

Her eyebrows were a thick black line drawn in an arch above her eyes. A tattoo marred the inside of her wrist. Grafted. Unlike the sweepers, she could not use her factional nature. The idea sent a tendril of tingles deep down inside, squelched immediately when I refocused on the ripple of faint light as it ran across her shield, the lesser sort of shield, one more easily penetrated. But I could not puncture her shield quick enough before the sweepers retaliated.

"Take her through." Voice like a blade, it was as though she'd read my hastily scrambled then scrapped plan.

Her eyes settled on me as we passed, echoing disinterest, but the sort of disinterest that made someone apathetic to injustice. I held her gaze, but nothing new flickered behind her eyes. Maybe she didn't even see me as a person.

When we entered the tunnel, I looked up at the ceiling high above us to the collection of piping and beams and God knows what else running its length. The harsh lighting heated the top of my head. Our boots smacked in stereo around the curved walls, a countdown to us reaching the other end. What would I have to do to bring all this down? Could I do it? And who would I sacrifice for my escape?

This was what it meant to be dangerous; all of a sudden, it became an attractive option. I could justify the end result, but it would still amount to the same thing. Worst of all, one day soon, I wasn't going to be questioning myself on this issue, because the time of choices would be gone, replaced by the time for action.

The sweepers' long strides swallowed the distance of the tunnel, and we stepped out into a cavernous room, so large a handful of trucks could maneuver in here with ease. The bright light reflected off the floor like glare from the sun, but it did nothing to disguise the deep gray of everything around me, a color to suck the fun from a soul.

The sweeper behind nudged me in the back with a hard point, which had to be his gun. All this looking meant I lost my pace, and that was his friendly reminder.

We continued across the cavern, heading for a small black panel at the far side. With the faint *scrape* behind, I turned my head. The sweeper blocked my view then nudged his weapon forward and took a step. I was forced to comply if I didn't want him walking over me. I spun back and staggered forward through the open door, only to pull up short to stop myself from bumping into the sweeper in front.

The door behind us closed with a soft suction sound, locking me into the confines of a small gray space with six sweepers circling me, each facing inward. Destruction flared up with the sudden arc of adrenaline now lacing through my veins. I fisted my nails into my palms, looking for that pain, anything to steal my attention, harden the barracks. I couldn't win this. *Don't even try.* The gentle shift under my feet meant we were moving.

Shields up, weapons held to their chests, intimidation that worked. Destruction didn't cower, which meant the fight against it became harder. My balance gently shifted again as we came to a halt. Behind me, the sudden wash of new air followed the noise of the door opening.

"Get out."

If not for the energy ripple from their shields, my face would reflect in each of their helmets. My head reached the level of their chins. My eyes reached the level of their weapons. Cocooned within the circular wall, this should be intimidating. It would be if destruction obeyed. It didn't. Instead, it formed its own wall, cutting me off from common sense, which would keep me alive.

Get out.

My feet wouldn't listen, because they were no longer on my side.

The sweeper in front butted me with his weapon, sudden and hard, to push me backward out the door. I saw his weapon coming with time enough to snap out both hands and latch onto its girth. The move was so sudden I succeeded in yanking it free. But he was a sweeper. I was surrounded by a wall of them, each trained like any battle-hardened soldier back home. The weapon was in my hands, but he reacted as fast, his fist colliding with my jaw. I reeled backward as the weapon was snatched from my hands. I fell and fell, nothing behind to stop me except the solid, cold surface of the floor. When it hit, the wind was punched out of my lungs.

I curled to the side, gasping for air, my jaw throbbing from his fist. The pain, the shock, the suddenness, and destruction lagged behind. But with the sound of boots smacking nearer, I remembered; destruction remembered. I slammed a palm onto the floor—I couldn't let it loose. It welled up my throat with such force I rolled to my stomach, thinking I would vomit. Coughing, gasping, I curled my fingers inward with the effort to claw it back down, drawing my nails along the concrete.

A hand clasped my shoulder, yanked me onto my back.

"I can't," I gasped.

On his knees, the sweeper leered down, shoving his helmet-covered face into mine. His shield wrapped around his body, skimming the surface of my body. "You're right about that. And you won't ever again. We'll see to it."

It slipped out before I could snatch hold. Destruction powered forward and slammed into the wall of his shield with the force of an explosion, and it sent him airborne backward into the lift where he collided with the far wall, his weapon clattering to the lift floor. The barrel of five weapons filled my view with inches to spare from my nose.

"Do it. One. More. Time," a sweeper dared.

The sweeper in the lift rose from the floor, rolled his neck, then scooped up his weapon. "This is why I love my job," he said as he stomped toward me. The others in the huddle surrounding me spread, creating a runway for him to follow.

By the time he reached me, he ripped his helmet from his head so I could see his eyes, now soaked red. He kneeled down beside me again, clutched the front of my shirt, and pulled me off the floor to meet his face. Nose-to-nose. "You have nothing," he whispered over my face. "Nothing compared to me." His breath worked its way into my mouth, sweet, spicy licorice. His free hand made its way into my hair, fingers curling inward to scrape across my scalp as he grasped a fistful of hair and pulled it down, arching my head backward, tugging farther until it hurt. "You are nothing compared to me." His breath dusted along my cheek.

Something pricked at my temples. Intensifying, it stabbed like needles on my brain, jabbing and jabbing, then it won through, piercing inward, down and down, funneling through the center of my mind, dragging with it a searing pain.

Oh, god. I lashed out with my hand, clipping him on the side of the shoulder, only because he moved in time. He still held my hair, my head at a painful angle, but I thrashed out with both arms regardless, punching wildly at his face while he laughed.

I knew what he was doing. I knew what he was capable of. But it didn't make sense.

He let me go by throwing me to the ground as he stood. I fell back, curling my knees up, fists to my eyes as the radial spiral of pain in my head ebbed away.

"Girls need lessons," he said as footsteps approached.

"What is going on here?" A woman's voice.

"Reeducation." The sweeper grabbed my wrist and pulled me to my feet, limp muscled and floppy. "She's ready for you now." He pushed me toward the woman.

Reeling from what happened, I staggered forward like a blind person. Once again, the shock subdued destruction, leaving me empty, feeling like I didn't even have a skeleton to hold me up.

Beautiful green eyes framed by long black eyelashes, but that's where her attractiveness ended. Her vitriolic stare cored me through. She dismissed me with a tilt of her head, spun on her heels, and clomped away. I watched her go. Which was better, her or the sweepers?

The woman's shoes smacking on the floor blanketed the sweeper's approach. "You should follow," he said over my shoulder.

I walked after her, casting a glance over my shoulder to see the sweeper had returned to normal, eyes now their usual color. He winked at me, licked his bottom lip, and that was all I bothered to see before I hurried after the lady.

She stopped in front of a vacant station receded into the wall. Long nails strummed on the smooth countertop as she tapped out an agitated tune. She looked sideways at me then shifted to face me, taking my chin between her fingers and turned my head to the side. The shield surrounding her flowed with her outstretched hand. When she spied what she was looking for, she recoiled her hand as if I'd bitten her and screwed her lips into a puckered O.

Another lady appeared from behind a partition. Without a word, she focused on the monitor in front of her, fingers feathering across the screen. "D4," was the first thing she said. "She'll have to be taken through for now. We're not ready for processing."

She disappeared behind the partition again, but the lady standing next to me stayed put. The other woman returned with a set of what looked like handcuffs and slid them across the counter.

Before we went any farther, the woman next to me cuffed my wrists. With the soft mechanical *click* of the lock engaging, she said, "Now let's see how brave you are."

"Anyone would fight if provoked."

"Only the foolish would try once in those." She nodded toward my wrists then turned and marched away.

The other woman disappeared behind her partition again.

"I'd hurry if I were you. There isn't much time left," she spoke over her shoulder but slowed, allowing me to catch up.

Why put the cuffs on me now, after I already walked through half the facility to get here? The sweepers left us. It was just her and me. "These suppress my factional nature."

"As if you were any match for me." She stopped in front of a door. Not bothering to wait for my reply, she faced the panel next to the door, placing her hand on the black screen and staring into the rectangular box above it.

The door slid open. "You don't have much time left."

"For what?"

"To reach your cell."

"What do you mean?"

"You can stand here and find out."

I didn't, because her face, for once, took on the jubilant expression of anticipation. Something bad was going to happen, and she couldn't wait to see it.

Chapter 23

IT WAS BRIGHT—FLUORESCENT, fake-light bright—the sort that highlights all your facial flaws and makes you look sick. That was as welcoming as the place got. Rows of open doorways ran the length of the room. A metal balcony dissected the second story from the first. Piping tangled along the ceiling. No windows, no hope of seeing natural light, no way of marking the days from the nights. Austere, quiet, smelling like someone dumped a bucket of ammonia, this was my home. I moved farther into the space, peering inside the closest rooms as I passed. This was the cell block, and somewhere amongst these doorways I would find cell D4.

There were ten rooms downstairs, matched by ten upstairs. Above the first doorway was a plaque etched with C1. Through the metal grille of the landing, I read the plaque above the first doorway on the second story, D1. I didn't have far to go.

The woman had not removed the cuffs, because they suppressed destruction. How long was I expected to wear them? Although I'd never been great at anything, now that destruction was truly chained, I felt totally useless. Once they grafted me, it would be permanent. And would I be prepared to risk reversing the graft, if I ever managed to get out of here?

Ignoring the women's preemptive order, I explored downstairs. There was one bed in each room, wide enough you could fall out during the night if you rolled over. The walls were white, not gray like the rest of the place, which was something. This was the sort of place that would have you climbing the walls in boredom ten minutes after entering.

A single doorway opened to a passage at the opposite end of the large room. I headed over, casting glances into the rooms as I went in a futile hope that it wasn't just me in here; isolation was a good way to foster despair. Every room looked the same, empty except a cot.

In the passage, I found two doors; left was the toilet block, right the showers. That was something, at least. I turned back and looked down the length of the room and stared at a whitewash of emptiness. I'd felt hollow in the courtroom the day Dad was led away. But that was nothing compared to now. Fully clothed, I felt bare. I wouldn't last in here alone.

I marched down the length of the room to the only exit. Perhaps there was an intercom system, a way of connecting with someone in case of an emergency, maybe a camera that monitored my movement.

"Hello?" I banged on the door. "Anyone?" If I made enough noise, someone might've come. And then what? I could've asked why I had to be locked away alone. Maybe there were other women I could be put with. Anything was better than this. I used the cuffs to *clunk* a dull, reverberating tune against the door, but after forever, no one came.

The cuffs became suffocating, more suffocating than the room, the isolation. Not only was I trapped within a room with no possible chance of escape, but I was physically bound. I blamed everything that happened to me so far on my factional nature. I'd grown to hate its constant presence. Without it now, the void I felt within grew like a chasm. Without it, I felt utterly alone.

A blaring sound punctured the quiet. Short, sharp bleeps pitched to pierce your eardrums. Handcuffed, I could only cover one ear. Was this an indication something was wrong? A warning for me to back away from the door?

Then the tingle in my wrists started. Light at first, increasing with each bleep, until it swept up my arms and into my shoulders. There, it rested. I shook my hands, rolled my shoulders. What the hell? It had to be coming from the cuffs. Moments later, the tingle was off across my chest, engulfing my upper body, morphing from tingles into a vibration.

I staggered from the door with no intention of heading somewhere, just doing something that wasn't standing still. The pain slammed into my head like a bat across the skull, sending me stumbling backward onto my ass. When I hit the ground, bum first, the jar hammered up my spine. I fell sideways, one elbow spearing the floor as I curled into a ball, squeezing my temples between my forearms. Endless waves of agony radiated from my wrists to my head.

The bleeping stopped, but the pain did not. And my crime for this punishment was dawdling. The only way to stop my torment was to reach D4. As if infected with a migraine, times ten, my vision tunneled and wavered when I unfurled my head from the protective cover of my forearms, searching for the stairs.

They were meters away but closer to miles. That's how long it would take for me to reach them the way I felt. I was Daddy's little girl, so Elva taunted me, which meant I was made of the same steel. I gave myself one deep breath and one more weak moment before I got to my knees. Halfway to standing.

The pain, the wavering vision, made me squint at the stairs. They seemed to ripple and stretch farther away from me, which was impossible. I closed my eyes, another deep breath, and then I pushed to my feet, hunched but standing all the same. My first step and my foot felt like it didn't belong to me. The vibration, which claimed my upper body, had spread throughout, making my legs quiver.

I looked at my feet and willed them to move, take another step, and one more. Ahead, the stairs stayed at a distance. I closed my eyes and shook my head. This was an illusion, a product of the agony in my head. Concentrating on my feet again, I forced more steps. My whole world became those steps. An explosion could decimate this room, and I would still be looking at my feet and willing my legs to make those few steps.

Eternity came and went, and I was still walking. A moan of relief escaped when I glanced up and found the rail within reach. I grasped for it, leaning over too far, and tumbled forward. Mind slowed by pain, I realized I'd fallen once I felt the sharp stab at my hip, which then jarred through the rest of me.

It was like starting again. I had to pull myself from the floor, had to find the mental willpower to drag my heavy, unresponsive body to stand. Lagging limbs meant when I grasped for the railing, looking for help to stand, my coordination was out, and I ended up tipping forward and banging my face on the metal. I reeled back and landed on my ass then tittered to my side.

My yell sprung the lid on my tears. It ratcheted the pain, but screaming felt good, because it drove fire into my veins, buried my despair under a blanket of rage. I was on my knees without willing it. I knelt and screamed throaty, hoarse screams that flushed raw emotions out of every possible hiding place. For those few seconds, I was immersed in something more powerful than my pity.

When done, I crashed back into reality and hunched forward, so my forehead rested on the floor. The only way out was to reach my room. A climb was all it would take. I lifted my head and found a small pool of blood on the floor. Using my tongue, I found blood on my top lip. Soon, it ran into my mouth, coating my tongue with a metallic taste.

In one push, I reached my feet. Hands white-knuckled on the railing, I took my first step. *Don't look up.* If I did, the wavering stairs would send me back on my ass to the bottom. Keeping my head down, I took the next step.

With every gain I made, the agony would intensify as if it sensed I was nearing my destination and wanted to make the most of the time it had. My legs still quivered and threatened to collapse. By now, though, I found my rhythm, two breaths for every step. It became my challenge to keep to those two breaths and not let my pacing slip.

Risking a peek, I found only a few steps to go. This buoyed me on. One more step and then the next, when a sudden noise behind me made me lose the step. The front of my boot banged into the grille stair, and I staggered forward. I had a hold of the railing, but my partially disorientated mind wasn't strong enough to enforce the grip, and I lost my hold. My knees hit the step. Next, the *clank* of the cuffs on the metal, and I was falling. Hip, elbow, head, most parts of me met the stairs on my way down, tumbling, rolling until I bumped into something soft.

Terrified there was yet still falling to be done, I stayed in my semi-curled position like a corpse.

Someone rolled me onto my back. A man leaned over me as he scooped his hands under my knees and back then hoisted me up to his chest. His boots thunked heavy on the steps. It could not have been easy, carrying me up the stairs, but he kept going, powering up without breaking a sweat. At the top, he stomped across the landing and entered the door of a cell. The moment we crossed the threshold, the pain in my head and body stopped. He laid me down on the bed then stood back, hands on hips, and assessed me with analytical eyes.

"You've had a bit of trouble, haven't you?"

I rolled to my side and pushed myself up, gingerly at first in case the thumping agony came back. When it didn't, I pushed all the way up and shuffled on my ass to the wall. No one in this place was trustworthy.

He was dressed like a sweeper, minus the helmet and the accessories they hung from their belts, in particular a weapon. His faded gray eyes reminded me of a multifaceted crystal. Penetrating, they dissected everything. Without a blink, confidence kept his gaze on my face, made me feel like a peculiarity or a lab experiment. His short, military-style cut failed to obscure his tattoo. Set. A liar. The friendly smile had to be deceit. The sleeves of his uniform covered his wrist, so I couldn't tell whether he was a liar in full control of his factional nature. What else were Set masters of? Jesus, I couldn't remember.

"I think we can dispense with these." He knelt at my feet. Knelt like he was about to pray or beg for my forgiveness. I pressed farther to the corner. *Set, remember?* A display of compassion was likely a forerunner to a stab in the gut.

He opened his hand, revealing a slim, silver device. "If you wouldn't mind." Palm held out, facing up, and a welcoming smile. Did he really expect me to give him my hands? Set would slice them off at the wrists. Wouldn't they? This was a ruse to win me over. Like the good cop/bad cop routine, send in someone caring and I'd cave.

He quirked an eyebrow. I didn't want to suffer again if any alarm went off, so I stretched out my hands. Turning it into a magical stunt, theatrics and all, he flicked his wrist then waved it over the base of the cuffs. There was a small *click* then the cuffs disengaged and fell to the bed.

Because he was kneeling, we looked eye-to-eye. "That should feel more comfortable. I will have a word with intake about your treatment. These cuffs were unnecessary. They should never have been left on while you were alone."

He held my eyes the whole time he spoke. Instead of dark and surly like Jax, he was blond and full of smiles with a nose too big for his face and wide lips.

I arched away from his hand as he drew it near to my face. At first, his smile dropped, and he genuinely looked worried as he withdrew his hand. "I'm sorry. I didn't mean to alarm you. I was going to clear some strands of your hair, which were stuck to the blood on your face. How'd you get that, anyhow?"

"I fell down the stairs." Now that he'd drawn attention to my injury, my nose throbbed, which it had likely been doing all along, but I'd been distracted with other more life-threatening issues to notice.

"I'm sorry you had to experience that."

Was he for real? "You keep apologizing."

"I'm appalled at your treatment."

"I'm a prisoner, so why do you care?"

"It's not our way to treat anyone like this."

This is all a lie. "The lady who brought me here was under a different impression." I wasn't going to bother mentioning the sweeper. They would treat anyone like that, regardless of who they were.

He heaved a sigh, like it had been the hardest thing in the world to hear. "I'll take care of intake. Perhaps some retraining of protocol is in order." He fished around in his pocket as he spoke. "Would you like to go to the bathrooms and clean yourself up? You'll find towels on the shelving to your left when you first enter. I'll see to it some clothes are sent down the chute before you get out of the shower. Soon, we will have a chat."

"You're kidding, right?"

His attention had been on whatever he was searching for in his pocket. Now, he focused on me, eyebrows raised high on his forehead, waiting for me to elaborate.

"After everything that's happened, we're going to have a little chat? I kind of thought you'd torture me first and ask questions later."

"If that's what you want, I'm sure I can organize something. But in general, we don't torture here."

"What do you do?"

"This facility is for reeducation."

"What does that mean?"

"Sometimes people forget the reasons why we exist as we do. They forget the importance of the senate's mandates and the danger of disrupting order."

He found what he'd been searching for, a thin, black bracelet similar to the cephulet Jax wore on his wrist. "If you don't mind." He extended his hand, another encouraging smile, which creeped the itches over my body, but mostly because I longed for something warm and welcoming from someone in this world. Like a simple smile. *Don't.* He was dangerous, and not just because he was ungrafted and worked for the senate; I wanted to believe someone cared.

"What is that?"

"This is what they should've used instead of the cuffs."

I had no choice but to give my hand. He took my wrist. Instead of attaching the band, he turned my hand over, exposing the pale skin on the underside. With a finger, he traced a pattern feather-soft, following the swirl with his eyes. "It's miraculous, really."

My own eyes followed the trail of his finger then flicked up to his face, but I couldn't read his expression. The distracted awe in his voice, like he'd forgotten I was there, was the only hint I got. I was an anomaly, an experiment, something to be caged for dissection.

His one finger turned to more, creeping their warm, soft touch over the non-grafted area. I inched my arm away, but his hand viced to my wrist. With its suddenness, I jumped. Slowly, he relaxed his hold to one finger, which rested across my wrist, pressing firmly into my flesh. His eyes found mine. "Your pulse is fast."

"Yours would be too in the same situation."

He gently shook his head with a smile to ease my seized heart. "You don't need to be afraid of me. I want to help you."

The crystal of his eyes became the twisting facets of lies. This understanding must've reflected in my eyes, for he broke eye contact and slipped the black band on my wrist. Once done, he pushed off the floor with casual, easy grace.

"This does the same thing as the cuffs."

"In a more comfortable way, wouldn't you say?" His smile was back, so alluring. I wanted to believe it.

"Why must the people remember the senate's mandates?"

"They must remember why they agreed to be a part of this society in the first place."

"Why did I agree?"

"To stop fearing yourself. To feel like you belong."

In the entrapment of his stare, time wound to a halt. He started the clock ticking again by moving to the door. "I'm Archon, by the way."

Chapter 24

THE WATER SPRAYED hot and needle-hard, hammering into my scalp and across my back. I stayed still, savoring the punishment while I thought of Jax. What were he and the others doing now? Jax would've told Alithia about her daughter. I turned around, pressing my hands into the smooth surface of the wall, feeling the same awful desolation Alithia would be feeling, the same feeling I felt when I read Holden's message on Jax's phone.

What did they do with the children? *Stay true to your word, Holden. Look after my family.*

The hot turned warm, which soon turned cold. Once I stepped off the plate at the base of the shower, the flow stopped—a neat trick, which had taken me a while to discover. True to Archon's word, my clothes arrived down a chute in the bathroom, wrapped in a thin, rubbery film. Overalls, socks, and boots. Instead of abandoning my clothes, I pulled the overalls over the top, since they were baggy enough. If the opportunity arose, I would escape in my normal clothes. No doubt, they'd tell me soon enough if it was unacceptable or not to continue to wear my normal clothes.

In the mirror, I surveyed my nose from different angles, and each way told me it was swollen and ugly, same as my top lip, which was twice the size of my bottom one. I also found bruising along my jaw to go with the dull ache. If I saw that intake woman who brought me here, I'd ask her to recite the protocol. Then again, she'd probably feel smug at my appearance. I had no friends here, especially Archon. He was a rat, a snake. I was sure of it. The way he fondled my wrist like I was a rare specimen to explore spoke of his greed. He wanted to know me, but not as a person, as a possibility.

He looked youngish, maybe in his late twenties, much older than me, but not so old that his hair was about to turn gray, which meant he wouldn't know what it was like to be graft-free. Or maybe he wasn't grafted. Maybe he was trusted by the senate. I'd been unable to tell, because his sleeve covered his wrist. How many of the staff were grafted?

No one is your friend here. My face told me what I needed to hear. An ugly, fat nose and lip, because no one cared what happened to the people inside. If they did show interest, then it was time to be worried.

A repeated *dong* echoed through the empty chamber of my cell block. I left the bathroom and moved out into the open space. There was no one there, no indication to what it meant, except when the door opened with no one on the other side. The warning *dong* meant get out before my brain was fried again.

In the corridor, I saw no one. I also saw nowhere to run except the way I'd come, and I knew where that led, the way they wanted me to go.

At some point, I'd fallen asleep—how I managed that was a mystery. As if sensing I'd awoken, my cell door slid aside the moment my feet touched the floor, releasing me from the confines of my cell, but the door to the block had stayed shut until now.

I found Archon standing in front of the lifts. Hearing my approach, he spun on his heels, his expression that of a welcoming host seeing a visitor arrive. His eyes darted over my outfit. "Seems I misjudged your fit."

"It's comfortable. How long has it been since you left me?"

"Sounds like you fell asleep."

Stop making this a pleasant conversation.

"Twenty hours. You must've been tired."

Twenty hours! How had I managed it? With a little assistance perhaps? That would mean Nada and Azrael spent that long in the senate's hands. Alithia spent that long going out of her head with grief. Jax and the team spent that long cursing my name for ruining their plans.

"I'll get someone to look at your nose."

"That's not necessary."

"It is. I don't want everyone else on the reeducation program to think you have been deliberately abused."

He didn't care, but he wanted the people to believe he did, which made no sense. Archon didn't need to win their trust. They were all powerless to whatever he chose to do with them, whatever he chose for them to believe.

Hands clasped behind his back, he stepped into the lift. "Come. I'm keen for that chat I promised, but we have to make a stop first."

This wasn't an invitation. It was a command.

The lift doors closed on an empty corridor. Not even the woman who'd given me my cell number could be seen behind her desk recessed into the wall.

Archon didn't bother to make small talk while we rode the lift to the surface. Thank God. He was much better silent, and in that time, I could try for a few seconds to pretend he wasn't there. The high-polish, reflective surface of the door turned into a mirror of sorts. While not clear enough to show his face, I could see his body, as a blur, standing less than a meter from mine. Close enough that if I snapped out my arm, it would collide with his face. Then what?

Chaos. I remembered. Set was in control of deception and—

"Excuse me?"

"Chaos." *Oh, Jesus. You bloody fool.*

"I'm sorry?"

"My head feels full of it." I wanted to slap myself. But he'd distracted my thought with his sudden question.

The lift stopped, but Archon moved to stand in front of me rather than exit from the now open lift doors. My breath rolled up my throat when he placed his palms on either side of my face.

215

"That's why you are here. I will calm this chaos. I will give you peace."

Get your hands off me.

Spring filled the space before me, the smell of a gentle breeze as it passed over budding flowers, of crisp, ripe red apples ready for picking, of sweet, spicy, earthy amber sap oozing from the trees. I opened my mouth to suck it in as a subtle joy spread through my chest, the sort that comes with the glimpse of sunshine washing the long, dark cold away. I closed my eyes and stepped forward, drawn by the allure of what I felt. But when I opened my eyes and stared into Archon's face, I remembered where I was. I stepped away from the cocoon of his warm hands. What was going on here? This was not what I smelled when I first entered the lift. This was not the way I should feel, like my heart was bursting with joy.

Archon's lips twitched at the corners as he lowered his hands. My confusion muddled his smile—genuine or smug? Smug, of course. He was Set, manipulating me into a position of his choosing. *He wants me to trust him.* Was this what it meant to wield deception? Phonus had the ability to make me see night when it was day. Could Archon, a Set, twist my mind, force me to see only his reality?

And what did it mean to wield chaos?

With a slow, fading smile, Archon led me out of the lift and into a pristine white corridor with squeaky floors and not the vast open space I passed through when I first entered the facility. This had to mean we'd not reached the surface. Another man coming our way, dressed in blue scrubs, flicked a glance at me, snapped his eyes to Archon, then stared ahead without acknowledging him.

Still spinning from the incident in the lift, I had to skip a few steps to keep pace with Archon's stride. His uniform might've looked like it had yet to experience a fight, but the way he moved spoke of a military background. This was not a man who spent his time behind a desk all day enforcing senate laws to a bunch of recalcitrants via paperwork. He was much more dangerous.

Farther down, we stopped in front of a door that took form from the wall once Archon palmed the panel. A man dressed in white scrubs met us inside. My muscles twitched to turn me around and sprint me out the door. To where? A corridor sunk beneath the desert.

"Let me know when you're finished," Archon said to the man in white. He didn't bother to look my way before he marched out the door.

There was one piece of furniture in the room. A long metal table reminiscent of a hospital surgery bed.

"Please." He gestured toward the bed.

This man was going to graft me. Once he did, I would be helpless in this world. I would become another citizen slotting into a society I wasn't a member of and didn't want to be a member of.

"It will not hurt." His eyes were kind. Genuine. The first genuinely warm expression I'd seen since arriving here. His gray hair, full beard, and rounded stomach reminded me of Santa Claus.

"What if I don't want to?"

His smile dropped. "Sadly, that is not a choice."

"Do you believe in what you're doing?"

"Of course. This will bring you peace from the threat of your factional nature."

"Not all see it as a threat."

He came around the bed, resting his hand at my elbow, his touch light as a moth. "What have you done to end up here?"

I sucked in a breath, stepped away from his hand.

"Aris child." The voiced sentiment sounded fatherly coming from his mouth. "You have committed a terrible crime to be here. But not from your choosing. It is our factional nature that drives us to do evil things." He straightened. "Ah, yes. I see it in your eyes. You know it is true. Do you always want to be at war with yourself? Continue to feel fragmented and lost? Let us welcome you back to where you belong. Let us help you find that stillness inside that resides beneath the desire of your factional nature. It cannot be so while you are split."

His expression was mournful, but his smile was welcoming. "Let me help you."

He held out his hand; I placed mine in his. There was no manipulation in his words. They were true and honest and came from his heart. I wanted to be a part of that. Everything in my life was bad; I wanted him to help me.

"That's it, my child. Let me stop the confusion, bring you peace. It is what you deserve."

It had been so long since I felt anyone's concern for me. What he said was addictive. After everything, I didn't want to be me, fighting destruction, fighting Carter, fighting the senate, fighting innocent people. Fighting, fighting, I didn't want to do it. Destruction felt more a part of me with every day. It gave me courage and strength, but it also turned me into someone else. I'd made one terrible mistake after another since destruction awoke inside me. I'd killed someone, destroyed another's mind. I didn't want to be that other person, because in a crisis, the bad choices were always made. I wanted to be normal.

"This fight inside you will only get worse. If you allow your factional nature to become you, this part, the part of you I am talking to right now, will disappear. The two cannot coexist, not in harmony. And the softer side will lose. Do you want to become that person?"

No, never, not destruction as it wanted me to be. He was right. I was split in two, always this war inside, always the darker side of me wanting to win through.

But once I lost destruction, would Jax and the others still want me? Would they hate me?

I allowed the man to guide me to the table, helpless in this final decision. I lay back on the bed, stared up into his eyes. "It will not hurt at all. And once it is done, you will be welcomed back into society."

His face disappeared, leaving me staring up at the ceiling. *I'm sorry, Jax.* This was a betrayal to him, a betrayal to everyone in the fringe, but I wasn't a good Persal. I didn't have to agree with the senate, but I didn't want to be a lethal killer; destruction wanted me that way.

The man reappeared, holding the grafter up for me to see. "Once this is done, you'll feel good again. You will no longer be exposed to the dangerous urges of your factional nature. You will be safe."

He moved my wrist with the tattoo farther away from my body in preparation for the grafter. I placed my hand over the tattoo.

His brow creased. For a breath, we stared into each other's eyes. "What is your factional nature?" I asked.

"Does it matter?"

"But it is a part of you."

"This is who I am. That other part doesn't belong. I renounced my factional nature the day I used it to hurt someone I cared for."

"You weren't grafted at birth?"

"I was born in the fringe."

"How are you working for the senate?"

"Once upon a time, I believed in the rebellion's rhetoric; I believed in the fight. But I saw many terrible things done by those who claim the senate is the evil in Califax."

Was this the truth?

He nodded his head. "I understand your confusion. It is hard to accept the reality of their lies. I did not want to accept myself. But I could not pretend, nor could I turn my head from the things I saw. The senate's rule is just in comparison to what is committed by the rebellion."

Carter was guilty, yes. And Dad, where Dominus was concerned, he acted no better than the senate. But I couldn't believe Islia or Alithia were guilty of anything more than wanting freedom.

"There are no innocents when you fight a war. Do you want that war?"

Don't ask me that.

He maneuvered the graft over my tattoo then clamped it down in place with side levers that held snug to my wrist. I surrendered. A few simple button presses illuminated a display on the back, and the grafter made a faint whining sound.

A faint buzzing vibrated through my wrist and then up my arm. After the last time I'd felt this vibration, my panic swelled. I inched my body away from the machine, but my wrist would not move. Not only was the grafter clasped to my wrist, but my wrist was immobilized to the table.

"It's all right. It really doesn't take that long, and then you will be one of us."

No backing out now, not that I could.

I stared down at the grafter as a vibration hummed in the place the grafter touched my skin. The restraints fueled a sudden growing panic. Again, I jerked my arm against the bind.

The man pressed his hand onto my arm. "Calm. It is all right. It will not hurt, as I promised. The vibration will relent soon enough."

I stopped fighting against the restriction, but my body remained tense, muscles twisted, ready to launch me off the table.

As he promised, the vibration eased, leaving prickles that spread up my arm.

"See? It is as I said." His grandfatherly smile calmed my residual tension. Like a big exhale, my body relaxed onto the bed.

"We must leave the grafter on for a few more minutes and then all will be done." He patted my hair like a parent.

I released a long breath, rolling my head to the side. The illuminated display had faded to black, the prickles lessening as well. Once the man removed the grafter, I raised my wrist, touching the red mark left on my skin.

"It looks like you may need a touchup on the tattoo. I was hoping there would be minimal damage to the design, since the craftsmanship was so good. Unfortunately...."

Islia's tattoo, the one he'd given to protect me.

"I shall give you something for your face."

The swelling and bruising. "No."

"But child—"

"Leave it that way." *Let everyone in here see.*

"If that is your wish. You don't need this anymore." He removed the black band from my other wrist. I wouldn't need anything anymore to suppress destruction, not even my will.

I welcomed this in the end, but now that it was complete, I felt like a traitor.

Chapter 25

ARCHON RECLINED IN HIS CHAIR, fingers steepled, gaze fixed on me. Like everywhere I'd been so far, his office resembled a morgue minus the bodies. Surfaces gleaming pristine, stark, sterile, unwelcoming, the sort of place that made you feel you were dirtying it by your presence alone, the sort of place that made you want to keep moving and not stay awhile or grow roots for a decent duration. Two glasses half full of amber liquid sat on the table in front of us, unlikely to be scotch or whiskey.

My body felt heavy, my heart as well. All I wanted to do was curl up on the cot in my cell and pretend nothing happened. Regrets sucked. Being free of destruction seemed like the right choice while in the grafter's room. Everything the grafter said made sense. He made freedom from destruction reasonable, more than that, desirable, the only sane choice to make. His words offered a sanctuary from the shame I harbored inside for all the things I'd done under the control of destruction, a chance to be normal again. Away from him now, I felt different. Half of me was missing. At what point had I come to accept destruction as me, a vital part of myself that belonged?

I loathed the things I'd done since discovering my factional nature, but to turn my back on that side of myself was to turn my back on everything that brought me here. Jax, Dad, Elva, and the team, Dominus, the reason I was thrown into the game, the reason I began this fight, the reason the fringe dwellers struggled to live, the reason the children were stolen. I never wanted to be a part of any war, but I could never undo what I now knew; I would never stop knowing what it felt like to be destruction. I would never stop feeling like I lost an important part of myself. I would become one of the many who filled the streets of Califax. The outsider, I was no longer like Jax, Elva, Islia, Nuke, and Patrick, my friends.

I stared at a spot above Archon's head, avoiding his stare, my mind empty.

"It will take some getting used to."

I shifted my gaze to him. "You know, do you?" He wasn't grafted. He couldn't be, not with the way he manipulated my feelings in the lift.

He dropped his hands and sat forward. "What if our factional natures weren't a gift? What if they were a curse?"

"That's a matter of perception."

"Maybe not. I want you to look at something." His eyes were weirdly unfocused. Something I'd become accustomed to when people consulted their cephulets. On the wall behind him, images moved into focus. The clarity of the images increased until I stared at a street scene in the aftermath of a terrible tragedy. A few supporting walls remained, but the streets were mostly destroyed. Everything was coated with a fine film of ash, shrouding the city of Califax in a gloomy gray. Even the sun's rays couldn't penetrate the heavy layer of destruction floating as a cloud over the landscape. Bodies were visible, a leg poking out of a pile of rubble, a mangled torso and head, two people seeming locked in an embrace, their bodies partially melded together as if they'd been made of wax and left in the sun too long. Blood, blood, blood, staining everything a dirty, dusty reddish-brown.

Archon didn't turn his head to see the images behind him. His gaze stayed on me, catching the flinch in my expression, because he wanted me to suffer. This was about reeducation, fearing who you were. *Put your trust in the senate*, the images demanded, *for this was the only way.*

I'd had enough, turning my head from the images to stare at the floor.

"This is your *gift* to Califax."

It was as though I could feel the shards of crystal in his eyes gouging deep into my skin. I longed to touch the tattoo behind my ear. Not in front of him. Islia was ungrafted, an Aris, who lived peacefully with his factional nature. He wasn't an uncontrollable monster. And what about the other fringe dwellers who lived alongside each other without conflict? I'd been so afraid of myself.

"Why won't you look?" His voice was soft, kind.

"I know what you're doing."

"Is the truth so hard for you?"

From your perspective, yes. But there was truth to what he showed me. Were these not images from a time when no one was grafted? Had the people of this world changed enough from then to live in peace with one another if they were free to use their factional natures? The people in the fringe managed it, but they had a reason to unite. Take that reason away, and would they still see their neighbors as their friends? Was the man who grafted me right?

I didn't have a cephulet flicking images in front of my eyes, but I didn't need one. My memory did a great job of haunting me with the plea in Jax's eyes the day he told me he didn't want to be the monster inside. Rather than be free of it, he committed the ultimate sin. As Aris, he killed someone, as had I. There was no going back for either of us. Our souls were burned. When I was destruction, the right judgment didn't matter, neither did morals. Winning was everything. But at what point do you give up, stand aside, and let someone dictate your life, and what do you have to fight?

"There is no real right and wrong. All we can do is make the best choice for the greater population," Archon said.

The images behind Archon disappeared, so too the lies hiding in his crystal-like eyes. "I think we understand each other."

I blinked. *He's twisting my mind. This is nothing but Set deception.* It had to be.

Archon came around his desk, close to me, resting back like he was preparing for a long and comforting chat. Everything in me twitched and tightened. I tried not to react and push myself back into my seat like it would gain me distance. No way would I be that transparent. *We're not friends.*

"It's within these walls unity begins."

Was he for real? Delivered like he was reading my mind. Set couldn't do that, could they?

"It's through trust, Sable, that we make a difference. As a community, we win."

The use of my name, as if calling my eyes to his, pricked my attention. How did he know my name? Instead of doing what he wanted of me, I stared at his hands clasped in front of him, resting casually in the semi-bend of his legs as he leaned on his desk. His nails were trimmed, manicured. Soft hands, a man that didn't do the heavy tasks. Why would he, when he had others to do it for him? Archon pulled the strings, and everyone danced. Under his sleeve, I'd find nothing, no tattoo over a graft to signal his sacrifice, because he didn't have to make a sacrifice. His harmony came at the detriment of everyone else's freedom.

How did he know my name?

"What happens now?"

Archon rose. "How about I show you around?"

"I meant when my reeducation is over. What will you do with me?" I didn't belong here. Would they force me to stay?

"Let's take this a step at a time."

"Why am I the only one in D-block?"

"D-block is for those who need… encouragement. I think you've passed that stage already."

"Does that mean I graduate to a new room?" I didn't want to be in there all alone.

"I'll certainly put forward the request. It may take a day or two, but I'll get you out of there."

"Are you like this with everyone?"

"And how is that?"

"Accommodating."

"When it is warranted, yes."

His eyes called to me, reaching out and sweeping me close. Why was it warranted with me? "What time is it?"

"Late, if you're to see what I want to show you." He glided off the table and headed for the door.

In the corridor, he gave time for me to catch up with him. I had no idea which way we headed, if back toward the grafting room or in another direction.

"The man who grafted me, what was his factional nature?"

"Why do you want to know?"

"Curious?"

From his profile, I caught the smile. If I looked closely enough, I'd probably read it as a smirk. Around a corner, we found a woman waiting by the lift at the end of the corridor. Appearing like a wax statue, or maybe a cyborg, her expression was a mask, disinterest painted on every inch of her face. Her eyes mapped Archon's approach. It was like I wasn't even there.

Archon opened the door to the lift with his palm. "Wait inside." A command dressed as a suggestion.

I caught Archon's profile as the door slid closed. While not as useful as seeing his expression front on, I saw enough to know he wasn't happy. I didn't know what Archon would look like angry, but in the short seconds before the metal doors shut me in, his body turned rigid, arms slapped to his hips, already knowing he wouldn't like what she had to say.

My warped reflection stared back at me. Not quite that perfect mirror, my features were a blur; no swollen nose and top lip to be seen here.

As I was staring at my reflection, the sudden *hiss* of the lift door opening left me facing Archon. The woman had disappeared. The smile made its usual reappearance. Even his body language had flipped, looking relaxed and limber yet poised and ready.

"Sorry about that." He stepped inside. I took a few paces left, creating distance.

The lift left my stomach behind on its upward flight. As quickly, we slowed to a stop. When the door opened, I felt the subtle pressure of Archon's hand at the small of my back. I took a large stride out into the corridor to rid myself of his touch.

"We should be in time," he said as he headed off down the corridor.

"For what?"

"That would ruin the surprise." His sideways glance was enchanting, a boyish upward sweep of his lips, like a hopeful date eager to impress as he matched his steps with mine. The mercurial turn of his mood screamed caution. Before the lift door closed him out, I got the sense Archon could turn to steel and that a steely Archon was not a nice person, only to be confused by this playful side, light and airy like a summer breeze.

He was a man well-schooled for his job. His manner made people feel comfortable and relaxed in his presence. Such consideration as matching his gait to mine rather than forcing me to keep up hinted at a man who paid attention to those around him, more than most. What I couldn't decide was whether that made him dangerous. In the beginning, Jax had said to win Dominus, I was to lie, cheat, and deceive. I would assume he was preparing me for life in Califax, else why have Dominus played that way?

Archon guided me through another door to a landing. From this high, we looked through a glass wall over the vast open space I passed through when I first arrived, or something similar. It was still vacant.

"This is where everyone gets some exercise."

"Is there any chance to exercise outside?" They weren't big on windows in this place. But maybe we were too far within the compound to have windows.

"There are select times for outside activities."

"How long do people stay here?"

"That depends on them. Those who accept the truth early, leave early. We have a high success rate, which means most don't stay too long."

Once grafted, there was likely little reason to keep them. "Is that why D-block is vacant?"

"The last left a moon span ago."

"Where are the children taken?"

"This facility is not appropriately equipped for children."

"What happens to them afterward? Do they ever see their parents again?"

"We try our hardest to locate the parents. It does society no good to create parentless children. We want the best for the children. We want all our citizens to understand that we work for the betterment of Califax and the surrounding provinces. We want everyone united."

"The parents would have to be grafted to get their children back."

"Don't make it sound calculating. It is the best solution. Everyone comes to understand and accept that in the end."

Archon's nurturing scenario was not Jax's Califax, nor the Califax they'd built in Dominus. I'd been given opposing views, but which one was I to believe? Did people like Carter and my father, people who built Dominus to train emotionally distilled warriors, develop this facility, govern these rules, even encourage rebel families to be together?

"Come on. I promised to show you something."

Archon led me along the landing. We passed out of sight of the expansive room, and the glass became a solid wall, but farther along, it opened up to glass again, and we looked down on a room full of tables. At the tables sat people dressed in gray overalls, prisoners like me.

I stopped and placed my hands on the glass as I peered down on them eating.

"The dining hall. It's late, and I'm keeping you from your dinner. I hope you don't mind."

There had to be hundreds of people down there. "That's a lot of people."

"Most of them are from outside Califax."

"The provinces?"

He nodded. "There are pockets of resistance to our ways in Califax. Some who have slipped through our yearly census. These are people looking for a better life but need to understand the rules governing the city. Once they are reeducated, they will be welcomed into Califax and given homes."

"How many people from the countryside come to the city?"

"Enough to fill our tables. Certain times of the year, it gets tough in the provinces, creating an influx of people. Most are grafted. It tends to be those from the far reaches of the countryside who have the most resistance, places like Uradra and Guilia."

A jolt sheared through my body upon hearing the name. My knuckles turned white as my hands pressed into the glass wall.

"But come, we're dawdling." He picked up his pace, forcing me to jog. A few more strides and we left the dining hall behind and slipped through another door. Dry wind parched my face, bringing with it the clogging smell of dust. I'd made two steps out the door, no farther, before I stopped short, gaping like a toddler. The sun hung low on the horizon, but already a few stars were visible. Along with three moons. One big enough to dwarf the other two and fill a good part of the sky.

"Riddean." I breathed the name, awed by its beauty. This big, it seemed a bridge was all we needed to get across.

"She is beautiful, isn't she?"

We were standing by the railing, the vastness of the desert below. Archon stood close enough for me to feel the heat of his arm through the sleeve of his shirt. It was a distraction, but I didn't want to draw attention to the fact by moving away. Instead, I stared at the ground below. Given Riddean's closeness, the murkiness of dusk had disappeared.

The expanse of the desert spread to the horizon. No place to shelter from the heat for anyone out there. "When will you release me?"

"Steady. It's not that easy. We have to be sure you are one of us now."

My breath stopped. "And how will you do that?"

He took my hand and moved it toward him. Ignoring my first desire to yank it away, I watched his expression. Wasn't that what you did with an opponent? Wasn't that what Jax and Holden tried to teach me through all our sparring matches?

He pulled the sleeve of my gray overalls up and bared my wrist. "You do not have a cephulet."

"Do I need one?"

"You will need to be monitored during the initial phase of reintroduction into society. It's a precautionary measure. We like to make sure everyone is acclimatizing well."

Maybe it was a false memory, but I was sure in the early days Jax said for some the grafts failed. There was nothing but emptiness inside me. Nothing roamed under my skin, roiling to be let loose.

"We will give you one soon. It's important you are connected to the biostream as part of our reeducation and reintroduction program. From time to time, you will be requested to meet at your HQ for further education. We want to make this as problem-free as we can."

"Once I have the cephulet, you will release me?"

Archon turned back to the moon. "There are a few more things that need doing before then."

"Will you tell me what is going to happen?"

"No, but I will tell you one thing. The man who did your graft, Martimon, is a Set."

Chapter 26

A HARSH LIGHT bored through my eyelids. I opened them to find I was not in Alithia's safe room curled around Azrael. Instead, I curled around the standard issue, rough, gray blanket, which smelled like tens of dozens of unwashed bodies and a stale stuck-in-a-cupboard stench.

I'd spent what seemed like most of the night in the dark, staring up at the ceiling. The utter silence left me alone with too many thoughts, too many regrets, too many seething emotions. All directed at Carter. To be fair, my dad should cop half my fury, since he was part of the Dominus mastermind. But there weren't enough people left in my life for me to cut any of them out.

The same beeping from last night sounded again. I untangled my legs from the stale blanket when the lock to my cell door *clanked* open. Already, I was moving to their rhythm, responding to the heavy horns and beeps as if they were voiced commands. Without the black bracelet, I doubted I'd suffer the same excruciating headaches, but I wasn't about to take any chances.

Out on the landing, I peered through the metal grille to Archon standing below, hands akimbo, looking up at me. As a high-ranking official, he was free to go wherever he chose. If only he treated me like everyone else in here, showing disinterest from a distance.

"You must be hungry."

"Do I get a shower first?"

"If you're quick. Our schedule is pinched."

What do you want from me? Did he plan on standing there while I had a shower? As if reading my thoughts, he said, "I'll be back in ten minutes," turned on his heels, and marched out of my cell block. Ten minutes. I scooted to the showers, stripping as I went. In the chute waited more clean overalls, so I trod all over the ones I'd worn then used them after the shower as a bathmat to keep my feet dry. When I left the shower room, Archon returned. I was sure I'd been quicker than ten minutes.

To hide my awkwardness, I asked, "Will I be eating with everyone else?"

"In the dining hall, yes."

Another night on my own and I craved to talk to someone other than my incarcerator. I'd hopefully get a chance to learn more about this world, especially the provinces and what it was really like in here. Maybe someone would know where they sent the children.

"How long do I get to eat?"

"Long enough, if you don't dawdle."

End of discussion, he swiveled and led me out the door.

The babble of chatter from the dining hall could be heard from this side of the door. Keen as I was to meet other people who resisted the senate, my steps slowed alongside Archon as we neared. The last thing I wanted were a dozen questions focused on me. Archon stopped before the door and turned to face me.

"Word of advice. Keep quiet about your true identity." This was the first time he admitted any knowledge about me. Needing to know how much of my history he knew, I held his eyes, a silent inquisition.

Quirked eyebrows, he said, "I thought you were hungry."

"What is my true identity?"

"I would love to hear it from your perspective."

"You must have everything logged on some database somewhere." *How do you know my name?*

"Not the important things."

Such as? The extended quiet became uncomfortable.

"Still mistrustful. That's to be expected." His one step toward me upped my heartbeat. "No matter. All in good time." Halfway through turning to the door, he stopped and faced me again. "One thing I would like you to tell me very soon is the whereabouts of your father."

All the saliva in my mouth dried.

"The location of your mother and brother would also be handy, your brother more than your mother."

I took a step backward, needing a chasm of distance before I could school myself into controlled neutrality. Archon allowed me no space at all, following in my wake to eat any distance I created. A jerk of his arm and the vice of his fingers locked mine in place.

"It will make things easier. But it's your choice how I am to proceed." No more Mr. Nice Guy. This was him, the real him. No more Set falsity wrapped in treacle.

Wrist released, he swept his arm sideways in an elaborate gesture of welcome. "Your breakfast is getting cold."

Not waiting for me to lead the way, Archon strode through into the dining hall and up the center of the benches arranged in neat rows, heading for the front of the small queue.

I melted under everyone's gaze. Scurrying behind gave me little time to look around. As I passed, my eyes landed on the faces closest to the aisle to see hungry, curious, suspicious eyes gobbling me up as we soldiered past.

"Grab a plate from here." Archon pointed to a stack in a metal cradle at the bottom of a chute. The plate felt warm in my hands.

At the end of the two-person queue, a woman dished food onto offered plates. In front of her was a large pot on a metal trolley.

"I'll give you half an hour to finish your breakfast," Archon instructed before leaving me alone. I stared at his back, his strides forceful as he pounded back down the room. In a roomful of strangers, aliens, I should panic about now. Instead, with every step Archon made away from me, the tightness in my chest eased. I was finally amongst the right sort of people. Being with Archon, his personal attention, made me feel dirty, like I had betrayed Jax and the team.

I hate you. If only I could say it to his face.

The grafter lied to me. He used his factional nature to get me on that table without complaint. He turned me into a puppet, manipulated my emotions, much as Archon had done in the lift. Set were deadly, worse than all the other factional natures put together, to bend someone's will to their choosing, to control another's emotions as he'd done. It was the most personal violation.

With Archon gone, the chatter in the room resumed. I was forgotten. The person in front of me shuffled ahead one space, holding out his plate. The serving lady dolloped a ladle full of what looked like scrambled egg onto his plate.

When it was my turn to offer my plate, the serving lady's eyes skimmed my face for a brief moment before she hefted the same-sized pyramid onto my plate. The food had no smell and looked dry, but I was hungry enough I was bound to eat it. I withdrew my plate and turned to go.

"This might come in handy," she said with a voice sounding like she smoked two packs of cigarettes a day. In her hand was a spoon of sorts, broader and flatter for big mouths.

"Thanks." Being polite earned me an amused expression.

Two rows down, a man waved me over with an encouraging smile. One quick skim around the room showed there were few spaces left and no one else welcoming me. What did I have to lose? And I wanted to ask questions.

The moment I slid myself along the cold metal seat, the man who waved me over held out his hand. "Jerome." His beefy, clammy hand enveloped mine. With a neck as wide as his head, he looked like a pole stuffed in overalls with a face drawn on the front.

"Sable."

"Special treatment, ah. None of us got a personal introduction to the dining hall." He winked at me as he shoveled a spoonful of scrambled egg into his mouth. My neck heated. The heat then inched its way up into my cheeks. The last thing I wanted was for anyone here to think Archon thought me special. That was bound to isolate me from the prisoners. No one wanted to befriend the eyes and ears of their jailers. "It's rare the likes of him come into the dining hall."

"What does the *likes of him* mean?"

"The guy runs the place."

Just great. That was the last thing I wanted to hear. "Maybe he doesn't trust me to get myself here."

"They don't trust any of us." His bald head revealed the tattoo of Perun behind his ear. With his next mouthful, he exposed the underside of his wrist, showing me his graft. Seeing where my eyes fell, he said, "Got this soon after I arrived here. That's how much they trust us. Caught in the sweep, I was."

The man beside him extended his hand toward me. "Fethon. All trades merchant. They caught up with me at one of the outer stations. The senate had placed sweepers there some months back after there was a noticeable discrepancy between the cargo in my wagon and what was recorded on loading." By the way his face twisted up in disgust, I'd expect him to spit on the floor if we'd been anywhere else but the dining hall.

Outer station? I wasn't about to ask. I'd have to listen well and catalogue a map of all the names I learned for future reference.

"How 'bout you?" Jerome asked.

Seemed initiation into life at the compound involved sharing your capture story.

"The fringe. There was a sweep a few days back. I was one of the unlucky ones."

Jerome and Fethon nodded their understanding. In contrast to Jerome, Fethon looked as though he stuck his finger in a power socket with all his wild, stringy hair. Given his skin looked like crinkled parchment from a long-lost scroll, I'd say the outer station was in the desert or close to it, and he spent all his time sucking up the rays. His wild hair hid his tattoo.

"I was running supplies for the mines when they caught me," the guy sitting on my right said. "Ishren." His long hair was tied behind in a thin plait, and his goatee and mustache were trimmed neat. My height while sitting, he had to be a small man, wiry, with shaped, clean nails and pianist long fingers. He'd shaved his hair around his tattoo to ensure everyone saw the symbol of the family he belonged to. Phonus.

"Where does everyone else come from?"

"Mostly the fringe or the transition zone."

Another name I'd have to remember. It sounded like the place bordering Califax and the provinces.

"How long have you all been here?"

Jerome shrugged. "Weeks, months. Long enough."

"I was told most stayed a short time."

All three made their own sort of derisive noise.

"Had to be one of the intake crew. They love to see us suffer," Fethon said.

"It was Archon."

I got their full attention for saying that.

"He gave you his first name?" Fethon said.

Careful. Too many of those slipups and no one would want to talk to me. I could lie, say I overheard his name called by someone else. No good would come from lies, so I kept my mouth shut.

"You know what I think? You have or know something they want to have or know," Jerome said.

"I couldn't think what." *My family.* "Besides, why would they put me in with everyone else if they wanted to break me?"

"Reasonable question," Fethon said.

Jerome leaned across the table, casting a not so subtle glance around first before he spoke. "You're a part of the rebellion." He sat back, looking like he just convinced himself. "Either that or you have intimate knowledge of who's involved. Looks like intake area is a little biased against you." He motioned with his finger toward my nose and mouth.

Jesus. I forgot about my face, and only now, with the mention, I felt the faint pulse of pain. I continued the conversation as if he'd never drawn attention to my fat lip and nose. "You know of the rebellion?" Which rebellion was he referring to? Carter and Dad? Or was there another brewing separate from the Dominus plan?

"Everyone knows someone who is part of some rebellion," Ishren said, sounding dismissive.

"Aye, but have you heard of the whisperings coming from Persal province?" Jerome questioned.

"What whisperings?" Perhaps I replied too quick, sounded too eager for the information.

"Talk of an army built from people freed of their grafts."

This was it. Holden had returned to Uradra as Dad had thought. Was he successful at reversing the grafts without a high death tally, or were the people willing to risk their lives for a cause they believed in much as Holden had been?

Fethon sighed. "More rumors. Can't see how that's possible."

"Doesn't sound right to me either," Ishren said.

I'd forgotten my breakfast but took a spoonful now to save myself from having to respond. It had to be true. I knew Holden had the grafter. Dad knew Holden would return to Uradra. No way could rumors surface naming these specifics and not be true. Mum and Ajay would be there. I ate the flavorless egg, staring at the mound on my plate while my thoughts raced off on possibilities. I let myself be robbed of destruction. My hands clenched around my spoon. If destruction was still a part of me, I'd end this charade, pull down this compound, and go to Uradra to rescue Mum and Ajay. I'd beg Holden to at least return them home. He owed both Dad and me that. But Archon had seen to it I would never be able to free my family.

My hand clenched around the spoon. Lies, lies, I'd drowned in them, lost my ability to make the decisions I would choose to make. Instead, I'd willingly allowed myself to fall for the deception of Archon and Martimon. And now I was Archon's puppet. Jax would've known straight away what Archon was capable of, never believing a word that crossed his lips. He would've fought, not climbed on the table like I did, nor offered his wrist up with resignation to be grafted, not like I'd done. How many times would I fail him, fail them all?

I couldn't help them anymore. Never would I be a part of their team, fight on their side. Separated, permanently. I asked to be tattooed Aris so this would never happen. And now I was grafted, there was no greater separation. Not only was I separated from Jax, I was separated from myself, carved down the middle so that one part of me sank deep within, severing me in half.

I didn't stay long, locked in my dark pit, when a question formed in my mind. *How did Archon know about Mum and Ajay?* With my hair analysis, he'd know I was Nixon's daughter, but how could he possibly know about Dad's life on earth? The same way he knew my name, which would also not be found with hair analysis. He'd been told.

"How long have you guys been here?"

"Plenty of time for them to conduct their experiments," Fethon said.

"Experiments!" *Jesus.*

"Don't worry. It doesn't hurt. Not always. Sometimes, you're left feeling a bit groggy for a few days. Your memory slips as well. Most of it will come back. But some have lapses that are permanent," Ishren explained around a mouthful of egg.

"What memory, short term or long term?" The panic was there for them to hear.

"Short mostly. But some don't remember patches of their childhood either," Jerome said.

I didn't want to forget Mum or Ajay or anything that happened to get me here. "They're trying to scrub our memories?"

Jerome snorted a hard laugh. "If they are, they're doing an awful job. Nah, they're trying to achieve something else, and temporal or partial memory lose is the byproduct. All speculation, mind you. I've got no proof. No one can guess what they're up to."

Ishren slapped me on the back like I was one of the boys. "Cheer up. No one's died, as far as we can see."

This was the mysterious *other things* that needed doing Archon had referred to. "Two children were taken with me. Do you know where they go?"

"It's not right they take the children," Ishren said.

"Nobody can say. They're never seen again. Not by their parents. This gives rise to some of the rumors about the experiments. A not so vocal few think they're trying to work out how to strip the memories of the children. With a blank slate, they can assure the children will remain loyal citizens to Califax. But they obviously haven't succeeded, seeing as they're still experimenting on us," Jerome said.

I was an Aris, according to my tattoo, so it would be reasonable I should know nothing of the Persal province, which meant it should not be weird, me asking subtle directions. "I've never left the fringe. How do you move through the desert to the outer provinces?"

No one seemed to find that a peculiar question. "You catch a lift if you can," Jerome replied. "Some merchants are willing to ferry people as well as cargo. Though none will take you from the city into the provinces without a pass. If you've been in here, you won't get yourself a pass; that's for sure." He glanced at my wrist. "The senate will monitor your movement once they give you a cephulet."

"There's no way someone can tamper with the cephulet to ensure it gives a false report?"

Jerome smiled to himself as he munched on his mouthful. Fethon leaned across the table, waving his spoon at me. "You're going to get yourself in deep trouble with thoughts like that."

I focused on my food again.

"Once it's on you, it's on you. That's what I hear," Ishren said. "You can't take it off. They do something to it so that any attempt to remove it does something to your brain. Messes it up real bad." He scooped in another mouthful.

Jesus. Was there no end to the senate's cage? I could barely breathe with the suffocation in knowing all the ways Archon chained me. This was why the people fought to free themselves from their grafts. This was why I would do the same.

"But I love your spirit, girl. None of us are hero material. We can't help you with these ideas you're having," Ishren continued.

"Is there anyone here who could?"

Chapter 27

POUNDING of boots on concrete drew me away from my half-eaten breakfast. Behind, six sweepers entered wearing no shields, because none of us here were that sort of a threat. They still carried their weapons, which probably meant some of the prisoners rallied against the reeducation process.

Islia's tattoo, now a disjointed mess, reminded me of who I was—one of the grafted. When Islia had asked me what I wanted for my grafted tattoo, I'd thought of what Jax had said the first time he'd shown me his tattoo in the lift on the way up to the top of the Adolphy Tower. To him, the graft tattoo was a sign of enslavement, and so I asked Islia to tattoo a series of chain links. At the time, the image held no real significance. It was only now that the tattoo had been destroyed did I feel chained.

My three new friends set their utensils down and rose from the table. Around me, the noise of scraping chairs followed the rest of the prisoners as they too left their places and filed out of the rows toward the exit, passing the line of sweepers who formed a guard at the door.

I wasn't sure what was expected of me, so I followed everyone else. Shuffling forward in the group, I spied women amongst the predominately male crowd. Like everyone else, they weren't looking at me. I'd become another number, one more captive and now recruit to the senate's freedom eradication program and propaganda.

Picking up my pace, I moved closer to Jerome as the crowd slowed to funnel through the doors. "What's going on?"

"Exercise time."

"What does that entail?"

"Depends on the weather. If the storms are blowing, we're forced inside. They'll send us to the velodrome. If the weather's good, we'll lap the compound until we drop."

"Storms? It looks pretty dry out there. I didn't think there would be storms."

"Not storms that bring showers. I'm talking about dust storms. Ferocious things, they are. If you get caught in one, it will cut you to pieces."

Something to remember. If I ever did manage to escape. Not only would I have to deal with the life-sucking heat with no shade, but I would also have to deal with dust storms.

"How often are there dust storms?"

"Often enough to force us inside a lot of the time." Jerome shrugged. "Or maybe that's just what they tell us to keep us in. Seeing the sun, smelling the fresh air, even if it's full of dust, gives us hope. It saves us from feeling caged and keeps us believing there is another life outside the compound and that we'll be living it real soon." The closer we came to the exit and the guard of sweepers, the lower Jerome's voice dropped. "They don't like that much. Hope fosters resistance, and they want to wipe that from our psyche."

Outside the dining hall, the prisoners filed off to the left, not needing any prompt from the sweepers, moving as one. Not seeing Archon—he said he would give me half an hour before he came and got me—I followed, sandwiched between Jerome and Fethon. Ahead, the prisoners were parting around an obstacle, which turned into a sweeper standing in the middle of the corridor. His eyes scanned over everyone as they passed. When we neared, those flat gray eyes fell on me, and that's where they stayed. After eyeing my approach, he jabbed a finger my way before I split with the rest to move around him. "You're coming with me."

I glanced at Jerome, but he was already on his way past the sweeper, as was Fethon and Ishren, leaving the sweeper and me as an island amongst the moving sea of prisoners.

"You will follow me."

By now, a few stragglers were left. The sweeper ignored them and set off at a brisk pace, expecting me to keep up. We headed in the opposite direction. The last prisoners at the back of the line stared at the two of us passing, open curiosity to why I should be so special. Amongst them, there may be those who would be willing to help me with my *spirited* ideas. I watched them back for the microseconds I had, asking questions in my head. Would any of these people be willing to take the risk and escape with me?

These people were all grafted, as was I. We were helpless. But the thought of giving in made me feel mummified, suffocated under the binds of the senate. If I wanted to get out, I needed to recruit others to help. Maybe everyone in this place had been broken—they moved about as if they were—but I had to try. At times like this, destruction would be thrashing beneath my skin, a constant reminder of my potential, who I was, and what it meant. Who was I now? Nothing. The same girl I was months ago when Dad was taken from us, leaving us struggling to pay our rent. I didn't want to be that girl anymore. I wasn't special with destruction, but I had choices. I could save Mum and Ajay. There was nothing I could do now. *Damn you, Archon.* He was going to cage me. The senate would not tame me.

There were no distinguishing features to guide me from one corridor to the next, one level to the next. I didn't need to ask the sweeper where we were going. He stopped at a door, Archon's office door, skimming his eyes over the top of my head like I wasn't there. I took that to mean I was to go inside. The *hiss* of the opening door, without his prompting, confirmed it. Archon was waiting.

Archon sat behind his desk, an illuminated display of what looked like data in front of him. He looked through the scrolling data to me. In an instant, the image disappeared, and he rose from his chair. "Breakfast was to your liking, I hope. You made some friends, I see."

Them watching us didn't surprise me. "I'm a gregarious person. Was I meant to sit on my own?"

"Friends are encouraged. These are bonds that may stay with you once you are released. It makes integration back into society run smoothly."

"Then why am I not exercising with everyone else?"

"That is not on your schedule for this morning. You have plenty of time to further your friendships."

Did they want to experiment on me?

"Sit, please." He motioned to the chair I sat in yesterday.

Once I slumped into the seat, he wove back around his desk and relaxed into his comfortable-looking chair. I blinked once then stared as the back of the chair outlined the contours of his body like it was snuggling him close. One mental shakeup drew me back to more important things.

I was not going to play his games. "The men I spoke to at breakfast mentioned experiments."

He huffed to himself. "I suspected the conversation would come up soon enough."

"It's true then?"

"We prefer the word trials." He eased farther back. "The grafts are an effective but outdated technology. Over time, our understanding of the way our biosystems work has improved. It stands to reason we would continue to study, develop, and implement the latest technical advances for the betterment of our people."

Weird way to put it, but biosystems had to mean the body. He made it sound positive, improving their understanding of the body for the betterment of the people, but really he meant improving their understanding of people's factional natures and how to suppress them.

"The grafts were a great advance at the time, but their effectiveness is decreasing over time. Plus, there were and still are implementation limitations."

Meaning many in the fringe or outer regions were missed. And what did he mean by the graft's effectiveness decreasing over time? Were people becoming immune?

"We're in the process of researching different ways of producing the same outcome without the need for grafts, less evasive technologies that are easier to administer."

He made everything sound harmless and reasonable. The research was driven by the senate's need to maintain their rule. I did not for one moment believe any altruism on their behalf to make living together harmonious. It was the outcome, sure. But now that destruction and I were separated, I wanted back the part of myself that made me a better, stronger person, the part that meant no one could cage me. Holden was driven by his belief in everyone's right to be whole. Stuck in this compound, listening to the insincerities preached by Archon, I sided with Holden. After what he'd done, I never thought I would feel that way. But the senate had no right to graft me against my will, not while they were willing to avoid the same measures for themselves and other key people who helped keep them where they wanted to be.

"Am I here in your office rather than joining everyone else because you're putting me in the trials?"

"It's a great opportunity."

"For who?"

Archon bowed his head. I caught the sly smile.

"I'm impressed by you," he said once he resurfaced from his private chuckle. "Few are so forthright. Are all your people like this?"

This was the first time he directly admitted knowing my citizen status, namely alien.

"I should very much like to meet more of your kind."

"But the senate forbids dimensional shifts. Is that right?"

"For now. But you, Sable, may change their minds."

"How?"

"Once we see what you're capable of."

Jesus, what was he saying? "No more special than anyone in your world." They could not be thinking of invading earth to gather innocents to trial in their laboratories like rats. "There are few people like me in my world."

"I know someone who would refute such a claim."

The saliva dried in my mouth, gluing my lips together.

Archon's gaze skimmed over my head to the doorway. I'd not heard the *hiss* of the door opening, but someone caught his attention. "Isn't that right?" He spoke to whomever else had entered.

I turned. Carter advanced into the room, and all I could do was watch him while a hot, black anger boiled through my blood, turning it lava. At the sight of Carter, I craved violence. If destruction were still a part of me, it would be making its way along his neural pathways by now, severing every connection his brain made. I would destroy him as eagerly as he'd chosen to destroy my family, and there would be no remorse for what I'd done afterward.

I followed every step he made, fed my loathing and promise his way, and now while he stood by my chair, looking down on me like the victor over the defeated, I stared up, unleashing the force of my hatred. It was just a gaze. That was all I had. *One day, Carter, one day. I promise you, I will make you pay.* This was how Archon knew my name. This was how he knew so much about me.

He swooped down and took my hand too fast for me to react. My attempt to rip my wrist from his grasp was met with pain. Carter turned my wrist over, ran his eyes over the destroyed tattoo. Again, I renewed my attempt to be free of his hold; again, he resisted, squeezing my wrist, fingers indenting deep into my skin.

"There was once a time when your freedom made you interesting. Now, your enslavement makes you valuable," he said then threw my arm back down to me.

"There will come a time when you wish you never met me." A hollow threat. It sounded pathetic coming from the girl with the tattoo binding her factional nature, making her a prisoner to the whims of people like him.

To prove the point, Carter laughed. Malicious and cold, it crept underneath my clothes, right into my heart, turning it to ice. "It seems my world has done great things to your character," he said as he strode around toward Archon. Archon responded to whatever private signal Carter made by vacating his chair for the other man. "I like this much improved personality." He seated himself. I was distracted from Carter's speech long enough to watch the chair reconfigure itself to conform to the new weight and breadth of Carter's body, snuggling him in. "If you prove yourself worthy during the trials, you shall herald in a new direction in our research."

Settled back, fingers steepled in front of him, he peered across the desk at me. Archon hovered to the side, keeping himself out of the conversation but still very much a part of the atmosphere, which was suffocating in its tension. My stomach ached with how many knots now twisted in it. My muscles ached too, because they bunched and coiled, wanting to leap me out of this chair, explode me into action. For months, I'd been trained to fight. For just as long, I'd done exactly that, in the depths of a game that gave you two options, life or death. Sitting opposite Carter, it felt as though I'd been born to fight. I could remember the ease at which I fought in Dominus the last time I'd been inside. My body remembered the moves as though I was doing them right now. My mind played without instruction, running on an instinct I only just developed. Destruction too had been a part of my fabric, working ahead of me, independently but still as one.

The memory crushed me. A heavy weight rolled over, sinking me down into the chair. Destruction was lost.

But not my hatred, not my motivation to win my freedom, to defeat Carter. I'd do it. Some way, I'd do it.

"Before we proceed, I am curious to know one thing. How did you do it? How did you win over my best?"

He was referring to Jax. I stayed mute.

"I must say, I was convinced he would let you die. I've never seen so much rage caught within one person."

Carter only knew one side of humanity. Maybe I shouldn't classify these people under the umbrella of humanity, but they thrived on the same emotions as us, and those emotions were always dualistic. Carter knew hatred and revenge, but he didn't understand compassion and love. He would see them as weak emotions, but it was because of these *weak* emotions Jax had the strength to save me. It was because of them he was defying Carter and the senate to save Alithia and Azrael. It was because of those emotions I would not give in, for Mum and Ajay, for Jax and the others, for Nada and Azrael.

"I would very much like to know where he is."

I pressed my lips into a firm line. Seeing my resistance, Carter glanced at Archon. Summoned by his silent request, Archon came around the desk toward me. I followed him with my eyes, my throat turning into a straw with the diameter of a pin head. Archon sat on the desk in front of me, and I couldn't help but stare into his crystal eyes. The lies were already forming on the many facets within. Set was coming out to play. Much like I'd done when I'd been forced to contain destruction, I fisted my hands, fingernails digging into my palms. It would likely have no impact against the power of a Set, but I would fight all the same.

"The question is made with good intentions. It is important that we find Jax and help him. From the start, he was suffering from his factional nature. It tormented him, as I am sure you well know. And his father's murder made it even harder for him to be able to control his factional nature. You know, Sable, that he is struggling, that he is in mental torment. All we wish to do is help him."

"Liar." I spat the word out then clenched my teeth. I could feel the heat in my cheeks from the effort it caused me to resist his lying lure.

But he'd been right. Jax was struggling with his factional nature. He loathed that part of himself. I couldn't stop the image of his badly beaten body the night we hid in Alithia's safe room. The agony in his words when he told me what he'd done, behind those words were pleas for my forgiveness and his need to forgive himself.

I roiled at the feel of Archon's gentle touch on my upper arm. With the sudden touch, the image of Jax was gone. In front of me was Archon, only Archon. His eyes were no longer the harsh dissecting shards of crystal I had always thought they were. They were now a multifaceted mirror opening doorways to different shades of my personality. Within, I could see the girl I had been before any of this began, before I knew my father was a murderer, before he was taken from us, back when I was innocent and thought my father would always protect me. There was another mirror that was the lonely, desolate girl who lost the man she loved the most, trusted in all ways. And yet another mirror showed the girl forced into Dominus, who now knew too much, who had killed someone. In his eyes, I saw a girl become someone powerful, someone feared, someone ripped from who she'd been. This had been her destiny. This had been Jax's destiny.

"Only you can save him, Sable."

I felt them rolling up my throat. Felt the sting of the tears, because I knew the words would flow out. "We separated at his apartment."

Archon caught the escaping tears with his finger. "Where did he go?"

This time, I shook my head violently, but it was no use. "He was heading to Aris HQ."

"What did he hope to do there?"

"Find out about Carter."

Archon did not break eye contact to look at Carter. He had me now, and doing so would weaken his hold. I tried to be the one to sever our link, but I was not strong enough.

"He never made it. No one saw him there. He must have gone elsewhere instead. You wouldn't happen to know where that would be?"

I forced myself back in my seat. "You won't win," I hissed. I wouldn't tell him.

"Sable." His words were so gentle, sounding like a warm embrace. A finger under my chin brought my face to his. "Your struggles hurt you both. They upset me too. I want to help. Everything I do is for you. All you have to do is give me the right location."

"The fringe." I folded forward, feeling like a tsunami washed through, dragging me away.

"Was he alone?"

I shook my head. It served as both a denial to answer and the answer itself.

"Who was he with?"

"What did you do with the children?"

"Yes, we did want to ask you about those. But first, you must answer my question."

"I won't."

Archon sighed. Carter launched to his feet. "Finish this," he growled.

Archon dived forward, arms spearing to the armrest on either side of my chair. I gasped, pressing backward, but he caught my eyes with his.

"Tell me," he demanded on a deep growl.

"Elva and two other recruits" came out between clenched teeth.

"And did he introduce you to anyone while you were in the fringe?"

"A woman."

"Make her speak," Carter growled from behind him. I couldn't escape the bond of Archon's gaze to look at Carter.

"Be specific," Archon said.

"Alithia."

Archon sat back, jerking his head over his shoulder to Carter.

"Have someone look into it," Carter commanded.

With Archon diverted, I launched forward off the chair. I had no plan in mind, just to escape Archon's toxic enchantment, stem the flow of my traitorous mouth. What evil had I brought down upon Alithia by revealing her name? She'd been born within Califax to respectable parents, which meant her name would be held within the senate's database on its citizens. How easy would it be for them to track her down? How easy would it be for them to make the connections between Jax's father, Jax, and Alithia?

Archon moved faster than I expected. He grasped my shoulders and threw me backward into the chair with such force the chair went over, me with it. The wind punched out of my chest as I hit the floor.

I rolled to the side, diving deep for destruction in a nanosecond before I remembered it was no longer a part of me. Footsteps sounded as Archon approached. His shoes came into view, stopping short of my face. Behind me, Carter had also come close, no doubt to pick over what was left of his catch. I heard a rustle of fabric, and then he spoke close behind me, which had to have meant he crouched down, as if wanting to make this intimate.

"Now, you will ask her to tell us where the grafter is."

Chapter 28

MARTIMON WAITED FOR ME, grandfatherly smile welcoming me onto the trolley table. I knew his lies; he knew I knew, and he didn't care. Like destruction would've become a part of me, Set was a part of him, the greater part it seemed. His smile, which had seemed kind and generous the day before, now looked smug, because he knew what he was capable of and what I was no longer capable of, thanks to his Set trickery yesterday. This was not the benevolent smile of a kindly helper—more the smile of a man who believed himself superior. And the fact that I was here meant Archon and Carter wanted me to start the *trials*, whatever that meant.

Neither had bothered to bring me here; instead, they signaled a sweeper—that was after Archon had me give up the location of the grafter. And it hadn't been easy. I'd fought him all the way, discovering that if I hurt myself, it helped me stay focused, sealed my lips, enough to force Carter to kick the back of the chair and swear in frustration at my resistance. Archon, though—creepy in his intensity—found my resistance intriguing, if his look was any indication. From his quizzical brow raise to the slow twitch of a sly smile, he found me a worthy toy. It seemed few, if any, people were able to disobey a Set's evil beguilement. It hadn't lasted. Archon had won through. Biting my inner cheek until the metallic taste filled my mouth then switching to gouging small bloody grooves into the soft skin at the base of the collar at my neck helped me fight the initial gentle commands. His words had become more intense, ringing through my ears, ripping through my brain, an aggressive recital of what he wanted me to surrender. And I'd done it, caved to his voice. The horror I felt as I heard the name coming out of my mouth.

The sweeper deposited me at the door and left without saying a word, the door hissing behind him.

"Lie down on the table." That was Martimon's welcoming words this time around.

I complied, but not because of his bewitching Set words. I complied, because to refuse was to delay the inevitable, and I wanted to be away from him as soon as possible, away back with the others, so I might learn as much as I could about the desert and how I could get out of here.

Destruction may no longer have been a part of me, but I was not going to accept this fate, not if this fate meant I would be forced to join society, an alien society, as someone I was not; there was no going back when you knew too much. Never, never would I allow Mum and Ajay to suffer this life, to live controlled as they would. And what if the senate forbade us from assimilating into this world? We were aliens, after all. The senate would not want the people to be seduced by the possibility of leaving this world. Would that mean we would be locked away for good?

I lay back on the trolley bed and stared at the ceiling, resisting the urge to turn my head and see what Martimon was clanking onto the cart beside me.

"Cooperation is in your best interests. The procedure will progress quickly and painlessly if you comply with my requests. I will be forced to take certain measures if you do not cooperate."

"I'm lying down, aren't I?"

Standing at my head, he paused for a moment, bending over so his beady eyes could peer all over my face. From this angle, his cheeks became jowls, loose flesh drooping toward the bed. How did I see him as Santa Claus? Crowding me as he was, the strong astringent smell, like fruit left to ferment longer than required, flowing from his breath and pores reduced my breathing to tiny inhales.

He placed small discs at my brow and temples, much like the ones I had worn when playing Dominus, the ones Jax said connected to my neural pathways and dictated the way I saw reality in the game. They also read my brainwaves and body, collecting information on the use of my factional nature, my physical and mental health, and a myriad of other useful data I was sure they would gather and study during these trials.

Discs on my head, he moved farther down my body, strapping my arms then my legs to the bed. Feeling helpless like this, I couldn't help but delve inside, looking for destruction, and found nothing, which turned into a hollowness so profound it felt like I was crumbling into the bed. Destruction was the essence of me. That's what it felt like right now, when I needed it so much. I was cast outside myself, a stranger in this body.

It's not true. I had to remember that. I was someone before I knew about my factional nature. And now I had to become someone better, more resourceful, cunning, and determined. Isn't that what Jax instructed me to do the instant before he jumped from the Adolphy Tower? With no superpowers to help me in a world full of them, I would have to do as I was—for Mum and Ajay's sake.

"How long will this take?"

"You needn't worry. You will not remember the passage of time."

"You won't take any of my memories, will you?"

"It's not our intention to remove your memories. It is an unfortunate side effect. For most, it is temporary. Relax during the procedure, and all will be well."

"Will you tell me what you're going to do?"

"It's a very complex and detailed study. Something you will perhaps not understand. But we are just gathering our knowledge, broadening our understanding."

"Of factional natures and how to suppress them permanently?"

"Something like that. Now turn your head slightly to the right and fix your eyes on the corner of the ceiling."

"Why?"

"Question less and it will go smoother."

I did, finding the joint between the wall and the ceiling when he placed his hand on my temple and pressed my head down into the bed. At the same time, something sharp pierced the skin on the side of my neck, the pain just a pinprick. Minuscule but enough to make me jerk. Thanks to his hand pinning my head to the bed, I didn't move.

"I said relax, girl. You will only make it worse for yourself."

"I'd like to see how you'd react if something sharp pierced your skin when you weren't ready. What is that?"

"It's quite harmless, though vital to our study." That was all I got out of him.

An anesthetic numbness diminished the sting at the point of entry. Martimon moved in close, feathering his breath on my throat. Because the skin was numb, I felt nothing around the needle site. Beyond that, the skin felt warm and moist in a pulsing rhythm with his exhalations.

Soon, I felt a heavy sensation across my neck, but not as it would feel if someone or thing was laid across me, more from some invisible pressure within. The pressure spread a warmth along my throat, moving upward to my face, wrapping around to the back of my skull. More heat moved from my throat down into my chest. I could feel its incremental spread like a trickle of water streaming down the skin. No longer just warmth, the invisible flow heated further, and with it my arteries throbbed. I could feel them as if they were swelling to twice their normal size and forced to pump a thick sludge along through my body.

I tried to raise my arm, forgetting he strapped me down only moments ago. As with my arm, my leg flicked outward only to be hampered by the band wrapped around my ankle. With the jacking of my heart rate, the sludge bulging my arteries spread fast. Without even concentrating, I could trace the direction it traveled, how far it reached down into my toes.

What is happening? Did I say that out loud or in my head?

The room coalesced into a spinning cloud of white. I turned my head to the side, searching for Martimon—at least, I thought I turned my head to the side. Too confused, I wasn't sure what I wanted. I licked my lips, and my tongue ran over the swell, which now felt ballooned.

Someone returned to my side. I couldn't see them, because my head was in such a jumble, my mind unable to make my eyes focus. And the noise, not an audible noise but a chaotic tumbling in my head, distracting me so anything going on around me became a background tinkle. But whoever it was, I sensed their presence. Like a snake, I felt their body heat and their breath shimmying over my face. With it came a fragrance steeped in leathering oils but also mixed with the smell of sweet molasses.

I jumped when, through the fog in my brain, a hand touched my arm. The hand smoothed its way down my arm to my exposed skin and rolled my wrist over, so it faced the ceiling, revealing my tattoo.

"What is happening?" Again, I couldn't be sure if the words managed to leave my mouth. "Can someone tell me what's happening?"

Silence.

The effort of trying to turn my head was like moving a solid block of lead. Any minute, I'd perhaps go through the table and crash to the floor; such was the weight of my body.

Seeing movement in my periphery, I doubled my efforts to look, putting all my effort into inching my head to the side like it was my life-line. I felt the move like rocking on a turbulent sea, nauseating my stomach. Until finally I succeeded, feeling the cold, hard metal of the table touching my cheek. Through the haze, I stared into eyes, the gray so faint it was like someone sucked the color away, eyes churning and roaring like a wild storm.

"Sable."

I knew that voice. From Dominus? No. Contacts Jax knew? No. At what point had I heard this voice, met this man?

"I want you to tell me about yourself. I want to know everything there is to know about you. All the special things that make you unique."

My name was Sable. The questions were directed at me. He had it wrong. I wasn't unique. But the questions pulled at the back of my mind, made me think of my life, my family, everything I experienced and had seen, the ache of losing Dad, the struggle of supporting Mum, the hatred at meeting Jax. And Dominus, the fear, the rage, the feeling of being tricked, trapped then reborn anew, the loathing and addiction toward destruction.

Words spilled from my mouth. I didn't know what I was saying, just felt them moving up my throat and slipping off my tongue. A jumble perhaps incoherent, perhaps poignant and on point. I followed none of it. It spilled too fast for me to keep up. Out it poured while the hand stayed at my wrist, to soothe, encourage, or warn me to keep revealing the depths of myself.

The words seized in my mouth when an instant agony seared through my head. It stabbed, burned, brutalized my mind. My body arched off the bed, ripping out a long, throaty scream, sounding like it came from deep in my lungs. Colors swirled in front of my eyes. Gone were the images I replayed with everything I said to the mysterious man to be replaced by flashes of scolding red, and blinding white, and every mix in-between. It was like the pain had torn the images apart, leaving a disjointed jumble of colors.

A sudden pressure on my forehead seared like a branding iron. I tried to thrash my head, but the pressure held my head in place. Anymore, and it would puncture through the trolley. The touch felt cold. Either the hand had come out of an ice bath or my head was on fire. More hands reached for my wrists, also cold on my bare skin. My body was on fire. I remembered the time in the tunnel under the Dome, swimming through the fiery pool and how it felt to have my skin barbecued from my body. Was this it? Was I about to burn internally, charring from the inside out?

Someone pulled the discs from my head. The moment they were gone, the pain receded, ebbing rather than disappearing completely. My body collapsed back onto the bed, and only then did I realize how long I remained coiled, muscles tensed and fighting. Fumbling at my wrists and then ankles, and then I was released. My head lolled to the side. I felt too exhausted to do anything but sink, sink, sink, hopefully disappear into oblivion, where I could sleep for eternity.

Hands slid under my body and lifted me from the table. I was too weak to fight against it. And then I didn't want to, as I was pressed against something firm but giving, warm and smelling of life. Carried away, the gentle rhythmic rocking of my body lulled me to semi-sleep. Once or twice, my head jerked backward before I righted it again, then unable to keep my neck up anymore, I allowed my head to loll backward, arching over someone's arm. Too tired, I didn't bother to look where I was taken. If only this journey would end.

A harsh metallic ring pounded through my head, and then I was lowered onto a firm bed. When the arms released me, I curled to my side, rounding into a ball. No one touched me. I wasn't moving. I was blissfully free to fall, fall into the darkness.

Chapter 29

WHEN MY EYES OPENED, I stared ahead for a long time, orientating myself within the room. Nothing about it was familiar. Even the nose-tingling smell of menthol, which made it feel like each inhale was opening up all my airways and expanding my lungs, gave me no memories. I pushed up from the hard, thin bed and looked around me, but found each direction had the same view. This was not my cell.

I slid off the bed then swayed, my knees buckling once they hit the metal of the bedframe and sat back down. My fingers felt thick. Opening and closing them was an exercise in slow motion. It was like they'd been held in cold storage for days, thinning my veins so no blood could flow through. Repeated scrunches and the blood shot through to my fingertips, bringing with it pins and needles. That's when I noticed the same effect in my toes, prickling as though millions of needles were being jabbed into the soles.

What happened to me? The sweeper separated me from everyone else after breakfast. I remembered watching Jerome's back as he skirted around the sweeper in the corridor and kept on his way. A wave of them, casting fleeting glances while they flowed around the two of us like rushing water around an obstruction in a stream, that was my last memory. Memory loss could only mean one thing. I'd been forced into one of their experiments.

And the rest of my memories? Jax, Elva, the team, Dad in prison, destroying the Amex, Holden betraying me, Alithia, Nada, and Azrael. They had the children. I sagged where I stood, the exhale of relief caving me forward. The important memories were still there. Was it intentional to wipe out everything from the experiment, or was this an unavoidable outcome?

I was still staring at my feet, wiggling my toes within my boots, when the door *hissed* open. On seeing Archon's face, an image cut through my mind. Filling my mind's eye, dark lashes, crystalline eyes, silent echoes of demands calling out hidden secrets. His eyes did that to me, always made me feel anatomized. Knowing he was an ungrafted Set was perhaps most of the reason I saw sharp-bladed lies in his gaze.

"You look rested."

"What did you do?"

"Nothing harmful or permanent." He came close, standing as someone would who knew you well, not intimately close, but uncomfortable enough for me. I would not take a step back. I would not give Archon the satisfaction of knowing his effect on me. Every action full of provocation, every look full of scrutiny. He wanted to shred me, layer by layer, deep down into the ticking beat of me so he could understand how to twist me, how to make me cry, scream, or plead. Benevolent words shared from a poisonous heart. Was that the gift of Set?

For the first time since meeting him, his eyes dipped down the length of my body, a look used to belittle someone. "I trust you feel recovered."

"When will my memories return?"

"It's hard to know. You're not like the rest."

Because I wasn't from his world.

"I'm told the similarities between your kind and mine are astounding. It explains the ease of breeding between your world and mine, even with missing loci of key genetic markers within your code. More in-depth analysis will need to be completed before we fully understand the differences."

"What experiments did you do on me? I think I have a right to know that at least."

My question surprised him. He took a moment to drill those dissecting eyes a little further into mine like he was determining the true meaning of my simple questions. "What do you remember?"

I didn't want to tell.

"I am not your enemy, Sable. I wish there was a way to make you understand."

"You're Set. I'll believe nothing you say."

"That's because you've been misguided."

"Jax sees things clearer than any of you."

"I was not referring to Jax, although your association with him has been an unfortunate mistake. But is it any wonder he is lost?" He shifted his gaze to the side, staring at the floor as he inhaled as if clearing his thoughts in preparation for what he had to say. My breath stalled, hanging on the silence. "It could not have been easy to discover his father's deceit. It would've torn his family apart."

My body turned cold, starting in my heart, frosting outward until my limbs were frozen in place.

"Everyone lies to some extent. But lies about love are an insidious breach." There was no innocence in those eyes that bored into mine. "Wouldn't you say?"

He knew. How did he know? It would mean the senate knew. For how long? Not long enough to stop Alithia and Jax's dad from having a child, which surely meant they didn't know. Was it his mum? Was she the one guilty of betraying his dad? Azrael would never have survived free as long as she had if Jax's mother was guilty of revealing the secret. It had to be someone else.

"Jax needs the right assurance and guidance now more than ever. Given what he has been through, his judgement is clouded. He is unable to make right decisions for himself or for those who have unwisely chosen to follow his rebellion."

Again, he turned his head away. His sigh sounded as though it dredged out the weight of his heart. "It was a terrible tragedy. Such violence has echoes from long ago when killing each other was akin to sport. Harmony between factions has and will always be the senate's only goal. The murder of Jax's family finds its precedence in pre-graft days."

Everything he said fogged my brain. His words become chatter, filling the quiet while my mind swirled inward, spiraling and spiraling until it felt as though it was being flung apart. Or trapped within the Adolphy maze. Each struggling thought showed the same path, any new ideas nothing but dead ends.

"Of course, your father will be trialed according to our laws."

Palms pressing to the sides of my head did nothing to free my mind. A pain hatched at the center of my brain, throbbing to existence. I felt hollow, insubstantial; one gust, and I'd topple.

I jumped with Archon's touch. "Do you feel all right?"

"I don't."

"Perhaps I should take you to the medic. There could be side effects we are yet to understand, given your genetic makeup."

"I don't want to go anywhere with you."

He lowered his hand. The lower it got, the wider his smile grew. "But you already have. And you will again. You'll follow me to the very end."

Now was not the time to pretend he didn't frighten me. He reached for me, but I stepped away, step, step, step, until the *hiss* of the door made me spin. Spinning unsettled my balance, my head still mucked up from whatever they had done to me. Hands at my waist brought my equilibrium back, but I fought against his intimate touch, lurching myself free from his steadying hold.

"She needs to eat," was all Archon said as he moved past the sweeper and out the door, trailing the remnants of a voice devoid of compassion.

Eat? No, thanks. But my stomach indicated otherwise once it heard the magic word. The sweeper spun and marched out, pausing at the door to ensure I followed. He waited for me to lead the way then smacked along behind, occasionally scuffing my heels if I lagged my feet. My head felt like it was attached to my body by string, which allowed it to bob about on my shoulders like a tethered balloon.

Was it lunchtime the same day? Maybe dinner… or breakfast time the day after? Trying to work that out took me the entire walk to the dining hall.

The doors opened to a rowdy room of prisoners already eating. A wave of the sweeper's weapon at the doorway ushered me into the dining hall. The room was full, the air thick with body odor and the rich aroma of roasted fatty meat slathered with spices. I hovered in the entrance, my head going light, my vision wavering for a flash, until my stomach's churning, driven by the delicious smell, grounded me back in place. The hush was brief. Being no one new now, the chatter resumed soon after as everyone dismissed me.

My eyes scanned the rows for my friends. Through a gap between two men sitting on the nearest row of bench seats, I spied the long plait of Ishren. Rather than head to the front for a plate of food, I squeezed along the aisle toward him. Fethon sat next to him and Jerome across from him.

Jerome saw me first, eyes widening a fraction before he said something to the other two. Both turned; on seeing me, Fethon scooted over, saying something to the man on his other side, making him shuffle along so both Ishren and Fethon could create space between them for me. I sat heavily, feeling like I'd only just made it into my place before a dark wave swallowed me up.

"They got to you, didn't they?" Jerome asked, dropping the bone he was holding back onto his plate.

"Your face is whiter than our plates," Fethon said. "You need something to eat. It will make you feel better. You wait here." He pushed to his feet and headed back through the row then up to the front of the dining hall.

"I don't remember what happened." I sounded panicked.

"It happens," Jerome said, his tone like a shrug. "You got all your other memories?"

"Everything, right up until I left you guys in the corridor. What time is it?"

"Dinnertime same day. I s'pose you've been out for the whole of today. That happens too. Don't worry. You'll feel fine after some food."

I glanced at his plate piled high with hunks of meat and bone. Beside me, Ishren had half the serving size plus some added greens, which looked like chopped spinach or seaweed. I covered my mouth, not knowing if the gurgle in my stomach was hunger or the threat I was about to throw up. The pain that hatched in the center of my brain had not gone away, and now I felt a tingle running down my arms. Not running, sprinting, moving so fast my skin should be turning red or catching fire with the friction. I pulled the sleeve up on my left arm to take a look, amazed the skin remained pale.

"You sure you're doing all right?" Ishren said, staring down at my forearm to see what it was I fixated on.

"Am I supposed to feel bodily effects?"

"Like what?" they chimed in unison.

"Headaches."

"Maybe," Jerome said. "I've never had a problem, but a few have mentioned something like that."

"How about tingles on my arms?"

"Never heard of that," Ishren replied.

"Maybe it's nothing."

Fethon returned carrying a plate stacked high with meat. Bone stuck out from between the meaty layers, along with gristle and a healthy dose of a rich, thick gravy, which added depth to the smell. The gurgle most definitely turned into a cry of hunger as the spiral of steam wafted up my nose once Fethon set the plate down in front of me. "The meat's a bit tough, but I doused it in plenty of sauce, so you shouldn't notice overly. Make sure you eat it all. Get some color back in them pale cheeks of yours. Looks like you could do with a decent feed as well. I know meat can be a rare commodity in the fringe for some."

I didn't bother to reply, spearing the fork he'd brought back with him, which looked like a miniature trident with its deep-grooved prongs, into the topmost layer and hefted a chunk into my mouth. Suddenly, I was starving. Perhaps that was why I felt so lightheaded. The flavor of the meat was strong, stronger than our usual meat back home. I'd never tried game meat, but the flavor was likely closer to that than cow. And it was good. So good, I speared another large hunk and tore a mouthful away. Sauce dribbled down my chin to drip to the plate, and I didn't bother to clean it away.

"You still thinking those dangerous thoughts?"

I'd been too interested in my food to notice Jerome had leaned across the table. His elbows rested either side of his plate, his head ducked in a conspiratorial whisper. The other two had also moved close giving the discussion an intimate and dangerous feel.

I lowered my fork. He took that as an invite to keep talking. A quick look either side of himself and he continued. "Made a few enquires—"

"We may be able to help you out," Fethon cut in. "Didn't want to say too much this morning because…well, you can't tell who's your friend and who's your foe in this place. But we, as in us three, have been discussing things and we figured you're just what we need."

This had to be related to this morning. We'd talked, but I couldn't remember what we'd said. Introductions but that was all? "What was I saying?"

The three sat up, the eagerness in their expressions gone. Instead of replying they repeated their conspiratorial glances around them, making me follow their lead. Everyone seemed intent on their food and chattering to their neighbors rather than paying us any attention. "Nothing. Forget I said anything at all." Jerome resumed his eating. I looked to Fethon then Ishren when Jerome stared at his food.

"What were we talking about this morning? I have no memory of it. I thought I remembered everything until the sweeper took me away, but I don't remember saying anything to you that could be dangerous."

Jesus, did I mention Jax and Elva?

"You didn't, love. No one is that stupid," Fethon said, casting Jerome a frowning glance, which told me he was lying.

"Please, I know you're lying. I want to know the truth. There is enough lying done by the people who run this place. It's not going to help if we lie to each other."

The faces of all three shadowed, shutting down or feeling ashamed, I couldn't tell.

"Give it until tomorrow. If you remember everything by then, maybe we can talk," Jerome said.

I wanted to argue with him, but when I opened my mouth a lump from my stomach rushed up my throat. I slammed my lips closed, smacking my hands over my mouth as the tide rose up then receded.

Ishren touched a finger to my elbow. "You going to be all right?"

I closed my eyes as a hot wave simmered up to the top of my head. My pulse pounded through my ears. After a couple of swallows and a calming breath I removed my hand. With the settling of my stomach, the heat washed out leaving me feeling cold. My hands felt clammy against my cheeks.

"Some get effected more than others," Fethon said.

Three pairs of concerned eyes met mine when I opened my eyes. Concern, that was not good. If it happened to enough people there should be no concern. Did this mean it was only happening to me?

Too late to worry any further. My stomach turned again. Like a giant tidal wave, the contents of my stomach rolled up my throat. This time with enough force I knew closed lips and a hand over my mouth would stop nothing. I spun from the table in time as I heaved my guts out onto the floor behind me. Gasps and moans of disgust filled my ears, bench seats scraping as those around me darted to move clear. The heat rushed upon me again, as too the horrible clammy feeling, all over my body. My clothes under my overalls felt plastered to my skin. Another wave. But the damage was done the first time, so what came next was a weak watery after flow.

Coughing and swallowing my way through the after effects, I raised a shaky hand to press against my forehead. The violence of being sick triggered my headache. The dull throb turned merciless, jackhammering through my skull. Following the pounding, rippling down my neck, racing across my chest and out to the ends of my fingers, the tingles started again.

Chapter 30

MY EYES FLUTTERED OPEN. The light was too bright, so I slammed them closed again. My stomach felt raw. How many times had I lost everything in my stomach? In front of everyone. At least that was something I did remember from yesterday. It had been yesterday, right? I'd not blacked out again, surely, losing yet more days, more of my memory?

I remembered two sweepers descending on me, hitching me under my armpits and dragging me out of the dining hall. It would be a mercy to forget the faces of the prisoners as they dragged me down the aisle between the rows, everyone craning to have a good look. Residual saliva dripped from my mouth while my clothes clung to my clammy body and my hair to my forehead.

They wanted to take me back to the medical room, back to Martimon, but I protested, attempting to right myself in their arms so I could walk on my own. At one point, Archon intercepted us, his usual cool charm in place. Had he been watching from through the glass paneling overlooking the dining hall? Maybe they monitored the prisoners with higher tech surveillance. He'd seen; they'd all seen, and this would have me back on the trolley table, Martimon anticipating another shot at experimenting on me.

"I feel fine. I just need to lie down in my room," I told him.

His eyes meandered down the splash marks from my vomit on the front of my drab uniform, then to the moisture on my lips, the sweat caking my hair to my forehead. I wrenched myself out of the sweepers' hold and wiped my mouth using the back of my sleeve.

"Leave us." Archon motioned with his head, sending them in the other direction. Archon waited, eyes on the backs of the sweepers. Once their heavy smacking boots receded, his eyes moved back to me. "What triggered this?" *This ugly display* were the words used in his expression.

"Maybe you should ask the people who run your experiments."

"Did you manage to eat anything?"

"Why is that important?"

"You'll feel a lot better once you do."

I remembered asking myself if he *was* really concerned about that. "What I ate is being cleaned off the floor as we speak."

His nose and top lip crinkled—subtle, but I saw it. The idea made him squirm.

"I just want to go to bed. I'm not too bad now, and I'll feel better after I sleep."

"It's likely a minor aberration due to your biosystemic structure. It is something we'll have to study in greater detail."

"Does that mean more experiments?"

Archon had signaled for me to go in front. As I passed him, he said, "We've only just begun."

My mouth tasted like I'd eaten rotten meat. My body smelled like I'd never washed. I swung up, putting my feet on the floor, and my door *hissed* open. At the railing, I looked down to an empty cellblock. Good, Archon wasn't lurking.

I hurried down the stairs and beelined for the showers. As was the way, a new set of clothes waited for me in the chute. I undressed and took a whiff of the clothes I arrived in, the ones I kept on under my uniform. As expected, they stunk of sweat. Leaving them in the pile along with my worn uniform, I stepped onto the plate that started the water flow. Maybe it was time to ditch my clothes and just wear the gray scrubs.

I lathered myself hard, scrubbing my hair and body with the liquid that came out of the dispenser on the back wall of the shower. Soon, I became buried in a foaming lather, smelling of chalk and flowers. I arched my head back and filled my mouth with water, swilled, then spat, repeating a few times. Skin pink, I placed my hands on the wall, head bowed, allowing the hot spray to rain down my back. The needle jabs of the water massaged along my spine, soothing and hard, so hard it felt like they were penetrating through my skin and into my body. But it wasn't just on my back. The needle-jabs were hammering at my chest, the part of my body protected from the spray by the curve of my body.

I pushed away from the wall, stepped off the plate, and stood staring down at my naked body. Now that I was no longer under the hard jets, I felt the sensation within, a seething, restless motion punctured by jabs pricking at my skin as if something inside wanted out. My concentration on it now, the intensity built, racing around the top half of my body, churning my stomach into wanting to heave once more.

I slammed my palms together. Just like closing a circuit, the wild motion took flight across the link formed by my hands. My heart staccatoed a heavy beat, *bam, bam*, as if it had no ribcage to keep it in.

I closed my eyes and pressed my fisted hands to my temple. The energy was so great I could practically feel it penetrating from my hands to my skull. Slowly, I lowered my hands to my lips and kissed the knot of knuckles, felt the tremor on my lips, felt the current flooding below the skin, felt the tickle of tears in my eyes.

Destruction was back.

Somehow, it had burst through the control of the graft. This had to be related to the experiment. The grafter had done its job initially, but whatever they had done lessoned the grafter's effect. This had to be an abnormality in the experiment and something that had only happened to me, or the experiments would've been stopped, surely, if everyone's grafts were made redundant as a result.

Destruction was back, and as much as my joy was bursting to overload, I had to keep it a secret. This was my advantage, and I would find the greatest joy turning it on Archon.

I swiped the towel from the recess in the wall and used little care drying myself. There were places still damp, but I dumped the towel and climbed back into my clothes, my arrival clothes, and then the uniform. I had the edge that would get me out of this place, and I meant to do it in my normal clothes. Their sweaty stink was like the best perfume, because it came from me. The smell was my body, now strong and capable, and not the antiseptic odor of gray scrubs they forced me to wear.

Whatever I did from now on, I had to do with care. No mistakes, no accidental slipups with destruction. They must never know. *Never, ever, know.* This was my only chance to escape and find Mum and Ajay. I slowed for a moment, head bowed as the reality washed over me. I was one of them again. I was like Jax and Elva and all the rest. I was back amongst them again, not physically, but I could be a weapon. I could do what they needed me to. Azrael and Nada were prisoners of the senate because of me, and now I could undo what I had done.

I left the shower area and found the door to the cellblock open. I headed out into the corridor and found it empty. Forward was the only way I could go, right to the lifts. They too opened as I neared. Were they following me through surveillance cameras, some sensitivity to footprints on the floor, heat sensors through the walls? Big questions I needed answered if I hoped to prevent every move I made being monitored.

The doors opened soon after I felt the subtle change under my feet, the signal the lift had arrived.

"You're late."

The sight of Archon had destruction rising in a wave, washing up out of the depths. I inhaled the beauty of the feeling, wild and restless, aching for release. If it were physical rather than a feeling, I would caress it like a treasured possession. "For what?"

"The arrival of another mislead soul. The utility will be docking shortly. We need to be in place."

"What does that mean?" What did this have to do with me?

"You'll have to wait and see." As an afterthought, he said, "I hope you're feeling well."

"I would feel better after something to eat." And a chat with my three friends. Should I tell them what happened? Would they be willing to follow me out of the compound? Escaping was one thing, but surviving the desert was another. Since all three were from the outer provinces, they would make the perfect companions.

"There will be time for that after this."

Why did he insistent on me being there? The only thing I could think was the capture of one of the fringe people I'd met. Islia or Alithia, someone like that. But how would they know I had links to any of these people? Unless they were able to get something out of Azrael. If they did, it would be Alithia. She was grafted, so why would they want her? She knew things, things about Jax and his father. Did she know about Dominus? And perhaps there were other secrets she could spill the senate would find fascinating, links to rebels, plans, how far the rebellion reached.

The trigger released the moment I chased Arlo out of his safe room, giving the children an excuse to go too. I should've known Azrael would never obey me. She didn't even listen to her mum. And now the fringe would unravel, the people exposed. People Jax cared about, everything destroyed.

No more. Right the wrongs. Do what needs doing. Keep going. Be smarter. Learn what's on the other side of my fear. Jax said those words. My dad said similar words. I had to embody those words. Because I was capable now. Destruction was me.

Archon was staring at me, using those splintering eyes to chisel out answers to his ever-consuming fascination with me and need to master me. For a moment, I stared back, leveling my eyes on him, my daring enabled by my secret, the powerful feeling of a hungry ache to destroy, the addictive understanding that I could end him if I wanted to, sabotage the neurons in his brain, sever his ability to function, terminate his *biosystem*. For a moment, my mind raced through the delirious knowledge of my power then quelled those thoughts, wrangled destruction behind the barrier, and looked at his feet. The expected action for me to take. "I hope it doesn't take too long. I'm feeling pretty hungry."

"Once this is over, you can have your breakfast with me."

He didn't give me a chance to catch his expression before he marched away down the corridor. *I'd rather eat snails.*

Now was not the time. There were too many obstacles, too many questions about how they ran the compound, security, number of employees, routine. I'd need to make a mental list of everything challenging I'd possibly encounter that I would need to know prior. I needed to learn, be smart. Most important of all, I needed friends. People who knew how to survive in the desert and direct me which way I should head.

Archon led me back to the vast open space I entered when I first arrived. Was he going to take me all the way out to the docking platform? If my wish were to come true, he would. That way, I'd get another glimpse of the desert and what waited on the horizon. I would look differently at the view than I had when I first arrived. Back then, the desert was the final barrier. Now, it was my escape route.

We didn't go any farther. Archon positioned himself in the middle of the vast space, me by his side. Hands clasped in front of him, he said without looking at me, "You're scheduled for another trial today."

"What's a trial?"

Eyes sliced to me, darting back and forth over mine. "How much do you remember of yesterday?"

"Nothing." No point in lying.

His chin crinkled as he gently nodded his head, taking the information in like a doctor hearing symptoms from a patience. "That's a mercy for you." He breathed it out. Not a surrendering sigh, a grateful one. I'd say it was a disinterested sigh translated to mean *don't expect any more of those.*

What did he do to me? I wasn't meaning them, Martimon and whoever else were likely involved in administering the experiments, *trials.* What was between Archon and me was personal to him, an intimacy that had nothing to do with emotion and sex, or rather any emotion that extended to me. It was like he saw me as a personal challenge, climbing Mount Everest, conquering the wild seas, but it was a personal challenge fettered in malevolent intent. It can't be hard for a Set to master anyone, yet Archon found it particularly interesting to master me, and he wanted to do it through friendship and beguilement, which made his actions depraved.

Something happened yesterday that I couldn't remember, something Archon did. While he watched the entrance, I cast glimpses at his profile. He'd know I was watching him. Archon was always aware of his surroundings and everyone near him. A man as perceptive and cunning as he was would feel the burn of my gaze on him. Let him feel; let him think I was afraid or in awe. Let it bolster his arrogance. Let my glances bore into him, because soon they would, *literally*. Soon, I would look at him with more than my eyes. Destruction would be there as well. But I needed to know first how many sweepers there were, how many ungrafted, and what factional threat did they pose.

My glances were disrupted by the echoing sound of boots marching down the tunnel. In my periphery, I felt Archon's eyes land on me, wanting to capture my instant reaction to what I saw. Transfixed, I couldn't turn to him. My heart timed its beat with the stereo march. A tingling started in my stomach and lower down, like I was about to wet myself. *Alithia, I'm so sorry.* How would I feel when our eyes met? The accusations, and I deserved them. I couldn't shut out the big, black eyes of her little girl nor my promise to bring her back.

They came into view. Sweepers surrounded their prey, shields up, weapons held at the ready. The large sweeper at the front blocked the person immediately behind. For a held breath, he obscured my view. For the grace of one second, only until an equally imposing man came into view, stepping to the side of the leader so he could be seen or see.

Jax.

Chapter 31

ARCHON MADE me wait so I could watch Jax pass me caged by a wall of sweepers. There were six of them, the same number who'd arrived with me. To me, their details were blurry, nothing more than meaningless figures obscuring where my eyes lay.

Jax's gaze stayed on me, leveled, intense as he passed. His expression like granite, nothing to read, but his eyes were telling me things. I wanted them to tell me things, like "I forgive you." *I blame myself for everything, Jax.* And now I blamed myself for this.

Now past, Jax couldn't turn far enough to keep our eyes locked, so he stared straight ahead. I ducked my head, staring at the floor. Destruction heaved up like the vomit of yesterday, worse, the billowing rage of heat and flames from an explosion, punching me through the chest, and I felt about to topple backward. I was switched to full wattage; the excess would soon zap out of my fingers.

I clenched my teeth. *Don't.* This was my weakness. Blame, it cored into me, debilitated, diminished, destroyed any strength I had. That's why destruction was here, tail lashing and whipping below the surface, my wakeup call. While destruction could not change the truth in my heart, it could force me to change my mind, think powerful thoughts.

Archon moved behind, expecting me to follow alongside him. I ignored his stare, blatantly fixing my eyes on Jax's back. How many times had I marched beside him or scurried in his wake as he strode forward, driven by his intent? Enough times to know the emotions warring inside that made him move the way he did now. His was a stride with purpose. No way would someone like Jax get caught. Was there a reason? Or was my stupid heart begging for a reason? His walk could be nothing more than a man refusing to be humbled by fear in the face of defeat.

We all gathered at the lift, but the sweepers positioned themselves to block my view of Jax.

"I will take him now," Archon said.

With helmets on, it was impossible to know what they thought, but turning their heads to each other said what didn't need saying. Confusion. This was not how the rules went.

"You may log your data and then leave." Archon's voice hardened with an edge of steel.

The lift opened with the sweepers remaining where they were. Archon ignored their stymied departure, touching my back to prompt me forward and into the lift. "You too." His eyes moved to Jax.

My eyes remained on Jax for most of the charade, but he was watching Archon, even caught the hand he placed at the small of my back. I darted forward, freeing myself from the contamination of Archon's touch and into the lift.

Archon followed me in, sweeping Jax up as he went. The lift was big enough, but we crowded inside. My body hummed. It was like someone plugged me in. The distance between Jax and me was mere meters, but it might as well be brimmed by a chasm for how much I wanted to touch him but couldn't, not with the greedy eyes of Archon yearning for ammunition.

One of the sweepers whipped out his hand to block the sensor at the door. "This is unregulated, sir."

The conversation brewed, taking Archon's attention. With his back to us both, it freed us to share a glance. There was too much cramming my head to be said, so I said nothing at all. In typical Jax style, he just stared. We weren't in Dominus, so I should be able to read his expression, but the black of his eyes was still nothing but a deep well, and I'd yet to learn how to climb out.

What happened? Why are you here? The others? Too much to say. But he only needed to know one thing. We were back in the Amex Tower on the cusp of my explosion. I'd given him one look, and he had understood. I needed to give him more than that now.

A slight nudge and destruction purred, arced, lashed. My mental hold was tight. It was like chains yanked through a fisted hand, a little release on the stream of my stare, a piercing jab through the pits of his eyes, funneling, funneling inside. Jax stiffened, his eyes flaring wide. I reeled destruction back, blinked to sever the link, stepped back with the force of fighting to leash it again. Jax ducked his head, his body exhaling, the whole of him. His understanding lapped outward like the ripple on a pond, caressed over me. And for the first time in so long, it felt like we were joined.

How many seconds had passed? A few and the conversation was over. The sweeper relinquished his hold on the door. They hissed closed, locking the three of us inside. Mere seconds was all to reach our stop, so Archon didn't bother to look at us. But we looked at each other. Jax's eyes were on my nose and lip, still showing signs of my kiss with the stairs, and maybe the bruising was still visible on my jaw. How long had it been since we last saw each other? My eyes were ravenous.

The feeling that washed through my body was not the sensation of descending. We were going up. The lift doors opened to a maze of white corridors and paneled doors creating dead ends as we walked. It felt like we were crossing the circumference of the compound when Archon finally entered an open doorway. The view slowed me to a standstill. The desert expanded across the entire wall like the window in Jax's apartment. What we saw was the distant horizon, inhospitable and unforgiving. And I hoped to cross it.

"Please, take a seat." Archon was all smiles and hospitality.

Jax led me in. This was a place within the compound I'd never been before. Situated above everything meant the person who occupied the room had to be important. Yet Archon's office was a level or two below. Or at least the one he'd taken me to. Compared to the other rooms I'd been inside so far, this place oozed comfort from the chairs and couches to the muted color of the sparse furnishings.

Archon moved around like it was home. Jax did as told and headed for a chair, but I was drawn to the window. I'd never seen a desert, except in books back home, but even then, there'd been some stumpy, sick-looking vegetation managing to get a foothold. In front of me, there was nothing but red dunes looking like an endless roll of waves. Up close, I looked down the wall of the compound to the desert below. Violent sandstorms had built a giant mound of sand up the side. No wonder there were no windows below. The compound looked to be in the process of slowly being buried. I pressed my palm flat to the glass, but the thickness meant the heat from outside couldn't penetrate. There was nothing but madness in my plans to escape across the desert. But desperation made mad plans the best plans you could make.

"This all seems like déjà vu to me."

I spun at the sound of the voice, seeing Carter in the doorway. Two emotions distilled all others away. The warp of déjà vu was also real for me, only this time the fear, present and churning my still unsettled stomach, was soon eclipsed by the furnace of hatred. My veins burned with the emotion, and destruction fueled the fire.

Jax had risen from his chair, and our eyes met for a brief moment before both of us turned back to the doorway. Carter! Here, mixed up with the compound, Archon, and the experiments. We now had our answers to what he was up to. Where was his legion of recruits from my world?

"You were always so good at hiding your emotions," Carter addressed Jax as he advanced into the room. Jax eased back down into his seat, but I wasn't as skilled with my acting. Barbs should be showing through my clothes from the number of prickles I felt.

"And you," he said, settling his gaze on me. "I guess it's to be expected."

"Her memories may return in a few days," Archon said.

"How much has she lost?"

"I'm not sure. Seems the most recent ones. She remembers nothing of the trial." Said like I wasn't in the room.

"And meeting me, it seems."

Sweet Jesus. What happened?

This nauseating tête-à-tête infected me with some disease of their making, slicing a divide between Jax and me. They'd done something to me, and now I couldn't bear to look at Jax and see his scrutiny. I felt like a traitor, like I'd given away something important. Maybe I had. Myself. Without a choice.

I kept my eyes on Carter as he strolled toward a recliner. The large room wasn't large enough. This world wasn't large enough. Would we ever be free of him? As in Archon's office, the chair responded to his presence by molding to his body, looking like a giant hand cupping him in comfort.

His predatory eyes ate me up. "I must thank you for your interesting insights. We are mobilizing as I speak."

Stomach acid burned up my throat. The desert was in my mouth, dry and scratchy, and my lips felt sealed tight. Mobilizing? As in attacking the fringe. They did that all the time. Razing it out of existence? I had given something away, and it was more than myself. This time, I couldn't stop my gaze from seeking Jax out. More controlled than I could ever be, he showed no outward sign of emotion from what Carter said. I knew Jax enough to know his mind would already be ahead of mine.

I could do it now. Learn first. "Where are your followers, all the people you brought back from my world?"

Carter tapped his time out with his fingers. "They have not been assimilated into daily compound life as of yet."

Holy crap. Yet again, I couldn't keep my stare from seeking Jax out, but he kept a steady gaze on Carter.

"They are here?" What a pathetic question. It reflected the daze in my head.

"To do anything else would be premature. And the work here is very important. Your kind have proven interesting subjects. We are similar in many ways, but the differences are enough to provide interesting outcomes." Carter shifted his gaze to Archon. "Any updates on our progress?"

"We have pleasing results from the latest test subjects. It seems you were right. Their biosystems are easily manipulated."

Carter's eyes were back on me. "You will undergo your second trial today. I'm afraid that will really fog your brain, but I'm assured it will sort itself out over time." He settled his hands in his lap. "Jax, Jax, Jax. It's good to see you again."

Jax stared but didn't reply. Here was the mentality that made him a prized fighter. The force behind his silence pounded my heart. Slouched in the chair, he could be here for a friendly chat. I read something else. I didn't need to see his expression, dive into his eyes, to understand what his body was saying. He was not cold-hearted like Carter, but he was unremitting and resolute and like granite to crack.

"Your sudden arrival has messed with our schedule. You'll be happy to know you've been bumped to the front of the line. We've had little success with our own kind, but there have been the odd positive result. Enough to make me keen for your results." Bumping his thumbs together, he said, "Should I let you know the reason I lied to Nixon about your father?"

For once I caught the first crack in Jax's face, nothing more than the finest veining on Jax's marbled expression. The slightest twitch in his jaw muscle. A faint glimpse was all, but I felt the fury, the wild turbulence of it, enough to turn stomach acid to poison, enough to annihilate any previous plans or thoughts, twist them into revenge, revenge now, revenge absolute. My breath was bound up in that small twitch, concealing to everyone but me what dark drive Carter's words festered within him. Archon wouldn't see. Jax was a stranger to him. Carter would miss it because he only saw what he wanted to see.

"Renus was proving as much a problem for me as Nixon." Carter continued oblivious, as I suspected, to the warning signal seeping from Jax's expression. "You were meant to have passed through the trial long before now, but Renus refused to allow it. As did your mother. Familial bonds are tiresome."

Jax was motion before I managed to force the breath through my tight throat. Destruction was not delayed by my paralyzed reflexes. It rose. As a wild cat it lashed its tail. The sudden force of its impending burst and I was on the verge of peeling my lips back and snarling.

Jax was over the table, nothing but a blur of furious motion when Archon shouted, "Stop. You won't do this."

Too late, the impact of Jax's weight toppled the chair backward. But both were Aris and Aris, as I'd learned, came with agility and sped beyond normal. Either Carter had lurched himself sideways or Jax had dragged him, but both missed the impact of the chair on the floor, so that they were sailing backward, backward until Jax had Carter against the wall, hands clasped at Carter's throat, nails indenting deep into the flesh. He could do it, gouge a hole through Carter's throat, mute his toxic words, mute the torturous taunts. His eyes would be shot with bloodlust, thoughts lost within the insatiable desire for bloody death. But he was caught, his hands tremoring over Carter's throat, his mind now locked in a war. Set words shackled him.

"Release him."

I could cry with the restraint of tying destruction down. Feral, it thrashed inside, churning me up like a tin boat bucked on a stormy sea. *Be smart, Sable.* Neither Archon or Carter knew destruction was free. Now was not the time.

Distract. "What are the trials for?"

Carter pushed Jax backward. Seized in his internal struggle, Jax staggered away, but kept his feet. Carter straightened his clothes, adjusting his collar as if to emphasis he'd won, as in kept his throat intact, and returned to his seat without bothering to look at Jax. "He needs to sit."

"Return to your seat," Archon commanded. While not directed at me, my legs buckled with the need to find a seat. *Dirty Set asshole.*

I couldn't watch Jax shuffle to the seat he'd just vacated, hated to witness how easy he was tamed by Archon's voice, hated to see the anguish in his eyes brought on by his internal fight. How could anyone want to see Set free of their grafts?

Jax sat heavy, his hand frozen in a claw, just as it had been at Carter's throat. It was as if his muscles held onto the memory of Carter's flesh captured underneath.

"Maybe it's time this one left. I'd like a chat with Jax."

Archon moved toward me.

"Just a minute." Carter held up a finger. Finally he gave me his attention. "I'm curious to know how it felt when you discovered Holden had betrayed you."

What did he mean? How would he know? My mind was on a sprint.

Carter snorted a laugh. "Never mind. But I am curious to know why you didn't get Jax to bump your dad from goal."

I would speak if I had the saliva to lubricate the words.

"You've saved his life, you know. Tucked safely away in prison, he's no threat to me now, so I have allowed him to live. The senate paid tribute to his death, of course, and has now replaced him with someone else. Unfortunately it meant I had to foster knew relations, which take time. But things are progressing with the senate member for Negal." A flick of his finger, "you can take her now."

Archon came alongside me resting a hand at my elbow. "Your next trial starts soon."

I jerked my arm away. "I'm not going anywhere with you." No way would I leave Jax.

Destruction was in my throat squeezing it shut. It was hammering against the barrier of my skin and turned my heartbeat into a spastic gallop. Now. It had to be now. Destruction flooded up into my head. I was on fire. I was going to explode.

I glared at Archon. I wanted to dagger through his eyes into his mind and heart. The force of my hatred prickled my eyes. Glee, there was glee. I fought not to laugh. It tickled up with triumph. Luscious and compelling.

What was in my stare? Whatever it was forced Archon back one pace. The shift in his demeanor was like a storm descending. He inhaled himself taller, broader, crueler. Lethal shards scissored in his eyes.

Jax caught my attention. Released from his paralysis, he pushed up from his seat. His movements were like a big cat readying for the prowl.

"This is all very amusing," Carter said.

Jax spared a few more seconds with Archon before turning his gaze to Carter. "Oh it will be."

Since entering the room, I saw the smug smile on Carter's mouth slip. Jax was his prize fighter, his pet. He knew Jax little, but well enough to know the edge in his voice was something to concern himself about.

Was this Jax's signal? Was it time for destruction?

I was the one who saw it first as I was facing the window. There was no noise because the glass was inches thick. Archon saw it next. Following Archon's frown, Carter turned in his chair to also look.

Time suspended as we stared out the window at the nose of the STU utility, hovering threateningly close.

Jax dived for me, slamming into me with such force I was thrown backward. At the same time a thunderous sound punctured the air, roaring through my sanity. The weight of Jax crushed me, but there was glass splintering like rain drops onto my face and wind ripping around us and grit scratching at my eyes.

Chapter 32

THE FURY of the wind whipped around the room, fierce gusts ricocheting off the walls within the confined space, abrading the skin of my cheeks, filling my mouth with the desert. The unplugged ferocity of the wind swelled the simmering giant inside me.

"We've got to leave!" Jax yelled into my ear over the roar of the wind and the tinkling of billions of specks of sand pummeling every surface in the room. His weight lessoned over mine. "Get up!"

Hands on my upper arm, Jax dragged me to my feet, bracing against the onslaught. Eyes scratched up, I blinked through the curtain of sand and caught movement in my periphery. Jax pulled me one way. My eyes followed in the direction of the movement to see Archon racing for the exit. Watching him dash for the door, destruction raged a silent roar of its own.

"Jax!" I yelled over the noise and the concealment of my hand over my mouth so as to keep the grit out. My voice tilted up to a manic pitch. Was now the time to reveal that destruction was no longer bound by my graft?

Jax's mouth pressed against my temple. "We need to get on the STU." It was only his proximity and the agitated tone of his voice that gave me the strength to keep the thread of destruction from arching forward in a deadly stream and taking Archon out as he fled.

"Archon's getting away."

The wind whipped my hair over my face. We knocked heads as Jax pulled me close so he could use me as a barrier to the wind as he spoke. "He's not our concern."

I pushed him in the chest. Unhinged from his hold, I staggered sideways against the ferocity of the wind. Not willing to let me go, Jax wrenched me to him again. "They're here for us. We have to get on that STU."

"Carter's here. You can stop him."

Jax's face remained fragmented through the sandstorm. I'd been a recipient of his frustration enough times to know what I'd see in his eyes if I could peel back the curtain. In this, the storm protected me. He was right. This was the chance I thought I'd lost only a day ago before destruction returned, when I was stripped of my factional nature and left helpless. But I was destruction again. To remind me, it thrummed and pulsated throughout my body, aroused by the chaos surrounding us. It was time to force Archon and Carter to pay their dues.

"You're not listening to me." Jax's fingers dug into my arm, tearing my mind back to him and not Archon fleeing, back to our escape.

But I didn't want to escape. Archon had to pay for all his deceit and for puppeteering me and stripping me of myself. I wanted to look in his crystalline eyes and watch the smirk slip slowly from his face when he realized I'd been the one to deceive him. "You know what revenge feels like."

"I also know what it feels like to be free of it," he said.

"Then help me end this, and we can both feel that freedom."

"It won't end, Sable."

Neither will destruction. The storm inside my body was bigger than the storm in the room, drumming faster than my heartbeat, energizing me to life. Now that it was with me, a part of me, I couldn't—refused to—ignore its desire. Was this the precipice, the edge of my choices? To be destruction or that other girl. A day ago, I'd been that other girl, and I couldn't, wouldn't be her again.

"I can end this!" I yelled back at him.

I pulled myself free of Jax. No, he let me go. I spun toward the now closed door, unprepared to chance catching his expression. Jax understood. He knew, because he'd been here himself, more than once, this place of defining decisions that altered more than the outcome; they also altered you.

Rather than run, I chose to fight.

Nearing, the door slid open. I stumbled out into the corridor, blown from behind and into the wall opposite. The wind escaped with me, showering me and the wall with fine grains of sand. The wind blasted off the wall but lost its impact down the vast corridor, leaving trails of sand in its wake.

Archon had vanished. But which way? *Think*. Left. Yes, definitely left.

Sand shed from my hair and clothes as I ran. I tasted desert, bit into grit as I clenched my teeth to entrench my decision. Tears from the sand blurred my vision. Keeping my sprint, I wiped at the tears until my eyes burned raw.

How many doors had there been? Too many. He would've gone for the lift, not sheltered in one of the rooms I passed. But how was I to get inside the lift? How did I expect to move around within this compound? Stupid, I'd not thought of that.

Before I reached the lift, it *hissed* open. A bunch of sweepers rushed into the corridor, protective energy rippling in rivers in front of them—the tough sort that shielded them from physical as well as factional attack—weapons clutched to their chests. I skidded to a stop but felt a detonation puncture through my chest, expulsing a wave toward the sweepers. I could feel my body in place, but it was like I hadn't stopped at all. This other part of myself exploded outward. Unhinged from my mind, it fed on instinct.

The force at which destruction hit stripped the wall paneling like it was sheets of paper. Storms of debris replaced the storms of grit of moments ago, choking the corridor with a fine powder and missiles of rubble. Pummeled as they were, the sweepers remained on their feet, thanks to their shields. Destruction pulsed below my skin, the throb like a heavy drumbeat, finally subdued by my mental control. I couldn't bring the ceiling down or I'd block the lift, but how would I get past the wall of sweepers who'd weathered the storm I unleashed?

"Get down, Sable!" someone yelled from behind me.

Hearing my name in the forceful cry, I went down, hands smacking the floor first. The residual injury in my left wrist flared a sharp twinge to life. Before I could turn to look over my shoulder, a sizzle flashed over my head, leaving a trailing smell of ozone. The sweepers scattered like ten pins.

I scrambled up, half looking over my shoulder. Someone collided with me, scooping me under my armpit, helping me to my feet. "We have seconds," Jax said.

Elva appeared on the other side of me. "This stinks of your doing," she all but snarled.

Sweepers were finding their feet. Two had lost their shields, disintegrated in the weapons fire.

"Duck," came the voice of Patrick from behind.

Jax dragged me down to my knees as another bolt blew over us, nearly scorching our hair. The sweepers who'd found their feet were sent backward once more, blown by the impact then sliding farther down the corridor on their backs.

"The lift," I panted, pushing to my feet.

"No. We need to get back in the STU and disappear," Elva said.

"Carter's here," I said, hoping that would fire her own need for revenge as I sprinted for the lift, dashing inside like a tidal wave was about to sweep down the hall and flush us all away. Elva, Patrick, and Nuke burst in behind me, but Jax disappeared. I lunged forward out into the corridor to see Jax dragging one of the sweepers who'd lost his shield in the first blast. Blood followed in a trail behind them. Not a river of the stuff, but enough for me to suck my breath in.

This is what you're doing.

Destruction pawed impatiently inside my skull, incited by the sudden slap of reality at the sight of the injured sweeper. Unleashed and wild, it would not give in or allow me to falter.

Patrick came forward to stand with me in the doorway. One sweep of his arm, he shoved me backward into the lift. I tumbled back onto my ass, biting my lip as he swung the barrel of the stolen weapon up and forward and released another arcing shot. The smell of electricity burning the air, the noise of the impact as the stream collided with the sweepers down the hall, and I turned to stone. This was the game, for grownups only. For those willing to step beyond the boundary and into freefall. I'd made the first move over the line, and the others had followed. I'd plunged them into my decisions.

Elva pushed past me, darting down the corridor. Soon after, Jax crammed the doorway with the wounded sweeper as Patrick bent and swept me up off my ass. "Sorry about that," he said with a wink. There was no missing the red bruise in his eyes. Bloodlust was assuming control.

"Why him?" I asked, staring at the sweeper.

Elva reappeared carrying extra weapons. "How do you expect to move around in here?" Venom tinged her answer.

Destruction lashed under her remark.

Nuke helped Jax maneuver the sweeper toward the panel. They were going to use his palm print to operate the lift.

"Why can't we shift from level to level?"

Elva turned her body toward me, pulling herself up to her impressive height. Destruction read her body language as an imminent attack, writhing and flaming for release. "Don't you think it's a bit late to be asking those questions now?"

"It won't work inside the compound," Jax said.

"This is a prison, sweetheart. Do you think the senate would be so stupid as to allow something as risky as shifting?"

I tried to dismiss her by looking to Jax and Nuke as they moved— which felt painfully slow—the sagging sweeper so they could place his hand in the right position over the panel.

"You better make this worth it."

I ignored Elva's acid and willed the guys to hurry up. The door *hissed* closed, and my stomach rose as we dropped. I held my breath for the time it took to travel into the bowels of the compound.

"Do you know—" Too late. The lift stopped.

The doors opened to silence. Patrick was the first to leave the lift, moving with the same skill and grace as he'd shown countless times in Dominus. This was what we'd been trained to do. Only now, we fought with weapons more lethal that did not require us to get close to cause injury or death, but our enemies were better protected. And our enemies were real people. I could make the moral choice—we all could —and step back from this fight, refuse to do harm to a living soul. And what would Archon's choice be? And Carter's? Was there room for moral choices in this game we played?

"The others will meet us on the docking platform," Jax said, arranging one of the weapons Elva retrieved in his hand. Nuke carried the other.

"Others?" I asked, but everyone hustled out the door, leaving my question to sink in the emptiness of the lift, bar the sweeper now propped against the wall. I hesitated for a stilted breath. Destruction warped through my head, flushing a color of white across my vision. *Get going.* That's what it said. Like lowering the googles and descending into Dominus, there was no turning back, no time for regret.

I joined the others in the corridor led by Jax's hurried march.

"How long will they hold?" Nuke said.

Jax swiveled so fast I bumped into him. It was like he transformed into a granite wall. The force of his coal eyes, emanating the power of his will, bared down upon me like a sledgehammer. "You want Archon, you've got fifteen minutes."

"I need more. I'm not sure how to find him."

"Take it down, one level at a time."

I flinched at the edge in his voice, sharpened to a fine blade.

"The compound." My words came out in a shocked rush.

"Start at the top and work your way down."

"There are prisoners in here."

"You've made your choice, Sable. You can't save everyone. You should know that." The first signs of red filmed across the white of his eyes.

He was right. The choice I made to chase Archon meant he was right. The burn inside me for revenge meant he was right.

I knew Jax; I knew his heart. The redness of his eyes was not because he longed for the fight, nor because bloodlust was on the verge of winning control. He was pulling down the boundaries, letting his factional nature through, because he understood what a fight meant. We both understood, because we both knew the depth of the words "kill or be killed." *I'm sorry, Jax.* But he would do it too. They all would. That was why they stood with me now.

"He'll go to the docking platform." Of course. "That's his and Carter's only escape."

"The others will cover that. No one will leave alive, but I wouldn't put any faith in that being their only way of escape."

"What if there are people in the—"

Jax fingers manacled around my arm as he gave me a sudden shake. "You need to do it."

Destruction had arced wild, empowered by the maelstrom, amped by the sound of the shattering glass, the fury of the wind, and struggled to break free and smash up the room. It was feeding through me now. I glanced around to the wall of my friends, each Aris, each with eyes flushing red.

I arched my head back, stared at the ceiling, focused on the stream of destruction. It fled out of me in a glorious surge, poring straight from my core. This is what it mean to be united and whole. It was grounding, blissful, consuming. The ceiling above us vibrated with the immensity of my release. Cracks corded outward from a center directly above my head, spreading down the corridor and outward to splinter down the walls. The force of destruction and the walls shuddered, and the floor vibrated beneath our feet.

"How about we get moving?" Nuke prompted, bringing me out of my excited fascination with what I'd done.

Nuke was right, no point hanging around in case I'd been stronger in my release. I was sure Jax had taken us down to the level of the platform, which meant there weren't too many more levels above our heads, and that is why I'd been steady with my release. I had to be careful not to bring the floors above down on top of us but needed to make enough of a mess to cause Archon and Carter a lot of pain in their plans to escape, if Jax had been right and they disappeared via another route.

A heavy monotone siren sounded in stereo.

Our eyes sought each other out. "Looks like the clocks wound down to zero," Patrick said.

"You know what to do!" Jax yelled, sweeping us all up in that command. Just like in Dominus, now was the time to engage.

With the sound of rushing feet behind us, we launched into a sprint around a bend. In front was the vast open space that served as the reception for new arrivals and the indoor exercise area for the prisoners. It was filled with prisoners corralled into the middle of the cavernous space by a wall of sweepers, the exercise for the day violently disrupted. Behind us, pounding feet meant more were on their way.

None of us broke our stride, running into the enemy at full sprint. In front, to the left of me, Patrick rose his weapon to his line of sight. Before he released a shot, a wall of bluish-white expanded out in front of us, warping the vision of the prisoners to a rippling glow. One of the sweepers had released his own shot.

Destruction flowed with the barest touch. It raced out in front of me, poured down the corridor, and slammed into the bluish blast of energy, expanding it farther into a blinding light. The thunderous sound felt like a detonation held to my ears.

The others continued running toward the mouth of the corridor and into the turmoil I created. I spun, emboldened by destruction's release, and sent it funneling back the way we'd come, severing the path of the sweepers behind. The energy collided with the walls, puncturing through into the rooms and cavities and bleeding debris into the corridor. Expanding upward, the energy punched through the ceiling then rushed as a line of devastation toward the oncoming sweepers, creating a chasm through which the level above fell through. I coughed, pulled my overalls up over my nose to protect me from the billowing dust, now a thick haze in the air.

The grit from the sand was joined by fine particles of dust as I ran through the cloud toward the noise up ahead. I managed a few strides when something collided with the back of my head and sent me tumbling to the ground. I hit hard, sliding forward on my stomach, with the pain radiating through to the front of my head. On my stomach, vulnerable, destruction seared a line down my arms and out of my fingertips, splintering cracks along the littered floor, radiating outward from each finger.

I inhaled the dust, because my overalls mask had slipped. Coughing,

I rolled to my back and looked back down the corridor. Expecting to see a sweeper, someone who'd thrown the lump of ceiling or wall at me, I saw nothing but my own devastation. I scrambled up onto my ass, peering into the hazy gloom, breath seized in my throat so I could hear clearer. Nothing.

I touched the back of my head, resting my palm over the smarting pain, then pulled my hand away to see blood. Behind me, the others had already broken free of the corridor. The sounds of fighting echoed down toward me. By the sounds of the commotion, I'd say the prisoners, encouraged by the attack of Jax and the others, had decided to join in. At least I knew where they were. Safely away from destruction's attacks.

I climbed to my feet, about to join the rest, when I heard a faint *clink* behind me. I turned but couldn't see anything through the dusty haze. It was a stray piece of debris falling onto of the rest. About to turn around and head for the fight, the floating haze in front of my face began to swirl. No longer was it wafting through the air, because it was light enough to resist the gravitational tug to the floor. It was moving in a coordinated circle. As it went, it gathered more, sucking in dust from around it to spiral a wider vortex. As the particles spun, they expanded, taking in more. Soon, the dust was spinning around my head, whipping my hair into my mouth and eyes.

Staggering back, I couldn't draw my eyes from what I saw. The vortex had grown, vacuuming up the debris from the floor and corkscrewing it up into a tornado that expanded up through the chasm I created in the ceiling. The noise was like a million hammers pounding on a tin roof, blowing out my already sensitive ears.

I kept pacing backward but felt helplessly held by the horror-tinged fascination of what I was witnessing. I knew what I was seeing. I knew what this was.

Chaos.

Chapter 33

HE MOVED through the chaos of his making, waving his arms to gather more and more of the debris littering the floor. I stumbled over the lumps of wall and roof scattered around my feet as I staggered away, unable to turn and run, unable to do anything but focus on Archon and the majestic way he manipulated everything around him.

Chaos and deception, the two abilities involved manipulation, one physical and the other mental. And Archon was a master of both. I spun and ran. Knowing a storm was about to break, I wanted to be with the others, out in the open, ready to take Archon on. The cavern was just up ahead. The haze disappeared now that Archon had sucked everything up into his deadly tornado, which was this minute shearing through the spaces I created with my carnage. Up ahead, I saw havoc, silenced by the storm behind me. As I thought, the prisoners were playing their role. None had their factional natures, but they'd kept their spirit, and seeing a possibility, they were willing to risk the fight.

Dread rushed through me as fast as destruction on flicking a look over my shoulder. The tornado of debris expanded, coring out more of the walls and sawing through more of the ceiling, growing larger with every spin, eating and eating like a black hole does to light. Archon was building it to gigantic proportions with each forward step he took. Soon, it would be large enough to smash through into the cavern and fill it width to height until there was no space left free of its lethal bite.

I burst out into the open space, ducked, and spun away from a sweeper sent tumbling backward from a shattering blow of fire. He clipped me on my shoulder and sent me tumbling to the floor. Seconds I stayed before I scrambled to my feet, eyes darting for the others. There wasn't just chaos behind me. It was everywhere. The inpouring of sweepers from other entrances other than behind me meant the space was filled. As sweepers lost their shields through the savage attack of Jax or one of the team, a prisoner was fast to scoop up their weapons, turning it on the next sweeper to come near. The fight was a frenzy of bodies and shouts, but nothing, nothing compared to what was brimming at the mouth of the large corridor.

Caught up in their own survival, few had seen what was eating up the walls and verging on busting through. I couldn't let it happen. If Archon unleashed his spiraling doom, everyone would be scattered like poppy seeds, sliced and diced as they went.

The noise was so great it had now caught everyone's attention. The sounds of fighting subsided, which meant all eyes were on Archon's toy. I stood my ground and gathered destruction, pulled it from every recess in my body, wound and coiled the stream into one thick pulsating thread. Such was the depth of chaos, I could no longer see Archon on the other side.

Chaos burst through into the cavern, splintering the walls and sucking them up into its ferocious twist. But as quick as they'd disappeared into the deadly tornado, the whole wrapped rope of it began to unravel. The speed at which it happened seemed milliseconds-quick. Destruction moved as fast. The untangling mass shot forward, giant arms of debris haloing out toward us. Destruction rose up like a solid blast wall, sending the splintering debris upward toward the ceiling, careening miles over our heads. The force of Archon's release, coupled with the force of destruction and the debris punched upward, cratered a massive hole.

"Everyone, get out!" Jax yelled. He moved closer to me. I could tell, because when he cried those words of escape, he sounded near.

The stampede began, a chorus of shouts and cries, the noise of pounding feet. Jax was right; the place had to be cleared, because at some point I would have to release this up-flow, and all it could do was come down, bringing the entire ceiling with it.

"We have to leave, Sable." He was beside me.

"Archon's on the other side of this mess," I said, not removing my concentration or eyes from the stream of debris funneling its way through the ceiling.

"Come on!" Elva screamed from over the noise. I never thought hearing her voice would make me feel happy.

I allowed Jax to tug me across the open space, guiding me around strewn bodies. I didn't have the heart to look down. But as I went, I saw there were more gray than black amongst them. So many had lost their lives. Who between them would've chosen to die rather than live suppressed? Probably not enough.

We managed halfway toward the exit, and the wall of debris was lessening. Through the haze, I saw Archon. As if sensing there was no use, he released the last of what he'd gathered in his chaotic spiral. I finished off the rest before it pelted us with lethal chunks by exploding it into fine pieces.

Archon and I stared at each other through the raining dust. Beside him stood Carter. I looked over my shoulder at Jax, but his eyes were already staring across the distance to his enemy. One look behind, everyone had cleared the open space and into the tunnel beyond; perhaps the surviving prisoners were making a break for the platform and freedom beyond. Hopefully, they were. At least we helped some of them.

"This is how it will end." Carter had to raise his voice to be heard. I couldn't see his eyes from this distance, but I was sure they'd be tinging red.

Would this be the Amex all over again? Only this time, Jax could not pull me to safety as I brought the place down.

"I never expected a woman to bring you this low," Carter continued, advancing slowly into the cavernous space, Archon moving alongside him. "I had plans for you, Jax. You proved my best man, the one willing to make the sacrifices of your own free will. You could've been so much more."

"I'm enough," Jax breathed. Neither of the other two would've heard. They would not have understood the sentiment.

"How is this to play out?" Carter asked, splaying his hands wide.

Jax half turned his face to me. "Reinforcements will be on their way."

How were we to move this along? I shifted my attention to Archon. Both were my enemy, but Archon had a special claim over my revenge right now. As always, he kept his eyes on me. When my gaze met his, he smiled, quirking an eyebrow at the same time, like a nonchalant *fancy meeting you here*. Always the arrogant asshole, even when facing the possible end. But whose end?

"I'm curious. At what point did your graft fail?" Carter said.

The question was directed at me. I'd been too busy staring hard at Archon to notice for a good few heartbeats.

"Or were you pretending all along?"

"You really think I'm going to tell you?"

Carter chuckled to himself. Like Archon, you couldn't shake his arrogant belief in his own assured survival. Jax had to be right; reinforcements were likely heading this way as we wasted our time with these two.

"We need to end this," Jax whispered again.

Was I ready to do this? The choice was in front of me. There would never be another time. It felt so much easier to allow revenge free rein when I was chasing Archon. It seemed his flight fanned the emotion. Once he was standing in front of me, he became less a nightmare and more a human.

I didn't get to think another thought. Hell rained down around us through the devastation of a wall to our right. Jax crashed into me, dragging me to the ground as a shower of wall flew over our head. In no time, Archon funneled the loose chunks up into a spout and barreled them down toward us like a javelin. I lashed out with my hand and sent destruction through the middle of Archon's weapon, fragmenting it into a fine cloud. But whatever had created the explosion drew my attention. A sweeper stood in the cavity he made. A Persal. Of course there had to be one of those around.

We were still on the ground, Jax partially across me. The weapon in his hands pressed into my belly. He turned his head from the new arrival back to me. We didn't need words.

He rolled from me, keeping the weapon tight to his chest. Before he was on his back, the weapon's barrel was facing the sweeper, a shot of bluish light igniting from the end. Destruction met it halfway, but my own ability slipped through all the way, diving deep, deep down. A great wave of power, instantaneous and absolute. There was no time to allow judgment through or to juggle my emotions. It had to be now, hard and fast. The sweeper's body went rigid. Rising up on his toes, his muscles seized, his eyes bulging. The eyes of Aris, shot through with blood.

I sucked destruction back, fueled with the sudden shock of what I'd seen. I recognized his face, the sweeper who'd given me an aching jaw on my arrival. What happened was not my imagination. He had funneled destruction into my head while wearing the bloodlust eyes of Aris. A man of mixed faction, ungrafted, free to work his twin abilities. Working for the senate.

Noise erupted around us, snapping me into the present. More sweepers arrived from different entrances to the side of the cavernous room, but so too the others. Elva, Patrick, Nuke. Even armed prisoners poured back through from the docking platform. Enough of them to make the fight even. Jax was already halfway up, the sounds of fighting already erupting. My eyes flittered through the jumble of bodies alive and dying. Light emitting from the side, behind, overhead. It was starting all over again. Still on my back.

One swift move, and I rolled to my feet as everything went dark, complete darkness. A collective utterance of horror swept through the cavern, its echo trailing long behind. From my left, a bluish blaze *sizzled* through the air and the sounds of a man dying. This tipped everyone else into panic. A Phonus sweeper who was not blinded by the dark, who could move around and pick off those who weren't one of him.

Someone grabbed my hand, yanking me toward them as another *sizzle* firing of a weapon lit the cavern like a display of lightning. We were going to get picked off one by one.

"You get one chance." It was Jax, his face close to mine.

Despite the blanket of cries and shouts of desperation, the sounds of stampeding feet as people tried to escape to somewhere in the inky dark, I heard Jax prepare his weapon for release. A bright bluish-white light surrounded us. Jax had aimed his weapon to the ceiling, releasing one laser blast that provided a shower of light spanning out from the stream of energy punching upward. This was my one chance. I scoured the side of the room where the sweeper had been firing. He was there, on the outer rim of the light thrown by Jax's release while those around him bumped, stumbled, tripped, and scampered away as far as they could, clambering over each other, pushing others aside in their fear, only thinking of themselves. A natural, understandable instinct.

The sudden light drew his attention. He released one hand from his weapon. Lips pursed, face full of savagery, he reached out, snapped his hand into a fist, and wiped the light from my eyes. But he'd been too late. I'd already seen him, already sent destruction his way, in a single burst directed straight for his weapon.

The darkness was crowded with noise. It was so easy to lose your head, scatter like everyone else, but the one thing that kept me grounded and sane was the pulse of my factional nature. The Phonus sweeper was still alive, or else I'd have my vision back by now. I reached out my hand, thinking Jax was still nearby, but my frantic swipes found only air. I took a step, but arms wrapped around me, strapping my limbs to my waist.

"Shh." A whisper close to my ear.

"Jax?"

"We need to get out." Harsh whispers this time.

He dragged me along, forcing me backward, making me stumble. "Stop. I'm going to fall."

"I have you." His lips were close, breathing warm air, which fast turned cold across my ear.

"Wait. What about Archon and Carter?"

"It's done." His mouth still close, his voice kept to a whisper.

"What's done?" As in neither of them survived. "When? How do you know? Can you see?"

"Yes."

"Stop, Jax." I attempted to wrenched myself out of his control.

He tightened his grip, pinning my arms to my side. This wasn't right. I curled my legs up, at the same time kicking out behind with one.

It entangled with his own, pitching us forward. I landed first on my stomach, him coming down on top, punching the air out of my lungs. Pinned, destruction riled, whipping up in a vortex of agitated fury.

Hands gripped my shoulders as his weight lessened, giving me the space to gasp in a much-needed breath. Those same hands flipped me like a sack onto my back. "Jax!" I shouted. A hand smacked down over my mouth.

"That won't do."

"How about this?" I was blind, but destruction didn't need eyes to find a mind, especially when his breath was all over my face, filing my nose with acetous smells.

I'd expected his mind to be a convoluted mess of angles and mazes, something destruction would have to wind around and hurdle through in order to find purchase because of all his Set lies and fabrications he used to twist the truth. As always, it was frighteningly easy to pierce down into the very fabric of a person's mind.

His hands on my shoulders, I felt their sudden jerk. "You don't want to do this, Sable."

"It gives me great pleasure."

"I always knew you had something special in you. It's why I convinced Carter to give you a chance."

What was he talking about? I faltered in delving deeper, stripping the inside of him open. "This is all Set—"

"Sable." His voice rose. "Listen to me. Your mind is strong. Much stronger than Carter gave you credit for. But I protected you from his plans."

Don't listen. "Shut up." This was what he did.

"Stop. Listen to me, please." His words pierced me, loosened my control over destruction. "You never understood what I did for you, what I hoped to do for you."

"Your words are poison." I grappled for my hold on destruction, grappled to direct it to where I wanted it to go.

"My words are the truth. You have always known that. It is why you have hated me as much as you have. You fear the truth."

It wasn't the truth. Nothing that came from his mouth was the truth.

"I'm your ally."

The word resonated around in my head. "That's a lie."

One hand released my shoulder; next, fingers feathered along my cheek. I jerked my head away.

"You didn't need to fight me. I was always on your side."

Was that true? Was that why he gave me more attention than the others? Jerome had noted the special treatment he was giving to me. "I don't understand." My voice was not my own. It sounded fogged and distant.

"You never wanted to believe what was there in front of you. Jax has made you fear so much. Everything you had to go through while in Dominus. It wasn't necessary."

At times, it had been terrifying. I argued against Jax at the start about forcing me and everyone through Dominus. And look what it turned us into.

"Dominus should never have been. There is a gentler way to learn your factional nature. What he did was brutal and cruel."

"It was." The words were a whisper.

"I can help you, Sable. You want that, don't you? You want to be free. Your family free, all your family. Your dad too. I can save you all, reunite you."

My throat thickened as the sting made its way into my sinuses. I wanted it so much. I was nodding, nodding fast, sweeping the floor with my hair.

"That's my girl." He patted my hair, brushed my forehead like my mum did to me when I was young, like I would do to Ajay for no other reason than because I wanted the connection.

It ended so fast. One minute, he was there, his hand comforting me with parental pats, and then he was gone. The warmth of his body over mine vanished so fast I gasped with the sudden emptiness. And with the emptiness, reality crash-landed into my brain. I'd been bound tight in his evil lies. But he was gone, and now my awareness, corralled by his words, expanded to the distant sounds of fighting.

Rough hands pulled me to my feet, latched onto my shoulders, gently shook me. "Sable."

"Nuke?"

"Any minute now."

Was he talking to me? The black was wiped from my eyes so instantly my knees buckled as if I'd fallen from a height.

"Striker just took care of that pesky Phonus sweeper."

I glanced around me. The cavernous room had cleared of the survivors, but the distant sounds meant we'd not won a solid victory.

"We need to get going." He took my hand and led me along.

"Wait," I said, jerking back, losing Nuke's hold.

"Islia just informed us reinforcements are on the way. The others are holding the docking platform, but we've got to leave."

"Archon." I craned my head around. "I have to finish it with him."

"He's gone. And not looking too good as he went either."

"What happened?" I'd been so lost to Archon's words I'd forgotten where we were, what was unfolding around us, and that I was blinded because of a Phonus sweeper.

"The sweeper blanketed everything, but once Jax released a blaze of light from his weapon, everyone got the same idea. We hunted him out by copying Jax. He couldn't maintain his control over us all while trying to protect himself, but of course he'd been specific with you two. He kept control over both your sight, because... I guess it felt personal. But you're released now."

"Because he's dead?"

Nuke ignored me.

"What happened to Archon?"

"Now that was my doing," Nuke said, raising his weapon. "He saw me at the last, enough to save his ass, but I did clip him as he dived. I should've followed up on that, but I was more worried about you. Thought you may have been injured. And I guess I'm not as merciless as I should be. He was on the run, wounded. I couldn't...." He shrugged to fill in the gap he couldn't say in words.

"Where's Jax?"

"Elva dragged him out. He was a helpless babe. But don't tell him I said that. Sorry if I interrupted something you felt needed doing, but we've really got to go."

The choice to relent and go with Nuke should not be a difficult one to make. Soon, the compound would be overran. But it was. This was revenge taking over.

Be smart.

I turned my back on the destroyed corridor leading farther into the compound. Archon was in there somewhere. Carter as well, no doubt, unless someone had a different story they could share. They ended up here at the exit to the platform, which had to mean they had no other way out of the compound. Stuck in here or not, they were no easy targets. Besides, these guys had come here to rescue me. I couldn't risk their lives or their freedom by dragging them further into my revenge.

"Let's go," I said.

Chapter 34

Jax was on his way back inside, skidding from a full sprint when he saw Nuke and me rushing toward him. Seeing him, this gentle heat bloomed inside me. His eyes raked over me in one swift sweep before settling on my face, holding my gaze for a fraction of a moment, relaying nothing of his emotions.

"They'll be here soon." He didn't need to elaborate.

He waited for us to draw alongside then we all raced toward the opening and the platform together. The sun reached inside, casting the gray into a dazzling light. At least that's how it looked to me. Sun meant open space. It meant freedom. This was the first time in however long I'd been stuck here I'd seen natural sunlight and it was the most magnificent sight.

I wanted to ask about Carter and any other news of the fight while Archon had me twisted up in his mind games, but that would have to wait until we were away from this place. Instead, I concentrated on sprinting from the tunnel. The heat of the sun hit my face. The rays were scorching, but I tilted my face upward, allowing them to bathe my skin. I'd risk extreme sunburn just for the ability to have the heat touch my face. I thought I would never see the sun a free woman again.

The skirmish continued up ahead. Jax and Nuke picked up their pace, forcing me behind, raising their weapons, readying to engage. I scanned through the prisoners, my heart relenting its knotted hold increment by increment every time I caught sight of one of our party. Elva and Patrick in particular, but I was also relieved to spy Jerome bravely fighting amongst the remaining prisoners.

The sweepers had been outnumbered when the fight broke out. It seemed the compound operated on the belief the prisoners were no threat once grafted. No weapons, no factional nature, they weren't much of a danger. Lucky, because anymore sweepers and the outcome of today could have been miserable for us.

No weapon, but I was by no means unarmed, Jax and Nuke left me behind and joined the fight, engaging like they had just arrived fresh, fighting with the knowledge that we had perhaps only minutes to be on our way before we would lose our chance to escape.

"Sable."

My run faltered in seeing Islia in the opening to the only utility at the docking platform. Nada was a prisoner because of me. No. It was time I stopped wearing all this guilt and shame. I didn't always make smart choices, but I'd made the best choices I could.

"Come, get in," Islia yelled, waving me over with a frantic jerk of his arm.

I should join in. Persal was as effective as any sweeper's weapon, but one glance toward the prisoners told me perhaps I wasn't needed. Dominus had trained Jax and the team to move against the clock. Judging by the way they fought, swift efficiency and accurate strikes, they'd imbued the skill. But we'd suffered on our side. Of the prisoners who'd risen up against the sweepers, few remained.

"Come, child. Time is not our friend!" Islia shouted.

I diverted toward the docking arm and the utility, leaping inside once near. My momentum tumbled me into the seat opposite once inside. Islia remained by the entrance, keeping an eye on the finishing fight and also darting looks to me. "They will succeed. Have no worry of that."

Said half to ally his own fears and half to calm me, no doubt.

I came alongside him, unable to take my eyes from his face despite what was happening outside. "I'm sorry." I would no longer carry regrets or shame, but it didn't mean I would not accept my responsibility in screwing up.

My apology was enough to steal his attention. Tenderness was what I got from his expression. The relief sprung a tingle at the back of my nose, pressure at the corner of my eyes.

"It is only you who blames yourself for what happened. It does not come from me. Nada was a willful boy. I knew the day would come. The senate is greedy for our children. Each year, they send more and more sweepers, and each year, they grow more ruthless. There is no other way but this. My gift to Nada is to fight as Aris, as I never have before."

"I hope you're willing to fight alongside a Persal."

"It is my greatest pleasure to have you beside me."

Islia took hold of my hands, squeezing them gently between his. The warmth soothed a tightness within me, unlocking the doors Archon had closed. With my hands in his, Islia's gaze wandered to the graft tattoo he completed less than a week ago. Releasing my other hand, he turned my wrist up, exposing the mess of his inkmanship. He lifted his face, meeting my eyes. And for the first time, I saw surprise on his face.

"They tried. But failed," I said.

"But this is a wonder."

"It worked at first. But then...." I shrugged. "I'm not sure if my ability was able to overcome it, or if their experiments nullified the graft."

"Experiments?"

"I don't remember any of it. It happened only once. You guys arrived before they could do it again."

"What is it all about?"

"I was told they wanted to study our factional natures so they could develop more sophisticated ways of subduing us. That's all lies, of course. I believe they are experimenting in creating mixed factional fighters."

Islia let my wrist go in his horror, pressing himself up against the door.

"We came across one just now. A sweeper who was both Persal and Aris."

Islia turned his head away, looking out over the platform.

"I believe that's why they take the children," I said.

"They brainwash them and train them to be their army when they come of age and develop their factional natures. The people of the fringe have long believed this."

"I think they are also studying them. Learning how to genetically enhance the sweepers they have."

Islia shifted his eyes to me. I knew the look of determination, of a decision made, of finality closing all doors except one. "Then it is good we have started this."

I was cut off by yelling, which drew both Islia and me to the opening of the utility.

"Go!" Jax was shouting at Islia as the remaining fighters made their way toward the docking arm and our utility. No sweepers left to run from, this was sprint against the clock and the arriving reinforcements.

Islia left me as the others leaped through the door. My eyes gobbled up the sight of Jax flying through the opening, followed by Elva. I withheld the urge to fling myself at Jax, feel his solidness, the warmth of his living vitality, and the beat of his heart. And Elva. I wanted to sweep her in for a hug as well, which she'd likely slug me for. Nuke and Patrick came next, the four of them fit from their days in Dominus. The rest of the prisoners stumbled and panted through.

I had no problem sharing my joy with Ishren, taking his hand only to have him sweep me in for a hug. Fethon had made it too, tumbling down onto the seat beside us, panting as blood stained his clothes. In no time, it was dripping onto the seat. I crouched down beside him.

"Don't worry about it. It doesn't feel serious."

The sudden relief was crushed by the sight of the blood. There was nothing we could do, not when sweepers were about to arrive and we had to depart. "There's a lot." It was all I could say. No one had special pills, but if we made it out of here, we could find some fast.

"I have a lot to share," he replied, gently squeezing my hand, disguising his want for me to stop prying with a gesture usually reserved to reassure people. Maybe this was his reassurance, the gentle squeeze his way of telling me he didn't care about the outcome as long as he could die free.

"You hold on," I said. "We'll find something for you once we get out of here."

He nodded, grimacing behind a weak smile. "Don't you worry about me, child. I'm were I want to be."

"Come here, girl." I turned to find Jerome as well. He opened his arms to me. I rose from Fethon's side and walked into him, craving more hugs, more physical reassurances that we were going to make it.

"Everyone, find a seat!" Jax yelled from the front.

Jerome pulled me to a seat next to him, but with a quick glance to the front, I noted the seat next to Jax was vacant.

"I'll sit up front." I patted his arm and left him.

I never thought I would feel this happy to hear any sounds of take-off, but the engines thrumming to life, the mechanical whirring that signaled the utility was about to depart, and a big exhale rushed out. It was like I was exhaling the last few days of my life. Maybe I shouldn't feel like this. We'd yet to clear the compound and lose ourselves in the desert. Reinforcements were on their way—an army of them, no doubt. But I couldn't stop this feeling. I already reached a low point, lost half of myself, thought I lost my friends. And yet here we were, having survived our first fight.

While Islia maneuvered the utility away from the docking arm, I made my way for the spare seat. Islia knew how to fly, but given his age and how long he'd hidden in the fringe, those days were a long time ago, so it was no surprise the departure was a little rough. Twice I fell into the lap of a prisoner I did not know but welcomed seeing.

Jax reached out, giving me a hand to steady me with as I drew close. I slipped in beside him as the utility pitched sideways, nearly sending me pinwheeling across the space into a prisoner's lap sitting opposite us.

Jax helped me with the harness. I gave up and moved my hands away, allowing him to clip me in, because my eyes were too busy drinking him up. Once his task was complete, he turned his attention forward and stared at the wall above the guy opposite. It took two breaths before he inched his head around, sliding his black eyes to me. The smile was for me. After what was behind us and what was still to come, he gave me the warmest smile. I stared at his lips and then into his eyes.

We were getting good at sharing looks that spoke things we would not say. And then, hopefully because he could no longer keep it welled inside, he patted my thigh, a gentle, warming pat. One, two pats. He didn't remove his hand when it was over, his eyes on some place in front of him but his hand on my thigh. I sealed his welcomed invitation by placing my hand on top of his.

I looked down the length of the utility at the survivors. A pitiful number. From the hundreds I'd seen in that dining hall, the survivors did not even fill the utility. And there were no guarantees we would make it clear of the compound. Even if we did, would we reach our destination, reach the very end, be victors in this fight? Perhaps for the remaining prisoners, that didn't matter. After their incarceration, maybe this was freedom enough for now.

We'd not won. Archon and Carter were still alive, so perhaps one could say we failed. But I could not think that while we were free, nor while I sat beside Jax, his hand on my thigh, feeding me those silent words about his feelings. As subtle as the gesture was, it was everything to me. He'd come for me. Elva, Nuke, Patrick, and Islia too. Five Aris had rescued me. Dad and Holden were wrong. This was my family. My new family.

And I was destruction, and it was me.

Author's Note

Of all the millions of titles on Amazon it's great you found mine.

Sometimes the hardest part of publishing a book is the reviews. They can be like any developmental editor, shredding. But despite how tattered they can leave you feeling they really are a gift.

In many ways they are even more valuable than a developmental editor because now the people we write for, the readers, get a chance to let the author know what they thought. It doesn't matter how many times you rewrite, reedit and perfect your work, if you're not writing what the readers want to read then you're not doing your job. And the only way a writer can know this is through reader reviews.

And so my dear reader I would greatly appreciate it if you would kindly leave me an honest review. I say honest because I want to know what you really thought. If you loved it, please be verbose in your critique. If you didn't, I welcome you to be as verbose, but please be honest and respectful. I can improve my craft only if I know there is something wrong with it (and an author is the last person that can tell, we love all our babies).

You can leave your review at all stores

Thanks heaps. See you in The Dome

The Dome

About the Author

When I wasn't riding a camel through the Rajasthani desert, white water rafting the rapids on the Zambezi, bungee jumping off the Victoria Falls bridge or hiking the peeks in Pakistan, I was piloting a twin prop into remote aboriginal communities in northern Western Australia or staring down a microscope in a laboratory.

Now somewhat tamed, the microscope has morphed into a computer and I spend more time plotting dire situations for my protagonists than being in them myself.

I am the author of books that won't stay normal.

facebook.com/terinaadamsbooks

instagram.com/terinaadamsauthor

amazon.com/-/e/B088NQVG7L

bookbub.com/profile/2890827497

goodreads.com/terinaadams